THE LAST LIGHT

K. N. TIMOFEEV

DEDICATION

For the members of the Alphabet Mafia.
You are seen. You are heard. You are loved.

Also by K N Timofeev

The Lost Guardian Trilogy

The Lost Guardian

Souls in the Dark

Time of Prophecy

A Tale of Blades and Darkness

The Serpent's Coils

The Hidden Temple

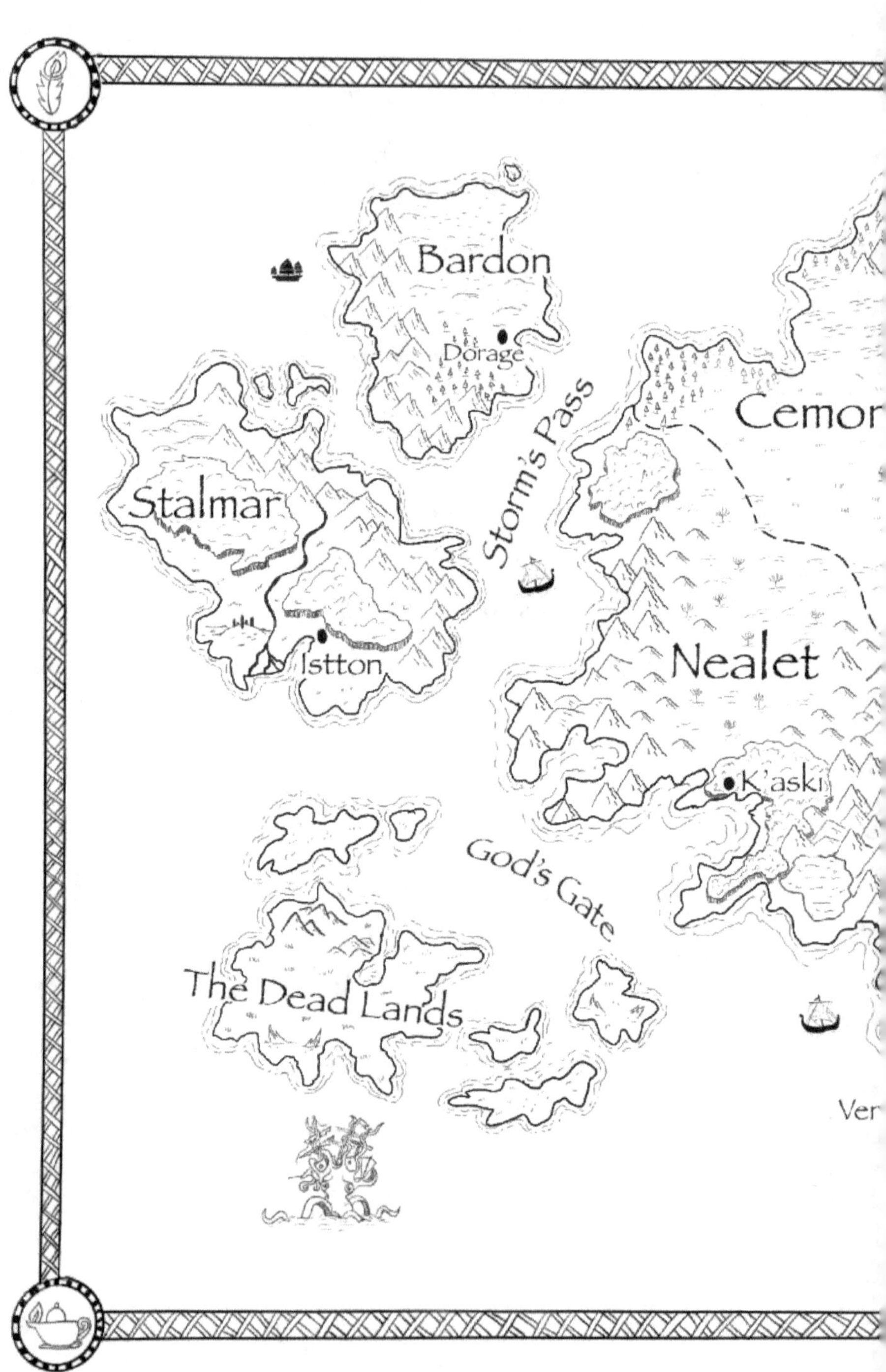

Bardon
Dorage
Stalmar
Istton
Storm's Pass
Cemor
Nealet
K'aski
God's Gate
The Dead Lands
Ver

N
Paddniq
Vilnia
The Gray Seas
Lorcea
Eddany
Black Marsh
The River Lands
Zallino
Three Kings Bay
Xhu'Rozo
The Keep
The Holy Isle

CHAPTER ONE

A PEAL OF LAUGHTER RAKED ACROSS BRAELYN'S NERVES, turning her delicate mouth into a sneer. Vapid courtiers tainted her mother's sacred gardens, once a place of serenity and protection, already scheming their way to new power. Her frown deepened as she counted how many had already traded their mourning garb for the lighter hues of half mourning. The sun caught on precious metals and glittering jewels worn by a few of the more brazen courtiers. Those undoubtedly wholly in Lord Julian's pocket.

Braelyn took a long drink from her cup. Her father's finest brandy, once only saved for special occasions, burned her mouth and throat. Facing the vultures that picked at the carcass of her life with relish, she needed something stronger than a delicate rosé.

"That color does nothing for your complexion, your highness," Julian said as he saddled next to her.

She straightened her shoulders, keeping her eyes focused on the far side of the garden, picking a spot on a distant tree to direct the anger in her gaze. "I'll shed my mourning garb the day my brother lays your head at my feet."

Julian looked at her from the corner of his eye, a slow smile breaking across his face. "Are we being truthful at last, princess?"

"I've never hidden my contempt, you conniving bastard. You clarified that if I failed to comply, you'd inflict more harm."

"And yet you still tried to run. Subjecting them to my whims without a backward glance."

Braelyn bristled. "In my actions, I sought to do what was best for my people. What good is a ruler who allows others to control them?"

Julian remained silent, staring out at the courtiers enjoying the first social event of summer. A few courtiers and visiting nobles cast apprehensive glances at the pair, picking up on the tension between the pair. Uneasy whispers ran beneath the cheerful event like a foul odor.

"And how were your actions for the benefit of Lord Tolin?"

For a moment, her façade cracked. Gasping for air, her grip on her cup slipping, Braelyn stumbled forward a single step. From somewhere inside, a demon roared, demanding the blood of the man who dared to harm what was hers. Braelyn latched onto that anger like a drowning sailor to a scrap of lumber. She turned on Lord Julian, her teeth bared like a cornered beast.

"Lord Tolin was a good man; they all were. They remained true to the crown until the very end. You may paint them as traitors and conspirators, but I know the truth. And I will not forget the debt I owe."

Downing her cup in one large gulp, she stormed away from Julian before she lost all semblance of control. Not one more inch would she give him. Courtiers scattered as she passed, bowing their heads in shock.

Julian frowned at the princess's retreating back. Why hadn't the curse taken hold of her mind? Only someone who had magic could resist his incantations, and he was fairly certain that the princess didn't even have a drop to shield her. His frown deepened. He had thought the same about Mirra and that turned out to be false. Julian quickly dismissed the idea. He'd been near Braelyn her entire life and she had shown none signs of magic. Something else must have happened. Perhaps one of those buffoons that nearly allowed her to escape had crushed his curse beneath their shit caked knees.

"She's quite a remarkable young woman."

Julian turned to the middle-aged merchant standing next to him. "I surmise in some ways she is, despite the limitations of her age."

The merchant chuckled into his wineglass. "Either way, she is as fine and as spirited as the mares I travel the world to secure. I breed horses, and while having a good stud is important, it's the mare that really determines how the offspring will turn out. I wonder which of these young stallions will try to bend this mare to their will." The merchant took a long swig of his wine. "I bet her children will be something to behold."

The merchant wandered off, calling out to a friend, his face already fading from Julian's mine, though his words remained. As much as he loathed to admit it, the princess was right. His position was only secure to her coming of age in a year's time. He knew that her first proclamation would be his head on a spike. Julian unconsciously rubbed his neck, weighing the strength of his network to the loyalty of the court. The outcome could go either way, but there were things he could do to shift the scales to his favor.

Enjoy your little rebellion while it lasts, your highness. I will bend you to my will one way or another…or break you.

BRAELYN SAT IN WHAT SHE THOUGHT OF AS "HER window seat," staring out at the rain splattered glass with a book loosely gripped in her hands. The garden party had been the first of many events that required her presence, demanding the projection of stability and security. Dances, dinners, promenades; she dutifully attended each one, the singular dead tree amidst the budding forest. And then the summer rains started providing a few moments of respite and solitude. Her thoughts were dark and painful, yet she preferred them to her court's insincere attendants.

"Pardon the intrusion, your highness, but your carriage to Yulla's temple is ready."

Braelyn set aside the book she had only been pretending to read and brushed the wrinkles from her skirts. She followed the servant to the awaiting carriage. She didn't bother to hide her contempt for the burly guard already seated inside.

"I'm only going to the temple," Braelyn snipped.

The guard said nothing, slightly flexing his thick arms. Braelyn rolled her eyes at the silent threat. The worse the guard could do was throw her over his shoulder or possibly knock her out. He wouldn't dare leave a mark where anyone could see or end her life; no matter how much she wished for it some days.

Braelyn got into the carriage with a sigh, putting as much space between her and Julian's watchdog as she could in such tight quarters. Braelyn nearly vaulted from the carriage even before it slowed to a stop at the stairs of Yulla's Temple.

Priests and priestesses in dark robes bowed to the princess as she walked up the steps. A young novice led her up the stairs, holding an umbrella over her head to keep the worst of the rain off. Braelyn walked as quickly up the slick stone steps as she dared, hoping to spare the poor novice from becoming thoroughly soaked.

Once inside, she purchased offerings of incense and red-black bread. She tried to not wonder, as she had so often before, what gave the bread its slightly reddish hue. She heard once that before burning the bodies of the nameless dead; they drained the blood and used that to add to the potency of the bread. For blood is the water of life, and even in death, some life still lingers. The very idea had terrified her when she was younger, but now, having stained her soul with the blood of the innocent, it didn't twist her stomach as it once had. With offerings in hand, she walked through the main temple space. Her eyes flitted over the grieving people at the smaller altars nestled in small alcoves as she looked for an open one.

"There's a free altar just behind the main worship space," a helpful novice said, pointing.

Braelyn nodded her thanks, her steps quickening to reach the semi private altar. Behind her, the watchdog hesitated briefly before resuming his slow, steady pace, allowing the distance to grow between them. Perhaps he had the tiniest sliver of decency after all.

A thin film of ash and wax coated the altar. A singular candle burned in its holder, thick rivers of wax flowing down the side. Braelyn set the bread in the middle of the altar, lighting her incense with the candle's flame. Twin spiraling streams of smoke rose from the sticks, filling her nose with their pungent aroma.

Braelyn then placed them in their holder, a small bowl of graveyard soil, and picked up the bread, tearing it into smaller pieces. She left most of it on the altar, keeping only a small portion for herself.

"Separate yet together. Linked by bonds of blood, soul, and sustenance."

She quickly tossed her chunk of bread into her mouth, her jaws working to grind against its toughness. When she swallowed it, the bitter bread stuck in her throat, sending her into a coughing fit, tears streaming down her face.

"Drink this," said a familiar voice behind her.

Sasha knelt next to Braelyn, holding a small flagon in her thin, pale fingers. Braelyn took the flagon, tipping back its contents without a second thought. Mulled cider poured down her throat, softening the stuck bread, bringing sweet release as it finally moved down to her stomach.

"Thank you," Braelyn coughed, handing the near empty flagon back.

Sasha smiled, tucking it away before turning her gaze to the altar. Braelyn stiffened, though her face remained neutral, or as neutral as one could be recovering from a near choking.

"As much as you might wish it, your highness, you mustn't be so eager to join the dead."

Braelyn blinked at the priestess, spying a tucked away smile in the corner of her mouth. "I didn't think the priestesses of Yulla made light of death."

Sasha released a breathy laugh. "Why ever not? We see death in all her many forms every day. I dare say we know her intimately enough to have a friendly relationship."

"Delightful," Braelyn mumbled.

Sasha folded her hands in prayer, her head bent. Braelyn watched her at first, then joined in.

Hamath, Shooth, Prenn...and Tolin.

Her throat constricted. If it wasn't for me, you'd still be alive today, scheming behind Julian's back, but you're not. You'll never be again, all because of me. I should have known that he'd never let me slip through his grasp. I'm sorry. I'm sorry. And what's worse, I don't even know how I can ever repay my debt to you.

A rustling of cloth told her that Sasha had finished her prayer.

"Take care, your highness, and please remember my words. You have so much you need to accomplish before the Mother welcomes you into her halls."

Sasha bowed, leaving Braelyn with more than the taste of cider in her mouth. The man Julian sent as a watchdog leaned awkwardly against a pillar as he waited for Braelyn to finish with her prayers. She smirked, half tempted to kneel before the altar until she no longer felt her limbs. She quickly let the wicked thought go. Julian would undoubtedly do something terrible to the temple to keep her from ever being able to visit again. Her hands were already stained red and dripping, and she didn't want to incite the wrath of the gods by causing harm to their servants. She stuck her blood-stained hands away from the robed figures around her, freezing on the spot when her fingertips touched the edges of a piece of paper, someone slipped into her pocket.

The guard turned, his brows furrowed at her sudden stop and the pallor of her face. Braelyn swallowed down her alarm, schooling her face into royal indifference once more despite the frantic beating of her heart.

THE BELL TOWER CHIMED THE MIDNIGHT HOUR. BRAELYN slowly crept from her bed, tip-toeing over to the box that held the items for her monthly cycles. It was the only place she could think to hide the letter that Sasha had slipped into her pocket until it was safe to read.

Creeping to a window, she knelt on the cold stone floor in a beam of moonlight. It was pale and flickering because of passing clouds, but it was better than lighting a candle whose light would stand out like a beacon in the night. Her fingers were near ice, and not just because of the night air. The letter's seal remained unbroken to her eye. She couldn't read the emblem of the seal until she cocked it just right to catch the light. Her eyes went wide at the seal of the Holy Isle. Only the Abbot could use the seal, and he rarely used it.

Breaking the seal, Braelyn hastily opened her letter, half hoping, half dreading its contents. A swirling mass of black covered the page. Braelyn blew against it and the swirling mass settled into. After reading a few sentences, Braelyn had to press her hand to her mouth to muffle the sound of her cries.

On the night everything went to shit, I was supposed to drive a knife into your back. Instead, I jumped into the shadows and took out the goons Julian sent along. All because we became friends after I called you out on your privileged ideology and you called me out on my cynicism.

Your brother asked be to write that he never thanked you for taking the blame when he broke your mother's crystal dancer figurine when you were six.

I hope that those are enough to convince you we're us and not some ploy by Julian. Because, in all honesty, we don't have the time.

There's a demon inside Lord Julian. The Ilmarrions imprisoned this demon ages ago, you'd call them Mystics. Luckily, some survived the Purge and are living in secret. They say I'm one of them and that's why I have magic. I'm still trying to wrap my head around it. We already know about two relics they used, and the people who will use them. We have to find the rest.

Braelyn could feel Mirra's hesitation through the ink. She briefly ran her fingers over the words, keeping herself grounded despite the fantastical revelations.

I have friends in the city. I've reached out to them to see if they will help you. They have an extensive network of people possibly well suited to giving that demon a run for its money. If they decide to help you, and it's a big if, they will reach out to you. Gaitlan's hovering over my shoulder, incessantly saying to remind you about a Codex? He said you'd know what that meant. In the meantime, keep your chin up, princess. We're counting on you to carve out a hole for us to end this bastard once and for all.

Since her parent's murder, her dreams were filled with the sounds of screams and the scents of smoke and gore. Her waking life did little to ease her suffering, introducing one fresh horror after another. Leaving her no place to escape the travesty of her life.

However, the dream she had after reading Mirra's letter was different. Calmer. Brighter. It soothed her frayed soul like a salve to a wound. Braelyn felt the ever present lines of tension ease throughout her body as she allowed the dream to pull her deeper.

Bright lights blurred her vision, leaving only the impression of objects and people. She only knew that she was in the palace. Flecks of gold, like minuscule floating suns, caught her eye, leading her to a set of doors she would recognize by touch alone.

With hands much smaller than hers in the waking world, Braelyn pushed the door open and the world around her thrown into sharp clarity. Laughter greeted her first, drawing tears to her eyes. She never thought she would hear her parent's laughter again.

"Braelyn, my love, there you are." Her mother opened her arms wide.

Braelyn ran toward her mother as fast as her feet could carry her and threw herself into her gentle embrace. As she burrowed her face into her mother's hair, drawing in its light floral aroma, she heard her father laugh behind her.

"What a little savage you've become whilst we were away. I should fire your tutors."

"Whatever for", her brother said with all the dignity a fourteen year old could muster. "It's not their fault you indulge her."

Her father ruffled Gailtan's hair affectionately. "Then I suppose you're too old for presents?"

Gaitlan pushed away, a smirk already forming at the corners of his mouth. "It would be rude to refuse them now."

"Well, then come and see what we've brought you," their mother said with a laugh. She shifted Braelyn next to her on the couch and rang a bell. Two servants, each bearing a medium-sized, ornate wooden box entered the room.

They set the boxes before Braelyn and her brother, who waited for their parent's approval before flinging open the lids. In Gaitlan's was an emerald halter for his horse. For Braelyn, it was a collection of myths and legends from across the continent from before the fall of the Mystic Empire.

"I'll never understand why you like those manky old books," her brother said, his nose scrunching at the sight of the books' frayed bindings. "They're nothing more than a bunch of fanciful stories."

"Fanciful or not," their mother said, her face growing stern, "there's always a bit of truth buried beneath the fanciful. And we should always strive to remember it."

"Just like with the Codex," Braelyn said in a prim voice not quite suited for an eight year old.

"Quite right, my little scholar," her father beamed. "These books hold secrets like the Codex hidden somewhere in the royal libraries."

"Can't you tell us where it is, father?" Braelyn pleaded.

Her father laughed and shook his head. "I'm afraid I can't, my love. I've never seen them myself. The only clue I can give is the same one my father gave me. The…"

Braelyn sat up in her bed and wiped the tears from her face. "The keystone is kept by starlight."

Throwing back the covers, she slipped into the simplest dress she owned, quickly braiding her long, golden hair. It was time for her to once again resume the search for the Codex. As she hurried down to the first of the three royal libraries, she pondered over her brother's message.

Had he somehow discovered the location of the Codex and never told her? She quickly dismissed the idea. Her brother's interests hardly changed from childhood to adulthood. He cared more for fighting, hunting, and having "relations" with any woman he could get his hands on, than uncovering mysteries from long forgotten pasts. Perhaps he thought that she still pursued it as ardently as they had as children. Braelyn huffed at how little her brother seemed to know about her. Then again, she also never attempted to preserve their connection. She too had grown too wrapped up in her own personal interests and goals to give her brother anything more than a passing, judgmental thought. She swore to remedy that if, no, when, they set things right again.

Chest heaving, Braelyn stood before the heavy library doors and felt the first stirrings of hope. Finally, something to do that didn't involve running away or leaving her fate in the hands of others. She could do this. She had no other option.

"Pardon me, your highness."

Braelyn loosened a breath before plastering a bland smile on her face. Her fire from the morning had fizzled out before lunch time as mindlessly picking through the astrology section. Her fingers were coated with the same dust that burned her eyes and caused her to sneeze relentlessly.

"It is time to get ready for the evening meal."

Braelyn's smile fell beneath furrowed brows. "It must be later in the day than I realized."

The maid's face paled while her gaze remained pointed at her feet. "Tonight's meal will be of great importance. The Lord Regent has requested that you take the utmost care in your attire."

Clenching her jaw, Braelyn stood, setting her book on the seat behind her, and returned to her room. Lord Julian had held three other events of "great importance" already. She suspected each reason was to assure those presented that she was safe and healthy before aligning themselves to Julian. Her dismissal quickly turned to alarm when the attendant presented her with the wrong gown for the evening. "What is this?"

"Your gown for the evening," one of her handmaids replied, her eyes lowered.

"No, it's not," Braelyn stormed over to her wardrobe, flinging the doors wide. The bottom of her stomach dropped at the rows of muted but colorful dresses. "Where are my clothes!"

The most senior of her maids stepped forward. "The Lord Regent decreed that the time of full mourning has passed and that now the kingdom is in half mourning."

Words typically only heard in the lowest streets of the city poured from her mouth as she slammed her wardrobe shut. Her maids blanched, slowly backing away from Braelyn as if she were a wild beast. She felt like one. She wanted to lash out at the women cowering before her, to tear at them until they felt the smallest measure of the pain that she carried inside. Just as her rage threatened to spill over, it crashed into the wall of ice that kept her emotions in check.

"I suppose there's nothing to be done for it now," she said, turning so her maids could begin undressing her. "Leave the adornments to a minimum."

As one, the maids breathed a sigh of relief before setting about their task. They silently worked, hoping for a quick end to the princess and regent's silent war.

Braelyn scowled at her reflection after her maids scurried out of her room. They had done their job well. Her golden hair sat on top of her head in a braided circle with the end trailing over her shoulder. They left her face bare, save for the slightest hint of blush to make her face look less wane. The only jewelry she wore was the pearls her parents had given her on her court debut. Braelyn absentmindedly ran her fingers down the string, drawing strength from the cool, milky pearls. She hadn't put on the dress that Lord Julian had chosen for her. Instead, she chose the most somber of all her new dresses. One of light gray heather with simple embroidery around the neckline and hem. The sleeves clung tightly to the elbow before belling out to drape over her hands.

One small act of rebellion.

That was all that she was capable of, and it tore at her like a knife in the dark. The bells chimed the hour. She stood with a heavy sigh, brushing the wrinkles out of her skirt.

"Let's see what he's after now," she said to her reflection before walking down the dining hall.

A riot of color assaulted her eyes the moment she entered the dining hall. At the top of the grand staircase, all she could do was stare down at her court. No, it wasn't her court anymore; it was his.

Braelyn descended the stairs with a forced smile. The courtiers nearest to the stairs noted her arrival and sank to their knees. Braelyn inclined her head slightly and continued toward the table set on a dais at the far end of the room.

All around her, people bowed, with a few scowling at her modest attire. Braelyn allowed a ghost of a smirk to tug at her mouth. Mirra's letter had rekindled a fire in her soul, that was only tempered by the still tender wounds of losing Tolin and the others. *Did you think after all this I would play by your rules?*

This time, Lord Julian left Braelyn's seat vacant, choosing to sit on the right of the place reserved for monarchs. Braelyn's heart leapt into her throat. To anyone else, Lord Julian's actions would appear to be a deference to the princess's position, but she knew better. If he was publicly relenting power, what was he about to grab from the shadows?

Spying her, Lord Julian's face lit up, and he hurried around the long table to greet her at the foot of the dais.

Braelyn cocked her head, halting her steps. The sour feeling in her stomach rose, coating her tongue in bitterness.

"I've forgotten how attractive you are, your highness." Lord Julian took her hand, lightly placing a kiss on it. "I must say that color looks well on you."

"Thank you," Braelyn said tersely, unobtrusively wiping her hand on her skirts. Stepping onto the dais, she took her seat. Now that she'd arrived, the courtiers quickly took a seat at their respective tables. Servers flowed into the room as if by magic, each bearing a heavy tray of steaming delicacies.

Venison, pork, soup, potatoes, carrots, and parsnips were served with red wines, ports, and ciders. The courtiers seated at the tables feasted, talking merrily amongst themselves, only sparing those seated at the dais a passing glance before moving on. Braelyn watched them, all the food turning to ash in her mouth. Beside her, Lord Julian laughed and joked with the courtier sitting next to him, not paying her one lick of attention.

Run, some part of her mind screamed. Run away before you get ensnared! Move, you fool!

They served all too soon dessert, yet not soon enough. She could leave without potentially insulting the nobles she needed to keep on her side once the last dish left the table.

The clanging of crystal rang out across the dining hall, as clear as a bell and as terrible as a tomb. Lord Julian stood, a small glass of sherry in his hand. A great hush fell over those gathered as they turned their faces toward the dais expectantly.

"A blow was dealt to our home. A blow that has shaken us to the core and yet, as I look out at those loyal to their kingdom, I can see that we have remained strong!"

A roar went up that drowned out the pounding of Braelyn's heart.

"Though we have weathered this storm, there are still many more to come. Our kingdom stands at a crossroads, and the choices we make now will echo throughout eternity. That is why we must look to the future."

Someone seized Braelyn by the elbow, urging her to stand next to Lord Julian before shoving a matching glass in her hand. Wide eyed, she stared out across the room spying one glass of sherry appearing after another.

Beside her, Lord Julian continued to speak, his words sounding muffled to her ears. The courtiers cheered again, clapping, toasting, their faces twisted . Braelyn could only stare out at the crowd, confusion and alarm written all over her face for anyone to see.

"I look forward to our union," Lord Julian said, clinking his glass against hers.

The crystalline sound snapped her back to reality. She jerked away from Lord Julian, setting her glass down hard enough that a few droplets splashed onto the white cloth.

"Have you finally gone mad?"

The band had picked up a merry tune, drawing away even the most curious of gazes while masking her voice.

"In what world would I ever agree to marry the man who slaughtered my family?"

His hand lashed around her wrist like an iron band, pulling her closer to him. Lord Julian leaned in, pressing his cheek to hers. Below, it looked nothing more than a suitor kissing his betrothed.

"Because if you don't, every person here will die in an unpleasant and painful way."

"Impossible."

"Did Mirra ever tell you of the training she received under my tutelage?" Braelyn blinked.

"No? Then I shall illuminate. Besides learning how to navigate court and how to move about without being seen, she learned a fair bit about poisons. Of course, she had to suffer through most of the poisons she learned about. I am of the mind that experience makes for the best teacher."

All color drained from Braelyn's face as she slowly turned to look at the celebrating people below. "Y-your lying."

"You don't sound so sure, your highness. Care to wager the truth of my words against the lives of your people?"

Uncertainty froze her tongue. With as much tenacity as she could muster, Braelyn lifted her chin, meeting Lord Julian's eyes.

"If you slaughter all the nobles in the court, the people will see you for what you are. They will rise against you and end your reign before it even begins."

Lord Julian's feral grin sent shivers down her spine. His tongue darted over his teeth like snakes, savoring her fear.

"Perhaps," he said, closing the gap between them. "And then what will become of you, my dear? You're still not of age and highly marriageable. Every man in this room knows that you are the surefire way to the throne. If not me, then someone else will lay claim to you, taking your only bit of value. Better the devil you know than another. He might even be worse than me."

Ice filled Braelyn's veins, yet she kept her composure, schooling her face into granite. "I highly doubt that. I refuse you, now and always."

Not caring about pretenses, she stormed out of the dining hall. Once alone, her hurried steps turned into a run that carried her all the way to her room. Covered with a fine sheen of sweat, Braelyn hastily ripped her hair down and removed her dress.

She stood in the middle of her room, feet cooling on the stone floor, until her tempest of emotions brought her to her knees.

BRAELYN STOOD STARING AT THE TOO SMALL FIGURE ON the altar, completely numb. Crumpled at the foot of the altar, the boy's mother screamed and cried, her anguish rippling through the silent gathering of mourners. The priestesses of Yulla sang around the shrouded figure, asking the Dark Mother to accept the child into her embrace and bring them to eternal spring.

Her fault. This was entirely her fault. When the first members of court fell ill after the banquet announcing her engagement to the Lord Julian, she chalked it up to coincidence. But then another fell ill, and another, and another, until she could no longer deny that Lord Julian had poisoned the entire Undrosean court.

And then Tobias fell ill. Tobias wasn't a noble son, but his brother worked in the palace as a server. During the banquet, his brother Johnas swiped a small bottle of sherry used during the toast. At first, only Johnas was ill, and then Tobias didn't wake up for his morning chores.

He would never wake again.

Braelyn learned all this from the whispering of the servants and her maids Julian used to keep eyes on her movements. Her spine stiffened when she felt his oily presence saddle next to her.

"No parent should ever have to bury their child," Lord Julian said. "Although, I guess your parents won't ever have to worry about that."

Braelyn closed her eyes, breathing heavily through her nose. "What do you want?" Her voice was as hard and dull as the surrounding stones.

"Still think I was bluffing, your highness?"

Shielding her face with her hair and veil, Braelyn blinked back bitter tears.

"No," she croaked.

Lord Julian placed his broad hand on the small of her back. "Good."

CHAPTER TWO

THE PREPARATIONS FOR HER IMPENDING WEDDING WERE well underway before her face was dry of tears. Braelyn languished in bed for a solid week, refusing all food and drink. Her spy-maids entered and exited her room, whispering to themselves. She didn't care. Let them talk. Let the whole kingdom talk. That's all they're good for.

The delicate scent of roses wafted into the room, enveloping her in warm memories of days in the sun with the taste of honey and hope on her tongue. Bitter tears welled in her eyes. Braelyn pressed her face into her pillow to smother the scent and the memories.

Her mattress sagged as someone sat next to her. Braelyn didn't move until a gentle hand brushed over her tangled locks.

Braelyn sat upright, coming face to face with the soulful eyes of Lady Nora. Red washed over Braelyn's vision as she pulled her lips back into a snarl before reaching out to rake the beautiful face with her nails.

Fast as an adder, Lady Nora latched her well-manicured fingers around Braelyn's wrists, pulling them down with more force than expected.

"Now, now, princess, this is no way for a lady to act."

"As opposed to a lying, backstabbing, two-faced guttersnipe!"

Hurt briefly tugged at the corners of Lady Nora's subtle mouth. "Not all of us can be brave like Mirra and defy pure power. But we can find our own strength and carry on."

Lady Nora's words soften Braelyn's rage, despite her attempts to harden her heart. Tears welled unbidden in her eyes, spilling over as great, wracking sobs shook her body. Strong arms wrapped around her body, bathing her in the delicate scent of roses in summer. Her mother's favorite scent. The once comforting aroma turned her stomach but instead of pushing the woman away, Braelyn pulled her in and hated herself for being so weak.

Braelyn sat in the steaming tub with her chin on her knees. She kept her focus on a cracked stone in the wall at the far end of the room. The bath attendants scurried around her, mindlessly chatting about something that she couldn't bother to listen to. The faint scent of roses behind her was the only sign that Lady Nora was still with her.

As the attendants washed her hair and body, Braelyn let her mind wander, relishing the only place where she was truly free. She would never allow herself to be shackled to Julian. She'd find some way to take her life before he ever could possess her. But how? There was no place she could go where someone wasn't watching her, reporting back to the monster dressed as a man.

A pitcher of warm water poured over her head, bringing her back to her surroundings. The bath attendants bowed in unison before leaving her alone with Lady Nora.

Lady Nora stood with a towel, waiting for Braelyn.

Braelyn rolled her eyes and stepped out of the tub, soapy water cascading down her body.

"The world has never been a kind place for those like us," Lady Nora said as she quickly whipped away most of the cooling water.

"We are nothing alike," Braelyn spat.

Lady Nora continued on as if she hadn't spoken. "But we are more fortunate than the common woman. At least we have resources at our disposal to either ease some of our suffering or remove it all together." Lady Nora gave Braelyn a pointed look. "Especially if you have the will to succeed."

Lady Nora maintained eye contact, putting the weight of her words into her eyes. Braelyn blinked for a moment until the words settled.

"Mirra said you gave good advice."

"Good advice comes from years of unpleasant experience. I don't want to see other bright futures snuffed out the same way my future was."

Pointed silence. "This changes nothing."

"Naturally."

With her looming marriage on the horizon, the palace transformed into a hive of activity. Merchants from all corners of the kingdom, and a few from neighboring kingdoms, vied for Braelyn's attention. They wanted to know what colors she wanted and a thousand other frivolous questions that she didn't want to answer. Instead of facing them, Braelyn sought refuge in the only place that gave her a morsel of peace — the library.

Wrapped up in the anonymity of semi-darkness between the shelves, her ears sharpened to the sound of approaching nuisances. Her steps became as light as feathers as she maneuvered around the tall bookcases. Though she would never admit it aloud, she rather enjoyed avoiding people. If anything, it kept her mind off of her impending doom.

All the while, she continued her search for the keystone. She'd given up on the most traveled portions of the library, opting to search through the older portions of the library. Every generation or so, the architects added new wings and destroyed old wings. It was plausible that they had moved the keystone from its home to be lost forever, or rested in a portion of the library that was no longer in use.

Braelyn prayed it was the latter.

Adding to her frustrations, courtiers had invaded the library. Nearly every young noble flocked to the library for the chance to "accidentally bump" into her. Braelyn groaned, pressing the heel of her palms into her eyes.

"Archive day it is, then."

The entrance to the archives was nothing more than a nondescript door that could have been mistaken for a broom closet. It took Braelyn three great tugs to open the door, revealing a semi dark stairwell. To the left of the threshold sat a small table with a box of half burned white candles with disks to prevent hot wax from dripping onto unsuspecting hands.

Braelyn sparked a candle, carefully fitting it inside the disk before descending the stairs, one hand firmly on the railing.

One of the many benefits of building a castle, or anything, on top of a hill or cliff, was all the available space below. As long as you could cut into the bedrock without weakening the foundations of the structure. The architects used bedrock and natural caves to build the castle, with tunnels connecting them. The larger caverns became storage for supplies, riches and, in this case, archives of partially forgotten knowledge.

At the base of the stairs, Braelyn discarded her candle and studied the cavernous space in front of her. The roof of the cavern was low, scant inches from the tops of the tall rows of shelves. Most of the back of the archive was cloaked in darkness, hiding just how far back it went. Golden lanterns bathed the front in golden light, illuminating several long tables covered with haphazard stacks of books, scrolls, and abandoned quills. Twin braziers burned, keeping back most of the chill, as long as you sat near them. But the half a dozen wizened robed figures didn't seem to mind. Only one bothered to look up as Braelyn entered, blinking at her with watery eyes set deep within a weathered face.

Light sparked behind his eyes when he finally recognized who Braelyn was. He hurried toward her as fast as his bow-legged gait could carry him.

"Apologies, your highness," he said, his voice sounding like wind through wheat. "We don't get visitors down here often, especially youngsters like yourself. No one cares for history anymore. They're all too worried about making it instead of learning from it."

"That's why I'm here," Braelyn said.

The ancient priest gave her a look that made it clear he didn't believe her half lie.

"I don't know if you've heard about what's happened in the past few months?"

The priest's face fell. "Ah, yes. Terrible thing, losing one's parents in such a violent manner."

"Yes, and that is why I've come. In all my years of study, I've never heard of a travesty like this happening. I hoped, and feared, that there might be some record of something similar in the archives."

"May I ask why?"

"I want to serve my people the best that I can. If there are concerns or situations that I need to be mindful of, I would like to, at least, be aware of them."

The old priest rubbed his stubbled chin with a gnarled hand. "Can't argue with that logic, can I?

Braelyn held her breath.

"Take one lantern with you. Some lamps may have gone out. They come once a month to refill them, but they're late this month."

"When I leave, I will remind them."

"How about some better food and tea?" shouted the woman with stark white hair. Her bawdy cackle brought to mind images of witches stirring black cauldrons over large fires.

"I'll see what I can manage," Braelyn answered, a bit more hesitantly. The priest she first met shook his head and led her gently by the elbow to the shelf.

"Look at this."

Carved into the shelf was a crude image of a cauldron or brazier. "If you see this, keep walking ahead. Eventually, you'll find your way back here. If you get lost, just know that it will be at least three days before someone will come looking for you."

With a hearty thump on the back, the priest left Braelyn, standing bewildered before the shelf. He rejoined his colleagues, a laugh at her before becoming consumed by whatever held their interest before her arrival.

Braelyn retrieved a lantern, ensuring that she had a couple of candles in her pocket and a means to light them. She ran her hand over the carving, then glanced at the elders before entering the archive.

At first, her steps had been hesitant, almost fearful, as if some monster was going to jump out of the crumbling books and scrolls around her. The cave walls forced her to take turns, even though she tried to maintain a straight path. Her breath came out like tiny clouds in front of her face, and she wrapped her arms around to stay warm. Just when she was about to turn back, she caught the scent of something burning. She followed the scent and soon noticed the glow of a fire. She left the stacks, entering a circular space. Near the center of space blazed another brazier.

Braelyn was too grateful for its warmth to question why one burned so far into the archive when no one seemed to be around. Once she could feel her face and fingers again, she took in the space. Her dress had left a slightly less dusty trail on the floor, hinting that the floor had some sort of design beneath the layers of dust. Unease settled around her like a blanket drenched in icy water. If no one had been in the space long enough for thick dust to accumulate on the floor, then who lit the brazier? Braelyn entered the open space, eyeing everything around her.

Curio cases formed a loose circle around a singular table and chair. Walking over to the cases, Braelyn peered through the murky glass. She couldn't make out much, but she saw a series of half scorched scrolls, a tarnished bracelet and a broken pot. She tugged on a glass shelf's door, but it didn't budge. Below the shelf, she spied a tarnished copper placard. She wet her thumb and slowly scrubbed away years of grime and neglect.

Recovered from the wreckage of Ilmarrion city, Dalen.

"Ilmarrion," Braelyn whispered, pressing her fingers against the glass. She was unfamiliar with the name. Was it a place or the name of the people who once lived there? Would this be the fate of her family? Forgotten save for a few pieces left to collect dust in some forgotten corner of a library?

Braelyn walked around the landing, mindlessly gazing at the glass faced bookcases. Her footsteps echoed on the herringbone floor. The heavy silence of the written word pressed on her from all sides. Her nose prickled with dust from the ancient tomes that surrounded her.

She walked over to the desk next. More utilitarian than ornate, it reminded her of her father's desk. She ran her hands across the top, a bittersweet smile on her face, until a secret compartment opened at the touch of her fingers. Braelyn lept back, clutching her hand to her chest. When nothing horrible slithered out, she approached the gaping hole slowly, poised to retreat at a moment's notice.

A single slip of parchment sat inside, far newer looking than it had any rights to be. With trembling fingers, she withdrew the parchment, unfolding it. It took her mind a moment to register what was scrawled across the parchment.

A map.

The parchment slipped from her fingers, gently gliding back to the desk. Braelyn didn't linger, turning heel and ran for the entrance, paying no heed to the direction of her frantic escape. Slowly, reason clawed its way to the surface, and she slowed, her chest heaving. Sliding down against a bookcase, Braelyn pulled her knees to her chest, her soul crumbling under the weight of unyielding darkness.

"THE TIMING OF YOUR WEDDING IS EVERYTHING, YOUR highness. Spring is beautiful with the fresh flowers and promise of hope, but the weather is unpredictable. Summer is most common and you are anything but common. Fall has a richer color pallet, and the weather is more agreeable. But winter weddings are almost right out of a story with the glittering snow and bright greens."

The wedding planner appeared the morning after Braelyn came across the map in the dust covered landing. She listened to the woman prattle on about one useless detail after another.

Braelyn rubbed her temples, wanting nothing more than to order the woman away and retreat into her bed.

"Which one?"

"What?" Braelyn said, blinking against the too bright light.

The wedding planner made a small face before answering. "The season, your highness. When do you want to have your wedding?"

Never.

"My eighteenth birthday isn't until the end of summer, so perhaps winter?"

Another face. The wedding planner set her notes to the side, taking Braelyn's hands into hers. "I know that this marriage is one of convenience, not love. That's one burden of privilege. The common folk can marry for love, but the nobles...they have to marry for the greater good."

Braelyn yanked her hand free. "I know that better than you. My entire life has been built around what marriage I could secure for the betterment of my people."

"And nothing has changed," said the wedding planner, retaking Braelyn's hands.

"Everything has changed."

The woman's eyes filled with pity. Her lips pressed into a thin line as if she fought to keep her true thoughts from spilling over. "Nothing has changed. You are a woman and the men of the court will not follow you no matter your lineage. A union with Lord Julian, a respected man with power behind his name, is the only way to keep your family on the throne."

Braelyn's lips curled back. "We're done for the day. Don't come until I summon you."

The wedding planner blanched, hastily gathering her belongings before backing out of the room with her eyes fixed on the floor.

The pounding in her head increased, yet she didn't return to bed. Instead, she splashed cool water from the wash bin on her face and readied herself for another day of forced smiles and secret barbs. Braelyn's first instructions had been in court speech, the art of saying one thing but meaning another. It was the way civilized people battled; with wit, not a sword. But Lord Julian performed on a level that Braelyn never knew existed. Not only could his words have a half dozen different meanings. She was ill prepared to fight against him.

Ever since she cut off her meeting with the wedding planner, Braelyn spent all her time searching for the keystone and the codex.

Hiding in the library searching for a fairy tale will not help you.

"I'm not hiding," she said aloud. "The Shadow Library will help to level the playing field."

Don't you think he doesn't know what you're doing? He had the entire kingdom under his thumb, long before he slaughtered your parents. What makes you think he's now blind to your actions? Doesn't that map illustrate the point?

The map.

Had Julian put it there to lead her astray or someone else entirely? Was it even for her? It could belong to thieves or a new servant unsure about their way. Braelyn shook her head. Thieves wouldn't leave anything behind, even in a secret compartment, and a servant wouldn't hide a map either. It had to be Julian with a fresh new torture for her. But how could he even know that she would find that place? She didn't put it past him to orchestrate the incident that led her to the landing, and yet - how could he have known her steps before she took them?

The air on the landing was as silent as the day she stumbled onto it. She followed the trail she left in the dust, looking for any signs that someone else had been there. Nothing.

She walked in circles around the desk, trailing her hands up and down every part. The only compartment was the one on top, still open. The folded scrap of parchment sat where she dropped it.

Braelyn worried her fingers. She still wasn't completely sure that the map wasn't some trap laid by Julian to crush her spirit. That also raised questions over the letter's authenticity again.

Braelyn slammed her hand on the table, crumpling the map beneath her hand. She could not give into despair, not hand her kingdom over without a fight, no matter how many times they knocked her down. She turned, folding the map and sliding it next to her chest. Her education may not have included lying and how to work in the shadows, but her tutors always said she was a fast learner.

"I HAVE TO LEAVE THE CITY FOR A FEW DAYS."

"Oh," Braelyn replied, keeping her face calm despite the frantic beating of her heart.

"Don't worry, my dear," Lord Julian said, reaching across the table to take her hand. Braelyn suppressed a shudder. "I will take a small contingent of guards with me and will return swiftly."

"Don't make promises you can't keep," Braelyn said with a small smirk. "Who knows what hidden dangers linger just behind you?"

Lord Julian's eyes darkened. "And don't you forget that you have no genuine power in this world save what I give to you."

Braelyn's smirk became feral. "And don't you forget that the power you hold is only temporary. Even with this sham of a marriage, it will fade away into nothingness, just like you."

"We shall see, my love. We shall see."

Braelyn watched Lord Julian's retreating back, wanting nothing more than to bury her knife into it. She finished her breakfast, ensuring that her motions were unhurried and natural. She couldn't afford anyone to suspect that she was up to anything.

After her meal, she took a jaunt around the gardens, a light cloak around her shoulders. The wind that morning was cooler with the scent of rain. The cloak perfectly hid the rolled up servant's dress she'd pilfered from the laundry days ago.

After walking, Braelyn went to the library with explicit orders to not be disturbed. For everyone knows rainy days are best spent curled up beneath a blanket with a good book.

"Do you need anything else, your highness?"

"No, thank you," Braelyn said, waving the servant away. "I only need one day of peace and solitude."

The servant curtsied, backing away slowly before turning to leave her alone. Braelyn pretended to read, slowly turning the pages of a book that she didn't see. When she was sure that no one watched her, she set the book aside, pulling the bundled up dress and cloak from beneath the blanket.

With soft but hurried steps, she made her way to the landing. She lingered in the shadows, eyes scanning the open space before stepping out. She laid her disguise on the table, her fingers hesitating over the laces of her gown.

Pinching her eyes shut, Braelyn undid her laces, letting her gown fall to the floor. The chill in the air drew bumps along her exposed limbs. She threw on the servant's dress, ignoring the way the rough fabric rubbed against her skin. She replaced her silk slippers with a pair of sturdy boots. Much too fine for a servant, but who spent their time looking to ensure a person's shoes matched their attire? She coiled her golden braid around her head, securing it with the plainest hair pins she possessed before wrapping it all with a simple linen cloth. Tying the cloak around her shoulders, Braelyn held the map in her icy fingers. She took one deep breath before taking a step either to her doom or to her salvation.

The map led her deeper into the forgotten portions of the library. It took her down a winding staircase, completely void of light. Braelyn kept a hand on the wall in part to make sure she didn't stumble in the dark and partly to assure herself that darkness hadn't swallowed the world.

The stairway ended abruptly. Braelyn walked right into the stone wall, stars dancing behind her eyes. Cursing softly, she rubbed her nose, searching for the opening. When only met stone met her fingers, fear rose in her throat.

"Don't panic, think."

She slowed her frantic groping, running her hands up and down the stone wall slowly. The rough stone dug into her fingertips and palms as she scraped her hands along, looking for something, anything, to show that she hadn't been duped again.

A stream of cold air met her fingers. She knelt down, putting her face in the air's path, taking gulping breaths to calm her frantic heart. She pressed the brick, leaping back when the wall shifted with a boom, showering her with bits of sand and pebbles.

Coughing and sputtering, Braelyn shouldered the wall, sliding through the narrow opening. The wall closed with a thud behind her. Braelyn swallowed, but pressed onward.

The ground beneath her feet was earthen and uneven. More than once, she stumbled over some unseen stone or crevice. But still she persisted until the surrounding darkness shifted to gray and the air grew crisper with the scent of wet earth.

The pathway opened up into a small cave. Braelyn clutched her cloak tighter and stepped out into the open.

"Hello," she called out, her soft voice echoing in the chamber.

She took another step forward, calling out again. Only fading echoes replied.

Braelyn fiddled with the strings of her cloak, turning about in a slow circle. She spared the cave one last glance over before pulling her hood over her head to exit into the pouring rain.

"Mirra said you were smart — for a noble."

Braelyn released a yelp, stumbled over a stone, and fell. She braced for an impact that never came. A set of firm hands gripped her arms, keeping her nearly parallel with the cave floor.

The man who had caught her smiled down at her crookedly. His round face was bright, with deep lines of laughter around his eyes and mouth. Though the furrows across his forehead hinted at long hours in thought.

Braelyn stared up at him, speechless, until a flash of light drew her attention to a medallion on a bit of leather string. The man hoisted her back up. He didn't step back, the two of them so close that she could make out the minuscule details on the gold coin around his neck.

"You're from Zallino," she said.

The man chuckled. "Only born there." He took a step back, giving her a bow that wouldn't have been out of place on a stage. "Allow me to introduce myself. I am Bao. Mirra's childhood friend and the Bossman of The Merchant District, at your service."

CHAPTER THREE

BAO LED BRAELYN TO A SMALL CARRIAGE WAITING NEAR A grouping of evergreen trees. The inside of the carriage was mercifully dry, but did nothing to cull the chill. Braelyn wrapped her damp cloak tighter and studied the man who Mirra had sent to help her.

At first she didn't believe him until he handed her a letter in Mirra's own hand. The creases betrayed the number of times Bao had read it. In it, Mirra explained what she needed Bao to do and how she'd sent a secret message via the Temple of Yulla.

"While I applaud the forethought," Bao said, gesturing at her disguise. "I'm afraid it's all for nothing."

"You're sending me back?"

"Yes."

Braelyn blanched. "But Mirra told you to help me!"

"No, she asked me to help you. To what end and how much solely depends on how this little jaunt about town goes. You don't get to where I am by blindly trusting everyone you meet. Even if they come with an endorsement. I have no love of nobles as a rule, but there's a debt I mean to repay and its success has nothing to do with you."

"And if it doesn't go well?"

Bao remained silent, staring out the rain spattered window slats. Braelyn knew little about the seedy underbelly of the city, but she had heard of "Bossman". Some years ago, her father and the lord provost spent many a night trying to discover why the crime lords' actions had suddenly changed. Bao was most likely the cause, taking control from the man that took the life of his best friend. That meant that he was willing to shed as much blood as necessary to achieve his goals. She shuddered at the thought of more dead at her feet, but if she wasn't willing to do what it took to save her people, then she wasn't worthy of the crown.

"I don't know how much Mirra could tell you. But I can't sit around and wait for Mirra and my brother to come to my rescue."

Bao had turned from the window. His dark eyes boring into hers, making the following words stick in her throat.

"I don't know the first thing about working outside of societal constraints. I don't know how to write or read code or how to recognize when I'm being followed, or even how to protect myself."

"Well, you are a pampered princess," Bao said with a smirk. Braelyn opened her mouth, but he silenced her. "But what you are isn't as important as what you can become, as my mother used to say. What do you want to become, princess?"

Bao's question cut through her like a well honed blade. What did she want to be? At the moment, all she wanted was alive and not alone. She cringed. Not exactly the best answer to win someone over to your cause.

Bao enjoyed watching the emotions play across the princess's face. She might hide her inner thoughts well enough for the pampered peacocks on the hill, but not well enough for someone like him. "Don't answer me now. Take some time and think. What do you need? What are you willing to do? And more importantly, what lines will you never cross because if you choose this path, you'll have to cross them at one point or deal with the consequences when you don't."

The carriage stopped. Bao opened the doors to reveal the same place they started. He helped Braelyn out of the carriage, but remained inside.

"I'll leave you a note in the desk when I'm ready to see you again."

Wait!" Braelyn cried as he closed the door. "How'd you do it? How did you sneak into the library without leaving a trace? Does this mean that you'll help me?"

Bao flashed another cocky grin. "That is a story for another time." His face turned serious. "Be safe, princess. Keep your eyes and ears open and a knife strapped to your side."

Braelyn nodded before turning to race back to the cave and back to the library before anyone became too suspicious of her absence. She left the soaked dress and cloak on the floor, quickly throwing on her gown, cursing where the delicate fabric clung to her wet skin. Her boots were near ruined, but there was nothing she could do about it. She threw them under the desk, wishing her slippers were warmer.

The old archivist barely looked up from the mountains of delicate tomes as Braelyn hurried back to the main section of the library. She absentmindedly pulled books from the shelves until she had a small stack in her arms. She plopped onto the window seat, setting the books on the floor, turning the pages.

The gray sky had just turned black when her maidservant appeared to get her ready for the evening meal. The evening meal was far more enjoyable without Lord Julian, but she wasn't in the right frame of mind to savor the evening. Her interactions with the other nobles and important figures were solely based on muscle memory. If you asked her later, Braelyn wouldn't be able to recall who had attended or what they'd discussed. Her mind wasn't on the dinner. It was still back in the carriage, with Bao and his question ringing through her mind.

Julian left the following morning, to where she did not know. Maybe if she was lucky, highwaymen or some other calamity would beset him would take his life. Braelyn snorted at her reflection. Since when has fate been kind to these past few months? She didn't have time to imagine all the possible deaths Julian could experience while away. Today was the one chance she'd get to garner support.

The Council of Lords would handle anything defense or diplomatic while the Regent was away. That left only The Hall, a place where the people could present their problems to the throne, available to her.

Standing before the large double doors, Braelyn brushed her skirts and adjusted the small circlet around her head. She took extra care with her attire today, trying to balance between projecting authority and approachability. Her mouth ran dry as she stared at the double doors that would lead her into the hall. She could count on one hand how many times she'd sat on a

Hall. Her mother insisted, stating that Braelyn needed to see how to help people achieve compromises.

Her first Hall meeting needed to be successful. Bao's question about who she wanted to be kept her up late into the night. She still didn't have an answer. In the past, her parent's expectations had shaped her image of her future as the second born and a girl. But that world was gone and would never come back. And if, when, they defeated Julian, and the demon inside him, the world would change again. There was no guarantee that the court or the people would ever welcome her brother back. Even if they had evidence clearing his name, the common folk would probably never trust him again. She might actually have to sit on the throne as Queen.

She could do it. Most of Braelyn's education ran parallel to Gaitlan, up to a point. But that was a problem for another time. She needed to keep her mind on the present task just beyond the double doors.

The doors swung open, and all thoughts vanished from her thoughts. Keeping her back straight and her head held high, Braelyn walked to the singular throne on a slightly raised platform. From her peripheral, the attendees of The Hall bowed as she passed. A sizable crowd, much to her surprise. But she could do this. Reaching the platform, she stepped up, fanning her skirts out before taking a seat.

"Come forward and be heard."

Braelyn swallowed once as a pair of noblemen dispersed from the crowd to stand before her. The crier read the challenge and her first ever Hall began.

By noon, Braelyn's head pounded and her stomach growled. But the number of people clamoring for her attention had barely dwindled. So far, she'd heard at least six complaints about land, fourteen about trade deals, two wrongful deaths, and three elopements.

She had drawn on every scrap of advice, lesson, and remembrance of her parents to solve each problem placed before her. She only hoped that her final decisions were right, and the people accepted her rulings.

"Come forward and be heard."

A balding man with an enormous belly came forward, his hat clasped tightly between his hands. He bowed deeply to Braelyn, his eyes trained on the floor.

"I beg yer pardon my lady," the man said, "but I dunno where else to go."

"What can we do for you?"

The man played with his cap, fear clear on his face. "I already gone to the lawman and to the head of me guild, but neither can help, so I have no choice but to bother ya."

"We understand, good sir. That is what this time is made for. Now please, tell us what brings you here today."

"It's them gangs, yer majesty. The gangs in the Merchant district that are makin' it hard for an honest man to make a livin'. Things were good for a time, but lately...Lately they knocking down me door in the middle of the night an threatening me and me customers. I know I ain't much but a simple shop keep down by the docks, but I pay me taxes and all I want is for me family to be safe and to make a livin'."

"As you should," Braelyn said, her knuckles white. "It is only right for a person to feel safe in their home and where they work. Those men who prey on those who've fallen on hard times care little for the peace and civility. And we fear that the recent unpleasantries have only made them bolder." She paused. The court collectively leaned forward, eager to hear her response. "We cannot offer what you have come here for." The man's shoulders slumped and an uneasy current ran through the watching crowd.

"If we flooded the streets with watchmen and guards, the criminals would only retreat until the storm died down, gathering more to their side. It is how my father dealt with such men as did my grandfather. But in the end, the crown lost interest and relented, allowing these men to return and prosper. We cannot continue to follow suit while our people suffer. We will need to take more time than a few moments to find a solution to this problem. But for now, we'll send aid to your streets, a small show of force to help ease the minds of your family and patrons. But I have something I need to ask of you in return."

The man clutched his hat. "An what is that yer majesty?"

Braelyn took a steading breath for the torrent she was about to release. "I ask that you, my people, remain diligent and do not let your fear allow these people to remain in power. Speak to your friends, to the members of your guild. The crown cannot hold your hand like a child, easing all your burdens. Some tasks you must do yourself, and for others you require aid. Sometimes we have to go outside what makes us comfortable in order to do what is right."

Confusion ran across the man's face. Braelyn stood and walked toward him. The man froze in place, his eyes wide, unsure of what to do. She covered his hands with hers, looking straight into his eyes.

"One must grow beyond themselves in order to protect those they love."

The man held her glance for a breath before lowering his eyes to the floor again. Braelyn released him, stepping away to give him room to breathe.

"In these times of turmoil, those who would ground us under their heel clamor for power. We must all maintain our diligence and compassion. We must band together to drive those who would see us in chains from our borders. It will take each and everyone of us; from the crown right down to the beggars in the streets."

The court shifted on their feet. Braelyn spied a few people with open disgust on their face. Not once has a ruler ignored the invisible barrier between the classes to touch the common born. The weight of the day came crashing down on her, filling her bones with the need to rest. She walked out of the hall, ending the day's session. Braelyn tried to not pay attention to the bereft faces sprinkled throughout the crowd. She was only one person, and just as much a prisoner of circumstance as the man was.

Who do you want to be? What lines are you willing to cross?

It might be time for her to set aside the constraints of her life and leave every avenue open. Julian certainly didn't mind committing the most heinous acts of depravity. She wouldn't stoop as low as him, but it might be time for a princess to learn how to play dirty.

Every day, Braelyn checked the desk for any message from Bao. As the week progressed, the more anxious she became. Each day dawned on the threat of Julian's return and the closing window of opportunity to move with freedom. Braelyn wasn't a fool to think that they did not watch her movements at all, but with their master gone, Julian's agents were also taking time to breathe. Julian's watchdog hadn't accompanied her to the temple at all while Julian was gone. But as time dragged on with no word from Bao, Braelyn feared he would wait too long and she wouldn't be in any position to do anything.

I will leave a message of my own, she swore as she walked to the landing. Placing her hand on the secret compartment and with her eyes closed, she pressed it. Inside the neat little hole was a slip of folded paper. Her throat constricted as she pulled it out.

Ready? Before.

The first part of the message was easy enough for her to figure out, but the second part? What exactly did "before" refer to? The only thing she could think of was the cave where she met Bao for the first time.

Not bothering to change, Braelyn threw on the plain cloak and hurried through the passageway to the cave. It was nearly as dark as the first time she'd been there, though the late afternoon sun's light shed small bands of gray light just up ahead.

"Hello," Braelyn called. Silence greeted her. She chuckled as she navigated the cave, watching her step and listening for others.

She lingered at the mouth of the cave and listened. The only sounds she could make out were the birds in the trees. There were a few homes near the palace, but they were too far away for anyone to see her or the cave. The guards that walked the outer walls of the palace never patrolled the area below the final cliff that they built the palace grounds on. A perfect blind spot primed for exploitation. That raised the question of how Bao knew about it to begin with. He was a crime lord with a vendetta against Julian. He could have spent decades searching for ways into the castle.

Braelyn kept to the cliff side, ensuring that her hood remained up as she headed for the small cluster of trees where Bao had hidden the carriage. This time, no carriage greeted her, only the sight of Bao sitting cross legged on a woolen blanket.

He smiled when he saw her, motioning for her to take a seat on the blanket. "Before I hear your answer, have a cup of tea with me."

Braelyn tried to argue, but Bao would not be swayed. "No business until the tea has been served."

An earthen teapot sat suspended over a large candle. Steam was already curled out of the spout. Braelyn sat with her legs tucked beneath and her hands in her lap. Bao sat with his eyes closed. He leaned back, resting his head on the gnarled trunk behind him.

She pressed her lips in a tight line, not wanting to be the first to speak, the first to relent. A corner of Bao's mouth hitched upward, but the silence continued.

"I don't have time to play this game," Braelyn snapped at last. "I hurried here as soon as I saw your message. They'll notice I'm gone soon. Not all of us have the luxury to go whenever and wherever they please."

"And that's your first mistake," Bao said, picking up the pot to pour a light green liquid into an earthen cup with no handle. "I bet you didn't even bother setting up an alibi for your missing time, or even to make sure that you weren't being tailed."

Braelyn clasped her hands together tightly. Bao's accusations were correct. Even more proof that she wasn't suited for this line of work.

Bao poured some tea into a cup, then poured its contents back into the pot. He did this three more times before he filled a cup, giving it to Braelyn before pouring his own.

"And what are my other mistakes?"

Bao took a sip from his cup before eyeing hers. Braelyn suppressed a sigh of frustration and took a sip.

The tea tasted of flowers with a strange, bitter undertone. "What is this?"

"Hashime. It's a flower that grows in the River Lands of Zallino. It has a myriad of uses, but more commonly it's used for stress relief. And you are nothing if not stressed, your highness."

"Growing more so by the day." She took another sip. "When last we met, you posed a question. I have the answer."

Bao's smirk widened. "You wish to "go outside what makes you comfortable," am I right?"

Braelyn blinked. "If you already knew, then why did you wait so long to reach back out to me?"

Bao shrugged. "I had other things to tend to. Jobs to organize, underlings to keep in line, the usual. So are you ready, truly ready? Once we start, there's no stopping. You will have to learn to put aside your morals to do what needs to be done."

"There are a few stipulations I want in place before we move forward," Braelyn said, setting down her cup. "I want to limit the number of people caught in the crossfire to minimize the collateral damage. I also want a better way to communicate so that nobody questions why I keep disappearing into the library."

Bao nodded his head. "I think we can manage the second one and I already taken the first care of. You'll find out later." He paused, thinking. "Possibly today."

Until now, Bao presented a lightly teasing persona. When this bright mask fell, replaced by one of stone, Braelyn could see how he could rein in the criminals under his charge. There was something about his expression, just at the edges, that promised a painful death to those that crossed him.

"In order for us to work together, you need to know what I know. Are you sure you can handle it?"

A chill ran down her spine when Bao turned that deadly face to her. "Do I have any other choice?"

A sad smile. "You always have a choice, your highness."

MIRRA EYED THE SURROUNDING DESTRUCTION WITH A heavy heart. It was because of her that the last haven for her people was exposed.

"They held them off, remember," Gaitlan said, reading the pain on her face. "No one was killed, barely even hurt. Only the buildings outside the barrier are lost."

"I know," Mirra said, fiddling with the copper bead in her hair. "But these people lived for centuries in peace until we stumbled in."

"Technically, they brought us here."

Mirra made a face. Gaitlan chuckled, gently bumping her shoulder. "Look, while we figure out if Usoa really has the Seed of Life and how to find the others, we can help them recover."

"I guess," Mirra said, her tone still unsure. Guilt compounded with each fresh scorch mark on the crumbling city.

How many more innocent people would be hurt by the end? What would happen to the world if they should fail?

"Mirra!"

The dark clouds of her mind evaporated against Oya's bright smile. Mirra's eyes scanned every inch of Oya that she could see, searching for any sign that she'd been hurt. Seeing none, at least on the surface, the tension eased between her shoulders.

Oya ran down the steps of the citadel, skipping the gaps. She threw her arms around Mirra's neck, bringing their foreheads together. Mirra closed her eyes, breathing in Oya's comforting scent. Another knot of tension eased.

"I can't tell you how relieved I was to hear of your return."

"I aim to please."

Oya softly laughed, shaking her head, various beads and charms clinking. She threaded her arm through Mirra's. "Come, the both of you need a bath and a good meal. Usoa will see you later."

"Can't we see her now?" Gaitlan asked.

Oya's face tightened. "After your letter, she sequestered herself inside her chambers. "contemplating the future," and hasn't been out since. I'm hoping that your arrival will finally draw her back to the world of the living."

Gaitlan nodded and slung his satchel over his shoulder before heading back to his old room, leaving Mirra and Oya alone.

"Come, let's get you clean first."

Grandmother materialized from the steaming baths, enveloping Mirra in an herbal scented embrace.

"You have a mighty burden now," she said, drifting backward. "Your task will take you to all corners of the world before it's done, mark my words. You will need allies."

"Not now, Grandmother," Oya said, waving her hand. "She's only just arrived. We should allow her to rest before making plans."

Grandmother frowned at Oya, fading away to nothingness before reemerging, her face softer. "All that I have is at your disposal, be well."

Mirra felt Oya rolling her eyes. "Now that we have that unnecessary blessing, strip and get into the water."

Mirra laid her bags to the side, choosing the same pool she used her first time in Moakwyd. Slowly she peeled off her sweat and salt stained clothes, gritting her teeth when they pulled at her wounds. Oya inhaled softly at the sight of Mirra's molten back.

Keeping her silence, Oya took Mirra's dirty clothes, setting them on a bench to be taken care of later by the attendants. She watched Mirra step into the water, wincing when the warm water hit Mirra's still healing injuries. Mirra leaned her head back against the rim of the pool, sighing as the warm water eased many of her aches.

The sound of splashing and rising water caused Mirra to open her eyes. Oya sat at the opposite end of the bathing pool, her crystalline eyes smoldering.

Oya reached one arm out toward Mirra, steam already rising off her midnight skin. "Come."

All thoughts disappeared from Mirra's mind as she crossed the pool. Oya gently guided her to turn around, seating Mirra in front.

The feeling of Oya's body against hers burned into Mirra's back. Without saying another word, Oya filled a small pitcher, filled it with water and then gently poured it over Mirra's head. Mirra closed her eyes, tilting her head so Oya could have better access.

Oya's deft fingers removed the copper bead she had given to Mirra, setting it aside in the grass where there was no danger of it falling into the water. She poured a sweet smelling solution over Mirra's head and then worked it into a rich lather.

Mirra lost herself to the sensation of Oya's fingers massaging her scalp. More warm water cascaded over her head, her eyes protected by Oya.

It was her body's turn next. Mirra was aware of every stroke of Oya's fingers. Every trail sending ripples of delight down her limbs. Though she couldn't see them all, Oya carefully avoided the worst of her injuries, only lightly brushing over them when necessary.

"Turn around."

Mirra obeyed, her skin flushed and eyes glazed over. Once more, Oya pulled her in close, forcing Mirra to straddle her. Heat, not from the bath, spread across Mirra's face. Oya lightly chuckled, reaching to grab a bar of soap from the side of the bath. She paused, her eyebrow arched.

"Yes." Mirra's words were barely above a whisper.

Fire raced through her veins the moment Oya's hands touched her chest, spreading the lather over every curve, every swell, and plane.

Mirra locked eyes with Oya, their expressions the exact mirror of the other. When Mirra caught the flush of Oya's face, a wicked smile spread across her face.

She filled her hands with soap, working it into a rich lather. "It's only fair."

Oya's breath hitched, her mouth forming a small o.

Mirra paused, her soapy hands hovering over Oya's skin until the other woman nodded her head.

They washed the other, their hands sliding from top to bottom, spreading fire in their wake. Mirra wrapped her arms around Oya's slender waist, pressing their slick bodies together. She leaned forward, resting her head on the crux of Oya's neck.

"I'm scared."

Oya stilled beneath her.

"I don't know if I can do this. I'm not a hero...but if I don't..."

Oya shifted, gently lifting Mirra's face. "You don't need to be anything but yourself. I don't know why the Ilieng brought you into this world, but I am glad. My life would be less bright for the want of you." She brought up her other hand to cup Mirra's face.

"You don't have to do this alone. But for now, set aside your fears of the future and enjoy the pleasures of today."

Mirra swallowed the lump in her throat before bringing her mouth to Oya's. Her kiss was as sweet as summer wine and just as intoxicating. As they tangled their hands into each other's hair, Mirra tried to take Oya's advice. But she couldn't ignore the reality of their situation. If they failed to imprison the Dark One again, she'd never get to savor Oya's kisses again.

CHAPTER FOUR

GAITLAN WATCHED OYA LEADING MIRRA AWAY, WAITING for jealousy to rear its ugly head. Instead, he felt the glowing warmth of happiness for his friend. Mirra's early years offered little comfort, if any. She was long overdue for a piece of happiness. Perhaps one day he would be so lucky to find someone who could ease his burdens as much as he eased theirs.

He inclined his head at every passing Ilmarrion, noting the stress around their mouths and eyes. The few children in the city clung tightly to their parents. He assumed they had hidden inside their homes. But despite their recent suffering, Gaitlan picked up on an undercurrent of resilience from the surrounding people. Despite the destruction of their calm world, they were victorious in the end, and they had a firm determination to protect their home at all costs.

Gaitlan fell face first into his bed with a groan. Every inch of his body hurt. He needed at least four days of solid rest and recuperation to feel like his old self again. He laughed into his pillow. Given how long that bastard had manipulated him, Gaitlan wasn't sure what his "old self" actually was. The carefree, entitled, self indulgent prince he used to be was no more. That version of him had died alongside his parents. But he didn't feel like an avenging prince or brother, either. He wouldn't have even made it out of the city if not for his sister's sacrifice and Mirra pulling him along, calling him a coward and demanding more from him.

He groaned, turning over, staring up at the beams above his bed like they had the answers to his problems. And he had a lot of problems. He wanted to rescue his sister as fast as possible. Who knew what that bastard was making her do? He wouldn't be able to sleep until that traitor's head rotted on a pike outside the city walls. Only then would he be able to rebuild the kingdom. Braelyn would help. She had hundreds of ideas about how the nobles could better use their power and wealth. And Mirra — would she even want to stay once they gathered all the relics and their wielders to seal away the demon inside Julian?

Gaitlan made a face. Even after seeing dark creatures made of smoke leap from one person to another, it was still a bit of a challenge for him to quell his anger towards Julian. Sure, he was possessed, but did that mean that it absolved him of all crimes? The face that haunted his dreams, the one that smiled wide when his parent's throats were slit, was Julian's. Mirra didn't seem to have the same problem, or perhaps she was better at hiding it. After all, they had much bigger fish to fry. As soon as Usoa confirmed their suspicions, they'd have to leave again.

His eyelids grew heavy as his breathing slowed. And in no time at all, Gaitlan fell into a deep and dreamless sleep.

INSTEAD OF A COMMUNAL MEAL, GAITLAN AND MIRRA SAT next to each other at a large round table with fully started members of the citadel. The food was simpler than before, though the aroma wafting off the dishes was enough to make Mirra's mouth water. Only one seat remained empty, as Usoa had yet to emerge from her room.

Mirra tried to not let the empty chair discourage her. She engaged in mindless conversations with the other people around the table, but all the while she was aware of every movement Oya made. It was as if their bath had seared Oya's essence into her soul.

Gaitlan's deep chuckle caught her attention. She turned to face him, her eyes wide and innocent.

"Don't even try," he teased. "Even a blind man can see the desire written all over your face."

Heat blossomed across her face. "I don't know what you're talking about."

Gaitlan shook his head. "Don't worry Mir, your secrets are safe with me."

Before Mirra could sputter a retort, the room fell silent. Usoa stood beneath an archway. Her face wane, the bones of her face more prominent than before. The light that always seemed to shine from her was gone, leaving only a tired woman who looked like she'd lived centuries beyond count. Her ever present smile was gone as well. Spying Mirra and Gaitlan seated around the table brought a ghost of a smile to her lips.

"Welcome back."

"I wish it was under better circumstances," Gaitlan said, standing to bow to the high priestess.

Usoa paused. "A good friend is a balm to any painful situation." She turned to the table, folding her hands over her heart. "I'm sorry for the worry I know I have caused during my sojourn. I have been converging with the Ileing."

Everyone seated around the table perked up, their faces turned toward Usoa like flowers. She closed her eyes, her shoulders sagging. "I saw and heard many things; not all of it coherent or clear. It will take time to detangle the web of visions. But for now, let us sup and take joy from being amongst friends."

Mirra scanned the table. Unease over the high priestess's vision written on all the acolyte's faces. There must be something more going on, something just below the surface that she wasn't seeing.

Gaitlan shifted in his seat, pressing his leg against hers. He was just as uneasy but would follow her lead, since these were her people. Her people. A giddy bubble threatened to spill over whenever she thought about it. It was the one thing she ever wanted when she was younger, and now she had it. But the impending threat of the Dark One inside Julian soured her joy, and the dinner.

All earlier conversations had died, leaving only the sounds of utensils against bowls to fill the air. Oya met Mirra's gaze across the table. She flashed a weak smile before lowering her eyes to her meal, shrinking beneath her worry.

Mirra lifted her glass, taking a long sip of wine. When she set it down, her mind set. "With all due respect, High Priestess, the world is hanging on by a thread. Our enemies are growing in both numbers and strength by the day. Take whatever time you need to detangle your web of visions, but Gaitlan and I do not have the luxury of time."

Usoa sagged in her seat, her right hand reaching up to touch the bright red gem at her neck. It sparked to life, briefly bathing the table and its occupants in rippling blood-red light.

"When I was a child, the relics were already a myth. A story about a time of great darkness that was defeated when humans and Ilmarrions joined together. My father said that the blood of both people were used to create the relics, but only the humans could use them. The universe has a way of balancing itself. As I grew up, I could only watch as the humans I once called friends turned. I watched my home and my family burn." She turned her gaze on Gaitlan. "Hatred grew in my heart for your people until I thought it would swallow me whole. Then, one day, many decades ago, a young nobleman stumbled into our city. Many of his injuries had become infected, and he was nearly gone with delirium. I nearly ordered his death that day until I saw what he clutched so desperately to his chest."

"The relics?"

Usoa shook her head. "The shattered fragments of The Dark One's prison."

A tense silence fell over the table.

"Instead of killing the man, I had him taken to our healers. When he regained his mind, he told me a story that still chills me to this day. The man wanted to hide the relics in Moakwyd because he'd believed it to be abandoned."

"Do you have the others?"

Usoa shook her head. "If The Eater was free, then no Ilmarrion city would be safe. I had the man scatter the relics across the continent, keeping only The Seed. A starting point, as it were."

Gaitlan's shoulders slumped. "How do we find them and the wielders?"

"You already know of another and its wielder."

Mirra shrank under the intensity of Usoa's gaze. Gaitlan turned to face her, his face twisted in confusion.

Who did she know? She'd met no one that pulsated with power. Not unless she counted Julian. But if he had a relic, he'd let them know just to watch their hope crumble.

"I don't…"

"You've forgotten him so easily, especially after how hard you initially hunted for him," Usoa said, frowning.

The bottom of Mirra's stomach dropped. "No…it couldn't be…gods above."

"What!" Gaitlan demanded.

"The man in the woods — Shiro."

The sound of wood striking wood filled the air. Mirra spun her glaive in a complicated motion around her neck, taking it from her right hand to her left. She brought it sharply down across Oya's staff. She winced at the reverberation, but didn't lower her guard. Spinning her staff, she led the leather wrapped end of Mirra's glaive toward the ground.

Mirra countered by stepping under Oya's guard, locking their weapons together. The women strained against the other, attempting to gain the upper hand, to no avail.

Oya retreated a fraction of an inch, giving Mirra the momentum to break their stalemate, pushing Oya back with her body weight. Instead of falling to the ground, Oya somehow snaked her staff around Mirra's glaive and wretched it from her grasp. Over extended, it was Mirra who fell face first to the earth, mouth full of sod.

"What was that?" Mirra sputtered, spitting dirt.

Oya's coy smile sent rivers of delight down Mirra's spine. "A trick I learned in the floating city."

"When were you in K'ashi?"

A soft chuckle. "I lived a life before we met, you know."

Mirra rolled her eyes. "Obviously, but you talk so little about your life "before". I mean, you know everything about me."

Mirth faded from Oya's face and her eyes turned distant. "You don't have to if you don't want to." Mirra scrambled to her feet, brushing her clothes.

"Perhaps one day, when the memories of those days don't hurt as if they were fresh." Oya seemed to shrink, wrapping her arms loosely around herself.

Mirra chewed her bottom lip, unsure of how to bring Oya back to the present. Crossing the distance between them, Mirra wrapped her arms around Oya, pulling her in until Oya's face rested in the curve of her neck.

Oya released a shaky sigh, uncoiling her arms to wrap them around Mirra. The two remained like that for some time.

"I met Shiro when I lived in a village east of here. He knew what I was, an agent of The Viper, right away."

"Did he know you were Ilmarrion?"

Mirra shrugged. "Oh, definitely. There's no way he couldn't." Mirra picked up her glaive, the wood of the staff creaking in her hands. Shadows danced along her fingers, trailing after her like whips of smoke. "But believe me, when I find him again, I will make him sorry he'd ever laid eyes on me."

"Why?"

"He knew. He knew. What I was and who had me bound in service. He could have saved me a heap of hurt if he only had the balls to reach out when we first met."

"Would you have listened?"

"Of course!"

Oya's face showed she did not believe Mirra's words one bit. "Honestly, my star. Would you have listened to a strange man in the forest telling you that you're a magical being thought long gone from the world and go with him?"

Mirra stared at Oya. The tension in her body eased. "No, I wouldn't have. I most likely would have run away and not listened to anything he'd said."

"There you go. It's pointless to agonize over opportunities missed in the past. The only thing we can do is to learn to recognize the signs and try to not miss more in the future."

Mirra huffed, walking over to lay her head against Oya's neck. "You're chock full of wisdom, aren't you?"

"Don't be too impressed," Oya softly chuckled and whispered to Mirra, "It comes from a lifetime of mistakes, my love."

Mirra straightened and cupped Oya's face. A strong but foreign emotion swept through her, filling her with dread and elation. "When this is over, will you sail away with me?"

The words were out of her mouth before her brain even registered them.

Oya's bittersweet smile was a knife to her gut. "Nevermind. Forget I said anything." Oya reached out for her, but Mirra couldn't stand to hear her refusal. Turning heel, she ran away like a coward.

SOMETHING HAD HAPPENED. GAITLAN COULDN'T QUITE PLACE what had occurred, but the way Mirra pushed her food around her plate meant that her mind was a thousand leagues away. He looked to Oya, hoping that she could provide some insight, but she, too, kept her gaze lowered.

He looked back and forth between the two women, who were pointedly avoiding looking at the other. Gaitlan took a long sip from his cup. He'd get the answers out of Mirra later when it was just the two of them.

The acolytes seated around the table stood as the high priestess entered. She motioned for them to sit, taking her place in an empty seat.

"Shiro and I keep our correspondences to a minimum, per my request. But he stops by from time to time when he's nearby. Other times, he sends a letter to let me know that he's still alive."

Usoa handed a salt stained leather pouch to Oya, who jumped in her seat. She quickly handed the pouch to the acolyte to her right before returning to the dinner she wasn't eating. Usoa shot Gaitlan a quizzical look as she noted Mirra's equally somber mood. Gaitlan shrugged, accepting the pouch from an acolyte.

"The last we heard from him, he was heading back north. He had joined up with a traveling band of performers and would winter in Eddany. It is likely that he is still in the city or has moved on. But you should be able to pick his trail up from there."

Gaitlan returned the letter to the pouch. "We'll need to travel north without drawing attention."

"Merchant bands are always looking for hired muscle," Mirra said dully. "Many don't want to, or can't afford to, hire permanent guards, so they hire on both sides of the pass."

Gaitlan nodded. "Do you mind if I keep the letters? If we miss him in Eddany, we might find clues to another place he might go."

Usoa waved her hand and dug into her meal.

Gaitlan leaned close to Mirra. "Do you want to go through these tonight? You're better at finding messages hidden between what's written."

Mirra turned her listless gaze toward him. "I guess."

Gaitlan pressed his lips together to keep back the question that threatened to spill out. Mirra didn't open up at the best of times, and trying to discover what had transpired would be like trying to wring water from a stone.

They finished their meal in terse silence. Mirra excused herself the second the last morsel of food passed her lips. It was then that Oya lifted her gaze and watched Mirra leave, her expression akin to one filled with regret.

Gaitlan chased after Mirra. He grabbed her arm, spinning her around. "Spill it," he demanded. "What happened between the two of you?"

Icy fire blazed briefly behind her eyes and the shadows swelled around Mirra, slowly encircling Gaitlan as well.

"Mirra, I'm your friend. I only want to help."

Mirra deflated, running her hand through her hair. "I messed up, I guess."

"How?"

"I asked…I asked…I asked her to come with me."

"That's all?"

"That's all," Mirra sputtered indignantly. "The look on her face." She shoved Gaitlan away with a groan before walking in circles in the hallway. "You'd think I asked her to change the stars or something."

"She said no," Gaitlan said slowly.

Mirra paused her pacing. "Not exactly." Gaitlan shot her a look. "I didn't exactly give her a chance to say no. I kind of ran away."

Gaitlan blinked twice before bursting out into a deep belly laugh. Mirra stood stunned in the hallway, a deep blush creeping across her cheeks and down her neck.

"Go talk to her," Gaitlan said after a while, wiping tears. "Give her a chance to explain her side of things. It's a big request to leave everything you know to travel the world."

"What if she says no?"

Gaitlan's mirth turned serious. "Then she says no. Once we leave here, we'll be in danger. We'll be able to handle that, will she?"

Mirra bristled. "She's a good fighter."

Gaitlan held his hands up. "I know. She's beat me more often than I'd like to admit. But power hungry demons, lost magical relics? This isn't something the average person deals with. And we might fail. Do you want her death on your hands?"

"No." Mirra sighed. "You know, you have a good idea princeling, occasionally."

Gaitlan flashed her a cocky smile before throwing his arm around her shoulder. "I know."

MIRRA FOUND OYA IN THE DILAPIDATED LIBRARY. SHE STOOD amongst the scattered remains of their people's history and knowledge with a faraway look. Mirra remained in the shadows, her uncertainty keeping her rooted.

A beam of golden sunlight broke through the leaves of the trees, accenting the bits of jewelry braided into Oya's hair, and grew to encase her in golden light. Oya tilted her head to the sky. When she opened her eyes, they were no longer icy blue, but pure molten gold.

"Abe, Hoyo," Oya said, her hands held lightly in front, palms up. "Awoya'al nä jeclaa, I seek your guidance and wisdom. I believe I've found my heart song, but the way forward is unclear. As a child, I never believed in NeNe's stories about the Dark One until this woman stumbled into my life. And now I am torn. Should I abandon my life's work to be with the woman I love? What if our plans fail and the world falls into darkness? Which regret am I willing to die with? Please shine your light and help me find the right path."

The molten glow of her power faded from her eyes in twin streams down her face, a river of gold against a night sky. When she was solely Oya again, she knelt next to one tree and placed a small bottle of brandy and a fruit tart near the roots.

Sorrow burned her throat as she watched. Mirra wanted to talk to Oya, maybe explain why she blurted out what she did. But watching Oya beseeching a higher power because she asked too much was more than Mirra could stand. And as much as she hated it, there was only one way for her to make it right.

Mirra found Oya in the kitchen later on, arms covered in flour. The noise of the kitchen masked her arrival until she tapped Oya on the shoulder. Oya jumped, turning her eyes wide.

"Oh you wicked soul," she cursed without venom at the sight of Mirra's smirk. "I could have blasted you to the Void."

"And yet you didn't."

Oya pursed her lips. "I'm still debating."

"Then wait until you hear what I have to say. Can you step away?"

"I can," Oya said slowly, trepidation spreading across her face.

Mirra led Oya to a small, quiet hallway not too far from the kitchens. "Gaitlan and I leave in two days."

Oya stiffened, but her face gave nothing away. Mirra closed her eyes and drew in a fortifying breath. "Stay. It was unfair and selfish of me to ask you. I can't expect you to give up everything just for me. You have your own life and the own goals you have to achieve."

"I do, but you are important to me."

Oya took Mirra's hand in hers. "But you're right, I can't come with you. Someone has to figure out how to fix the crystal prison."

"We can't make a new one?"

"The spells that went into making it were lost long before the Purge," Oya said, shaking her head. "I might mesh something together, but I need more than what we have here. Usoa has granted me permission to travel to the Holy Isle and search their archives for a way."

Mirra's face warmed like the first rays of sunlight after a storm. "That's perfect! The Abbot and the Masters are incredibly helpful. You'll find a way for sure and maybe find complete volumes to reprint."

"That's the idea. The Abbot's letter arrived just this afternoon. I was going to tell you after dinner."

Mirra shrugged. "Now…later it doesn't matter. It looks like we both have important journeys to make."

"And let us hope we meet again once they're over."

Oya brushed a strand of Mirra's hair behind her ear with a flour covered hand. Mirra wrapped her hand around Oya's wrist and pulled her in for a kiss. She hoped that the bitterness of leaving Oya behind didn't taint what could be the last time they'd meet in this life.

CHAPTER FIVE

It took every ounce of Braelyn's control to not gouge out Lady Nora's eye with a teaspoon. Everything about the courtier infuriated Braelyn. The way the sunlight made Lady Nora's hair look like spun gold right down the milky whiteness of her skin. Lady Nora was the picture of perfection, as if nothing in the world was wrong and how Braelyn wanted to shred that image apart with her bare hands. Yet, she didn't. She sat across from a known agent of Lord Julian, pretending that she wasn't preparing to tear them apart, root and stem.

One condition for their fragile partnership was her having to be pleasant with the unfaithful woman, though she didn't know the reason behind it.

"I do love these early summer days," Lady Nora commented while sipping tea from a delicate porcelain cup as pale as a robin's egg. "They're all too short, and too soon it will be too hot for moments like these. I guess that is what the summer nights are for."

Lady Nora gave Braelyn a coy smile that sent her hackles up. "You would know all about the pleasures of summer nights, Lady Nora. I'll just have to take your word for it."

To her credit, Lady Nora remained composed, undoubtedly used to such barbs from the women of the men who flocked to her bed. "With your upcoming nuptials and lack of a mother, your betrothed has asked me to offer you any support that I can. Ask me whatever questions you like and I will answer them honestly. I won't do you the disservice by using flowery language or metaphors. Too many young women enter the marriage bed absolutely terrified, unable to enjoy an action that is as natural as breathing."

Braelyn sputtered, nearly choking on her tea. Just the implications of sharing a bed with Lord Julian was enough to turn her stomach into a churning sea.

Smugness tainted Lady Nora's smile. "Of course, there's still enough time for that. I won't press you to ask. I only wanted to let you know I am here for you, should you need me."

Tapping her mouth with a linen napkin, Braelyn took some time to collect herself. "I appreciate the offer, Lady Nora," she said, placing the napkin on the table. "But my late mother was diligent with all my studies."

"Then she was a rare woman."

"She was. Now, if you'll excuse me, I have matters that require my attention."

"Of course," Lady Nora said in a tone that hinted at disbelief. "But before you go, allow me to present a small gift in honor of your engagement."

Lady Nora raised her hand and a young woman appeared. The young woman's hair matched Lady Nora's, but her tanned skin suggested she spent more time outside than indoors. Her dress was the color of bay leaves, not as ornate as Lady Nora's, but nicer than a servant's.

She curtseyed deeply when she neared the table. "Your highness, my lady."

Her voice was delicate, though there was something that lingered behind her words that spiked Braelyn's interest. Her voice almost sounded familiar; somehow.

"May I introduce Emyra. She came highly recommended by a mutual friend, but I have no use for a maid in waiting so young. I believe she'd be a better fit here, with you."

Braelyn eyed the waiting woman with suspicion. Emrya kept her gaze rooted to the ground, her hands demurely clasped before her. The woman's unnaturally still posture made Braelyn uneasy. This woman was a spy, of that she was sure. Refusing her would draw attention, so she had no choice but to agree.

"Thank you, Lady Nora. Your gift is too kind. Now, if you'll excuse me."

Braelyn rose from her seat and walked away. Behind her, she heard Emrya's light steps quickly catching up to her own. Gritting her teeth, Braelyn picked up her pace, taking one sharp turn after another. It wouldn't be her fault if Emrya failed to keep up.

Much to Braelyn's dismay, Emrya kept pace with her all the way back to her room. Braelyn spun around at her door, unable to ignore the woman any further.

"I don't want you, nor do I need another spy reporting my every move. "Let your master know and don't bother me," she said dismissively.

Emrya was a petite woman, yet she managed to appear haughty and look down at Braelyn. "If that actually worked, your highness, my boss wouldn't have sent me."

Braelyn shifted on her feet and glowered at the woman. "I honestly couldn't care less."

Emrya chucked, shaking her head. "She said you had a decent head on your shoulders. Even Bao said he thought you have half a brain. Perhaps they were wrong."

Braelyn blanched. Lightning fast, she latched onto Emrya's wrist, hauling her into the room. Braelyn slammed her door and locked it, using the time to calm the frantic beating of her heart and suppress the rising sense of hope. Leaning her head against the door, she took several deep breaths. Having Bao help her was one thing. But this woman, Emrya. Who was she? How did she know Mirra? And why did Mirra send another person?

The scent of blood-soaked earth and loam filled her nose, and she heard a cruel laughter that echoed through the forest. Lifeless eyes stared up at her from waxen faces. The whispers of the dead were relentless, clawing their way out of the dark and demanding to know why she couldn't save them.

A gentle but firm hand on her shoulder plucked Braelyn from her waking nightmare. Emrya's vibrant green eyes bored into hers. "Listen to my voice. Feel the warmth of my hands. Smell the smoke from the fire. You're not there. You're safe."

Braelyn blinked rapidly, slowly coming back to her senses. "Who are you?"

Emrya pursed her lips and led Braelyn away from the door. She sat her near the fire before picking up a music box from the mantle. She turned the key thrice before placing it on the small table by the door.

"Less likely for someone to hear. Won't work all the time but for now…" Emrya took the seat across from Braelyn, spreading her skirts as regally as any noblewoman. She folded her hands in her lap and studied the princess intently, as if she was still weighing her choices.

"Don't be too hard on Lady Nora," Emrya said after a while. "It's a hard life being a slave, especially to a cruel master."

"What?"

"Do you actually think that she would ever serve that snake willingly? She wears a brand, just like Mirra. The only people who follow that snake willingly are the worst of the worst."

Braelyn blinked. "Then why work for her?"

Emrya shrugged. "Why not? Julian would be less suspicious of a person placed by one of his most trusted agents. And Nora has a knack for dancing between complying and disobeying. She's learned how to work around the bindings of the brand."

"What are you…that's right," Braelyn said, straightening in her chair. "Mirra mentioned something about Lord Julian having magic and using that to bind people to him. So where do you lie in all this?"

Emrya pursed her lips, choosing her words carefully. "Since you were the first to put a crack in that wall of hers, I owe you."

Braelyn's brows came together at the strange remark.

"I used to run with Mirra when we were children. The name's Em. I offered Mirra and your brother shelter until…"

Em's face briefly twisted with sadness, betraying her emotion for only a moment. "Until the mercenaries Julian sent after them slaughtered my husband."

"I'm sorry," Braelyn said, hating how empty her words sounded.

"I don't want or need your pity, your highness. I need to avenge Micha so his soul can rest in peace. That is why I'm even entertaining the thought of helping you."

Braelyn swallowed, worrying her fingers in her lap. "I can understand having a thirst for revenge. I can only hope that you don't allow it to blind you to the surrounding dangers. Like I did."

Em studied Braelyn once more, understanding, softening the hard lines around her mouth. "This is how it's going to work. I will pretend to report your coming and goings to Lady Nora, who will pass it onto Julian. I can serve as your alibi when you see Bao, and I will get you caught when it's beneficial."

"How can getting caught be beneficial to me?"

Em smiled, a sharp, deadly smile that sent a shiver down Braelyn's spine. "Give them a taste of sweetness first and they won't notice the poison right after."

"The first rule of thievery is to always look like you belong."

"Shouldn't be too hard," Braelyn said as she stared out at the rain splattered window.

Em chuckled as she stuck her needle into her embroidery. "You'd think that, but what if you were in Julian's office? Or the office of a noble in league with him? Or even still, the chambers of a potential enemy or ally? Could you still act like you belong?"

Braelyn pursed her lips, turning her attention back to her forgotten needle work. "Possibly not."

"That's because you have an honest face. You couldn't tell a lie without giving it away if your life depended on it — and it does. There's no point in pretending to be meek or agree with Julian. A change in character now will only raise his suspicions. You kinda fucked yourself over, but nothing to be done for it now."

Braelyn hung her head. "Sorry."

Em made a face. "Why are you apologizing? The damage is done and all we can do now is move forward. Flexibility is the key here. Things go wrong, that's the nature of the beast, but the difference between surviving to see another day or the hangman's noose is to adapt, and quickly."

Braelyn studied the half finished design in her lap. If her mother could see her stitches, she would have had Braelyn practicing from sunrise to sunrise. She made a face and picked out the tangled garble of threads. "State work is much the same. A single word can have a thousand meanings based on who said it and who heard it. And with foreign dignitaries, one can never fully prepare for what will happen. My mother could quell any rising ire with a well-placed hand and gentle smile."

"Undoubtedly useful in the court," Em said, "but not so much on the streets. Here's what we're gonna do, princess. By the looks of it, this storm should last at least another day. Tomorrow you're going to need to move about the castle, not as Princess Braelyn, but as an ordinary woman. You have the rest of today to figure out how to manage that."

Braelyn blinked. "What about clothing?"

Em smirked. "Leave that to me."

Braelyn's heart leapt to her throat. How many times had she seen that same smile on Mirra? She would not fail, she couldn't fail. "I think I need to take a walk."

"As you wish, your highness."

The ancient archivist barely looked up from their studies as Braelyn and Em descended the stairs. Only the headman waved a hand in greeting.

"Mirra would love this place," Em said, eyeing the forest of books in front of her. "If we survive all this, you should bring her down. It might be enough…"

"Enough for what?"

Em shook her head. "Nothing important. So why'd'ya bring me here?"

Braelyn said nothing and continued to lead Em through the labyrinth of shelves until they reached the open landing with the desk. When they reached the landing, Em sat at the desk, her feet crossed on top.

Braelyn walked around the space, trailing her fingers across the shelves. "When I first read Mirra's letter, I didn't want to believe her. I mean, who would? Demons and Ilmarrions. Magic? But my time down here from when I was originally planning to run away has brought some things to light."

She hadn't wasted her time while waiting for Bao's response. She'd grown quite familiar with the shelving around the landing. Braelyn reached up, pulling out a book before reaching for the back of the shelf, revealing a folded paper. She replaced the book and disappeared down another. Em leaned in her seat to keep the princess in view. Braelyn climbed up a small ladder, retrieving a long scroll from the topmost shelf. She dumped the items on the desk before disappearing down another round of rows.

Em gently unrolled the scroll, mindful of the fragility of the paper. Her eyes narrowed as she tried to read the faded, scrawling handwriting. It was a map that she was sure of, but of what, she did not know.

"Humans were not the first inhabitants of this kingdom." Braelyn had returned with another stack of ancient looking scrolls and fresh papers. "Our ancestors came from across the sea. From where, it's never clearly stated, but the archivist we walked past earlier and I speculate it might be the Dead Lands. Either way, as legend states, there was a race of beings living here that could tap into and harness the forces of nature."

"Mystics," Em said slowly.

"That's what we called them, but they had their own name — Ilmarrion." When Em didn't show her the same level of excitement, she felt when uncovering the Mystic's true name. She suppressed an eye roll and pressed on. "They had several cities, places of concentrated power throughout the continent, including Undros."

Em picked up one of the newer sheets of paper. "And this helps you how?"

"Well, not me exactly," Braelyn said. "It could help Mirra, though. After my ancestors betrayed the Ilmarrions, they collected whatever trophies they could find and placed them here. However, much of the Ilmarrions' knowledge has been lost.

"I've been able to piece together a bit of information here and there about lost legends and entries, about the relics and their wielders. But the rest is locked behind that glass and I don't want to ask for the key in case it tips Julian off."

"Smart choice, princess," Em said, rising from the desk to study the lock. "It looks simple enough. I could probably pick this in my sleep."

"You will!"

"Not me, princess. You will. This is your lead. I'll just show you how to get there. You have to follow the path."

"I WOULD HAVE NEVER PEGGED YOU AS A STUDIOUS person."

Oya smiled down at Mirra as she ran her fingers across the exposed skin of her neck. Shivers of pleasure ran across Mirra's skin.

"One of my teachers was extremely diligent in my early education."

"One of them? How many did you have?"

Mirra shrugged. "I don't know if you could count Brian as a teacher, but he took care of me, showed me how to work the land, use a bow, and live simply. After that, Nora taught me the ways of the court, basic academics included, and Soren, well, let's say I don't think I'll forget his lessons anytime soon." Mirra shuddered as the ghosts of old pains caused by poisons set her joints aflame and twisted her gut.

Oya took the seat next to Mirra. "I too have had my share of hard teachers. Their lessons stick with us more than the happier ones."

"Definitely, but since we have some time before we can head north, I figured I might as well resume my training."

Oya picked up one of the many books strung about the table. "Infinite Seedlings. I hated this book. I thought I would die of boredom before the trials."

Mirra pressed her lips together to keep from laughing. "That's because you already had a firm grasp of the basics. I don't."

"Are you sure? From what you've told me, you've accessed a portion of your power since you were young. You acted on instinct. Naturally."

"Yeah, but I haven't been able to do it since. Even now, the only times I can really tap into my power are when there's danger. I know a little here and there, but I still feel…" She waved her hand, at a loss for words.

"You're overthinking things," Oya said. "You're acting like your affinity is something separate–it's not. It's as much a part of you as your heart, breath, blood. When you stop thinking, you can reach your full potential. You have to feel it, not wield it like humans."

Mirra played with the end of her pen. "Feeling isn't something I'm good at."

Oya snorted. "What horseshit. Honestly, Mirra, what in the world has gotten into you?"

"Look here, priestess, it's not like I've spent my life preparing to battle cosmic demons, reclaim thrones, falling in love…"

Her breath stilled inside her lungs. Oya stood as still as a statue, with only her slightly widened eyes as any indicator that she'd heard.

"We're all facing things that we never thought we'd have to," Oya said slowly. "But that is life, and all we can do is run from life or embrace it. I ran away in my youth, too afraid of standing on shaky ground to truly see what the Ileign sent me. And then one day I could finally see, and now—now I choose to embrace the world. The good and the bad."

Oya cupped Mirra's cheek. "Don't overthink it, my love. Have faith in the Ilieng and in your own heart." Closing the space between them, Oya lightly placed a kiss on Mirra's forehead. The pure love that emanated from Oya sent Mirra's stomach a flutter.

She sought Master Thrane, and before the sun had set beneath the horizon, Mirra stood at the Gates of Green, ready to face her first test of mastery. She had no doubt in her mind that she would succeed. Each door had its own test. The first door, just to get into the training tower, only opened with a gentle touch of power. And just like with that door, she had to find her way through it. But she could do it, had to do it. Oya's faith in her abilities left her with no other choice.

CHAPTER SIX

THE COURTYARD WAS ALIVE WITH THE SCENT OF SPICES, the sound of music, and the bright hues of flowers and fabrics. Dozens of caravans, tents, and troops loitered about, all eager for the night's festivities and the bags of gold for their efforts. The entire castle buzzed with excitement and anticipation. From her vantage point, Braelyn watched as the party came to life, her face contorted into a scowl.

"Better be careful princess or it will stick like that," Em teased as she laid out a selection of new summer dresses for Braelyn to choose from. The dresses were carefully crafted from the finest Zallino silk, and came with matching shoes. "I think the robin's egg dress would do nicely."

"Isn't there anything darker?" Braelyn sighed, turning away from the window.

"'Fraid not," Em said. "You should tone down your defiances," she advised. The darker tones of your dress only make the courtiers uneasy. They're getting conflicting messages, and if I can speak freely?"

Braelyn nodded and Em continued. "They know nothing of you except that you're the princess. You've held no seat on any committee your mother wasn't already on and served no cause of your own. If they had to place their trust in someone to run the country smoothly, they're going to bet on Julian."

Braelyn loosened a long breath, her shoulders slumping. "No adornments and minimal make up then."

Em quickly brushed Braelyn's golden hair, putting it into a long plait down her back with a small braid encircling her head. Next came the dark blue underdress. Em cinched it with a slender leather belt with a small dagger on each hip. "Now don't get any ideas," Em said, when Braelyn reached for both daggers. "They're meant for defense only and as a last resort. You don't have the training or the stomach to take a life yet."

"Is that to be another part of my training now?"

Em let out a bark of laughter. "Not in your life. You gotta walk before you fly, your highness. Now lift your arms, please."

Braelyn complied, closing her eyes as the dress slid over her head. Em cinched the dress with another leather belt, this one the same color as the underdress. She showed Braelyn the hidden slits that gave her access to her daggers. She made the princess practice over and over, drawing and sheathing the blades until she was satisfied.

A series of sharp raps at the door showed it was time to leave the sanctity of her chambers. Braelyn straightened, not bothering to check her reflection in the mirror as she passed. Em had proven to be a more than a capable lady-in-waiting and Braelyn had no energy to waste worrying about her appearance. Oh, how her mother would be appalled.

The spectacle that greeted her when she walked into the ballroom took her breath away. They strung brightly colored bands of silk from the ceiling along with rows and rows of paper lanterns, filling the room with a vibrant red glow. Lively music filled the air along with mouth watering food.

Em whistled. "You nobles sure know how to throw a party. I don't think I've ever seen anything…"

Braelyn's face was as white as a sheet. Her chest frantically pressed against the top of the dress. Em moved to fill Braelyn's line of vision and to hide her from any watching eye below.

Breathe", Em said, her tone firm and commanding. "Breathe through your nose and out through your mouth. Whatever it is, let it go. All that matters is getting through this. Don't let them see your cracks."

Braelyn's frantic breathing slowed, and the color returned to her cheeks. Tears lined her eyes, but never fell. She'd never let them fall where others could see them. The scent of phantom blood faded away to the dark recesses of her memories as her consciousness clawed its way back to the corporeal world.

"Thank you," she whispered, smoothing the front of her dress. Braelyn threw her head back, plastering a secretive smile on her face. "Shall we?"

She descended the stairs without waiting to hear Em's reply, trusting the woman to follow. Courtiers swarmed around her like flies to a rotting carcass the moment her feet touched the ballroom floor. Braelyn smiled and accepted their congratulations on her pending nuptials. She accepted them with grace and feigned delight. So believable was her performance that Em wondered briefly if the princess hadn't finally cracked under the pressure. Braelyn's facade cracked momentarily when she spied Lord Julian chatting merrily to a group of foreign dignitaries.

"Don't let it slip, princess," Em whispered into Braelyn's ear.

Turning sharply, Braelyn headed for the long tables that ran down the back length of the wall. Julian spared no expense. Each table boasted food and drink from each of the eight kingdoms, all the finest quality.

"Did our mutual friend tell you the story behind his name?" Em asked nonchalantly.

Braelyn shook her head. "I hadn't wondered."

Em shook her head and led Braelyn over to the table that bore delicacies from Zallino. She opened a bamboo basket, sending heavily spiced steam into the air. Using a pair of chopsticks, she plucked out a small white bun.

Braelyn arched a brow at the plain white bun. "This was the only food his mother wanted while she was pregnant with him. Luckily, you can stuff bao buns with just about anything, so her husband didn't see the harm giving into his wife's cravings." Em dipped the bun into a brown sauce before stuffing it into her mouth in one go. She handed her chopsticks to Braelyn before holding out the basket for her to try one.

Braelyn continued to eye Em, fumbling to hold the sticks the same way she'd seen her do it. She gave up quickly, resigning to use her fingers. Three buns sat on a bed of green. One bun, however, bore a small black mark on its twisted top. Braelyn's hand hovered over the buns, uncertain. Just as Em withdrew the basket, Braelyn snatched up the marked bun.

The outside of the bun lightly stuck to her fingers. "Should I shove it whole like you?"

With her mouth still full, Em shook her head. Braelyn
lightly dipped the bun into the same sauce, holding one hand
underneath to prevent any mishaps. Her eyes went wide for a
multitude of reasons. First was the flood of flavor hidden just
beneath the bun's light and slightly spongy skin. The second was
the small, cylindrical object buried in the middle that nearly
broke her tooth.

"Looks like you found a fortune, your highness," Em said in
a slightly raised voice. "I hope it's a good one."

Em wandered down the line, sampling dishes from other
regions, leaving Braelyn alone. Braelyn stuffed the remaining
portion of the bao bun into her mouth and pried apart the
impossibly small tube to get to the message inside.

To one man, the leopard is a sign of death, to another, a sign
of life. But to the leopard, it is simply itself.

Braelyn read the fortune three times before shredding it into
tiny pieces. Had it been a message from Bao? Or had Em
purposely misled her to test if Braelyn could discern a genuine
lead? Braelyn couldn't find Em, so she wandered around and
ended up watching Nealitian dancers..

The crowd moved out of her way and gave her a front-row
seat. She got there just in time to see a dancer leap gracefully, like
the creature her costume represented. White dots stood out in
sharp contrast to the tawny nature of her skin. Her costume was
simplistic, nothing more than a colorful band around her breasts
and a wrap skirt that left her thighs exposed as she danced.
Beads clicked with every movement, along with the light jingling
of bells around her wrists and ankles. Her hair was unlike
anything Braelyn had seen before, not falling down her back but
framing her head like a dark halo. Twin spiral horns arched

from the dark cloud on top of her head, wrapping the complete costume together.

Braelyn stood spellbound like the rest of the court as the woman and others, all dressed as animals, leaped and danced to the beating of drums. The musicians sang in a language unfamiliar to Braelyn, though she didn't mind. She allowed the music to flow through her and the dancers to entrance her until she had a generalized idea of what they were trying to convey.

A string of jarring notes changed the scene the performers had made. Their movements were more disjointed, anxious, as they mimicked looking out at their surroundings.

A dark form soared over the heads of the musicians, landing in the middle of the other dancers. They scattered dramatically as the music took on a frantic beat.

A man stood in the center, swaying from side to side, snarling at the crowd. There was no denying that this man was the predator in the performance.

The performer left and swiped at the crowd at random, drawing startled cries from the nobles. Even Braelyn jumped back, startled when the performer suddenly appeared before her, eyes wide and lips pulled back in a mock snarl.

"Barely above animals, aren't they?"

The cruel words and following snickering smothered the rolling of Braelyn's stomach. She turned with a scowl, locking eyes with a small cluster of unfamiliar noblewomen. The woman in the emerald dress didn't bother to hide her smirk behind her fan like the others cloistered around her like bees. Her scarlet smile took on a sharper edge when Braelyn continued to hold her gaze.

Over the lacy edge of her fan, one noblewoman's watery eyes went wide. She frantically whispered into the emerald woman's ear. Braelyn didn't bother to hide her feral delight as the other woman's face paled. She quickly dropped her gaze, bowing deeply to Braelyn, muttering a garbled apology.

Saying nothing, Braelyn turned back to the performance to see that it was over. Many of the viewers were now throwing small favors at the performers. Braelyn quickly reached for one ring on her finger, but was stopped by a dark, weathered hand.

"There is no need for that, your highness," said an elderly Nealitian noble. His ancient face shone with wisdom and kindness. "We are here for you, after all."

"That may be, but I still wish to thank them for a breathtaking performance. I only wish I got to see the end."

The Nealitian nobleman's face darkened for a moment. "Ignorance blinds many to the wider world and its pleasures. If you wish to thank the dancers, I can take you to them."

Braelyn hesitated. Was this man one of Julian's people, or Bao's, or was he simply a good man trying to do something nice for her?

"Ah, forgive me," the man said, bowing. "I was so taken in by your beauty and kindness that I forgot to introduce myself. I am K'hal Jabilo. I serve as an advisor to the king and queen of Nealet."

Braelyn curtsied. "I am aware of the wise men and women who serve under Oba Zulu and Mora Ujana."

K'hal Jabilo placed a hand over his heart. "As a daughter of Katherine, should be. Mora Ujana was and still is, beyond consolation at the news of your mother's death."

Braelyn blinked back at the mention of her mother's name.

K'hal Jabilo leaned closer, lightly kissing each of her cheeks, lingering to whisper in her ear. "You may call on her majesty if ever you need." He straightened, wrapping Braelyn's hand around his arm and guided her through the crowd.

They neared a small door with a single attendant dressed in a simple dashiki. He bowed deeply to K'hal Jabilo and Braelyn, opening the door without needing to be asked.

Braelyn swallowed once, her free hand sliding into the folds of her gown, her fingers lightly wrapped around the dagger strapped to her side.

Braelyn weighed her options. If K'hal Jabilo was in league with Julian, then this could be another ploy to get her to let her guard down. But if he was honest, then Mora Ujana really was trying to offer a way out. Then there was Em, whose continued absence nagged at Braelyn like a rotten tooth. If Braelyn miscalculated, she could only hope that Em could save her before things got too out of control.

The performers' cheery conversations died away at the sight of Jabilo and Braelyn standing at the threshold of their dressing room. Each one turned and knelt, bringing their heads to the floor. Braelyn bit back the desire to speak out, knowing it was their custom.

"This is princess Braelyn," K'hal Jabilo said in Undorsean for her sake. The translation of his words rippled through the performers for those unfamiliar with the language. "It pained her to miss the end of your performance and wishes to see it now."

"Oh no," Braelyn stammered, pulling away. "Do not trouble yourselves. The space is too small and you must be exhausted.

I've never seen such dancing before and only wished to tell you it was beautiful."

This time, it was her words that rippled through the performers. A few of their faces softened, though many still regarded her with stony silence. One man, the leopard, stepped forward. His yellow body paint smeared from sweat and movement. He placed his hand over his heart and bowed.

"We are honored that your highness has blessed us with her presence and undeserving praise. To thank you, would a small, special performance do instead?"

His voice was deep and slightly musical. Braelyn chewed the inside of her cheek. "As long as it's not too long. I will be missed eventually."

The leopard nodded, gesturing for two stools. Braelyn sat on one, while K'hal Jabilo took the other. He folded his arms with an indulgent smile and waited.

One drummer started with a slow, steady beat, much like a heartbeat. A flute joined in next, followed shortly by an instrument made entirely of bells. The music was as beautiful as the main chamber, but it had a hint of sorrow that tugged at Braelyn's heartstrings.

The leopard man danced with his whole being, not just his body. He conveyed emotions through his arms, legs, and face. Whatever story this dance told, it was one of sorrow and longing.

Just as her burning tears threatened to fall, the tune changed slightly, carrying a more hopeful ring. The anguish painted on the man's face changed, too. He locked his gaze on Braelyn as his movements became smooth and graceful. His face filled with hope and love, with only the slightest hint of fear, as if what he so desperately wanted was within his reach.

The last chord of the song ended abruptly, adding weight to the following silence. The leopard dancer now knelt in front of Braelyn. He gently took her hand in his, placing a ghost of a kiss on the back of her palm.

"Beyond words," Braelyn choked out. She stood, placing her hand over her heart the way she'd seen. "You honor me. I wish you gentle rains and good fortune."

Once again, her words rippled through the gathered performers. As one, they copied her movement, uttering the same blessing in their own tongues.

K'hal Jabilo studied Braelyn from the corner of his eye, not a single inclination as to his thoughts on his face. They remained silent the entire way back to the main chamber. The noise that crashed over them as they rejoined the party nearly eradicated the melody still coursing through her body.

"Thank you for that," she said with a curtsey. "I hope you enjoy the rest of the celebration and I hope to see you again."

K'hal Jabilo bowed. "The same to you, your highness."

Braelyn walked through the crowd in a daze. She found Em perched near a window. The small crack allowed a sliver of cool air into the sweltering ballroom. Braelyn opened the window wider, taking deep, gasping breaths.

"Quite a show, huh?"

Braelyn reached up with the hand that the dancer had kissed and tucked a golden hair pin he slipped her into her curls. "Illuminating."

THE ONE GOOD THING THAT CAME FROM HOLDING A multi-day celebration was that everywhere in the palace was full of unfamiliar faces. A guard's worst nightmare, but a boon for a fledgling…Braelyn wasn't sure what she was. She had no intention of being a spy, nor could she ever be an assassin like Mirra. She had enough that she felt no desire to steal, and yet, she was a student of the shadow world. Either way, she was grateful for the chaos, as she doubted her disguise would have held up otherwise.

She wore a maid's outfit, wrapped her golden hair, and went to the mausoleums using the scroll in the hairpin. Braelyn struggled to keep her face and steps light and carefree. She would go alone, at first, with Em following sometime later–just in case.

It took her some time to find the right name, and when she did, the door was slightly ajar. Hand wrapping around the hilt of her dagger, she pushed the door open as quietly as possible.

Inside there was nearly no light, save what found its way in through the opened door. Dust motes swirled lazily through the air. No signs of the dancer or anyone else. Cautiously, she inched her way further inside, her dagger hissing as she drew it.

A large hand latched around her wrist, wringing her dagger from her grasp. Braelyn glimpsed a light flash along its blade before it clattered into the dark recesses of the mausoleum.

Braelyn tried to swing around, bringing her knee up, just like Em had taught her, but her attacker was too quick. He kicked her other leg out from under her, using his weight to keep her underneath him.

Stars danced across her vision and all the air knocked from her lungs. She felt her head wrap ripped away, but could do nothing about it. Above her, a deep chuckle chilled her to the core.

"Good to see the honest life hasn't dulled your edge."

Braelyn blinked, confused until her vision stopped swimming and she saw Em's dagger glittering against her attacker's throat.

"Sorry to see that it has dulled yours," Em said, amusement coloring her words.

Much to her alarm, Em re-sheathed her dagger, stepping back from Braelyn and her attacker. To further add to her confusion, her attacker withdrew, extending a hand to her.

"Sorry for the rough handling. Can't be too careful these days."

Em shook her head. "Always the over cautious one, Sorro. You'd think you'd learn to relax by now."

"I let my guard down once and ended up trusted up like a goat in the back of a slaver's caravan."

"You won your freedom again."

Sorro stood as silent as the surrounding effigies. "After a time. Now let's get to the matter at hand. I received Bao's message. That's the only reason I'm here in the cursed land. I'm surprised you returned."

"That is a story for another time, my friend. Allow me to introduce…"

"I know who she is," Sorro said, cutting Em off. He turned, his dark eyes boring into Braelyn's soul. "Just so you know, K'hal Jabilo is here at Mora Ujana's behest. She was friends with your mother and has a deep distrust of those who engage in spy work, especially since the ellipse ten years ago. If you want it, all you have to do is ask, and K'hal Jabilo will secrete you away to K'ashi."

"I've already tried that and it failed miserably. I won't cause another's death because I can't manage my house."

The corner of Sorro's smile tugged upward. "That's what I figured. I will relay your words to K'hal Jabilo. Now that's finished, let's get to the real reason we're here." Sorro took a seat on top of a sarcophagus, seemingly uncaring that he was using someone's remains for such an undignified reason.

"You need allies, princess. And I owe a debt to Mirra and Bao. I have no love for this country or its people. I have witnessed the true face it hides behind towering structures and offal wrapped in silks."

Braelyn clasped her hands, worrying her thumb.

"But it also gave me my family. So for them, I stand here ready to save this godless country."

Braelyn bowed deeply. "I know my words hold no weight with you, but you have my thanks. To repay your kindness, I will strive to rectify the failings of my country and people. I too have seen the less pleasant facets of my home."

Sorro silently studied Braelyn before sliding off the sarcophagus. "Dignitaries will soon start flooding the capital. Your marriage is less than eight months away. They will come to see the quality of your character and just who will actually rule this country. We couldn't hope for better cover."

"For what?"

Sorro flashed his teeth. "Bao will teach you the ways of the underworld. Em will show you how to blend into your surroundings. I will teach you how to move your body. Be ready, princess, I am not a gentle teacher."

Sorro left, ignoring Braelyn's sputtering thanks.

Em chuckled, shaking her head. "He hasn't changed one bit since we were kids. Come along, princess, let's get ready to steal some shit to add to our disguises."

CHAPTER SEVEN

"I see Sorro has finally arrived," Bao said with a smirk.

Braelyn jumped, nearly spilling her wine on her dress. She turned, mouth agape, not quite believing what her eyes were telling her. Bao stood grinning like a fiend, dressed as a wealthy Zallino merchant.

"What are you doing here?" she hissed, gripping him.

"To wish a thousand blessings on you and your union, your highness." Though his words were light, his expressive eyes urged secrecy.

Remembering the hundreds of eyes upon her, Braelyn re-schooled her face, releasing her white knuckled grip on his arm. "Forgive me. I lost myself in thought and got startled. Thank you for your blessings. How are you enjoying your visit?"

"Quite well, thank you. May I be so bold as to request a walk around the gardens? Their beauty is legendary, even in my homeland."

"Of course." She handed her drink off to a waiting server and placed her hand lightly on Bao's arm. As they walked, they talked without familiarity with Bao, asking questions about Undros and the gardens. Braelyn played her part as host perfectly, taking comfort in a skill someone well versed her in. When at last they were far enough away from the crowd, Braelyn dropped her mask.

"Do you have a death wish? I don't care how good you think your documents are, Julian will sniff you out and then where will we be?"

Bao's face contorted into mock hurt. "Who do you take me for Braelyn? I am not some green boy fresh off the boat." His teasing tone fell. "And besides I've been working for decades for the opportunity to get back at that bastard."

"What?"

Bao's eyes darkened, all warmth and light draining in an instant. Braelyn swallowed and stepped back. Bao pulled back the threat of violence written across his entire being, bringing his carefree persona to the foreground. Not for the first time, Braelyn wondered if she'd made the right choice, throwing her lot in with him.

"If Julian should ever have the inclination to test my credentials, he will find a lifetime of proof that would fool the gods themselves."

Braelyn pursed her lips. She no longer believed in the gods, but she wasn't foolish enough to tempt fate by insulting them. Not when so much was at stake. "How do you know Sorro is here?" she asked instead.

"By the stiff way you're walking and moving."

Braelyn groaned. Em had to drag me out of bed and massage my limbs to bring life back."

"I'll send some restorative tea later to help."

"Thank you," Braelyn said, "but I doubt that's the reason you're here."

"I need something."

"What?"

"A key."

Braelyn narrowed her eyes. "A key to where?"

She felt her stomach drop at Bao's wicked grin. "Lord Julian's study."

She must have finally lost her mind. That was the only plausible reason she dressed as a servant and carried a tray of refreshments into the viper's pit. There was no way she'd be able to pull this off. Julian would see right through her, even with everything Em did to her. He'd see past her eyes, dyed dark from that stinging liquid, and the makeup applied to make her face look thinner and exhausted.

All too soon, the door to Julian's bedroom came into view. Now or never. Shifting the heavy tray to one hand, Braelyn rapped lightly on the door.

"M'lord, I 'ave the refreshments ye asked for."

Her words felt wrong in her mouth, heavy and fumbling. Even after the hours Em spent with her, practicing her common speech.

Silence answered her knock. She tried again and still no reply. With slightly trembling fingers, she reached out and touched the door handle. She half expected it to kill her on the spot, but the only thing she felt was the coolness of the metal. She gave it a tug, even more surprised when it opened under her touch.

"M'lord?"

Braelyn peered around the door, loosening a breath when she saw that the room was empty. Quickly, she closed the door behind her, setting the tray down on the first table she saw.

"M'lord," she called out, louder.

Not wasting any more time, she strode straight to the massive desk near the back of the room. As quickly and quietly as she could, Braelyn rifled through the desk, opening drawers and looking under papers. She tried to keep her calm, remembering to put everything back exactly as she found it. But as the seconds ticked by, her anxiety grew and she made careless errors.

Ten minutes.

That's all the time that she had to search the room. Any longer and the chances of her getting caught increased. Her heart stopped when she checked her time via a clock on the mantel and realized that she'd been in his room for twenty minutes. Hastily, she grabbed the tray and rushed out the door, crashing right into the one person she didn't want to see.

"Bloody hel, woman!" Julian bellowed as the porcelain pot crashed to the floor and the cakes smeared into his tunic.

Braelyn reflectively went to her knees, picking up the broken pieces, mumbling apologies in what she hoped was a convincing accent.

"What were you doing in my room?" His voice took on a dangerous and sharp edge.

"I brung the tray as ye asked, M'lord."

Braelyn stood, having gathered the last of the fragmented pot and plate. She sopped up as much as the teas as she could with a rag. Julian continued to brush off the smashed pieces of cake, not caring that they fell on her head. Her fear transformed into ire and she slowly rose, caution scattered to the winds. As she stood, her eyes caught the gleam of keys on his belt.

"Please, m'lord, allow me to make amends. Let me take your shirt to the laundry. They'd fix it in a jiffy."

Julian scowled down at Braelyn. She kept her gaze trained to the floor, keeping her face hidden.

"Very well", he spat, storming past her so swiftly that she had to leap to the side or risk colliding again.

Julian undid his belt, letting it fall to the floor, and then pulled his soiled tunic over his head. He scowled when he noticed that the tea had seeped all the way through to his loose linen shirt. Tearing it off with a disgruntled huff, Julian disappeared into an offshoot of the main room.

Braelyn heard the opening of a wardrobe and the rustling of clothing as he cursed loudly about incompetent servants. Seizing her opportunity, she snatched up the key ring, holding them tightly to prevent any noise. Reaching into her pocket, she pulled out a small silver case. Inside was a paste that would take the diameter of the barrel and the shape of the bit. Bao would use this to make a duplicate key.

Braelyn stared down at the three keys, panic rising in the back of her throat. She only had enough for one key. What if she got it wrong? Would there ever be another opening like this one?

She ran her fingers down each key, trying to discover any sign which one was the one she needed. Time slowed as the rest of the world faded away until the only things left were the three keys in front of her.

The pounding of her heartbeat filled her ears. As the beating continued, pressure built along the tips of her fingers. It grew until she felt as if they had been thrust into a fire.

Star-flecked darkness crept into the corners of her vision, blinding her to all the keys but one.

A loud crash broke the spell. Braelyn grabbed the left key, pressing it hard into the paste on both sides before slipping the casting into her pocket.

"M'lord?"

Julian re-entered the room, a strange look on his face. The weight of his eyes forced Braelyn's head lower. She quickly gathered the discarded tunic and shirt, backing away as fast as she could.

"Is there anything else ye need, m'lord?"

"No," Julian said slowly.

Braelyn backed out of the room, closing the door firmly behind her. She rushed to the laundry and back to her room. She felt weak in the legs when she realized how close she was to getting caught.

"THE TRIAL IS SIMPLE ENOUGH. YOU MUST CREATE A RUNE to open the door."

Mirra eyed the door apprehensively. "What's beyond the door?"

Thrane crossed his arms with a grunt.

Mirra rolled her eyes and turned her attention to yet another door she had to open. Unlike before, this time she opened her senses before pushing her magic inside. The first thing she noticed was the complexity of the spell work interwoven with the door.

In her mind's eye, she caught glimpses of runes for protection, endurance, reflection, strength, and stability. There were countless others that were unfamiliar to her. Frowning, Mirra withdrew her hand, taking several steps back.

"Take your time," Thrane said. "You don't have to complete the trial today, but if you want to advance to the next floor, this door needs to open." And with that, he left Mirra alone to puzzle out the key to opening the door.

Mirra sat on a table directly across from the door with her feet in a chair. She could spend hours carefully detangling the litany of rune work that went into the lock, but she didn't have the time for that. She couldn't force her magic into it to shatter the runes. Mirra hesitated before trying to open the door, knowing that brute force wasn't always the best solution.

"Key, key, key," Mirra muttered over and over. "I need a key. Wait…no I don't."

Mirra slid slyly off the table, disappearing into the stacks, the foundations of a rune taking shape in her mind.

When Mirra hadn't shown up for the evening meal, Oya entered the tower to find her. She eventually found Mirra scowling at the door, surrounded by the smoldering ashes of a dozen or more scraps of paper.

"You missed dinner," Oya said as a greeting.

"Huh…what? Is it dinnertime already?"

Oya lightly laughed, a bemused smile on her face. "And past. I sneaked something for you. Best eat it quickly. Thrane doesn't allow food in his library."

Mirra took the offered food, stuffing it into her mouth without taking her eyes off the door. "Almost there. Just need to figure out the binding."

"Binding?"

Oya knelt, picking up a stray piece of paper not completely burned to ash. Her brows furrowed as she tried to unravel the rune on the page.

"Where did you find this? It's not one I'm familiar with, though I have a feeling like I've seen it somewhere before."

"Pieces probably," Mirra said, picking up the wine skin Oya brought along with the food. She took three big chugs before tossing it to the side. "Rune work was the first form of controlled magic the Ilmarrions created. It was a way for us to harness our gifts in a more controlled manner. The key that unlocked our full potential."

"I know, but what does that have to do with all this?"

Mirra finally turned away from the door, her eyes alight with discovery. "How did they get the first runes? They made them. Rune work is the foundation of all Ilmarrion magic — our grounding. I just need to get the right combination and it's onto the next."

"Ambitious," Oya said slowly. "There are other runes that would open the door."

"Yes, but it would take me months, if not years, to find them. I don't have the time and I need to pass through to the next pillar before I have to leave again. Who knows when I'll have another chance or be back?'

The paper she held turned to fine ash in Mirra's hands. Oya scowled. "Don't say that."

"Why?" Mirra turned. Oya stood rooted to the floor like a statue carved from the finest obsidian. A perfect picture of an Ilmarrion priestess, save for the look of wild terror written across her face. The weight of Mirra's words settled around her like a flea-bitten burlap sack.

"I didn't mean it," she said quickly, tracking ashes across her scattered attempts. She took Oya into her arms, pulling her close. The familiar scent of magnolias and almonds filled her senses, soothing away the frantic search for answers that had consumed her all day.

Lifting Oya's face, Mirra stared into her eyes and promised, "I'll come back."

Oya turned away. "You can't make that promise. The road is dangerous enough without The Eater walking the earth. I nearly died twice after I ran away from K'ashi."

Mirra stilled. Oya talked so little about her life before Moakwyd. The only thing she knew was that Oya had been a slave in the capital city and was the first to escape the queen's clutches. The idea of Oya in a collar stirred a low growl in the recesses of Mirra's mind. Mirra buried her rage, focusing on Oya's words. There was nothing she could do about Oya's past hurts, yet.

"I understand that you and I have to travel our own roads for a time. I only hope that one day…one day we will meet again."

"Oya…"

Oya pulled away from Mirra, her eyes distant. "You mentioned a binding? Maybe I can help? Runes aren't my strong suit, but I live and work within the realm of theory."

Mirra let her arms fall, a heaviness settling in the pit of her stomach. "I thought I had to complete this alone."

Oya shrugged. "Yes, but I've never seen someone create a new rune before. I'm interested in seeing your thought process."

"It may only work for people like me."

"Nexian?"

"Thieves."

Mirra handed over a sheet of paper with every rune she'd been able to identify. "I don't have them all, but these are the basic runes for the locking mechanism. Now any good thief will do their best to leave no sign that they'd been there. It's much easier to create an alibi if the mark doesn't realize they've been robbed for a few days. That's why you always need two or three alibis. One for the day you actually committed the crime, just in case, and the rest until the item is discovered missing."

"But the major hurdle is working around the failsafe, setting none of them off. And that's where it's not quite working. I need something to bind all the fragmented runes together long enough for the central rune to work."

Oya could only blink, startled at the revelation of the significance of Mirra's crooked line of thought. A rune to bypass any magical enchantment. All one would need to do is sketch the main rune in the center and nothing would be beyond your grasp.

"Maybe grounding isn't the issue. Maybe I need a lure?"

"I'm almost afraid to ask, but what's a lure?"

"Sometimes security is too tight, so you need to use a lure to distract them and slip through unnoticed."

"Wouldn't the guards be suspicious about two disturbances in a night? The guards outside the slave chambers in the inner sanctum sounded the alarm for even one disturbance."

"We didn't always need to create an out," Mirra calmly answered, tucking away another kernel of Oya's past. "It all comes down to timing."

The sound of heavy footsteps signaled that their time together had come to its end. Oya kissed Mirra gently on the cheek. "Don't stay up too late. I'll be waiting for you."

Liquid fire pooled in the most intimate parts of Mirra. Suddenly, the puzzle of the door no longer held her interest. Oya tapped Mirra's chest with one long finger. "Finish what you started or you won't get your reward."

"Maybe I'll just steal it from you later," Mirra teased. Her wicked smile ignited fires inside Oya as well.

"Where would the fun be with that?" Oya asked breathlessly.

Mirra closed the space between them, gently taking hold of Oya's chin. "I can show you plenty of fun." Mirra captured Oya's mouth, pouring all her arousal into her kiss until they were both gasping for air.

"You have until the first watch," Oya whispered before striding away with more calm and poise than she felt.

Mirra watched Oya's retreating form, stunned by her newfound bravado. It wasn't like her to be so forward, so open about her wants, her desires. She couldn't quite pinpoint the exact moment the change occurred. The only thing she was sure of was that Oya and the other citizens of Moakwyd had something to do with it. Was this what it felt like to walk amongst one's people? To feel completely and irrevocably accepted for every facet of who you were?

Mirra's throat burned. She took another swig from the wineskin and resumed her work. First watch wasn't too far off and if she wanted her prize, then she'd better get back to figuring out how to pick a magical door.

"I HAVE A PRESENT FOR YOU," EM SAID CHEERFULLY AS SHE flounced into the room.

Braelyn looked up from her newly instated writing desk. She frowned, trying to not let her building migraine sharpen her tongue.

Em was a wonderful ally. She was always there to keep Braelyn from falling apart, and she was a ruthless taskmaster when it came to training. But she was too loud. Too excitable and overall just too much for Braelyn to handle in large quantities. It was at times like this when she missed Mirra's quiet, deadly presence.

"What is it?"

With an unnecessary amount of flourish, Em presented a newly forged key. Braelyn blinked several times before her memory caught up with her. "Oh, so soon?"

"Like Bao said, most of this plan has been in the works for ages. You're just moving it along faster."

Braelyn reached out and took the key. Nearly two weeks had passed since that day and burning pain still flared in the tips of her fingertips. She hadn't told Em about the strange feeling or the lingering pain. She didn't expect the woman to have answers, but was pleased to have her own secret that the "master spies" were unaware of.

"What's our next step?"

"All in due time. For now, let's play finding the copper."

Braelyn groaned. She hated playing, finding the copper. She always forgot to set something just right and Em would always catch her while she could never find the copper coin Em hid within the room.

"If we must, but let me finish with these. My courtly responsibilities don't stop because you want to torture me for an afternoon."

"But you make such an excellent victim," Em teased, flashing a cocky grin.

Braelyn shook her head, not bothering to keep the half smile from her face. She was convinced that Mirra's childhood friends were certifiably insane. There was no other explanation for it. And perhaps she was too, because they were growing on her.

CHAPTER EIGHT

The cool night air caressed Oya's flushed skin. For the past hour, she replayed Mirra's kiss over and over until every part of her throbbed with longing. It really was exactly like her Baba said. When you find the one you're meant to spend the rest of your life with, your very soul will call out for them like the flower to the rain.

Oya sighed, leaning her head back against the frame. If Mirra didn't come soon, she'd have to do something about the sweet fire burning through her. Loosening the topknot of her nightdress, Oya exposed most of her chest to the cool night air. With fingers that shone like stars, she traced patterns over the swell of her breast and the hollow between. Her every nerve was engulfed by the fire, bringing a pleasing and delightful ache. With her hand, she bunched the end of her nightdress around her thighs. Her knees parted slightly, and she trailed another stream of starlight down her inner thighs.

Heat pooled in her most intimate place, throwing her senses into stark clarity. The heady scents of magnolias and sun baked earth twined around her, the tendrils of her power coiling around her limbs like silken ropes. Molten fire seared her center with such longing, desire, need that she slid her hand up to the newfound slickness waiting.

Slender fingers stopped Oya's hand.

Her entire body deflated at the sudden withdrawal of the smoldering fire in her blood.

"Naughty, naughty." Mirra's eyes raked down Oya's disheveled appearance, lingering on Oya's exposed breasts and bare legs. Under Mirra's piercing gaze, Oya let her knees fall further apart, laying her desire bare.

"You promised that if I finished all my work before the first watch took their posts, you'd give me a reward." Mirra's husky voice sent shivers throughout Oya's body. Her eyes shone with something that Oya's center pulsing with the beat of her heart.

"And did you?"

A predatory smile as Mirra shifted closer to Oya. "What if I didn't?"

Mirra's other hand cupped Oya's breast and squeezed, erasing any rational thought in Oya's mind. Mirra pressed a light kiss in the hollow of Oya's throat. Oya arched back, giving Mirra more access to all the parts she wanted her to touch. A deep chuckle rumbled in the back of Mirra's throat. She trailed feathery kisses up and down Oya's neck and across her collarbone, sending wave after wave of fire across Oya's skin.

Oya's hunger for Mirra intensified, and she grasped her hair, drawing her mouth closer to hers. Mirra tasted like honey and smoke. Oya moaned, pulling her closer, not wanting any space between them. Mirra pulled back, laughing.

"My, my priestess, who knew you were so excitable?"

Oya put her hand in the middle of Mirra's chest and gave her a strong shove. Mirra's eyes widened as she stumbled back. Oya pressed her advantage, straddling Mirra on her bed. Sun gold light shimmered just beneath her ebony skin as she stared down at Mirra.

"There are many sides of me for you to discover."

It was Oya's turn to tease. With a smile akin to the one Mirra wore earlier. Kissing along Mirra's jawline. Oya trailed her fingers down the length of her body, mildly annoyed at the thin barrier of fabric that separated them. Running her hands back up, she grasped Mirra's shoulders and hoisted them into a seated position. Instantly, her hands went to the end of Mirra's tunic and ripped it over her head, leaving her in nothing but her breast band.

Mirra pulled the top of Oya's nightdress down, leaving her bare from the waist up. Her nipples tightened when exposed to the cool air. Mirra bent, bringing Oya's aching breast to her mouth.

Oya gasped, throwing her head back. Mirra's mouth burned against her delicate skin while her other hand kneaded the other. Liquid fire pooled between her legs, growing with every beat of her heart.

Mirra sat back on her heels, savoring the sight before her. Oya's eyes glazed over. The whiteness of her nightdress in sharp contrasted against the darkness of her skin, a swath of stars against a night sky.

A question hung in the air between them. "Are you sure?"
"Yes."

Mirra tore off her breast band, her hand going to her breeches. Oya stopped her with a hand. "Let me."

Mirra laid down, her own core burning as Oya fully slid out of her nightdress, tossing it to the floor. On hands and knees, she crawled toward Mirra, sitting back to undo the ties of her breeches with painful slowness. As Mirra attempted to remove the offending clothing, she felt Oya's power wrap tightly around her wrists, immobilizing her. Panic flared as the memory of old shackles filled her mind.

"Mirra?" The invisible shackles disappeared. Oya leaned over Mirra, her hands framing Mirra's face. "What's wrong?"

Mirra closed her eyes and grabbed Oya's hands and pressed them to her face, inhaling Oya's scent of magnolias and the lingering aroma of herbs. "Old wounds."

Oya said nothing but brought Mirra's wrists to her mouth, placing a kiss on both. "I'm sorry. We don't have to."

Mirra latched onto Oya's wrist. "Don't go. I don't…I don't want to keep giving him power over me." Oya's smile didn't quite reach her eyes, but she didn't leave. Mirra cupped Oya's face as if it was made of glass before placing a light kiss on her lips. When Oya didn't pull away, Mirra deepened the kiss, her hands running over the lines of Oya's body.

The molten pool of desire broke through again, causing Oya to squirm. "Please," Oya begged against Mirra's mouth, arching, demanding that Mirra finish what they started.

"As you command."

The worlds exploded to existence in a blinding light the moment Mirra's fingers finally slid into Oya's slick center. At first, Mirra's movements were slow and unsure. But as Oya's breathing sped up, her movements grew more confident. Oya pulled Mirra in close, eager to reciprocate. The world dissolved, leaving nothing but stars and fire in its wake. They left their mortal bodies behind as their souls partook in a dance that had been going on since the beginning of time. They were the Nexi and the Ileign, the eternal lovers. Light and dark, day and night, ebbed and flowed, building the other until they crescendo, birthing thousands of new worlds amongst the cosmos.

Sweaty and gasping for breath, Oya and Mirra stayed entwined long after they finished. Oya held Mirra tight in her arms, not willing to let her go lest Mirra disappear in the growing day like the tendrils of her shadows.

Oya brushed back Mirra's hair, placing a kiss behind her ear.

Mirra stirred and turned, her eyes heavy lidded. "What's wrong?"

"Nothing." Oya hid her face in Mirra's hair, her throat tight.

Mirra chuckled. "You can't lie to a lier. Oya, talk to me." She turned, lifting Oya's chin to meet her eyes. Twin rivers of silver ran down Oya's face. Mirra's face stilled.

"When I was young, I was a part of a gang. I did what I had to in order to survive. Sometimes things would get to be too much and I would run to the docks. I would stare out at the ships for hours, desperately wishing to be on them. I hated my life, hated everything. But Bao...Bao would always show up with sweet buns, and we'd talk. He always knew what to say to make me feel better, or at least, not as shitty."

Mirra brushed one of Oya's braids back. "I don't have his way with words or sweet buns to feed you. All that I offer is me. Have faith in me. I've survived this long through the gangs of

Undros and Julian's tutelage. Fought demons." Mirra huffed a laugh. "I even survived you trying to kill me."

Oya grinned weakly. "I wasn't really trying."

A sly half-grin. "Either way, I'm still here with you. Until now, there has been nothing that has actually made me want to live. I thought only of myself and didn't spare a thought for those left in my wake. Until this moment, I never wanted…"

Oya closed her eyes, bringing their foreheads together. "Me too."

"I will come back to you. I promise."

The damn burst. Oya clung to Mirra like she was the only thing that kept her tethered to the world. Mirra pulled her in close, murmuring words of comfort as she stroked her back until the sun chased away the night and its fears.

THE ONE GOOD THING ABOUT HER IMPENDING WEDDING was that the castle was filled with strange people. And as the bride to be and the heir to the throne, it was Braelyn's duty to be a delightful hostess. It also served as an excellent cover for her and Bao to meet right under Julian's nose.

He kept his cover as a Zallino merchant, seeking to secure a royal seal of commerce; and he wasn't the only one. Still, she didn't get to see him as often as she liked. They carried most of their communication out via Em and her uncanny ability to turn into anyone. Sorro spoke even less, only calling on her to twist her into some unnatural position that she'd have to hold for hours on end. He'd then turn the rest of the training over to Em, who was the harshest taskmaster.

But she endured it all and more, if that's what it took to rid her kingdom of that bastard.

"Lord Julian is here to see you, your highness."

Braelyn sighed, setting aside her work. Julian's brief visits had grown with every new arrival. Almost as if he suspected outside allies would try to reach her. It gave her no small measure of pleasure knowing that his worst fear had already come to pass and he knew nothing of it.

"What do you want now?"

Julian scowled, taking the seat opposite her. "Is that any way to greet your intended?"

"You're not my intended," Braelyn spat. "You're just the bastard that's trying to use me to get to the crown."

Julian's smile took on a razor's edge. "That's all you're good for, isn't it, princess? It's what you were bred for, what your mother trained you for. And it's what every person in this castle is trying to do. Why am I any different?"

"They didn't kill my parents and laid the blame at my brother's feet."

"Semantics," Julian said with a flippant wave.

Braelyn pinched the bridge of her nose. "Why are you here?"

"There's to be another ball at the end of the week."

"Just how many are you going to have? Are you trying to bankrupt the kingdom?"

Julian's eyes darkened. "You only need to concern yourself with making preparations for our wedding and answering your little letters. Need I remind you of what will happen if you choose to deviate from that path?"

Braelyn paled, her lips pressed into a thin line. Julian smirked, rising from his seat. "Make sure you wear something fitting for the occasion, and I can't wait to see what you'll wear for our wedding night."

Braelyn remained where she sat long after Julian left her room. Though her face had a greenish tinge, her fingers wrapped around the key in her pocket with nearly enough strength to snap the metal.

Mirra stirred in her sleep, cold. She reached out to pull Oya closer but only found empty sheets cool to the touch. She sat up, rubbing the sleep from her eyes. After falling asleep, she had the oddest dream. Most of it she couldn't remember. The only part that stuck with her was a blood red smoke and transformed into a spear.

"You're finally awake." Oya strode through the door and set a tray next to the bed. "You missed breakfast."

Mirra threw back the sheets, hissing when the cold air caressed her naked skin. Quickly, she threw her clothes on, stealing a kiss from Oya before digging in.

Oya picked at her nail bed. Her brow furrowed as she wrestled to find the right words. "I saw High Priestess Usoa this morning."

Mirra stopped eating and arched her brow.

"She says that you and Gaitlan need to leave…today. She warns that if you don't, you'll miss your chance to find Shiro."

The food turned to ash in Mirra's mouth. "Is she certain?" Oya nodded. Mirra stood and took Oya into her arms. "What I said last night is still true. I'll come back, I promise."

"You better," Oya mumbled into Mirra's neck. She pulled back and kissed Mirra hard. Her hands slid under Mirra's shirt, deftly pulling it over her head and tossed it to the floor. They didn't need to leave this very moment and Oya wanted another memory to cling to should the fates decide to be cruel.

Gaitlan tried to not stare at Mirra's brushed lips or disheveled hair. He couldn't resist wiggling his eyebrows when Mirra came up beside him. "Long night."

Mirra shoved him into his horse. "Shut up."

"You could stay, you know? Be here with your people, learn more about your abilities. I can find Shiro and the others."

Mirra shook her head. "You wouldn't last five days without me, princeling. And besides, you don't even know what he looks like."

"Perhaps, but you wouldn't have to leave her behind."

Mirra narrowed her eyes but said nothing, busying herself with last checks. Their mounts were smaller than the horses they arrived on, with shorter, stockier limbs more suited for rough mountain roads. The saddlebags were full of dried provisions, medicinal kits, and a small amount of coin.

The day was already warm, so she left her travel cloak rolled on top of her sleeping roll. She then lashed a quiver to one side, ensuring that the bow and arrows were secure.

"Oya told me how you got past the lock for the second pillar." Usoa handed Mirra a short, curved sword. "I would let you take the glaive, but it is a bit impractical on horseback."

"Only a little." Mirra strapped the sword around her waist before accepting several small daggers that she tucked into her sleeves and boots. She stashed the rest in another saddlebag. "I wish I had at least a little more time to learn something from the Düa."

Usao made a face. "Time is not always our friend and there will always be things we'll never get to do."

"Aren't you cheerful this morning?"

"It's not my place to make you happy," Usoa cut her eyes to Oya, who was busy explaining the different healing ointments to Gaitlan. "My place is to ensure that you're ready for the task set before you."

Mirra rubbed the back of her neck. "To be honest, I don't think I'm ready, but I don't think anyone would be. Are you sure Shiro's to the north?"

"This time of year he tries to check in on his family, in secret, of course. The passes between the black marsh and the river lands have yet to open. If you hurry, you might catch him in Eddany."

Gaitlan joined the conversation. He carried a long sword strapped to his back and matching daggers at his sides. "And if we don't?"

"Then you must figure out what to do, young prince."

"Are you sure about this?"

Sorro sighed, tightening the straps of his boots. "It's not what I think, little princess. It's what needs to be done."

Braelyn looked down at her attire for the evening, a direct copy of Sorro's, with a doubtful look on her face. She'd never worn anything so different in her life. For one, she'd never worn breeches in her life and didn't know if she liked them or not. Em had bound her breast, making her chest appear nearly as flat as Sorro's. The gloves had special rough patches at the tips and palm for grip strength. The same type of patching was on the soles of the boots. A tight hood covered her braided hair, leaving only her face exposed.

Braelyn fiddled with the strip of cloth that would go over the lower half of her face once it was time to leave. "But why me? Surely Em would be better."

"Then why did we waste all this time training you?" Sorro growled. "Make no mistake, princess, we're only here to repay a debt, nothing more. If you can't handle the work, then get out of our way."

Sorro pulled his hood over his face, fastened the face covering, and disappeared through the open window.

"You'd best hurry," Em said, blinking against the dye. Em dressed up in one of Braelyn's night dresses, her hair styled the same way. While Braelyn and Sorro were to traverse the castle's rooftop, Em's job was to make it look like Braelyn was in her room the whole night.

Braelyn waited for words of comfort or insurance, but they never came. Bile burned the back of her throat. With shaking fingers, she fastened her face covering. She didn't bother to mask the unabashed horror rolling through her. With calculated slowness, she perched on the window seal, peering out into the wide open world beyond her window.

The night air whipped and tugged at her, stealing the strength from her limbs and all thoughts from her mind. She couldn't stop herself from looking down. The ground was so far away, so unforgiving. If she fell now, she'd die.

Death didn't seem like such a bad idea. In the Dark Mother's realm, she'd be forever beyond Julian's grasp. Beyond all the hurt and pain. She'd even be able to reunite with her parents and Tolin. She leaned forward, the tips of her fingers and toes the only thing keeping her tethered to the world of the living.

"You coming, princess?"

Sorro's gruff voice cut through death's siren song. Braelyn jerked backwards, nearly tumbling back into her room.

Not now. Not yet.

Braelyn loosened a breath, letting go of everything thought whirling around her head. She stood tall, shifting her feet as wide as the window would allow. Squatting, she gathered every ounce of strength in her legs and leapt into the waiting abyss.

Hard stone met her fingers, the patches on her gloves helping her keep her grip as the rest of her body swung free. Braelyn took in a shaky breath before she rocked her body, gaining momentum to swing a leg over the roof's edge. She pulled herself on top of the roof, her chest rapidly rising and falling, already drenched in sweat.

Sorro cleared his throat.

Braelyn rolled over, pushing herself to her feet. "Shall we then?"

All she could make out of Sorro was his eyes. Though she couldn't perceive any change, Braelyn could have sworn mild approval shone through. Perhaps she'd imagined it, but either way she'd use it to carry her to the mission's end.

As fleet footed as deer, they ran along the rooftop. Sorro's footing was more sure than Braelyn's. He, however, was more patient with her than he'd ever been during their lessons. Perhaps it was because now, there was a serious risk of injury. One small misstep, one slip, one weak landing, and that would be the end.

Sorro stopped on the edge, standing as tall and stoic as the gargoyles perched along the rooftop. Braelyn's gasping breath was too loud for her liking. No doubt every sentry throughout the castle could hear her.

"Gather yourself, princess."

"What?"

Sorro backed up a measurable distance from the edge, turned and ran back. As the toes of his right foot met the edge, he vaulted into the sky as if taking flight. Braelyn held her breath as she watched him bring his knees to his chest, arms spread backwards like wings, before disappearing into the night. She scrambled to the edge on all fours, reaching the edge just in time to see Sorro land on the lower roof, curling into a ball as he fell. He rolled once before springing to his feet, and turning to see what Braelyn would do.

Of course, they'd practice this many times, with increasing distances and varying heights. She had felt confident then, but now, standing on top of the castle, the reality of what she had been training for settled like a sour stone in the pit of her stomach. I don't think I can do this. I can't do this. I'm not made for this. No. No.

Yes, you are, princess.

Mirra's voice cut through Braelyn's rising panic.

Listen to her, Bao's voice said. His trademark smirk coming through somehow. Would I let you even set one foot onto a single shingle if I didn't think you could do this?

Yes, Braelyn shot back vehemently.

You wound me, your highness. Now, are you going to prove what those sycophants think of you? That you're nothing more than a broodmare, a pawn to be maneuvered as they willed?

I'm nothing like that!

Then show them, Mirra said. Show them the fire that gave me the courage to break free. Break free, Braelyn. Fly!

Braelyn stood on shaky limbs. Closing her eyes, she breathed deeply, pushing down her fears until they were nothing but a pebble in her shoe — small, annoying, but manageable. She backed up, a bit farther than Sorro had, and ran for all she was worth. Her feet thudded against the narrow beam that ran the length of the rooftop. She didn't focus on the rapidly approaching edge, but on her imagined landing point. She saw herself make the jump and land safely on the other side. As Sorro always said, the body will go where the mind wills it.

Her toes brushed against the edge.

Braelyn willed all her strength into a single leg and pushed.

The world fell away, leaving only the star flecked sky around her and the gentle summer night air whipping around her ears.

For the briefest moment, Braelyn allowed herself to savor the joy of flight, albeit a short flight. Beneath her mask, a smile broke.

And then reality came crashing down. She wasn't going to make it. She hadn't gathered enough speed to cross the space.

The sour tang of fear coated her mouth. Braelyn clenched her jaw so tight that her teeth aged and clawed a sliver of rational thought.

She could still make it. She may not make the land as Sorro had, but as long as she grabbed the roof's edge, she'd be fine. Sure, crashing into the side of the building would hurt and most likely leave a mark, but she'd make it.

As predicted, Braelyn came up short, already falling alongside the building. She thrust her hands out, nails screaming as they dug into the unforgiving stone. Her body crashed into the side with more force than she'd expected, knocking all the air from her lungs. Stunned, her fingers lost their purchase, and she plummeted into the dark, too stunned to even scream.

Bao sat in the room appointed to him upon his arrival, scowling at the surrounding space. The room wasn't the most lavish by any means, and yet, its contents could feed a family of five for at least a year, maybe two. He saw beside a low fire and took a long draught from his cup.

How long had it been since he worried about a job? Had he made the right choices? Thought of everything? What if Braelyn failed? What if she got hurt?

He downed the rest of his drink, coughing as it burned the back of his throat. He poured another serving and downing it in three large gulps. The effects of the alcohol made his head swim and his eyes burn. He rubbed his face, pressing until lights danced behind his eyes.

Sharp tapping at his window sent him flying from his seat. A lone figure perched on the window seal. He couldn't make out much of the person's figure, but being hunched over it was hard to tell. Then Bao registered it was only one person. Bao's heart plummeted like a stone. Mirra's going to murder me.

He unlatched the window and stood back, ready for whatever calamity Sorro brought with him.

"I don't think I want to do that again."

Bao blinked. Since when was Sorro's voice so light, melodic, feminine?

Braelyn tore off her face cover, revealing a flushed smile. She pulled back her hood, strands of her golden hair stuck to her skin.

Bao blinked, and before he could stop himself, grasped Braelyn by the arms, searching for any signs of injury.

"I'm alright," she said, pulling back. Her brow furrowed as she studied him. Her head tilted to the side when she noted the lines of worry written across his entire face. "Honestly, I'm fine. Everything went off without a hitch. I almost fell, but Sorro caught me. I don't think I can stomach doing that again anytime soon."

"I don't think I could stomach it either," Bao said, stepping back. He poured another drink and downed it in a single go. He refilled the cup and handed it to Braelyn.

"No, thank you. I don't drink hard spirits."

The drink lingered in the space between them. "It's tradition. You survived. And what are we if we don't hold true to our traditions?"

Braelyn made a face and accepted the offered cup, ignoring the fluttering in her chest when Bao smirked at her. Her nose crinkled at the scent of the alcohol. She spared Bao one last, unsure glance before tipping the cup back. She sputtered and coughed, her already flushed face turning bright red.

"Gods, that's awful."

Bao took the cup back. "You get used to it."

Braelyn shook her head, unconvinced, and took a seat by the fire. "If you say so." She slumped in the chair, pinching the bridge of her nose.

"You'd best get back. There's a change of clothes on the bed for you."

Braelyn didn't move. "Give me a moment. Gods, I'm exhausted."

"You really shouldn't."

But Braclyn had already fallen asleep, worn out by the stress of the night and the lull of alcohol. Bao made a face but let the princess sleep. At least for a few moments. There was still plenty of time before the next bell. He sat at the foot of his bed and kept watch. The low flickering flames set her hair ablaze, throwing the planes of her face into sharp contrast. Her face softened as she slept, erasing the worry lines around her mouth and eyes and giving her a carefree appearance. Like she should have been if not for Julian and his twisted game.

Bao ran a hand through his hair. Just what was Julian's end game? What did the creature squatting inside him want? Despite his own far-reaching network, Bao couldn't find much information about The Dark One. Its appearance happened thousands of years before the slaughter of the Ilmarrion people and their cities. Nevertheless, not even a whisper? A scrap of paper? Some fragment of a larger story?

Braelyn stirred in her sleep, twisting to find a comfortable position. Bao laughed silently before walking over to the slumbering princess. He threw a lap blanket around her shoulders, gently brushing back a strand of sweaty hair from her face. You know, she wasn't half bad looking — for a noble, that is.

CHAPTER NINE

BRAELYN WOKE UP IN HER BED WITH NO MEMORY OF HOW she got there. She laid in bed, frozen, as she mentally scanned her body for any signs that she'd been abused. Her body ached from her crashing into a wall and nearly falling to her death, and that was it. Sitting up, Braelyn hugged her knees into her chest. She was left with a hazy memory of the night before, the only thing clear in her mind was the burning sensation of the alcohol Bao gave her. She recalled the sensation of her limbs relaxing, and then the world simply faded away.

"Princess?"

Em stood in the doorway. Her eyes were bloodshot, and still the same shade as Braelyn's. Dark circles stood out in sharp contrast under her eyes, the only sign that she, too, had a long night.

"What? How?"

"You were late, so I went to Bao. You were passed out….with Bao." A wicked smirk tugged at a corner of Em's mouth as she watched Braelyn's growing alarm. But the wild fear painted across her face soured any joy Em got from teasing. "He was on the bed and you were curled up in a chair by the fire. I think he intended to let you sleep a bit and fell asleep himself." Another smirk. "It was cute."

"So nothing happened?"

Em shook her head. "After I woke him up, we carried you back. I changed you and hid your clothes."

Braelyn was grateful that she was already on the floor as relief flooded through her. Her only value depended on remaining untouched. No man would want her after Julian violated the most private part of herself. Once he did, she'd have one less bargaining chip at her disposal. Though the thought of selling herself to secure allies twisted her stomach into knots.

Em knelt next to her, and the soft fabric of the robe felt warm and comforting against Braelyn's bare skin. The twisting in her stomach rose, cutting off her ability to breathe. Hot tears rimmed her eyes and Braelyn clung to Em like the other woman was the only thing keeping her afloat. Em wrapped her strong arms around Braelyn and told her to let go. Like a dam breaking, all the stress, anguish, and sorrow Braelyn kept to herself poured out until she was nothing more than an empty vessel.

"Are you feeling well, your highness?"

Braelyn plastered an empty smile on her face and turned to the diplomat from Bardon. He was about the same age as her father, and in some ways, he reminded her of him. They both had deep lines around their mouths and the threading of sliver around their temples. Braelyn blinked against the onslaught of memory, keeping her facial expression politely interested. "Yes, thank you. I think I finally understand why my father was always exhausted. There's so much more to ruling a kingdom than I ever knew."

The diplomat, whose name escaped her, patted her hand with the affectionate paternal air. "I'm afraid it only gets harder, your highness. But at least you won't have to manage it alone. Your fiancé is an old hand at all this."

Braelyn's smile faltered, taking on a razor edge. The diplomat paled, visibly swallowing. "I…um…what I mean…"

Cold fire filled her veins, spilled out the tips of her fingers and eyes. The thrumming of her heart filled her ears as the pressure built inside. She was going to either explode or burst into flames, taking everyone with her. The thought of burning the castle to the ground and denying Julian his prize filled her with a sickening sense of joy.

There came the sound of cracking, followed shortly by a great crash and cries of alarm. The great oak tree in the middle of the gardens swayed as if blown about by a storm. But the sky was bright blue and clear of even the tiniest sliver of a cloud. A single, massive branch tore divots into the ground around its roots.

"By the gods." Braelyn walked toward the fallen branch. She paid no heed to the scattered and frightened dignitaries, merchants, and courtesans flocking to safer ground around her.

"Careful, your highness." Bao halted Braelyn with a firm hand. He used the chaos to steer her away from the court to a small, darkened alcove. "What was that?"

Braelyn held a hand to her pounding temples. "What do you mean?"

"The tree. One minute it's fine and healthy, the next it drops a branch large enough to kill a man."

"Branches fall."

Bao scowled. "Not like this. That branch looked old and dead, and I highly doubt the royal gardeners would allow a branch like that to stay on the tree." Bao crossed his arms and scowled down at Braelyn. "We can't work together, princess, if you keep things hidden from me."

"Hel's Gates," Braelyn snarled, shoving Bao against the wall. "Do this! Do that! Oh, look at this poor, simple little girl in a crown! Everyone keeps making me feel inferior and I'm over it. The only reason this kingdom has a chance is because of me. I stayed behind so Mirra could get my brother out of the city. I've done everything I can to keep my people safe from a man who has no problem being the king of corpses. So you and your little band of miscreants can kiss my ass if I don't feel like sharing every last bit of myself."

The silence hung heavy between them. Braelyn remained where she stood, fists clenched and chest heaving.

Bao breathed through his nose, his gaze darkening. "Emotions have no place in my work, Braelyn. Don't let your feelings get you and everyone else killed.

Braelyn shook her head, her lip pulled back in a grimace. Turning on heel, she left the alcove and stormed back to the one place she could garner an iota of peace.

"You know, for someone who's supposed to be smart, you do a lot of dumb things."

Bao pinched the bridge of his nose and turned. "Not now Em."

"No, you're going to listen." She leaned against the wall, her arms crossed. "You know who she reminds me of?"

Bao rolled his eyes. "I give up who."

"Mirra." Bao blinked and stared at Em like she'd finally lost her mind. But Em wouldn't be swayed. "She's just like Mirra before she learned to let people in. And I wonder who was the one to finally break through Mirra's walls? Cause it sure as hel wasn't us." Em gave Bao one last pointed look before leaving him with his thoughts.

Braelyn passed around her room like a caged beast, cursing Bao under her breath. She turned when the door opened. Em walked in with her hands up.

"Don't take what Bao said to heart," Em said, taking a seat at the vanity. "He's always been like this; single-minded. You'd think he'd learned after what happened last time." A shrug of the shoulders. "But we both know that men aren't entirely the smartest bunch."

Braelyn fought to restrain the traitorous corner of her mouth that wanted to mirror the smirk on Em's face. "What happened last time?"

Em's face darkened. "We thought we got Mirra killed." Braelyn stopped pacing, her eyes wide. Em sighed. "It's not something I like to think about. Even though it turned out to be false, it didn't erase the decades of guilt. Look, Braelyn, you don't have to trust us. Hel, I wouldn't in your situation. But whatever happened out there, if it is what Bao suspects, we need to know. Julian went after Mirra because he believed she had magic even before she showed it. What do you think he'll do to you?"

Braelyn sat at the foot of her bed, her spine and resolution steeled. "Like I told Bao, trees grow old and break. That oak tree has been in the courtyard since my great-great-grandfather put it there in honor of his wife. A branch or two is bound to fall off, eventually."

Em sighed, her face disappointed. She reached into her pocket and took out a small leather journal. Braelyn furrowed her brow. There was something familiar about the book that tugged at the recesses of her memory. "What is that?"

"I found it under your bed." She carelessly flipped through the pages. "Nothing too odd about that, except that it's written in Zallino merchant shorthand."

"How do you know?"

Em snorted. Braelyn's cheeks heated. "Bao."

"He wasn't always an orphan. So princess, what do you want to know what's inside?" Em held the small book out for Braelyn.

Excitement thrummed through Braelyn's body at Em's tone and the mischievous gleam in her eye. "Definitely."

That night, Braelyn paced around her room, brimming with excitement. The book contained meticulous notes from previous queens pertaining to a secret account. At first, Braelyn had been upset that her mother never told her about the account or taught her Zallino merchant shorthand, but in the end, Braelyn let it go. It wasn't that her mother withheld the information because she didn't think Braelyn couldn't handle it. The account was only accessible to the queen. It was a safety measure against hard times and foolish kings. And now that she was a queen, in all but name, she could use the money however she saw fit. She paused by the window and stared up at the half-full moon in the sky. She clasped her hands and bowed her head in prayer.

Merciful Mother Yulla, Honorable Father Ydris. Please continue to look after my brother and Mirra as they seek to serve justice. Keep my parents well within your halls. I hope that they're proud of the path I've chosen to walk to protect our people. Continue to guide my way and forgive me for ever doubting you. Thank you for sending Mirra and her crew of miscreants my way. Thank you for Em's unwavering presence, for she has become my rock. And thank you for Bao and his never ending patience with me as I learn to walk within the shadows.

"I didn't take you for the praying type."

"There's much you don't know about me, Bao." Braelyn lifted her head and smiled up at the man perched on her window seal. She stepped aside, letting him in.

His boots made no sound when they touched the floor. He straightened his burgundy overshirt and brushed dirt from his loose-fitting trousers. He walked past Braelyn, taking a seat opposite her usual chair.

Braelyn sat in her chair. "I'm sure Em's already filled you in?"

"She's told me about the secret account. But not what you wanted to do with it."

Braelyn furrowed her brow. "You aren't going to lay claim to it for the rebellion?"

"Nope. It's your money, princess. You're free to do with it as you see fit. If you want to donate it to the cause, I'm all for it. You could also use it to hire mercenaries to fight for you, if it's a large enough sum. You could also make donations to various nobles and merchants to keep the court on your side. But at the end of the day, it's your choice. I already have my plans to get my revenge on Julian and, like I said when we first met, they don't need you."

Braelyn picked at her nails. "Right now, we both want to see that man suffer." Bao nodded his head, but his expression was impossible for her to read. "I see no need to diverge from that. Mercenaries are only loyal to the highest bidder, plus where would I house them? How could I ensure they don't cause more problems?"

"Fair points."

The next words out of her mouth left a bitter taste in their wake. "And as for the nobles and merchants…they're too untrustworthy."

A shadow of a smirk tugged at Bao's mouth. "And I am? A Bossman and known criminal?"

Braelyn barked a laugh. "Yes, you crooked man. You and the others are far more trustworthy than nobles. From the first moment we met, you've been upfront about what you will and will not do. You haven't bent or made concessions. Those are rare traits."

"So, what do you want to do?"

Braelyn chewed the inside of her cheek, her hand slipping into her pocket. Withdrawing the book, she gently ran her fingers over its edges and spine. "I need you to arrange a meeting for me with the other Bossmen."

Bao stilled, his dark brows drawing close. "Out of the question."

"It wasn't a request."

"You don't give me orders, princess."

"And I will arrange a meeting without you." Braelyn softened the scowl building on her face and kept her words soft and consoling. "I'm not asking without thought. I know the risks of going to see these people. They'd sell me out in a heartbeat if they thought it was more beneficial for them. I'm hoping to convince them otherwise…with your help."

Bao ran a hand through his hair. He chewed over her words and said, "not that simple, Braelyn. Most of them wouldn't want to meet you. There's no love of nobles, especially royals, south of the Divine District."

"I know that," Braelyn said. "But coming from you, the Bossman of the entire Merchant's District, they might be more inclined to follow your lead. At least to satiate their curiosity."

"Don't count on it," Bao said. "I made a lot of enemies on my way to the top. What's with this sudden desire to throw yourself into another deadly ring?"

Braelyn pressed her lips together to prevent the smile from building. He hadn't flat out refused this time. "I need people to make life hard for Julian and the rest of polite society. I need them to ruffle some feathers, break a few windows, and sow discourse."

"You want controlled chaos," Bao said. His eyes light up with a mischievous delight that caused Braelyn's heart to flutter inside her chest.

Braelyn clutched her mother's book tight. She needed to do something, anything, to weaken Julian's standing. Would there be some innocents caught in the crossfire undoubtedly? But if she continued to do nothing, then more would suffer. Braelyn swore silently to the future victims of her plans, promising to make the ends justify the means and to make it up to them one day. "Yes. Yes, I do as much as possible."

"I don't like this," Tull said from his position to Bao's right.

Pinching the bridge of his nose, Bao tried to ease the tension headache he had developed. "You've mentioned that about a dozen times already. Not to mention the three days Em chewed my ear off. Do you have any idea how annoyingly persistent she is?"

On his left, Sorro harrumphed. "Do you have any idea the amount of pain Mirra will inflict on you should things go south? She asked you to look out for the princess, not drag her deeper into a tangled web. And certainly not into our world."

"No one asked for your opinion, Sorro," Tull snapped, fingering the tops of his daggers, a telltale sign of his nerves.

Sorro glared at his onetime partner in crime with an unreadable face. Slowly, the corners of his mouth pulled back into a feral grin. "Never learned how to keep your emotions in check, have you, little one?"

"Little one!" Tull sputtered. "I'm older than you by a year and at least a foot taller."

Sorro snorted. "Three inches is not a foot."

Boa's tightly reined control finally slipped as he listened to his friends fall into old arguments. He covered his face with his hand and silently laughed, his shoulders shaking.

"To hel with both of you," Tull snapped with little anger, when Sorro joined in. He pressed his lips together to keep his own laughter in check, but soon the trio dissolved into a fit of laughter.

The years melted away, leaving them once more children joined together to challenge a world that sought to beat them down.

Bao wiped his streaming eyes. "I needed that, thanks."

Sorro grunted. "I think we all did. But that doesn't mean that I like your plan any better now," Tull said.

"It's not my plan, it's hers. The princess wants to meet with the underground and forge temporary alliances."

"They won't go for it. They barely tolerate you and the restrictions you put in place." Sorro's face hardened. "That's partly why I left. These people care nothing for those they consider less than them."

Bao ran a hand through his hair. "Some yes, but others have become fat on riches and complacent. It might help her or not."

"And if they tell," Sorro said, his voice dark and steady.

"Then they die," Bao said, his face void of all light and warmth.

The Gilded Lily was packed with people, yet the silence was deafening. This was not an evening for revelry or boisterous crowds, but for dealings and secrets. Bao surveyed the gathered bosses, mentally running through the list. Admittedly, it was a short list, but those gathered were ones he trusted, as much as one can trust criminals. Worry twisted his stomach into knots, making each bite of food or sip of beer recoil and threaten to come back up. He didn't think he'd ever been this nervous in his life. Not even during the first job he and Mirra pulled when they were eight, and that job earned him a scar across his left calf.

Closet to him sat Madam Tatinna and her Court of Silks; the other top madams and masters of the pleasure houses. She gathered and doled out nearly all secrets within the city. Her girls work from the lowest inn near the docs, grand estates, and even the palace itself. It was all thanks to her that Bao could get into the castle in the first place. And in return, Bao ensured that any man who hurt a girl met a swift and lasting punishment. His only stipulations were that the madams didn't push drugs onto the girls. If they wanted to, it was on the girls. The other stipulation was that no child under the age of sixteen could go up for sale. There had been some push back in the beginning, but Madam Tatinna was the first to use the age restriction to her benefit. Using the extra time to drive up interest and raising the prices for first blood rights. It was that willingness to work anything to her benefit that Bao was counting on.

Boss Quill played Xaingqui with the people he'd brought with him. However, Bao knew Boss Quill was taking stock of who was here to gauge what Bao wanted from them. Boss Quill had his fingers in all the forging rings throughout the capital. Money, identification, deeds, writs of sale, whatever you needed, his people could make it and none would be the wiser. The rumor was that in his youth, Boss Quill had either been a younger son of a noble or a merchant who had to run for nefarious reasons. The reasons varied depending on who told it. Some said that he owed a small fortune to the gambling houses. Another said he raped the magistrate's young daughter. Some even whispered that he'd fled after the brutal murder of his lover at the hands of his father. Either way, he was intelligent, meticulous, and, most importantly, kept his thoughts to himself. Of all his underlings, Boss Quill thought the most like a noble and might believe the sincerity of Braelyn's plea.

The only ones making any actual noise came from the table where Bosses Hal, Gale, and Halie sat. The siblings ran nearly all the gambling houses from the docs to the Noble District. People often gave Boss Hal and Gale wide berths because of their bulky, bruiser frames and scarred hands and faces, but it was Boss Halie that you needed to watch out for. Like Em, she used her pretty face and delicate frame to her advantage. Typically, she wore fine dresses to fit in with the other well-to-do merchants and lower nobles, but her "houses" were just as filled with vice as the ones in the Merchant's District. And she was far more lethal against those who failed to pay or damaged her goods.

Bao could have invited more bosses to the meeting, but the more people who knew, the greater the risk of someone speaking. Also, these bosses commanded the same level of respect and power as Bao; nearly. They also had the most to lose should the city fall. And they liked him, mostly. Bao stayed out of their affairs beyond what was due to him, and they, in turn, kept their scheming to a minimal.

"Bao, darling," Madam Tannia purred from her table, tapping her silk fan beneath bloody lips. "Are we here for pleasure or business? If it's the former, I have a rather substantial rate."

"I'm sure ya do, how bout I give ya a ride?"

"You couldn't afford me, Hal. Nor would you know what to do."

Hal's laugh boomed, his hand grabbing the front of his trousers. "Oh lass, ye wouldn't know how to handle a piece this big."

Madam Tannia rolled her eyes, flapping her fan open to hide her smile. Every time Hal was in the same room as her, he tried to get into her bed. Bao suspected Tannina enjoyed the attention, but would never give in.

"No one wants to see that, Boss Hal," Bao said with a laugh of his own. "To answer your question Madam Tannia, we're here for business." The room fell silent as all eyes turned to Bao. Here we go.

"However, it's not my business."

"Then whose is it?" Boss Quill demanded.

"It's mine." Hooded and cloaked, Braelyn stepped out from the back room that served as Bao's office. She lowered her hood, showing her face to the gathered criminals. At Em's urging, she wore a simple shirt and breaches, easier for her to run should things go south. The only signs of her royal status was the silver singlet around her head.

Sorro pulled a chair out for her, setting it next to Bao. She took it without acknowledging him, keeping her eyes forward.

For three heartbeats, no one said a word. And then, "Dark mother's tits, what is this Bao!" Boss Gale stood, his chair clattering to the ground behind him. He banged a fist on the table, his face crimson.

"The princess reached out to me some time ago, wanting to organize a meeting. She's already explained to me what she wants, and what she's willing to pay for our services."

"There's no amount of gold or jewels in the world that would ever make me want to work with a noble." Bao fought the urge to throw a piercing stare at the madam that spoke. As much as he hated it, Braelyn would have to convince them by her own strength.

"Believe me," Braelyn said undeterred, "the thought of working with the dregs of society isn't something I want to do either. But I have no other option at the moment."

A few more insults directed at Braelyn and her ilk were thrown. Bao dug his nails into his chair to not take them out. He had promised. Promised to not interfere, to let Braelyn speak her mind. If she won them over, great. If not, then he would quietly ensure that the details of the night's meeting never left the lower streets.

Boss Quill's calm and measured voice cut through the dim. "What exactly do you want from us?" The room fell silent.

"My brother didn't kill my parents. Julian did. I know you have no love for the nobles or the royal family, and frankly, I don't really care. But you care about profits. Julian will end that for you, permanently."

"How do you know that?" Boss Gale asked.

From her pocket, Braelyn pulled out a stack of folded paper. "I retrieved these from Julian's private study. They're copies, Sorro, who helped me get them, and Bossman Bao, who assisted as well, can verify their validity."

"Why would you help a royal?" Boss Haile asked, her tone calm and measured. She leveled a stoney glance at Bao. "I've always respected you, Bossman, but this is pushing too far."

"I know, Halie," Bao said. "Believe me, if there was another way, we'd take it. But it's not just the nobles future that's at stake, it's ours too."

Braelyn kept her face blank. "Julian has plans to do another cleansing, this time through the city. Those he has no use for or knows he can't turn, he will burn them to the ground, noble and criminal alike. And while I don't approve of what you do, I've recently come to the understanding that you provide a sadly necessary service. People aren't perfect. They will more often than not chase after whatever makes them feel better about their lives: drugs, excitement, money, flesh, or power."

"Hard lessons," Halie said. Some of the animosity had faded from her face as she regarded the princess with mild interest. "You're asking us to spill blood for you, our blood. Can you handle getting filth on your delicate hands?"

Braelyn met Halie's gaze dead on, her face filling with the all-consuming rage and fire bubbling just beneath a thin veneer of civility. "I have been covered in the blood of my family and allies. I hope that by the end of this, I'll be covered in the blood of my enemies."

A shudder ran down Bao's spine as he observed the princess with a new light. From the change in the air, he knew the others were thinking the same thing he was. The princess may have been a sheltered, delicate flower, once. But now, now, she was a pillar of vengeance and wrath. Would it be worth it, risking her fire or would go with the current preserve their life for another day?

"What exactly do you want us to do?" Boss Quill asked.

Braelyn leaned back in her chair, the very picture of a vengeful goddess. "Sow the seeds of chaos."

Bao kept glancing at Braelyn from his peripheral on the carriage ride back to the castle. Away from the eagle eyes of the crime lords, her body wilted. She'd undid her tight bun the moment she sat down on the carriage's cushioned bench. Her hair falling in golden waves around her pale face. She leaned back, head resting on the wall of the carriage, eyes closed.

"I can feel your thoughts." She sat up, staring with eyes appearing much older than a few moments before. "How can you do this? Put on this cruel mask, pretending to be like the rest of them?"

"Don't think they, too, are wearing a mask?" Bao shook his head. "Our world isn't an easy one. There's no room for weakness. That's not to say that some don't enjoy the pain and suffering they induce. But most of us are just trying to survive using the only education given to us."

"But you had a different start," Braelyn said, a furrow between her brow. "You started out on the right path."

Bao shrugged. "My life is as the fate's designed it to be. There is little I regret or spend sleepless nights worrying over."

Braelyn turned, mulling over his words. "What does keep you awake at night?"

"Are you making an offer, your highness?" The crooked smirk on his face was quickly becoming Braelyn's favorite part of him.

Scarlet colored her cheeks. "Oh, forget it, you crooked man." She turned, scowling out the window, but Bao could see the ghost of a smile in the lines around her mouth and eyes. And in that moment, bathed in the soft glow of the carriage lantern with her hair falling softly around her face, he realized just how beautiful the princess was. It hit him hard, like a punch to the gut.

CHAPTER TEN

Even though Mirra and Gaitlan had only been on the road for five days, she keenly felt Oya's absence. She missed the way Oya's eyes would light up whenever she discussed some old scrap of writing she'd been able to preserve. At night, Mirra dreamt of the soft and subtle lines of Oya's body, the way her breath hitched with each kiss and touch. She sighed in longing.

"If you don't stop sighing, I'm going to send you back." Mirra made a face, kicking her horse ahead to the front of the caravan they'd been paid to escort. Gailtan's deep laugh followed her up the line. She didn't bother maintaining the frown on her face. For Gaitlan to laugh, an honest laugh, soothed the edges of her worry. He was getting better.

The head merchant, a fat old Zallino man with a deeply lined face, slightly bowed his head as Mirra pulled aside his wagon. "Everything alright, pèngyǐg?"

"Yes, honorable govānxou. Just wanted a change in scenery."

The head merchant turned, tilting his face to the heavens. "Yes, The One has blessed us with beauty all around, if we only take the time to see it."

Mirra made a noncommittal noise in the back of her throat, her eyes and magical senses already shifting to the surrounding forest. The further they traveled from Moakwyd, the risk of bandits grew. "We should find a place to make camp soon," she said, noting the sun's position in the sky.

The merchant looked up. "There is a site a few more leagues ahead, near a small lake. We will stop there for the night."

Mirra nodded, turned her horse around and rode down the length of the caravan, informing the other hired guards.

"Couldn't stay away, huh?" One guard teased as Mirra trotted up. She rolled her eyes. From the day they joined, he pursued her, even though she made it abundantly clear that she had no desire to join his bed.

"We're making camp in a few leagues near a lake."

"Oooh, a lake. Does that mean we get to take a late night swim?"

The other guards riding within earshot let out bawdy laughter. The guard leered at Mirra, completely ignoring the ire painted across her face or the way her fingers inched toward her daggers. Her patience with the man was fast reaching its breaking point.

The guard yelped as a rock hit him in the back of the head. Gaitlan glowered at the guard, another sizable rock in his hand. "That's no way to talk to a colleague."

"Colleague!" the guard spat. "Since when is a woman a colleague? The only thing a woman's good for is on her back with her legs open."

A length of leather coiled around the man's neck, pulling him to the ground. Everyone turned. The wielder of the whip was a young man from the horse clans of Lorcea. His dark eyes simmered like a cauldron over the flames, full lips pressed into a thin line. Years in the sun had done nothing to his moon-shaped face, leaving it as fresh as a youth, though Mirra knew him to be several years older than Gaitlan.

"We were all hired for the same purpose." His voice was surprisingly deep for one who looked so young. "In this, we are all equal, partners, colleagues. Only a dishonorable man would scorn such ties."

"What is the meaning of this Altar?" One merchant, a leather worker, climbed from his cart, worry written across his features.

"This one needed to learn a lesson about respecting his fellow guard."

The leather worker's gaze cut to the guard, still gasping for air on the ground and Mirra. "I will speak to the headman tonight. This is not his only offense. Strip him of his weapons and horse. He can walk behind the caravan."

The guard's one-time friends all too eagerly stripped him of anything of value, tying him behind the last wagon with a length of rope. He barely had time to catch his breath before the caravan continued. The lurching wagon pulled him to the ground, dragging him for a couple of feet before he regained his footing.

Mirra took the reins of his horse and tied it to her saddle. The beast followed without complaint, its ears perked forward. "Thanks," she said to Altar.

"I was a few more moments away from knocking him out myself."

"It would have served no purpose," Altar said.

Mirra glowered. "Please don't misunderstand," Altar said quickly. "That creature has no respect for women of any kind. You lashing out would have only further fed the flames of his distaste."

"So I should just wait for some man to save me."

Altar shook his head and laughed. "No, my friend. I know you are more than capable of defending yourself. You are like the ice cats to the north. Beautiful to look at, but deadly to approach."

Mirra felt her cheeks warm. Unused to such an open flatter, she sputtered a thank you. Altar bowed, touching his fingers to his forehead, a sign of respect among the horse clans, and spurred his horse along to the front of the caravan. Leaving Mirra alone with her thoughts.

That night, Mirra tossed and turned in her bedroll near where the merchants slept with their families. Instead of luscious dreams of Oya, or the old familiar one of the burning city. Her dreams were a confusing jumble of images and emotions. In the morning she woke more tired than the day before, unable to remember what exactly kept her from her sleep. She could only remember fragments: the scent of spices, a red light and the sounds of battle, and a flaming spear drenched in blood.

Mirra tucked the images away as the caravan came to life, eager for the last leg of their journey. They'd cross into Lorcea in a couple more days. From there, the caravan would break apart, some continuing the trek north to Vilnia or cutting across the mountains into Nealet or Cemont. The rest would head east, crossing the Maiden's Tears, the only great river in Lorcea, making their way to Eddany, the capital city.

This was Mirra's and Gaitlan's path. Once in Eddany, they would need to find guides to lead them through the Black Marshes. Usoa said they would have a greater chance of finding Shiro on land than if they book a ship. His family's lands were firmly in the River Lands, though which river, she didn't know. Shiro never divulged, and she never pressed.

The next seven days were decidedly uneventful. During her turns for watch, Mirra practice more with her power. She shortened the time between reaching for her dark power and it manifesting in the corporeal world. She also practiced shadow stepping, moving from one patch to another. It was an easy way to ease the boredom of late night watch duty. And if she scared the disgraced guard from time to time, all the more reason to keep practicing.

At the first outpost they reached, the headman of the caravan handed over the disgraced guard, his weapons and signed testimonies of his transmigrations. The man seemed to have lost his wits, going on and on about whispers in the shadows and the faces of dead women with soul fire eyes clawing at him.

Gaitlan covered his laughter with a hand at Mirra's indignation. "I look nothing like a decomposing corpse," she hissed between her teeth.

"Are you sure," Gaitlan teased. "We have been on the road for a while."

Mirra kicked him off his horse and trotted ahead, his laughter ringing in her ears.

The crossing the border into Lorcea presented their first real challenge. Mirra and Gaitlan discussed many ways of getting around the border patrol. But when they finally reached the border, luck seemed to be on their side. Dark clouds released a light, but steady rain, so no one questioned their hoods, nor were the border crossing guards too keen on being out in the pouring rain for long. They passed without incident, their joy marred by the wanted posters bearing their faces nailed to the notice boards. At least their likenesses were faded from the elements and half covered by more recent news.

Crossing the Maiden's Tears was only slightly more daunting. The summer rains had caused the river to swell beyond its banks, making the perilous crossing even more hazardous. But in the end, those who needed to cross the river did so without the loss of life or goods. And soon after, the rains ceased as abruptly as they started and the sun returned with a vengeance.

The soft black earth grew hard and faded beneath the caravan's wheels and horse's hoofs. The lush trees thinned, becoming sad spindly branches with little patches of green too stubborn to wilt from the sun's relentless light.

Fortunately, they lingered along the coast. The ocean breeze kept them from feeling most of the heat, and the sound of waves crashing against the shore lulled everyone's tempers.

The first outcropping of sea stone huts was the first sign that they were reaching their destination. At each village, they welcomed the merchants with broad smiles and offers of hospitality. Mirra, Gaitlan, and Altar, however, were treated with marginally less hospitality. Especially Altar. One villager spat at the ground in front of his boots when Altar requested to water his horse.

Only Mirra's iron grip kept Gaitlan from smashing the villager's face against the hot, compacted earth. "We don't need to draw attention to ourselves," she hissed.

"So we're to do nothing?"

"Yes. Altar is not some fragile maiden that needs you to defend her honor. He is a son of the Horse Clans, raised in the saddle since birth, with a sword in his hand. The animosity between the clans runs deep. If Altar can stomach it, so can you."

Gaitlan frowned at his feet. "It's not right."

"No one said it was."

Like Verance, Eddany was also constructed on the coast, but the two capitals couldn't have been more different. The Great Hall, the seat of power for the ruling class, blended into the rest of the buildings that made up the city. The only buildings that were larger than the Great Hall were the temples of Dagga and Dannu, the primary gods of the Stone Clans.

All this, Gaitlan explained to Mirra as the caravan reached its final destination. Mirra doubted if he told her because of anxiety or if he forgot that when they first met, she pretended to be from Lorcea.

"They're actually a matriarchal society," Gaitlan went on oblivious to Mirra's barely contained laughter. " My friend Tarrent is the heir, even though he's second born. His older sister, Niamh, I believe, chose to serve their gods. Why anyone would give up power to serve is beyond me."

"There is power in serving something greater," Altar commented dryly. He shook his head. "You southerners are blinder than the stone people, surrounding yourself with things that cut you off from the truth of the world."

"And I suppose your people know best?" Gaitlan didn't bother hiding the scorn in his voice.

Altar shrugged. "All I know is that I can hear the voices of the Great Mother Sky and her children, and I can feel the embrace of Old Father Mountain and his children. Can you say the same for yours?" Without another word or waiting for an answer, Altar led his horse away in search of water.

Mirra hoped she would see him again before moving onto the next stage of their journey. Altar's no nonsense way of looking at the world was refreshing and something she appreciated. He didn't let the many minor injustices of the world affect him. On the outside, at least. Inside was a completely different matter. She could read the subtle lines of anger that ran across his face and throughout his body. Either way, Mirra wanted to keep him with them for longer. Maybe Altar knew of a way through the Black Marsh. She'd ask him later.

After another week, the caravan reached its final destination. The headman paid them the rest of their pay. Gaitlan went off in search of a drink to drown his anger. Mirra wasn't sure why Gaitlan's temper was so short lately, but that was for him to figure out. Mirra searched for a stable to tend to their horses' feet before sloshing through gods know what in the Black Marsh.

Gaitlan headed for the first tavern he saw, not caring what type of patrons it served. Atlar's jab, as he saw it, burrowed under his skin. Who was he to question a prince? Not that he knew Gaitlan was a prince, but that didn't matter. The noise of the common room hit him like a punch in the gut after so many weeks on the road. Jostling through the crowd, he claimed a sliver at the bar.

"The strongest ale you have."

The barkeep, a burly woman with a mop of graying copper hair on top of her head. She eyed Gaitlan, the lines around her mouth deepening. "Three coppers."

Gaitlan slammed the coins down, working his jaw. The barkeep shrugged before turning to get the ale. He drank half of it in three large gulps before his ire cooled. Taking deep, measured breaths, he worked to extinguish the embers of rage before they ignited and turned everything around him to ash. He'd never been good on long journeys. The monotony of traveling day in and day out grated on his nerves. He needed to do something. He wanted to take a ship to Rhu'Zoro, Zallino's capital, then traverse back through the river lands.

Usoa, however, argued against that course of action, stating that all ports were being watched and there was no way that they could slip through. She'd given them the last of the glamor charms and no one knew how to make more.

Gaitlan frowned into his drink for a different reason. Until now, he'd never thought too much about the Ilmarrion people, believing them to be myths. They weren't the first people to have their entire culture razed to the ground and forgotten. The ale soured in his stomach the more he thought about how everything he had was built upon the smoldering carcass of their civilization. Perhaps, once they defeated Julian and the demon inside him, if they won, he would help the Ilmarrion people rebuild. Surely there was something in the vast library and archives of the castle that could help them.

"Did you hear the news out of Undros?"

Gaitlan's shoulders stiffened. His grip on the pint's handle went white knuckled, and he froze as if turned to stone.

"What now?"

"So ya heard how the prince went crazy and killed his parents, right? Well, he almost killed his sister too, but some noble stopped him."

Gaitlan heard someone scoff. "I heard all that weeks ago. Old news."

"Did ya know the noble was the king's own spymaster? Eh, ya didn't. Well, not only is he being labeled a hero, he and the princess are gettin' hitched!"

"Ya don't say?"

"Not a bad reward for risking ya neck, am I right? To bed a princess." The men made vulgar jokes about the Undrosean princess's appearance and behavior during sex. Gaitlan's knuckles grew white as his body shook. If he clenched his teeth tighter, they would surely shatter.

The men's lewd conversation became too much for Gaitlan to handle when they suggested sharing the princess, causing him to stand up and spin around. He stopped short when Mirra placed her hand in the middle of his chest. Her eyes shone with more than her power and her lips pressed into a thin line. Invisible bonds kept him tethered to the spot.

"Let me go," he growled.

"No."

"Did you hear what they said about my sister?"

"Yes, it's deplorable, but what do you expect? To these men, the ruin of your family is nothing more than a passing thought. I've heard nobles say worse things about lowborn. So let it go, princeling and let's focus on doing something that will actually help instead of landing you in chains on your way back to Undros."

In that moment, Gaitlan hated her more than anything else in the world, even Lord Julian. Not because he thought her cold and calculating, but because her words rang true. If he wanted to help his sister, he needed to follow his quest to its end. Mirra released her hold when his body relaxed, his shoulders curling in on themselves. "Smart choice. Now come, we need to find guides."

Mirra led Gaitlan down a series of streets. He heard and smelled the market before he saw it. Grilled food and fragrant spices overpowered most of the other scents. Except for the freshly caught fish, their pink scales glistening in the sunlight. Vendors shouted to the masses, challenging anyone to find a better quality silk, fresher produce, or more beautiful craftsmanship.

Gaitlan followed Mirra, only half paying attention to his surroundings, his ears still echoing with the words of the men from the tavern. However, instead of the men committing the acts they so vividly described, it was Julian. The image of his sister's tear-stained face as Julian held her wrists above her head with one hand as he lifted her nightdress with the other. The most private part of her exposed to a man with the blood of her parents on his hands. Him positioning to enter…

His body rebelled, sending him sprinting down the nearest alley. His nails dug into the gaps between the bricks of the walls as his stomach heaved, spilling the ale and what lingered from breakfast onto the cobblestones. He heaved again and again until there was nothing left but bile and bitter tears.

Like in the tavern, Mirra's touch brought him back to himself. She said nothing, though her face was softer than he'd ever seen it. Without a word, she handed him a corked gourd. He accepted it. Fresh, herbal water cooled the burning in his throat and stilled his rolling stomach.

Gaitlan emptied the gourd, handing it back to Mirra. Still silent, she turned and waved her hand, erasing a wall of shadow he hadn't noticed until then. The sounds of the market filled the alley.

"Thank you," he said, his voice raw and hallow.

Mirra flashed him half smile before walking back into the sun.

THEY HAD NO LUCK FINDING SOMEONE TO LEAD THEM through the Black Marsh the first day, or the next day, or the day after that. Each day that they failed to find a guide, the more Gaitlan found relief at the bottom of a pint or bottle. On their third day of fruitless searching, the visions of Julian violating his sister were so graphic that he drank until he blacked out. Latching onto that small measure of peace, he spent every single waking moment in search of drink.

Mirra gave up trying to keep him sober after they fought when she'd resold all the liquor he bought. She touched her split lip, wincing at its tenderness. When she spat her blood onto the ground, Gaitlan's anger dissipated. He tried to apologize, but

Mirra's patience had run out. With two rapid strikes, she blackened his right eye and knocked the air from his lungs. She left him gasping on the ground, the sound of her blood drumming in her ears.

She sat on a low wall, resting in the shade with a drink of her own, worry gnawing at her core. She'd been losing sleep on top of everything. After her time in Moakwyd, she'd suspected that her dreams were more than they appeared. She spent hours puzzling out the meanings of the fragmented dreams, to no avail. But she couldn't shake the feeling that they held information vital to the success of their search. If they could find someone to take them across.

There were only perhaps a dozen or so people who knew the safe routes through the marshes. Some would stay on either side for a season, while others traveled back and forth as soon as they were hired. And because there were so few, the prices they charged were far more than what Mirra had on hand.

She supposed she could steal the excess, but it would take even longer to find targets worth her time and discover who she could sell them to without risk of capture. Mirra took another swig of the sour wine, grimacing. No, the safer course of action was their current path. All she needed was one person willing to show them the way without costing a king's ransom.

Braelyn.

Mirra scowled, her grip around the bottle's neck tightening. Was there nothing that Julian wouldn't stoop to? It sickened her as much as it did Gaitlan, only she didn't have the luxury of wallowing in guilt. Someone needed to keep their wits about them. She could only pray that Bao, Em, and the others managed to find a way to the princess and keep her safe for as long as they were able.

The clamor of bells drew Mirra's attention. Another band of travelers had made it safely through the Black Marsh. Like her, those closest to the arriving bands looked up with mild curiosity before losing interest.

The banners of the guides whipped about in the breeze. Most of the Mirra knew from her earlier attempts to gain a guide. A black sun on a green field. The twisting silver water dragon and the rearing gold horse. They were all expensive and only transported large groups across the marshes.

She had already slumped back when another banner caught her eye; a single blood red spear on plain linen. Mirra tossed the rest of the wine behind her. It shattered against the stone, but Mirra was already weaving through the crowd, her eyes never leaving the bloody spear.

The banner belonged to two women of the horse clans. Their faces were mirror images of each other and they shared the same height and build, but that was where their similarities ended. One sister was a warrior, as clear from the curved sword at her side, and the hardness of her gaze. Her clothing was cut similar to Altar's, loose around the limbs for effortless movement, cinched around the neck and wrists. Her breeches billowed over the top of her sturdy knee-high boots. The other sister greeted the elderly herbalist with a warm smile. She handed the herbalist a small pouch, receiving a smaller bag of money in return. Her clothing was more feminine than her sisters, a long overcoat stopping at her knees with form fitting leggings. Instead of a sword, she had several pouches fastened to her belt.

But there was something both women seemed to miss, a clan mark. Mirra scanned their horses' bridles and adornments for anything that could identify what clan they were from and found nothing. Shìzú. Clanless.

The warrior sister's scowl deepened as one member of the other guides walked over, his expression and gait full of swagger. He tossed a small bag at the warrior sister, saying something undoubtedly rude based on the way her hand tightened around the hilt of her sword. She glowered until her sister placed a hand on her arm.

"Let it go, Sadria. He's not worth the energy." The healing sister tugged gently.

Sadria sighed, turning to her sister. "He can't keep dishonoring us like this. We worked just as hard as the rest of them. He thinks he can pay us less because we're women."

"Excuse me," Mirra said as she walked up. "Are you two guides?"

Sadria's face was like a murky lake, unreadable. "Depends."

"I am Adria," the other sister said, stepping forward, "and what my sister, Sadria, means is yes, we are."

"Excellent. If you're otherwise employed, perhaps we can share a drink. I'm renting a room not too far from here. The ale isn't bad, and the food is decent."

The sisters shared a look before Adria motioned for Mirra to lead the way. Mirra led them to an inn in the opposite direction from the one she actually was staying at. This in however, was far more impressive, and she needed to make a good impression.

She ordered a jug of juice for the table and meals for the sisters. "I need a one-way passage through the Black Marsh."

"How many in your party?"

Mirra poured herself a drink from the jug. The lemonade was slightly tart, but refreshing after being in the scorching sun. "Two."

"Not worth our time." Sadria stood to stand.

"Do you honestly think that anyone will hire a pair of Shìzú?" Mirra shot back.

The women froze. Pain on Adria's face and rage on Sadria's. "What did you call us?"

"You wear no insignia of a clan on your clothing, horses or banner. I may be from the south, but even I know the signs of the clanless." Sadria's hand went to her waist. "I wouldn't if I were you," Mirra said calmly. She looked up at Sadria from her seat, nonplused.

"Perhaps we can strike a deal," Adria said, pulling her sister down with a single touch.

"Name your price."

"Forty gold braner."

"Twenty."

"Thirty-five."

"Twenty-five."

A pause. "Deal." Adria extended her hand across the table, clasping Mirra around the wrist.

"Excellent. I'll meet you at the edge of the city in three days. You'll receive half to start and half on the other side. Enjoy your meal." Mirra left enough money to cover the cost of the meal with a little extra as an apology for the low jab. Now all she had to do was get Gaitlan sober enough to stay on a horse.

Mirra groaned and wondered if she would have to lash him to his horse again.

CHAPTER ELEVEN

IT TOOK NO SMALL MEASURE OF CAJOLING, THREATENING, and magic to get Gaitlan marginally ready to cross the Black Marsh. Thankfully, Mirra managed to "forget" to pack the extra bottles of wine Gaitlan wanted. He'd be pissed as hel once he discovered the truth but he'd sober up.

The twins stood beneath the stone arch that indicated the end of Eddany's boundary. They had a pair of roans but different shades. A red roan for Sadria and blue roan for Adria. Both women sported recurve bows and quivers attached within easy reach on horseback. Tied to a led was a sturdy mule ladened with gear.

Sadria's mouth tightened at the sight of Mirra and Gaitlan. "'Morning," Mirra said with a wide, toothy grin. Sadria made a face then turned toward the gentle hills that housed the dead just outside the city's perimeter.

"Sadria's not a morning person," Adria said in way of an apology.

Mirra waved her off. But it was Gaitlan who responded, "Don't bother. This one has a knack for getting under people's skin. I think it's her only hobby."

Mild surprise and the tiniest sliver of impression made Mirra laugh through her nose. Adria kept her face blank, unsure of their dynamic.

"We'll follow your lead."

THEY WEREN'T THE ONLY ONES ON THE ROAD.

Merchants, caravans, and everyday people crowded most of the great road that ran the length of the Lorcean coastline. The congestion thinned out the closer they got to the Black Marsh. The twins proved to be quiet, choosing to keep more to themselves as they traveled. Although, Mirra did catch Sadria looking on with appreciation whenever Mirra and Gaitlan trained with their swords or hand to hand.

Even more surprising, Gaitlan hadn't thrown a fit when he realized Mirra had "forgotten" to bring the extra liquor. Instead he trained. Every moment they weren't in the saddle he trained, with or without Mirra. At first Mirra had been impressed at his dedication, but now, she realized he'd only traded one distraction for another.

One day, Mirra caught the whiff of something foul in the air. She couldn't tell if the stench belonged to a carcass, stagnant water, or some strange plant.

"It's the marsh," Sadria said when she caught Mirra lifting her nose like a dog. "The closer we get the worse it will be. Most don't bother traveling through the marsh during the summer because of the smell and insects." Her eyes narrowed. "Why are you? The two of you could easily book passage on a ship."

"I get terrible seasickness," Mirra lied. "And until now, I didn't really believe all the stories I heard about the Black Marsh."

A soft chuckle. "Neither did I."

Mirra eyed Sadria, mulling over an idea that had been rattling around her skull from the moment she hired the sisters. "If you don't mind me asking, why are you two…"

Sadria's face darkened. "Sorry," Mirra said quickly. "I didn't mean to offend."

"This time." Sadria sighed, muttering under her breath. "We chose to leave our clan behind. If we wanted, we could go back."

"Why don't you?"

Silence answered her question. Sadria scratched her horse between its ears before trotting along to ride next to her sister.

"Your ability to sniff out secrets is alarming."

Mirra scowled at Gaitlan. "I wasn't trying to."

He shook his head. "But that's what you are. You're like a bloodhound. The moment you sense that a person has a secret, you go for it relentlessly until you figure out what it is."

Mirra rolled her eyes. "Whatever, princeling."

"Leave them alone. They're here to take us across the Black Marsh, nothing more."

Mirra bit back the retort building on her tongue. Her dreams meant something, of that she was sure of. Whatever role the sisters had to play in the upcoming battle had yet to reveal itself. She would have to be patient.

Kasumi found Oya fast asleep amidst a horde of ancient books and scrolls. "Oya, you missed the evening mea."

Oya stirred, her eyes red and sleep lined. "What now?"

"The evening meal, you missed it."

Oya whipped her face and stretched, her spine popping. She stood and frowned at her notes. No matter how much she dug, she couldn't find a clue as to what the original spell that made the orb that originally held The Dark One. It would help if she knew what its true name was like the other relics, but that had been lost to time.

"Priestess Oya?"

She blinked. "Sorry Kasumi, lost in thought."

Kasumi peered at Oya's notes. "You're trying to repair the orb. For when Mirra and the Wielders challenge The Dark One."

"Yes, but like every other part of our history, it's either not here or has been destroyed."

"Why don't you go to the Holy Isle? The Abbot did extend an invitation."

Oya clutched her notes tightly, scrunching the paper. "I haven't left Moakwyd since…"

Understanding flickered across Kasumi's young face. She straightened, giving Oya a glimpse as to the woman and priestess the young acolyte would one day become. "Fear can become a poison if you let it. A little will keep you alive. Too much will leave you unable to avoid death's embrace. You must face your fears if you ever hope to be free from them."

Oya stared at the young acolyte, shame coursing through her. "You are wise beyond your years," she said to Kasumi, slightly bowing. "This task is greater than my fears. Thank you."

Kasumi beamed, a light blush on her cheeks. Oya drew the young acolyte close and began to list off all the things that would need to be taken care of while she was gone.

THE STENCH OF THE BLACK MARSH GREW SO PUNGENT that Gaitlan and Mirra gagged with each breath. Adria, the wonderfully merciful person that she was, offered a small jar filled with a cream that promised to ease the worst of the smell. The strong minty concoction stung their eyes, but did lessen the putrid odor from the marshy lands around them.

In the beginning the way through was clear, a large swath of land barely above the blackened water. But before long, the path narrowed to where they had to ride single file. Occasionally, the path was overcome by the foul black water. Most of the time the gap was small enough that the horses and mule could jump across. Other times, Sadria was forced to fling a series of planks fastened between two ropes in order for them to cross. More than once, the gap proved to be too wide, even for their makeshift bridge and they were forced to backtrack and choose another way. But every night without fail, a patch of land large enough for their party was found.

At the end of each day they set up a medium sized circular tent in the center of the patch of land before breaking up to finish setting up their camp. They tended to their horses, especially their feet, brushing the worst of the muck and mire off, checking for any signs of a stone or other injury. After brushing them down, bags with a grain and feed mixture were attached around their heads, since there was nothing in the marsh suitable for them to eat. Gaitlan helped Adria build the water filter every night, the two engaging in polite but restrained small talk.

Then Gaitlan would be left to hoist bucket after bucket of black slug into the filter until it ran clear from the other end. The trickle would be slow at first, but eventually turn into a steady stream they could use for drinking, bathing, and cooking. The first bucket of purified water would be dumped into the top of the filter to ensure that all impurities were removed.

The water was still slightly tinged gray, but if one didn't think too much about it, the water was quite refreshing.

Mirra removed the feeding bags from the horses, pouring any granules left clinging to the seams back into the feed bags. She then left a series of wide bowls filled with fresh water that would need to be refilled frequently.

It was only after their mounts and mule had been tended to were they able to look after themselves. Sadria would leave the camp in search of water birds or other small game for their evening meal. Sometimes she would be successful and other times their evening meal consisted of nothing more than small bowls of rice and dried meat or salted fish.

They would sit around the peat fire, its fragrant smoke driving away the mosquitoes and other biting insects. Due to both parties' secretive nature, conversations were short lived and simplistic. In spite of that, Mirra found that she actually liked the sisters. Adria was good natured right down to her very bones, open as a clear spring sky and the perfect foil to Sadria's quiet persona and reclusive tendencies. But when Adria was able to bully her sister into singing to pass the time before they tumbled into their bedrolls, her sweet voice soothed away the day's worries.

Adria proved to be a better balm for Gaitlan than Mirra. Slowly pulling out the wounds on his heart like a comb to wool. "My sister has a healer's heart," Sadria told Mirra after seeing her staring in disbelief at the way Gaitlan opened up to the young woman.

"The wounded flock to her like birds to water. She accepts them all without complaint, even when it leaves her too exhausted to do much else but sleep. And still they come."

Her face turned pensive as she watched her sister. "If I could take her place."

"There's no reason why you can't be a fighter and a healer," Mirra suggested.

Sadria's gaze snapped back to Mirra, too many emotions flitting across for her to read. Mirra held her hands up in placation and quickly found somewhere else to be. Later that night, while nestled with her back to Gaitlan for warmth, she realized that Sadria was afraid. Afraid of people looking too closely at her sister's abilities. But Adria didn't have the tell-tale ice blue eyes of the Ilmarrions so her uncanny healing abilities couldn't be magical; could they?

OYA STOOD ON THE BOW OF A SHIP, STARING OUT AT A rocky shore. There wasn't much by the dock and the stone cliffs still bore signs of charring. Pulling her cloak tighter around her, she turned from her viewing point and headed back down below to the passenger berthing.

Huddled in the poorly lit space, a small family huddled together, their faces too thin. Their youngest child had a hallowed look to his eyes that sent chills running down her spine whenever she saw him. There was still so much suffering in the world. Her time sequestered behind Moakwyd's protective walls had lulled her into a false sense of security. Even with knowing what happened to the Undorsean royal family and the impending battle with The Dark One, she'd thought that the rest of the world was milder. Embarrassed by her own naivety, Oya sat down on the musty mattress that served as her bed for the crossing and pulled her knees into her chest.

Across from her sat a small cluster of men, most likely academics by their garb, whispered excitedly amongst themselves, discussing what they hoped to find in the citadel's world renowned library. They didn't appear to have any desire to take up with the order in any capacity. Every so often one of the men would look worried, his hand going to wherever his letter of recommendation sat, wondering if it would be enough for them to gain access to the answers they sought.

She often wondered the same thing. Not that she would be turned away, she too bore a letter from the Abbot himself with a standing invitation. But that even the Holy Isle wouldn't hold the answer she sought. Oya closed her eyes and prayed to the Ilieng and to her vulnerable ancestors to not let her searching be in vain and that she'd be able to repair the orb before Mirra had to face The Dark One.

The sound of shuffling feet and shouting roused her from her slumber. She was the only passenger still in the berthing. All the others had left, taking their belongings with them. Oya stood, stiff legged and what she brought with her into her satchel before scurrying up the stairs.

The sea breeze tugged at her head and the only thing that kept it up, hiding her damning eyes from unfriendly eyes, was the spell she casted after the first time her hood had been ripped off her head.

A small group of people welcomed the passengers as they walked across the doc. Their belongings were thoroughly searched with little room for arguing. Not that any were offered. The entire world knew of the recent attack on the Holy Isle by unknown assailants.

Supplicants split the passengers up, taking them to their respective housing, except for Oya. The supplicant that approached her bowed deeply when she handed over The Abbot's letter. Oya kept her eyes trained forward as the supplicant led her away, straight to the citadel. The three scholars stared after her in awe, wonder, and jealousy.

She was given no time to marvel at the sea of books around her as she entered. Nor time to make herself more presentable, a proper impression of an Ilmarrion priestess. Let alone next in line to become high priestess.

Abbot Joseph leapt to his feet as soon as Oya walked into his study. "Welcome, welcome! Please take a seat, I know you must be exhausted from your journey. Should I have some refreshments brought up."

Oya blinked twice before answering. "No thank I'm not hungry at the moment. Um, Abbot Joseph, first I would like to offer you my most heartfelt thanks for opening the doors of your library to me."

"Think nothing of it. Most of it belonged to your people before the Purging. I merely serve as its caretaker and protector."

Oya laughed softly. "Mirra said you wouldn't be like I expected."

"How is our mutual friend?"

Fingering the hem of her cloak, Oya selected her words carefully. High Priestess Usoa and Mirra may have vouched for the Abbot. But she would make her own judge of his character. "She is with the prince, seeking allies for the task ahead."

If Abbot Josef sensed the hesitation or guarded nature of her words he said nothing. Instead he nodded, folding his hands on top of his desk. "That's good to hear. I will pray that they find them." He watched Oya for a moment. "But onto you, my dear. You'll be given a private room reserved for honored guests. We can provide clothing as I fear your normal robes might raise too many questions. And you are already a striking woman, especially with those eyes."

Oya jutted her chin forward, refusing to cow under. "Fear not, Abbot. I brought normal clothing with me."

"Excellent. One of the Master's will escort you around the citadel until you learn your way. They are most eager to meet you." He stood again coming around his table, extending his hand. Oya stood and took it. "We are here to assist you in any way possible. It is past time for us to heal the wounds of our collective past and move forward."

"It is the past that I seek to bring back into the light," Oya said. "Although it is a bit further back than most bother with."

Abbot Josef bowed deeply to Oya, much to her surprise. "As you wish. Shall we get started then?"

Oya folded her hands beneath her cloak to hide their trembling. Whether it was from fear of failure or excitement she couldn't tell. All she knew was that this moment was the one she'd been working towards her entire life. "Yes. I have much to do and not much time to complete it."

CHAPTER TWELVE

THE BALLROOM WAS FULL OF PEOPLE. A SEA OF BRIGHTLY colored fabrics, flashing gems, and the chorus of a dozen different languages. Young nobles seeking matches spun around the floor in intricate dance moves, their youthful faces flushed with more than exertion. With eagle eyes, the parents of the young nobles scrutinized the dance floor, calculating the benefits of each potential match.

Braelyn sat alone on the dais, watching everything without seeing. After she pleaded her case to the heads of the criminal underworld, they'd asked for some time to consider her offer. That had been two weeks ago, and still she heard nothing. She knew she couldn't force them to work with her. Even she knew that was the fastest path toward betrayal, and she'd been betrayed enough in this lifetime.

"Perhaps we should bring in tonight's entertainment?" Em sat on a small stool just behind Braelyn.

Braelyn loosened a long, suffering sigh. "I suppose so. The sooner we get it over with, the sooner I can leave."

Em pressed her lips tightly together. "You can't hide forever, your highness."

"I know that. I'm just…tired."

Wordlessly, Em stood, curtsied and disappeared into the crowd, leaving Braelyn alone. Braelyn's gaze raked over the gathered court. But they were nothing more than blots of color with flesh-colored patches. The weight of her burdens made her feel much older than seventeen and the hollow feeling inside her grew worse the closer her birthday creeped. Just this week alone, she hadn't been able to keep anything down that wasn't tea or simple broth. Of course, this led many to whisper that Julian had already found his way into her bed.

The mere thought of bearing the child of the man who murdered her family filled her with such rage that even Em was taken aback. She nearly ordered for anyone who breathed about her supposed pregnancy to be thrown into the dungeons until she felt less murderous. Fortunately, Em talked her down, ensuring that the rumors would die down after a time as long as she acted like they didn't matter and her belly didn't swell.

Movement drew Braelyn's eye. The crowd parted like winter wheat, clearing a wide area of the ballroom floor. From the rafters long, crimson bands of silk rolled down, earning noises of appreciating and mild clapping. The mild cheering fell silent as three young dancers in skin tight, brightly colored costumes took their positions at each band of silk. A slightly pudgy man in a gaudy costume bowed deeply.

"Your highness, it has been our greatest honor and privilege to celebrate your rise from darkness like the phoenixes of old. In honor of that strength to keep going, we," he gestured to the dancers behind him. They bowed and then climbed the silk bands. "Would like to dedicate this last performance to your indomitable spirit. May we all be so resolute before such tragedy."

The crowd erupted into applause. Braelyn numbly followed suit, puzzled by the man's words. She couldn't quite place it, but there was something about the man that made her believe his words carried more meaning than they appeared.

A haunting melody struck up from the orchestra. Braelyn's heart leapt to her throat the moment she heard the first few notes. She knew this song. She knew it as intimately as she knew herself. Her father had it commissioned for her seventh birthday. It was a musical rendition of her favorite story, the one she made her mother and nursemaids tell her every single night until she was nine.

She let the music wash over her, carrying her away from the crowded ballroom to the small bed in her nursery. For the first time in ages, she felt her parents at her side. Her throat and eyes burned with unshed tears for a time that she could never get back. Swallowing her sadness, she threw her chin out and focused on the dancer twining, swinging and falling in time with the story the gaudy man now told.

"A long time ago, there was a simple farmer. He had no need for money, fancy jewels or imported silks for all he needed his farm provided. Almost. The one thing the farmer wished and prayed every day for was a wife, someone to share in the joys, sorrows, and wonders of life. And then one day something miraculous happened: a star fell from the heavens right into the farmer's small cottage."

Braelyn silently laughed, remembering the look on her mother's face as she paused for dramatic effect every time.

The ghost of her mother's perfume wrapped around her like a warm blanket.

The dancer playing the actor released his grip on the silk and fell toward the floor, drawing gasps from the entranced onlookers. Braelyn included.

He stopped short of the floor, his hand reaching out to take the luminous star in the storyteller's hand. Applause erupted and the male dancer resumed his climb, twisting the silk as he went.

"Unsure of what to do, the farmer took the fallen star to town to visit the magistrate. Surely a man as learned as he would know what to do with the star. As simple as he was, the farmer did not realize that by touching the star, a bit of its brilliance flowed into him. The people of his village whispered behind their hands as a man they'd ignored their entire lives seemingly overnight became a being that enthralled all who looked at him."

One of the female performers, dressed in a brown and green costume, dropped near the male performer. The two clasped hands spinning around until they could sit within their bands of silk together. The magistrate's daughter fell in love with the farmer and brought her into her family.

"But the farmer was not happy. He did not want to live a life stifled by etiquette and breeding. And though he cared for the magistrate's daughter, he could not love her. So he left her a sprinkling of stardust in parting. The farmer then went to see the king, for surely a man as worldly as he would know what to do with the star."

Her father's chuckle at Braelyn's dismay over the farmer leaving his first wife in the middle of the night like a thief in the dark.

The second female performer, dressed in royal purple and gold, performed an upside down split, taking the star from the male performer.

"The princess coveted the farmer's star, but wanted nothing to him. She quickly realized that his splendor came from the star and wanted it for her own. The king ordered the farmer to give up the star to the princess, but the farmer refused. 'This star is not meant for those who make their life on the earth. This star must be returned to the heavens from whence it came.'"

The second female performer fell, catching her descent in the crook of her knee. She lost grip on the star and it fell into the male performer's waiting hand.

Her mother's reassurance that Braelyn would never be as selfish as the princess in the story.

"The farmer returned to his home, feeling right for the first time since the star fell into his life. He lifted his gaze to the heavens and held the star aloft. 'This does not belong down here in the land of mortal men. It belongs with you, in the heavens, where its light can shine on all.'"

All three dancers slid down their silk bands, moving their dance to the ground. The two women spiraled around the farmer, leaping and arching as the story reached its climax.

"A goddess who lived on the moon heard the farmer and called him to her ivory castle. There she blessed the farmer for the purity in his heart. She fused the farmer with the star, casting him into the night sky. The farmer became The Groom. The only star that never travels across the night sky."

The male performer handed the star back to the storyteller, who approached Braelyn. Guards moved to stop him but with a single gesture from Braelyn, they allowed the man to pass. He knelt on the step just below Braelyn and presented the star to her.

She stood and walked over to the kneeling storyteller. She took the star, made up of small triangular pieces of clouded glass, and held it to her chest. "You couldn't know, but this was my mother's favorite story. You have brought her back to me, if only for a moment. Thank you."

A surprised murmur echoed through the waiting crowd. Many were brought to tears by the sight of their princess standing before them with tears streaming down her face. She smiled down at the storyteller; her face a mixture of pain and longing.

The storyteller lifted his head, giving Braelyn the second shock of the evening. Bao beamed up at her, a player knowing he played his part well. She held the star tighter, knowing with certainty that it was more than a simple gift.

That night, Braelyn sat in bed, the only light coming from a single candle on the bedside table the star Bao gave her cupped in her hands. In the ballroom, she handed it off to Em as soon as she dismissed the disguised Bao. He vanished into the crowd and she didn't see him again for the rest of the evening. She unfortunately had to wait until the midnight hour before she could leave without causing a commotion.

Since then, Braelyn looked at the star in every way possible. She held it up to the fire, peered through it, even exposed it to the weak moonlight that came through her window. Nothing.

Fiddling with the end of her braid, the first inklings of doubt dug their claws into her. Perhaps she'd over read the situation? Maybe Bao was just trying to do something nice for her, to ease some of her sorrow? But why? It wasn't like they were anything besides two people using the other for their own ends. He owed her nothing, just like she owed him nothing.

No, this star had to be something more. It had to be.

The candle was nothing more than an inch long snub by the time she gave up. Blowing out the candle, she laid the star next to it, fighting back tears. Tomorrow, the visiting dignitaries, merchants, and others who celebrated her impending marriage would leave. Julian had left her alone while the castle was full. He didn't want outsiders to see how upset he made her and wonder if they should voice concerns. And who knows how many of his spies found their way into the departing guest's entourages?

There was nothing she could do about it tonight. If she wanted to have the strength to face Julian, she would need at least a few hours of sleep. Braelyn closed her eyes and tried to fall asleep, but the dim light of the moon refused to allow her mind to quieten. Throwing back the covers, she trudged over to the window, closing the thick curtains. When she turned, letting out a gasp as the star on the bedside table glowed in a soft green light.

"Gods above," she whispered, picking up the glowing star. She'd seen nothing like it before. As she peered closer, a darker blob near one point drew her attention. It looked like a bit of the bioluminescent coating on the star had been chipped off, or purposely left blank.

Braelyn brought the glowing start closer to her face, and she still had to squint to make out the image — an eight-pointed star. Using her nail, Braelyn delicately opened the invisible seam. The pane with the image came away. Too afraid to breathe, Braelyn peered inside the star. There, braced between two thin pieces of metal, was a rolled-up piece of paper. How it stayed in place during the performance, she did not know. Of course, Bao could have changed the star used during the performance with the glowing one with sleight of hand.

She couldn't get her fingers into the opening, not without breaking it. So instead, she retrieved a letter opening from her writing table and gently knocked the scroll free. Written on the scroll was a single word.

Agreed.

Sitting next to Bao in the empty Gilded Lily, Braelyn hid her quivering hands inside her robe. One step. She was determined to get one over on Julian, and each step brought her closer to achieving her goal. To take back a bit of her power.

"Mind your face, princess." Bao tossed an edamame into his mouth with a smirk. "Even a blind man could see your excitement and fear."

"I'm not afraid," Braelyn snapped, slipping on her blank court mask.

Beside her, Bao chuckled softly, leaning closer. "You look like a boy about to bed a woman for the first time."

Braelyn snapped her head in his direction, her mouth cracked and heat flooding her face. Bao's dark eyes met hers, sending shivers down her spine. The smirk on his face grew, setting her cheeks aflame. "I wouldn't know," Braelyn said, turning away.

"About the boy, or bedding?"

Braelyn huffed and turned to face him. "Why are you so interested in who I may or may not bring to my bed?"

"So there are people who get to enjoy your hidden sweets."

"You want a taste." Her words shocked them both. The silence grew between them, ripe with tension. Bao's tongue ran across his lower lip, and Braelyn couldn't help but watch it. Had his lips always been so soft looking?

A pointed cough finally broke the spell. They jerked back, falling back into the roles they had to play. Braelyn could only hope that the bosses mistook her flushed face for naïve excitement rather than…attraction?

Tull gave Bao a pointed look. Bao lightly shrugged. He did not know what had just happened. All he wanted to do was snap the princess out of her worry spiral. He thought that flirting with her would be the best way to distract her from her anxieties. No noblewoman in her right mind would want to sully her bed with a lowborn man from Zallino and a criminal to boot. But her response and the way she looked at him while she said it…Bao shifted in his seat, tugging against his breeches as inconspicuous as possible. *Get it together boy*, he chided, *she can dish it back as easily as she takes it. Nothing more. Get it together before the others arrive to sniff out your weakness like a hound.*

As if summoned by thought, Boss Quill walked through the door. His face was as unreadable as always as he took his traditional seat at the Xaingqui table. Bosses Hal and Gayle arrived together, followed by most of the enforcers. Madam Tatinna and Boss Halie remained absent. Though a member of the Court of Silks had taken the seat nearest to Braelyn.

"Forgive my lady's absence," the woman said to Bao, completely ignoring Braelyn. "She had business to attend to tonight."

Bao's brows pinched together. He shifted slightly in his seat, the aurora around him growing dark. "She agreed to this meeting in advance. And if I recall, she's the one that you lot spoke through. And now she can't be bothered to come?" His last words came out in a growl.

The gathered bosses visibly recoiled, with the exceptions of the five section enforcers at their backs. They'd agreed to Braelyn's demands the same night she made them. Not because they felt any kind of loyalty to the crown. They agreed because Bao asked them to. Out of all the Bossmen, Bao was the only one that didn't treat them like they were expendable. He helped them without asking or demanding extra payment in return. And for the few that wanted to leave the life, Bao ensured they could leave in peace with no fear of retaliation. All they needed was one look from Bao, and they would cut down the bosses without a second thought.

Boss Quill cut his gaze over to the looming enforcers and quickly interjected. "Many of the visiting nobles, dignitaries, and their people are leaving soon. If they have any pertinent information, this is time to gather it. Madam Tatinna is overseeing the collection and filtering what her girls gleam for you."

"So this means you've all agreed to my terms?"

"Not quite," Haile said when she breathed through the door. "Apologize for being late. My houses are overflowing with birds just dying to leave piles of feathers behind." She took a seat with her partners, stealing Hal's tankard from him.

Braelyn clenched her teeth and kept her thoughts to herself. "Is there something else you want?" A loaded question. A fool's question.

"Pardons", Bossman Quill said, placing a piece down on the board.

Braelyn jerked back in her chair, her eyes wide. "You're criminals. You've built your fortunes on the misfortunes of others."

The air in the room shifted, even Bao took offense. "Nobles aren't much better," he said. "Just who do you think we ply our wares to? And what else are we to do when there's no way out from the bottom? The rungs on the latter are too high for us to reach."

Ducking her head, Braelyn spoke softly. "I know. But I can't ignore all the hurt the people in this room have caused." She lifted her head and met his eyes. "Not even you."

A tense silence filled the room. Braelyn kept her head up, the bitter taste of defeat already claiming her senses. Grimacing, she lifted her head, looking each boss in the eye. "I cannot wipe clean your records. Especially if you intend to continue making a living outside the law. However, if you are ever caught or want to start over fresh, I will grant you a pardon and get you out of the city."

The bosses mulled over the counter offer, weighing it against the risks they'd be put through. The representative from Madam Tatinna spoke first. "I will relay your message to my lady and let you know her answer."

Braelyn nodded and raised her hand. Em entered the room carrying a small chest. She sat it on the table next to Braelyn with a grunt, flinging the lid back. "Take this then as a good faith gesture, or to buy your silence."

Em removed a bag from the chest and opened it, pulling out a small gold bar. This time it was the bosses turn to be shocked. Em returned the bar back into the bag and cinched it tight.

Braelyn loosened her breath and tried to not think too much of the suffering she was about to cause. "There's one for each of you. Use it however you see fit. Hire more people, increase the bribes on the city officials, whatever your wicked hearts want, as long as you don't betray me to Julian."

Em handed each bossman the largest sum of money they'd ever held, like they were nothing more than sweat buns.

"Should you betray me," Braelyn went on, "My other allies will see that your head and your body never met again." A bold faced lied but a necessary one. She needed them to have a fraction of caution to keep them from turning on her.

Bao surveyed his people, reading their faces and tells. She won them over; he thought proudly, suppressing a smile. Now all we have to do is follow through.

JULIAN HURLED THE MOST RECENT REPORTS FROM HIS CITY agents into the fire, snarling. The shipment of Bonedust he'd purchased through a proxy never made it to the city. He'd planned on flooding the streets with the narcotic to keep the masses too busy chasing their next high to bother with the affairs of the court. The missing Bonedust shipment was the most recent of his plans to have fallen through without a clear cause. It was as if there was another force working against him. Julian slumped back into his chair, his eyes landing on the chess board still set up from his last game. He picked up a pawn with mild disinterest.

He'd gathered many new pawns during the engagement celebrations. And those that he failed to win over completely or remained neutrally aligned, left with a set of eyes and ears that reported back to him. He set down the pawn, picking up the Priest.

Braelyn.

New to the world of spiders, snakes, and whispers, but highly intelligent, it was unlikely that she hadn't gained a few new allies during the festivities. At least, that's what Lady Nora reported by the proxy of the maid she'd placed. His frown deepened. Something had changed in Lady Nora since Mirra's escape. Seeds of hope were dangerous things, prone to driving rationally minded people into madness.

An authoritative knock dispelled his musings. "Enter."

The Captain at Arm entered, followed by two sturdy members of the castle watch.

Julian slipped into his friendly mask as easily as breathing. "To what do I owe this pleasure, Captain? Surely nothing has gone amiss now that the castle is quiet?"

The Captain bowed. "Forgive me, my lord, but I am to bring you to the Council of Nobles."

"Oh," came the reply. It became abundantly clear as to the meaning of the other guards. "Well then, best not to keep them waiting."

The Captain's shoulders sagged with relief when Julian stood to accompany him without a fuss. Though Julian's face remained pleasant as he chatted with the Captain about nonessential things, his inner persona was the direct opposite. The darker side of his consciousness roared for him to reduce the Captain and his pions to smoldering heaps of fragmented bones and ashes.

Julian rubbed his temple. That part of him had been growing louder as of late, especially since Mirra killed his sendings. Whether it was by design or pure accident, he doubted that her ignorance of her heritage and abilities would continue. Especially if she reached those fools clinging to the ruins of their civilization.

All things must die, be consumed, eradicated in the end. Nothing could live forever. A cruel, silent laugh. Except for him, of course. All things bound by life belonged to him in the end. All he had to be was patient, but sometimes it was more fun to speed things along. To have fear, panic, and despair season the essence of the living to delectable heights.

The two guards remained outside the council chamber, standing on either side of the door. The captain stepped into the room and motioned for Julian to follow. He closed the door and stood in front as if such actions could keep Julian contained. He scoffed inwardly as he strolled to his seat at the table as a man completely and utterly unbothered.

Most of the seats were filled with a few exceptions. He would have to replace the empty seats with nobles firmly in his control. Adding that task to his never ending list, Julian surveyed the gathered nobles seated around the table.

The air in the chamber was tense, nearly sour. Though years of service in the court made their faces unreadable, their disdain filled Julian's senses. He opened his mouth a bit, drawing in the flavor. Not his favorite, to be sure, but just under the disgust was the sweet taste of fear.

"Do you know why we've called for you today, Lord Julian?"

Biting back a scowl, Julian calmly folded his hands in his lap. "Not in the slightest. But I'm sure you'll tell me in due time. I suspect it has something to do with the vacant seats around this table. I had hoped you'd wait a little longer before filling them, but that appears to not be the case."

A confused murmur echoed around the table. "That's not it."

Julian frowned. "Then please enlighten me, my lords." He tried to rein in his glee at the lords' growing discomfort.

After a long pause, the eldest lord assembled spoke. "We have testimony that the death of Lord Tolin was not in defense of the princess, but murder to keep her from fleeing the kingdom…by you."

Silence fell on the gathered nobles. The sweat that beaded on several of the lord's brow had nothing to do with the heat in the room. The blackness in Julian rushed to the surface, baying for blood. It was only his white knuckled grip on his chair that kept it from spilling out and ruining his fun.

"And what does the princess have to say about this baseless accusation?"

"We haven't informed her. Given the complexity of the situation, her words cannot be trusted. There is enough suspicion that she will lie to avoid risking retribution."

Julian frowned, grateful that the weak light from the lanterns hid the darkening of his eyes. "So say you all?"

Silence answered.

"As the accused, I have a right to face my accuser." He surged to his feet, the chair clattering behind him. He felt the Captain shift behind him and heard his sword being pulled from its sheath.

Narrowing his eyes to slits, Julian turned his head a fraction, catching the Captain shifting to deliver a killing blow. Julian huffed. As if such pitiful measures could kill him now.

With a toothy grin, Julian turned to the gathered nobles. The men handled the running of the kingdom and managing affairs abroad. There wasn't one facet of life that didn't bear greasy marks left by these men's fingers. Their fear was palpable. The sweetest wine. The most fragrant flower in a garden of shit.

When Julian released the reins, the dark pit inside him erupted like an avalanche, causing someone to swear and the fear in the air to rise to near intoxicating heights.

"By the gods," one lord whispered.

Julian's grin stretched beyond what was humanly capable. "Your gods aren't here." His shadow stretched inhumanely up the wall behind him, slowly spreading until it encompassed the entire room. The lord's faces paled, with a few reaching for weapons they didn't have. Dark ropes lashed out from the darkness around the room, encircling each of the lord's throats. "I should kill you all now and be done with all this needless pretending." The ropes slid into the lord's open mouth. "But it's too soon. You have a purpose…for now."

Light crept back into the room as Julian's shadow shrank back into its original form. The lords slumped to the ground, their limbs twitching. Julian took his seat and poured a fresh cup of wine. As council meetings went, it was a good one.

"Did you hear that the Council of Lords placed Lord Julian in custody last night?"

A sharp gasp. "No, whatever for?"

The flap of a fan and a knowing smirk. "For murder."

The courtiers collectively gasped before pelting their friend for more details.

Burying her face into a bouquet, Braelyn hid her smirk. *I suppose the more tawdry the rumor, the faster it spreads.* She paid the flower vender, ensuring to keep her face hidden. *She may be dressed like a common woman, but the women would know her face when they saw it.*

They passed by her, chattering merrily to each other without a passing glance. Braelyn breathed easy. She could get used to being ignored by the nobility. She meandered through the market, perusing through the stalls, listening to the sounds of her people.

Not a single person around her appeared to carry any other worry than simply making it to tomorrow. Fathers, sons, and brothers labored tirelessly on the docs, in shops, and as day laborers. Mothers, daughters, and sisters tended to the needs of the family, often with a sea of howling children in their wake. They cared not for the comings and goings of "thems that live up on da hill" as she heard them say. They cared more for their landlords, ensuring that each month's rent was paid with little more than a few extra coppers left over; if they were lucky.

Braelyn shook her head, remembering how fervently she wanted to help "those less fortunate" than herself. Mirra had been right. Back then, she did not know what her people wanted, or would even be willing to accept. How could you worry about sending your children to school when you needed them to work the moment their coordination leveled out? With what money could they even put aside to dedicate any time to improving their lot? With what means were they meant to use to pack up and move? Who was to say that leaving the city would make their life any easier?

She had been foolish and too wrapped up in the idea of helping to actually be of any use. Braelyn pursed her lips. That didn't mean that she shouldn't try. It would take time, and a fundamental reorganization of everything, to even make a difference. Those at the top wouldn't give up a single fraction of their power and those below wouldn't take anything handed to them.

Perhaps once her brother reclaimed the throne, everything would be different. Surely his arrival and the truth brought to light would disrupt the balance enough for change, real change to take place. She sighed again. "Or perhaps not."

"Perhaps not what, my dear?"

Startled, Braelyn turned, coming face to face with the madam that had come in Madam Tatinna's place. Up close, Braelyn could see the deep lines of age around her eyes, mouth and between her brows hidden beneath the thick makeup she wore to make her face paler. The woman might have been a beauty in her youth, but now, the decades and strife had dragged down the corners of her face, leaving cruelty and bitterness behind.

"Nothing, ma'am," Braelyn mumbled, lowering her eyes. It riled against her being, but here in the Merchant's District, dressed as she was, she wasn't a princess. "Just problems at 'ome, if ya catch my meaning."

The madam's too red mouth stretched into an unnatural smile. "All too well. But I may have the answer to your problems."

Braelyn stood and arched a brow, honest confusion written across her face. She'd received word that Bao had a message for her. That was the entire reason she was dressed like a commoner. Initially, Em was going to meet Bao, but Lady Nora requested her presence earlier than usual. She wanted to wait, but Braelyn convinced her otherwise. She needed to get out of the castle, even for a few hours. Maybe Bao had sent the madam to collect her?

The woman's face fell a bit, sensing Braelyn's hesitation. "Forgive me, I have yet to introduce myself. I am Madam Ophelia. I run a small gathering hall called Oasis." She folded her hands, turning into the picture of sincerity. "I have a need of a new girl."

Braelyn took a step back. "I am a good woman."

Madam Ophelia raised her hands. "Undoubtedly, the girl I need isn't what you think. I need someone to assist with changing the bedding, carrying up refreshments, and the like. You wouldn't have to earn a single coin on your back and you'll still get to meet all sorts of interesting men from all over the continent. Who knows, maybe one of them will want to take you away from your troubles."

Braelyn paused, still unsure if she should follow the woman or head right for the Gilded Lily.

"At least come talk to my boss. He will ease the rest of your concerns."

Braelyn swallowed, but nodded her head. She followed Madam Ophelia, keeping her eyes trained on the other woman's trailing skirts. Even though the meeting was a complete farce, she couldn't keep shame from darkening her cheeks when she spied the pointed whispers as she passed. Even here, there were snakes ready to spew poison behind smiling hands.

The Oasis wasn't quite what Braelyn expected. Madam Ophelia led her up a set of stone steps to a handsome three story townhome. Window boxes full of calla lilies stood out in sharp contrast against the dark curtains pulled closed. Madam Ophelia opened the blush pink door and was greeted instantly by a young girl in a white dress.

Braelyn pulled back short, her eyes going wide at the sight of the girl who couldn't be any older than seven or eight.

"This way, my dear," Madam Ophelia called with a sickening sweet voice. That wasn't the only thing that was sickeningly sweet. The air inside the Oasis was smoky and sweet, burning her eyes and throat.

Madam Ophelia led Braelyn to the small room on the first floor that served as her office. She bade Braelyn to take a seat on the blood red velvet couch as she took up her place near a small set of cabinets. "I know we didn't start off on the right foot, your highness," Madam Ophelia said, turning around.

Behind her, bluish smoke rose from a copper sensor. "And to be frank, I still don't like you. But my Madam has chosen to take part in your suicidal escapade. I have no choice." The look she gave Braelyn would have caused a weaker person to crumble. Instead, Braelyn politely smiled, nonplussed and unbothered.

"I have business to attend to, so wait here until he arrives."

The young girl who greeted them at the door entered the room with a silver tray bearing an assortment of refreshments. She set the tray on the table in front of the couch and scurried out of the room. Madam Ophelia closed the door behind her, leaving Braelyn alone.

Huffing, Braelyn slumped back, her nose itching because of the smoke. Whatever incense Ophelia used, it was cheap. Her eyes burned and her head swam. She walked over to the only window in the room and struggled to force it open. She only opened it a sliver before her legs gave beneath her.

She caught herself on the ledge, saving her knees from the worst of it. The outside air caressed her face, diluting the smoke's sickly scent. From behind her there came raised voices, cries of alarm, and the stomping of heavily booted feet. Someone crashed against the door, banging loudly.

Braelyn released her grip and slid to the floor, her head rolling listlessly on her neck. She thought she heard someone shouting her name. Or maybe several people, she couldn't be sure. Her vision swam, darkening around the edges. And just as the door swung open, scattering fragments of wood, her world devolved into one of hungry shadows and blood-soaked tiles.

CHAPTER THIRTEEN

There wasn't a time that the Gilded Lily wasn't packed. Throngs of people, mostly members of the criminal world, took up every bit of available space. Multicolored smokes from the plethora of pipes fought for dominance in the rafters. In his youth, it made his head swim and stomach roll, but now he barely even noticed the smell. The source of his current headache came from an entirely new source; one with eyes the color of imperial jade and the fire of a dragon beneath moon rose skin. He could see how the princess got around Mirra's walls. For her, they simply didn't exist. The princess was the type of person who was easy to like, easy to… He never got to finish his thought. Standing in the space in front of his throne stood a member of the west market watchers. The watcher was a woman dressed as a flower merchant. "I need to speak with you, Bossman Bao."

"Speak freely."

"The Lady was in the market today, dressed as a commoner."

Bao jerked up. "Why?"

The watcher shook her head. "I don't know, but I think she was lured under false pretense…to see you."

Bao's eyes darkened as he leaned forward, and a palpable sense of violence radiated from him. "By who?"

"Madam Ophelia."

Ice flooded his veins. The tight grip on the arms of the chair was the only outward sign of the typhoon building inside. He thanked the watcher, flicking a gold coin at her for her troubles. Tull sidled next to Bao with a carefree smile and two tankards of ale.

"I take it you didn't summon the princess?"

Bao accepted the tankard, smiling through clenched teeth. "No."

Downing the tankard in four gulps, Tull slammed it down, drawing more than a few glances in their direction. "I'm bored. Let's go find some more pleasurable company and entertainment."

It was Bao's turn to down his tankard, tamping down his boiling anger. "Let's go."

A young girl in a white dress greeted Tull when he knocked on the blush pink door. She swayed slightly on bare feet, her eyes heavily dilated. She looked up at Tull with mild disinterest, her words slurring. "I'm sorry, sir, we aren't taking customers today."

Tull pushed past the girl, tossing her to the wall. She slid to the ground, curling her legs close to her body. When Bao strode through the door, death billowing with each step, the girl's face paled beneath her heavy makeup. She must have made a sound, because Bao turned his murderous gaze to her. She shrank even further against the wall.

"Bring Madam Tatinna to me." His voice reminded her of her father when he came home drunk and broke. But no matter how angry her father got, or how hard he would beat her mother and siblings, his rage was nowhere as bone chilling as Bossman Bao's was in this moment. Her belly fluttered and a small patch of warmth ran down her legs.

Scrambling to her feet, the girl fled through the open door, bare feet slapping against the cobblestone streets. Her lungs burned as she ran for all that her pitiful life was worth. She crashed into a large man, causing him to drop his belongings while she fell to the ground. He cursed, kicking her in the stomach once before stomping away, leaving her surrounded by soiled goods and gasping for air.

There could be no way that this was the real world. She must have already died and been sentenced to the Burning Lands within the Dark Mother's kingdom for her sins.

"Dove, what in the world is going on?"

The girl looked up at the elegant woman kneeling down to embrace her, heedless of the surrounding mess and her soiled dress. Dove's eyes prickled and the back of her throat burned. She launched at the woman, wrapping her tiny arms around the woman, and sobbed.

The house was silent as a tomb. Though the sweet scent of freshly burning dream weed clung to everything. Tull scrunched his nose, fanning the air in front of his face. "Gods, I hate this stuff. Why do you allow her to still use it?"

Bao stepped into the lounge, scanning for any sign of the princess with growing unease. "The girls and clients are already addicted. Coming off is worse than staying on. And at least Madam Tatinna moderates it usage."

A thump from the floor above. The two men raised their heads in unison. "You don't think…,"Tull said, worry creeping into his words.

Bao swallowed his own misgivings before answering. "I don't think so, but I also didn't think that Madam Ophelia would be this foolish, either."

They made their way to the foot of the stairs but halted as Madam Ophelia descended the narrow stairs. "Bossman Bao, Irrum Tull, to what do I owe this pleasant surprise? If you're looking for entertainment, you'll have to come back another time. It is our time of rest and recovery."

"Cut the shit,"Tull growled. "Where is she?"

Madam Ophelia tilted her head, tapping her red mouth with a fan, one corner pulling slightly. "I'm afraid I don't know who you're talking about. There are so many girls under my care. Could you be a bit more specific? Do you know her name?"

Tull bounded up the stairs, his hand wrapping around Madam Ophelia's throat, before she could even move to defend herself. Her face paled beneath her thick makeup, eyes wide. Tul pulled her close enough that their breaths mingled.

"Choose your next words carefully, woman." Madam Ophelia's red lips parted and Tull slammed her thrice into the wall. "No lies."

Madam Ophelia clawed at Tull's hands, her face turning red and eyes slightly glazed over. "Let go of me, you brute! You have no right."

"I have every right," Bao said with bone chilling calmness despite the promise of death in his gaze. "You broke the rules,

Ophelia. We don't move against people we've struck bargains with or our masters."

Madam Ophelia laughed bitterly. "Like you did with Bossman Jax?"

Tull pressed tighter, forcing her to cough and gag. Bao scowled. "He was never my master."

Scarlet lips pulled back into a sneer. "And you were never mine."

Her words stunned Tull enough that his grip around her throat loosened. Taking the sliver of an opening, Madam Ophelia struck, kicking Tull in the shin, forcing him back against the railing. Fleeing up the stairs, she stood on the landing, pulling thin stilettos disguised as hair pins. Her dark hair cascaded around her face, limp and oily. "Let's go, boys. I've grown tired of our little game."

"Then you should have played it better."

Madam Ophelia turned, her mouth dropping with surprise. Whether it was because of Madam Tatinna's sudden arrival at her side or the poisoned dart embedded in her throat, no one could be sure. Thick red veins spidered their way from beneath her fingers. She dropped to her knees, stilettos clattering to the ground. With ghostly pale fingers, she reached out toward the woman who had plucked her from the streets and raised her to a position of power. Through the haze of the toxins, Madam Tatinna transformed from the woman Ophelia knew to the visage of Yulla, the Dark Mother. She had come to claim Ophelia's wicked soul, tossing it into the Burning Lands for a thousand lifetimes.

"I'm sorry," she wheezed. "Forgive me."

Madam Tatinna stopped just shy of Ophelia's outstretched fingers. "It is for the gods to forgive, not mortals. I hope it was worth it, Ophelia."

Tears cutting paths through her makeup, Ophelia tried to reach out once more. "I never...was made...ta..." Blood dripped from her nose as her eyes rolled back into her skull and, with a heavy thud, Madam Ophelia was no more.

Madam Tatinna toed the corpse with mild disinterest. "I want to make one thing perfectly clear; I had no part in this."

Tull looked back at Bao. "Am I to believe that you had no involvement or knowledge of her betrayal?"

"You'll believe what you want to believe, Bao. You always have. But yes, I hope you do. Remember, I've stood by you for years, far longer than your time as Bossman. Don't let this sour what we've built together."

With the incline of his head, the tension evaporated. Madam Tatinna curtseyed. "Allow me to make amends. Let me look into what transpired today."

"Granted, now where is Braelyn?"

"The office, most likely. Be careful though, she's probably high out of her mind right now."

Bao ran down the narrow hallway, the odor of dream weed growing stronger. He crashed against the locked door. "Braelyn!" he bellowed as he slammed into the door over and over. Tull joined, backing up, they crashed into the door with all the force they could muster. The frame splintered as the door burst open.

Billowing clouds of dream weed flowed into the hallway, drawing coughs from Bao and Tull. Behind them Madam

Tatinna swore, reaching for a handkerchief to cover her nose and mouth.

Braelyn clung to the window seal, her face flushed, looking at them with eyes that didn't see them. Strands of her golden hair clung to her sweat soaked face.

"Braelyn," Bao said, rushing into the room without caring about the concentrated narcotic smoke around him. Her eyes fluttered close as she lost her grip on consciousness. Bao ran, falling to his knees, and scooped her into his arms. "Princess, princess! Answer me damnit! Stay with me Braelyn!"

Her eyes opened a sliver, revealing just a hint of their vibrant color. She smiled weakly up at Bao. Bao smiled, brushing back a strand of sweat soaked hair, and then she started screaming.

She pushed against Bao, tearing at him and kicking. Fat tears streamed down her face. It took all his strength to keep his grip on Braelyn's thrashing body. She bucked and kicked until Tul grabbed hold of her legs, keeping them in place. This only fueled her drug induced panic more.

"Don't go in there. The snakes. Don't leave me, mom and dad."

Pressing his lips into a thin line, there was nothing he could do, nothing any of them could do, but hold on to her as she fought against the darkest day of her life.

"Give her this," Madam Tatinna said, kneeling next to Bao. He shot her a suspicious glare. She rolled her eyes. "Do you really think that no one's accidentally overdosed here? This is a leveler. It helps to neutralize the effects of dream weed. She'll still have to wait for it to leave her body, but this should help to bring her out faster."

Bao took the vial, uncorking it with his teeth. With Tull and Madam Tatinna's help, he poured the greenish fluid down her throat. Madam Tatinna covered Braelyn's mouth and pinched her nose to make her swallow. As they waited for the medicine to work, Bao continued to hold Braelyn, cradling her head and murmuring to her in his mother tongue. When her thrashing stilled, Tull left to handle the body left cooling in the landing.

Madam Tatinna watched Bao with a strange expression that wasn't quite pity but something akin to it. "A beautiful face cuts both ways, Bao."

"What?" Bao asked, not looking up from Braelyn.

"Try to not get too close to the princess. She's from a whole other world, one filled with different rules and expectations. She's bound to them just as you are bound to this world."

Bao let out a bitter laugh. "Who'd'ya take me for Tatinna? I'm not some green boy fresh from the countryside. She's our main ticket into the castle, no questions asked. There's nothing between us but that."

Madam Tatinna huffed and rose, waving her hand. "Whatever you say, Bossman. Now, if you'll excuse me, I have some spoiled goods to deal with."

Bao's attention was consumed by the serene woman in his arms, ignoring everything else around him. No one could doubt that what Braelyn went through wasn't tragic. Things like that left a scar that never quite healed. Bao knew about tragedy. He experienced it on the day his parents died, trampled to death so far from home. He lived in it every time he had to sacrifice a bit of his soul to survive in this cruel world. Bao took a kerchief from his pocket and gently wiped away the tears left on Braelyn's face. Madam Tatinna's voice ran through his mind. Nothing more between you two, huh? Whatever you say Bossman.

"I got us a carriage", Tull said, walking back into the room. "To the castle?"

Bao shook his head, scooping Braelyn into his arms. Her head settled against his chest like it was made for it. "She's too drugged up to walk through the castle without getting caught. Send word to Em, let her know what happened. She can run damage control until we can get her back into the castle safely."

Tull nodded and led Bao to the waiting carriage. Not a soul wandering around in the streets near the Oasis showed that they'd heard the fight, or the princesses screams. Or after so many years, they'd become numb to such occurrences. Tull sighed. When would it end? When would they finally be able to rest, putting this shitty city behind them?

A good thief has at least two ways to enter their safe house. The paranoid ones had twice that amount. For the house on Silver Oaks, Bao had three — front door, back door, and a near invisible ladder running the height of the house nestled against the chimney. He carried Braelyn through the front door, leaving Tull to handle the rest of the cleanup and interference. Those who walked the crooked path never ignored a weakness to exploit. There were plenty who coveted Bao's position and power and plenty more that hated nobles with a fiery passion.

The Silver Oaks safe house was right at the border of the Merchant and Divine district, just one of many unassuming row houses on a quiet street. The city watch patrolled the area more regularly than they did in the lower streets, providing an extra layer of protection. Bao carried Braelyn to the lower back bedroom and laid her gently onto the single bed. She still looked too pale for his liking, a thin sheen of sweat coating her face and neck. Her brows furrowed, mumbling incoherently.

Bao shushed her, brushing back her hair with surprising gentleness. Her face relaxed as she drifted back down her drug-addled sleep. Bao kneeled next to the bed for several minutes, silently cursing himself for being so careless. He'd been too fixated on getting his revenge to even consider the fact that betrayal could come from anywhere. Braelyn was a distraction. She softened the edges he's worked so hard to sharpen. He would have to remedy that, and soon, before it landed them all in an early grave.

Bao stood to leave when Braelyn's eyes shot open. Abruptly, she sat up, hugging her limbs close, while surveying the room with wide, scared eyes. "Hey, hey, it's alright," Bao said, holding his hands up. "You've been drugged. I gave you something to help clear your head, but it's still gonna take some time. I need you to breathe and trust me. Can you do that?"

Braelyn rolled her head in his direction, squinting. "Bao?"

"Yes, it's me. You're safe. I'll get you back to the castle in a little while."

Braelyn stared at him, blinking slowly. "Water."

"As you wish, your highness."

Bao walked into the front room of the house. The room only had basic items like a table, chairs, and a fireplace. Dark curtains kept out most of the sunlight and protected the inhabitants from prying eyes. Bao paused, whispers of the past rooting him in place. He bought the house a few years after Mirra's "execution". It was in this very room that he swore to Em, Tull, Sorro, and Kril that he would get avenge Mirra's death. He shook his head and opened the cabinet, taking out a clay pitcher and cup. How naïve he was back then. Completely unaware of how low he would have to go to achieve his goals, of how stained his hands would become.

Out back sat a small communal water pump. He rinsed out the pitcher and cup as quickly as he could. Before any nosy neighbor looked out their window and spy a strange man entering a house that normally sat empty.

Braelyn hadn't moved an inch from where he left her. "Here, drink this." Bao handed Braelyn the cup, setting the pitcher on the floor next to the bed. As she chugged the water like a man in the desert. At the foot of the bed sat a linen chest. He pulled out the first blanket he touched and wrapped it around her shoulders.

Braelyn smiled drunkenly. "You're so nice."

"Thank you," Bao said after a slight pause.

"And smart."

He tried to smile, but it came out more as a wince. "I try."

"Loyal…pretty." She dissolved into a fit of giggles, while Bao sat as still as a stone. "Boys can't be pretty." She scrunched her face. "You're handsome, no matter what you wear. You looked nice as a mer…mer…chant. But I like you the best like this. You look like you." She dissolved into another fit of giggles.

Bao rubbed his sweating palms against his breeches. "Thank you, your highness."

Braelyn's smile dropped into a frown. "Braelyn. Call me Braelyn. I like the way it sounds when you say it. Much better than when he says it." She pulled her knees in closer, pulling the sheet over her head. "He wants to take my maidenhead. He wants to ruin me."

Beneath the sheet, her shoulders shook with bitter tears. Bao hesitated before reaching out to pull the sheet back so he could see her face. "You won't be ruined."

"Yes I will," Braelyn yelled, turning. "I'm a noblewoman. My only value is in being untouched until I wed and the ability to produce heirs."

Bao's face darkened. Reaching out, he took both her hands, forcing her to look him in the face. "Braelyn, your value comes from whatever you decide it is. You are worth more than what those sycophants on the hill want to limit you to be," Bao cursed sharply. "You're so much more. You're caring, fierce, deeply devoted to your people, and honestly a bit scary."

Braelyn blinked at him, her face unreadable. A lazy smile unfurled across her subtle mouth. "Why don't you take it?"

Bao jerked back, his mouth dropping. "Take what."

Braelyn laughed, her hands going to loosen her hair from the simple coiled braid she'd put it in. A river of spun gold fell around her shoulders, framing the gentle curves of her face. She'd undone half the ties of her dress before Bao's senses caught back up with him.

He pressed his hands on top of hers. "Wait, wait, wait, that's not what I meant."

She slid her hands free, her expression just as serious as the day she met with the other bosses. "It's what I want."

She slid from the bed; her dress falling to the floor. It pooled around her feet like a water nymph rising from her watery home to tempt the young hero. Standing in nothing but a simple shift that clung to her frame, she stepped over her dress and calmly stalked toward Bao.

For the first time in his life, Bao backed down. He backed up until he met a wall. "You're not in your right mind. Remember the dream weed, the smoke in the burner?"

She'd already loosened the string of the shift. Her pale shoulders peeked out with painful vulnerability. "You don't want me?" Her bottom lip quivered.

Bao ran a hand through his hair. "Gods, Ancestors, save me." Stepping off the wall, Bao straightened his shirt and took Braelyn firmly by the shoulders, ignoring the burning sensation when he touched bare skin. "This isn't the right time, princess. We have too much to do, and you need your rest."

Braelyn's gaze fell to his chest as she struggled to process his words, swaying lightly. She ran her hands over his chest, pressing her body closer to him. Bao gritted his teeth and pushed her back as gently as he could. This seemed to amuse her. Apparently satisfied with his reaction, Braelyn turned and shuffled back to the narrow bed as if nothing had happened. She grabbed the sheet and curled up, falling asleep the moment her body stilled.

Bao stared at her in disbelief, shaking his head. He ran another hand through his hair and walked back to the front room. He needed to put some distance between himself and the princess, for all their sakes.

Em arrived at the safe house with Tull long after the street lanterns had been lit. Bao considered it a small mercy that Braelyn still slept. The last thing he needed was for Em to get the wrong idea. He had no doubt that she would remove his manhood if she thought he had taken advantage of the princess.

"Gods Bao," she said, crossing her arms over her chest. "You look like hel."

"You have no idea."

She paused, taking in his haggard expression and mussed hair and Braelyn's discarded dress on the floor. A slow, rueful smile tugged at her lips. For the sake of her friend's pride, she kept it contained, barely. "Quite a wildcat, our princess is."

Bao growled, ignoring Tull's silent question. "Let's just get her back and from now on, she doesn't set one foot in the city. Disguised or not. We nearly lost her today and I won't risk her anymore than I have to."

Tull promised to see them safely back inside, as much as he could. He passed on two more doses of Madam Tatinna's medicine with her sincerest apologies. Bao watched the carriage pull away, feeling the weight of the day descend upon him. Running a tired hand over his face, he trudged back to the Lily for a drink and some well-needed rest. That night, he sprawled on his bed, unable to quiet his mind. Who was Ophelia working for? He didn't think Tatinna would move against him. It wasn't completely out of the question, but if he were to write a list of all the people he'd thought would betray him, her name would be near the bottom of the list. Ophelia might have been an agent of Julian; only a fool would think otherwise. Or she might simply just want to get back at him for something he did in the past. Bao groaned, there were too many variables to worry through tonight.

With a heavy sigh, Bao rolled over in his bed. The lone candle on the beside table burned low in its holder. When did his life get so complicated? Revenge was simple. You found your enemy's weakness and exploited it until there was nothing left. But add one tenacious princess with a fierce will into the mix and suddenly everything was as muddy as the surf after a hurricane.

"Gods." He threw the covers back, opening a drawer. He pulled out a small paper packet. Given the nature of his position meant that more than once, his mind was too full to allow him to think. But a little bit of powdered moon thorn, and it was off to the land of dreams for him.

Dumping the bitter, slightly sour powder in his mouth, he chased it with the remains of a tankard. The drug took effect quickly. Bao's eyes turned to lead as his body felt as if it was submerged in a warm, gently rolling sea. His bed enveloped his body, easing the day's aches and pains. He rolled onto his side, wrapping his arms around his pillow, and waited for oblivion to take hold.

The scent of roses and old, dusty books filled his sense. A delicate hand slid around his shoulder, gently tugging him onto his back. Soft stands of heaven fell around his face like a shield. A weight settled across his lap. His hands met thighs as smooth as silk. He felt the person lean down, their breath mingling with his. Lips as soft as rose petals pressed against his, hungry and demanding. He opened his mouth to comply, his hands sliding up the swell of hips to a narrow waist.

"I've wanted to do this from the first time I met you."

Bao's eyes shot open. Braelyn straightened, her hair sliding over naked skin, the swell of her breast to the blush of her nipples. He blinked rapidly, and the vision scattered like petals in the wind, leaving Bao alone.

"I'm in deep shit," he murmured, his hand sliding under the sheets to tend to . His breathing hitched with each stroke, the heat building. Leaning back, he summoned back the image of the woman he wanted most in the world but could never have. In his mind, he tangled his fingers in Braelyn's hair as he plunged deeper and deeper into her. She breathed his name, clawing at his back, bringing their bodies as close as humanly possible.

"Bao," she cried, his name sounding like a prayer on her lips. Her inner walls squeezed around him, drawing his climax closer. They crashed together, their cries of passion and pleasure mingling. Bao breathed heavily, his hand still wrapped around his member. The moon thorn and orgasm left his head swimming with crackles of energy dancing along his skin. Sleep, at last, dug its claws into him, dragging him down.

You're a fool. He told himself as oblivion claimed him. The crime lord that fell for the princess. It's like a tawdry romance story. And that's how it should stay, a story.

SHE USED TO BE AFRAID OF DEATH, BUT THAT WAS BEFORE she entered the Dark Mother's service. Now she saw it for what it was, peace and the stepping stone into something greater. It was the only aspect of life where all people were equal. It didn't matter that you were a noble, wealthy, or the poorest unfortunate soul, in death you were the same.

The priestess surveyed the corpses laying on the stone tables in the preparation room. The other brothers and sisters tended to the bodies with tender care, the last act of reverence of this life. Wealthy individuals were displayed for mourners at their funerals, while less fortunate individuals, such as the poor woman on the table, were cleaned and cremated. Poor woman had been found, stripped naked and dumped in waters by the docs. The priestess washed off the thick, pale makeup that did nothing to hide the angry red lines reaching over her face like branches. The woman had another curious mark on her, a tattoo of a serpent in the under crease of her breast. Perhaps it was the mark of whatever pleasure house she worked for in life.

The priestess closed her eyes and sent a prayer to Yulla for the woman in front of her to be forgiven of any transgressions she made in life. She'd suffered enough on earth and to only suffer through the afterlife would be too cruel. The great bell of the tower chimed, its low song reverberating through the stones. The priestess quickly set up the rolling table next to the preparation table and, with the help of another priest, hoisted the woman onto it. They covered the corpse in a black sheet and wheeled her to the cremation chamber, softly chanting prayers for her soul.

The crematorium was hot and smelled of burned hair and fats. She was grateful for the noxious odor as it lessened the aroma of roasted meat. The head priest in charge of the crematorium grunted, hoisting the corpse of the woman into the grate. He shoved the grate into the hungry flames, closing the great iron door before the black smoke could billow out. The fires would consume her body to cleanse her soul. They will burn away every mark, every scar, and every tattoo so that when she stood in front of the Mother, her soul would be pure and judged justly.

CHAPTER FOURTEEN

IF GAITLAN WENT THE REST OF HIS LIFE WITHOUT HAVING to enter a marsh again, he would consider it a good life. Between the stench of decaying plant matter, hopefully, the constant wetness that found its way to somewhere new each day, and the thrice damned mosquitos, he was ready to end it all. He looked at the sisters with a new sense of admiration. They made their living traversing the god forsaken strip of land repeatedly. He shook his head. The money couldn't be that good, not for a pair of independents like themselves. Suspicion nudged at him. Could they be agents of Julian? With the sleeves of their wrists bound, to keep out the pests, they said, he couldn't see if they had a tattoo like Mirra.

Sadria and Mirra got along well enough. Though there was a reservedness to Mirra that he hadn't seen, at least not since Oya tore her walls down. Sadria's aloofness could have simply been her nature, or perhaps it was something common to all those of the horse clans.

"Could you help me with this bit?" Adria stood on the tips of her toes, her hand stretched out for the tie that held a portion of their tent together. Wordlessly, he complied, coming up behind her to loosen the knot.

He felt her stiffen beneath him and heard a sharp intake of breath. When he stepped back, he could have sworn there was a faint tinge of pink to her cheeks. Ducking her head, she gathered the bit of tarp, folding it into a small square.

They were packing up their camp. According to Sadria, they should reach the end of the Black Marsh in a day or two, depending on the weather. The closer they got to the Zallino border, the darker the sky became and with it, the promise of rain. If they didn't reach the end of the marsh before the sky opened up, they would be stuck in the muck until it stopped and the waters resettled. Fearing spending one day more in the Black Marsh, Gaitlan redoubled his efforts to complete his portion of the packing.

They didn't stop until well after the sun had reached its zenith. Taking shelter under a small cropping of trees, they watered their horses, briefly checking their hooves to ensure that they hadn't picked up anything. Sadria had left as soon as they got settled, scouting ahead for clear pathways. Mirra sat under a tree, her eyes closed. Gaitlan noticed the unnatural way the shadows danced around her fingers. He cut a worried glance at Adria, who was completely involved in checking her medicinal wares.

Shoulders relaxing, he strode over to where Mirra sat, as casually as he could muster. "Don't do that so flippantly."

"Whatever do you mean, princeling," she replied, not opening her eyes.

"That," he growled. "In case you've forgotten, magic isn't common outside Moakwyd."

A heavy sigh. "And just like the sword, or hand to hand, I have to practice if I'm to get any better. Have you forgotten that Julian commands magic as well?"

His eyes darkened, and a muscle feathered at his jawline. "I forget nothing. That bastard has my sister."

"Yes, and he plans to break her, body and soul. So if you don't mind, I need to practice." And with that, she closed her eyes, dismissing him utterly.

A red haze settled around him as he stood, knuckles white as he stared down at Mirra. By the gods, sometimes he wanted nothing more than to pummel her into submission. But he wasn't fool enough to think that he'd actually win against her. She was just as twisted, if not more, than Julian himself. At least she was on his side, mostly.

Mirra listened to Gaitlan's retreating stomps with a heavy heart. He had so much rage inside, understandably, but if he didn't find some healthy outlet, it would consume him. And she would know. How many years did she waste letting her own anger fester inside before finally accepting help? She tucked away the problem of Gaitlan's anger for another day. There was another problem that demanded her attention.

How was she supposed to find Shiro once they crossed into Zallino? Usoa had only given a vague area of his family's home, not that it was definitive that he was there. And what if he didn't want to help? He knew probably better than anyone what that thing inside Julian was capable of. She recalled the way his eyes filled with fear the first time he saw the tattoo on her wrist. Absent-mindedly, she rubbed the inked serpent coiling around her wrist. It no longer had a hold on her, but she sometimes felt remnants of its power. After she'd destroyed the body snatchers, it felt as if her wrist was burning from the inside out. And every so often, she would get bursts of pain or a strong sense of anger or sick joy. She was still connected to Julian and the Dark One and it scared her. Would this link, no matter how faint, be the key it needed to claim her again?

Mirra released her magic with a sigh, stretching her legs out in front of her. Problems, problems, so many problems.

Warning bells clamored in the back of her mind. Scrambling to her feet, Mirra reached out as far as she could and her stomach dropped. A band of armed men had encircled their camp. Where is Sadria?

"Gaitlan!"

He turned, spying the alarmed look on her face. "To arms," she bellowed, making a dash toward her weapons.

Gaitlan pulled his sword from its sheath, creeping in a circle, looking for whatever caused Mirra to send up the alarm. He sent a brief prayer to the gods that what they faced was mortal and not some fresh horror sent to hunt them down.

Beside him, Adria stepped up, her recurve bow at the ready. "Bandits?"

"No idea. Mirra spotted them."

Adria scanned the open marshlands that surrounded the camp. They'd chosen it because the black willows and cottonwoods provided shelter from the elements and from prying eyes, but now, it shielded their attackers. She whispered her sister's name, hoping that one of the four winds would carry her call. Great Mother Sky had always watched over Adria and her sister. It was she who chose Adria to bear the burden of the healing flames. She resolved not to let anyone extinguish her light in such a pitiful way.

Mirra strung her bow. She pooled a sliver of magic into the arrowhead, just in case, and turned her gaze to the trees, backing up until she met Gaitlan and Adria. "I don't think they're like the mercenaries."

"Think or know?" Gaitlan asked.

"What mercenaries?"

They both chose to not answer Adria. The snap of a twig revealed how close their attackers had crept. Mirra and Adria loosened their arrows, both finding their mark. A strangled cry followed by the sound of splashing water revealed the fate of the unlucky person. A roar went up, pursued by others as a wave of people broke through the trees.

Their attackers were men and women in light leather armor over heavily patched clothing, but their weapons were in better conditions. They converged on the trio, wielding swords, spears, and long daggers.

"Bandits", Adria yelled, loosening arrow after arrow in rapid succession.

Mirra exchanged her bow for a sword, joining Gaitlan. The bandits weren't without some skill, but their numbers made up for what they lacked. Even Gaitlan struggled to keep the bandits back, his linen shirt already streaked with red. Mirra fared only slightly better with the thin shield of shadows that flowed around her like water, covering her vulnerable spots. Torn between quickly ending the conflict and maintaining their secret, she limited her spell work to covering her allies from the most damaging assaults.

"Where is your sister?"

"I don't know!"

One bandit locked hilts with Gaitlan and sneered, revealing a mouth full of rotting teeth. "The big one? We killed her first."

Adria's face fell. "No."

A bandit slipped past her guard, raising his blade to strike her down.

Mirra called out, drawing up her magic to throw a shield. Too late. She was too slow. The man brought his blade down, blood lust glowing on his face. Adria stood as still as the surrounding trees, grief stealing her thoughts.

The tip of an arrow burst through his throat, scattering droplets of blood over Adria's face. The bandit's body fell, landing with a thud at Adria's feet revealing a blood, but undeniably alive, Sadria. She called out to her sister in their mother tongue.

Adria whipped her eyes, nodded and rejoined the fight. Sadira didn't join the trio. Instead, she launched herself into the thick of the bandits, breaking their line, thus ending their advantage. Gaitlan rushed forward, cutting through the scattered bandits like winter wheat. Mirra picked up her bow again, assisting Adria, who took out the retreating bandits with cold indifference.

At last, the clearing was quiet save for the ever present buzzing of insects. Sadria was the first to lower her weapon, dropping it onto the blood-soaked dirt. Adria threw her bow aside, running to meet her sister. They crashed into each other, clinging as if they were bits of driftwood on a rolling sea.

Mirra and Gaitlan stood awkwardly to the side. "Are there anymore?"

Just as Mirra called up her magic to search for survivors, a lone boy, barely out of adolescents, stepped into the clearing. "You killed my family," he snarled, his tears cutting lines through the blood on his face. "Blood for blood!"

Time slowed as the arrow flew straight for Mirra. Sadria threw her sister to the ground, diving for her sword. Gaitlan surged forward, running for Mirra. On instinct, Mirra summoned a wall of adamant and shoved arrows of night toward the boy.

Her arrows struck true, each one clustered near where the boy's heart would be. He fell backward, his anguish and shock forever etched into his face. The boy's arrow bounced off Mirra's wall, striking Gaitlan in the shoulder.

He cried out, his hand going to pull the arrow out when Adria cried out, "Stop!"

Adria ran toward him, scooping her medicinal bag as she went. Gaitlan said that he was fine but the words wouldn't come out. The world around him swam, the ground beneath his feet rolling like a turbulent sea. Cold fire spread out from the area where the arrow pierced. The last thing he saw before the darkness claimed him was Adria, shining in a red gold light reaching for him.

Mirra turned to run to Gaitlan, but Sadria's iron grip on her arm held her in place. "What was that? The truth or you and your companion will join that boy."

Scowling, Mirra wretched her arm free, darkness gathering at her fingertips. No use of hiding anymore. "Sister, there's no time for that," Adria said. "It's poisoned. Bring it to me."

"No," Sadria snapped. "Not until this woman explains why she wields the night."

"It's not the night," Mirra said through clenched teeth. "Let me try to save my friend and I'll tell you all that I can. But if he dies because you stood in my way, you'll find out the full extent of what I can do."

Sadria glowered, but let Mirra go. Mirra ran to Gaitlan, whose face was now paler than hers. "Do you know what poison they used? I have some background in poisons."

Behind her, Sadria muttered, "Of course you do."

Adria shook her head. "There are as many toxins and poisons as stars in the sky. All I know is that we have little time left. His heart is slowing." She turned, glaring at her sister over her shoulder. "Now!" Sadria refused to move. Adria rose, cursing her sister's stubbornness.

Sadria followed her sister, angrily calling after her in their native language. Mirra could only make out one word out of three, but her attention was more on determining how to save Gaitlan's life. Kneeling next to him, she laid a hand over his wound and sent her power into it. She didn't know if the Nexi could heal or if it would push him further toward death. All she knew was that she had to try something, anything, to keep him tethered to the world of the living.

"Here, move aside," Adria said, gently nudging Mirra away from Gaitlan. In her hand she held a small, terra cotta clay lamp. Not unlike the ones they used every night for light. Adria set it near him, drawing a knife from her belt. She cut her finger, pressing it to create a crimson pearl at the tip, before dropping it into the spout.

Mirra watched with a mixture of anticipation and revelation, looking at the woman who knelt next to her, eyes closed in prayer in a new light. After what felt like a lifetime, the lamp ignited, but instead of a typical flame, this one burned the same shade as blood. Adria opened her eyes and picked up the lamp. She tipped the lamp over the wound and blood red flames poured out, much more than she put in.

Gaitlan arched, his mouth open in a silent scream as the lanes of his lifeblood glowed through his skin. He thrashed about until Sadira took hold of his feet, motioning for Mirra to do the same with his upper body. She put all her body weight into holding him down, and it was barely enough.

Adria continued to pour the liquid fire into the wound. Dark circles formed around her eyes, her skin turning ashen and her hair losing its sheen. "Stop it," Sadira begged as her sister continued to waste away before their eyes. "That's enough!"

But still Adria poured. Sadria growled, letting go of Gaitlan to pull her sister away, shattering the connection. An invisible wave threw Mirra across the clearing, knocking the air from her lungs.

When she gathered her senses, she crawled back to Gaitlan, who laid as still as a corpse. "He will live," Adria croaked out. She stood with Sadria's help. The fire requires time to work through his body completely, but he will survive. "Sorry. I was lost to the pull."

Sadria brushed a tendril of Adria's hair from her face. "I know. But it's alright now." She led her sister over to the same tree Mirra sat at earlier, placing a kiss on top of her head. When Sadria faced Mirra, her face was a mixture of pride and sorrow. "Your story for ours."

"Shouldn't we move camp in case the rest come looking for the others?"

Sadria frowned. "It is usually best to let them both rest undisturbed, but yes, we should move."

They quickly lashed Gaitlan to his mount and helped Adria mount hers. In a single file, Sadria led the way leading her sister's horse while Mirra led Gaitlan's.

Another relic and its wielder.

They rode through the night, relying on a mixture of moonlight, bioluminescent algae, and a large bit of luck. By dawn's first rays, they arrived at a small house that was barely large enough to house them. Inside was simple, with nothing more than a stone lined open air hearth and worn reed mats for sleeping.

As soon as they laid Gaitlan down onto the mat, his coloring still a bit too pale for Mirra's liking, they sat around the empty hearth. Mirra sat with Gaitlan at her back, facing the sisters with her arms crossed.

"Our clan's holy man trained me," Adria said to her folded hands. "Not to be bound to the lamp, but to become one of our clan's holy people. Someone to help heal the sick, tell the stories of the gods and ancestors, and to divine the future. As part of the last trials, we offered a drop of blood to the lamp."

She pulled the now ordinary looking lamp from its pouch. "This powerful artifact has been in our clan since the time of our grandfather's grandfather. We lost it once, but two decades ago, a man returned it to our clan. He told us to keep it secret, especially from those with eyes the color of the northern ice."

She lifted her head, meeting Mirra's unfaltering gaze. "If you suspected me," Mirra said, "then why did you agree to guide us through the marsh?"

"We need the money," Sadira said with a shrug. "My sister doesn't use the lamp often, only in life or death situations. So unless you already knew we had it, you'd never know. It was worth the risk."

A deep line formed between Mirra's brows as she mulled over the sister's tale. "Where's your clan?"

Adria's eyes brimmed with tears. "Twins are unlucky. There were many who wanted to give us to the gods before we could cause misfortune. But our headman, our uncle, wouldn't allow it. He took us in after our mother died, giving birth to us and raised us like his own."

"What happened to your father?"

Adria fell silent, leaving her sister to answer. "He was the one that tried to kill us, multiple times, until one day he walked into the grasslands and never returned. Now, what is your story?"

A hundred more questions bubbled on her tongue, but she let them fall away. There was more to the sister's story, of that much she was sure, and it was undoubtedly painful. It would take time to earn back their trust, if she ever had it at all.

Mirra chose her next words carefully. "My people made that lamp many ages ago. My companion and I are on a quest to find the other relics that go along with your lamp," she turned her gaze to Adria, "and those who can use them."

"Why?" Adria had her hands folded in her lap.

Mirra shot Gaitlan a quick glance before continuing. "There is a demon, a creature cursed with a hunger that will never be satisfied. These relics can imprison him again."

Adria's eyes lit up as if a piece of a puzzle fell into place. She turned to her sister, and they rattled in their native language. Because of their speed and dialect, Mirra struggled to follow along. The only words she caught were "drought" and "sickness".

Sadria scowled, but relented to her sister's demands. "We left our clan because of all the calamities that befell our people as of late. The winter rains never came. Then the spring melts were larger than ever before, rotting the few fields we have. More people got sick and more mothers lost…"

Mirra nodded. "His influence extends to both nature and people. Right now, he holds an entire kingdom in his thrall. Gaitlan is from that kingdom. He fights to save them."

"Who do you fight for?" Adria asked.

A long pause. "At first, I fought for selfish reasons. I was this creature's slave until I broke free. I didn't want the world to be destroyed before I ever had time to enjoy it."

"And now?" Adria's question was simple enough, yet carried immense weight.

A soft smile spread across Mirra's face as the image of Oya flashed across her mind. "I have friends, found my people, and I want…more…"

The sisters exchanged a look. Adria silently pleaded with her sister, who looked like she wanted nothing more than to end Mirra's and Gaitlan's existence and disappear. Finally, Sadria rolled her eyes and slouched, crossing her arms over her chest.

"Fine."

Adria beamed. "We're with you, Mirra. The evil that has taken control of your home has poisoned ours. We would shame our ancestors if we did nothing to set it right."

There wasn't a part of him that didn't hurt. Even the tips of his hair felt raw. He tried to call out for Mirra, but his mouth was full of cotton and his bones had turned to water.

"Don't move yet. Your body is still healing. Drink this."

Adria appeared in his line of sight, holding a small steaming mug of something that smelled atrocious. Gaitlan wrinkled his nose, drawing a whisper of a laugh from her. "It tastes even worse going down."

He grimaced, but let her assist him into a seated position. With one surprisingly powerful arm around his waist, she held the mug to his mouth. The pungent odor was enough to send his stomach rolling. He turned his head away, desperately breathing through his nose to keep the bile down.

Adria clicked her tongue and shifted. Gaitlan thumped heavily against the wooden wall of wherever he was and gripped his face with iron fingers. She pulled his face back toward the cup, forcing its contents down his throat.

It tasted like marsh water left to fester in the sun for days on end. He held it in his mouth, refusing to swallow. Adria pinched his nose, forcing him to choose—suffocation or swallowing the putrid concoction.

His need to breathe over road, his desire to not swallow. With one large gulp, the thick, slightly oily liquid slid down his throat, settling in his empty stomach like a stone. His body rebelled, his stomach rolling and bowels threatening to loosen. But as soon as the revulsion arrived, it vanished, leaving him feeling more like a human than an exposed nerve.

Adria smiled, helping him to lie back down. "When you wake again, you should be able to eat."

With eyelids already growing heavy, Gaitlan smiled drunkenly at her. "I miss your glow."

Adria blinked back, not quite knowing how to respond. Before she could ask him what he meant, Gaitlan drifted back off to sleep, looking more at ease than she'd ever seen. Cocking her head, she studied him for a moment.

When she first met Gaitlan, he hadn't made the best impression, just one of a dozen men drowning their sorrows with drink. But as they made their way through the marshes, his attitude and bearing had changed. Clearly he was an adept warrior, sparring with Mirra nearly every day. The way he carried himself reminded her of her uncle. Her throat constricted.

Even though her uncle had died three years prior, his loss still affected her greatly. She suspected it affected Sadria more, but her sister was like stone, unreadable and indomitable.

She brushed back his sweat soaked hair, running a cleaning cloth over his brow. She guessed he was handsome, in the way the people of the Stone Clan were. From outside, her sister called. Adria rose to her feet, stocking the small fire as she went. As her mind drifted to Mirra's tale, her heart thrummed against her breast. For so long, she'd blamed herself for the misfortunes that had befallen her people. They called her cursed, and she believed them. Course she would never tell Sadria that. Her sister's fierce protection of her did nothing to quell the whispers or the jeering. All it did was further drive a wedge between her and the rest of her clan.

But now she redeemed her birth. To make her life mean something more than a series of heartaches and calamities. And

for the first time since the lamp chose her as its keeper, Adria's
heart was light as a feather.

CHAPTER FIFTEEN

"Thank you doctor for your help," Em closed the door with a heavy sigh. Masking Braelyn's true condition from the court physician proved harder than expected. But she pulled it off, barely. *Damn you, Bao, you were supposed to keep her safe!* It wasn't entirely his fault, though. Madam Ophelia summoned Braelyn to the Merchant District under false pretenses and drugged her up. Em ran a hand through her hair. *But why? What purpose would kill the princess? Even Julian wanted to keep her alive.* But if she died because of an overdose, there would be no one to stand in his way. She shook her head. *That wasn't his style.* He liked to make his prey suffer, and overdosing wouldn't fulfill his sadistic nature. But Ophelia… Ophelia delighted in the suffering of others. Julian would be pissed beyond all measure once he learned of Braelyn's death, but the man would twist it into his favor.

Braelyn mumbled incoherently in her sleep. Em turned, chewing on her thumbnail. There was something in the air that raised the hairs on the back of her neck. If her city senses weren't lying to her, trouble wasn't too far off.

"Where am I?" Braelyn pushed up on her elbows, looking like someone had stolen a part of her soul.

"You're back in the castle. What's the last thing you remember?"

Braelyn frowned. "Madam Ophelia's office, then the room filled with smoke. After that, some shouting and that's about it."

"You don't remember Bao and Tull coming to save you? Or anything else Ophelia said before she drugged you?"

Her frown deepened. "Sorry," Braelyn said, shaking her head. "It's all fuzzy still. You said Bao…". Her eyes went wide in a mixture of remembrance and horror. She groaned, covering her face with her hands. "Please tell me I didn't try to seduce Bao."

"Don't worry, princess, Bao may be a criminal overlord, but even he wouldn't take advantage of a woman not entirely in control."

"That didn't answer my question."

"Would it make you feel better knowing?"

A long pause. "No." Braelyn sat all the way up. With each passing moment, her eyes grew clearer and her typical rosy complexion returned. "Will there be any lingering effects?"

Em sat down on the bed next to her. "Honest answer, I'm not sure. Dream weed is a powerful drug. Most people who take it spend the rest of their lives trying to replicate the euphoria of their first taste."

Braelyn pulled her knees into her chest, her long hair falling around her face like golden curtains. "All I felt was anguish, fear, reliving the worst moments of my life repeatedly. I don't think I'll ever want to feel that way again."

Em reached out, clasping Braelyn's hand. "Then you have nothing to fear. Madam Tatinna also gave us some medicine that helps to stop the addiction from fully setting in. As long as you stay away from it, you should have no long-lasting effects."

Braelyn nodded absentmindedly, pressing her lips into a ghost of a smile. Her eyelids grew heavy, and she laid back down. "I'm going back to sleep now. Can I have something to eat when I wake up?"

Em huffed a laugh. "Sure thing, princess, anything you like."

SOMEONE WAS POUNDING ON HIS DOOR, DRAWING HIM from his sleep. Bao clung to the fading images of his dream like a feral alley cat. To no avail, it would seem. The last tendrils of his dream drifted away, taking with them the goddess with sunlight in her hair and gems in her eyes. Growling, Bao flung back the blankets, fastening up his trousers.

"What is it now?" he spat, throwing his door open.

Tull stood on the other side, uttering unimpressed with the daggers Bao threw in his direction. "Everything's been taken care of," he said as he breathed into the room, claiming a spot on Bao's unmade bed. "Tatinna's closed down all of Ophelia's houses and scattered the girls after questioning them. Most of them weren't even aware of what happened yesterday. So whoever Ophelia worked with or for died with her. All we can do now is speculate."

"Great," Bao said, running a hand through his hair. "I love speculation." Turning, Bao opened a wardrobe, grabbing a clean, nondescript shirt. Today, he didn't want to be Bossman Bao.

Today, he needed to be no one. "Take care of things for me. I'm going for a walk."

"Don't I always," Tull said with a smirk. "Oh, and by the way, Em sent word, the princess is awake and is no worse for wear. Definitely hung over, but Em said she'll be fine in the end."

Bao paused, not turning around. "Good," was all that he said before slipping out of the Gilded Lily, just another faceless person in a sea of people. He mentally ran through the ever growing list in his mind, but there was somewhere he needed to stop by first.

With how quickly things in the world can change, you must take solace in what remains the same. Bao sat on the roof of a dilapidated warehouse, one foot swinging in the open air, with a half eaten box of sweet rolls. He stared out at the ships entering and leaving the harbor without seeing them.

This had always been Mirra's favorite spot in the city. No matter how they fought, they could always come back together here, with a sweet roll shared between them. It was on this rooftop that they shared their hopes and dreams, fears, and planned their most daring capers. When he thought he'd gotten her killed, it had taken some time before he could even approach the warehouse. But quickly it became his place to feel close to her and to be alone with his thoughts. None of that changed now that he knew she was alive. It simply took away a fraction of the bitterness in his heart.

Everything, all his plans, sat upon the edge of a dagger. One misstep and the whole thing could come crashing down, drowning them in a sea of blood. What to do? I don't think staying in this city is going to work out for much longer. The others will be fine. They have their own means of escaping or bunkering down, but Braelyn, no, the princess, isn't as free as the rest of us. If we leave, who's protecting her from Julian and that demon squatting inside him? Who'd be there to ease her burdens, her fears?

Bao flopped back, landing with a thud, small clouds of dust billowing around him. Staring at the clear sky, he scowled at the fluffy white clouds. He couldn't leave her behind, not for a second time. She'd never survive on her own, not with things ramping up. Plus, Mirra would beat him senseless if he left the princess to fend for herself after everything she'd been through.

"Welp, there's nothing for it," he said to the sky, shoving the last roll into his mouth. He would need the sugar to fuel his latest, impossible bit of thievery. The thrum of excitement filled his limbs. How long had it been since he had to organize a job of this complexity and danger? A feral smile spread wide. At least my life isn't boring.

THE PINPRICK OF PAIN IN THE CENTER OF HER FOREHEAD now spread to encompass her entire head, painfully pulsing with each beat of her heart. Oya pressed her eyes until lights danced behind them, desperate to relieve the pain so she could continue her quest.

A sea of scrolls nearly covered every inch of the table set aside for her use. What remained had been claimed by mountains of books, precariously stacked on top of another. She groaned, crumpling the bit of parchment she'd scribbled on with a stick of charcoal, and tossed it to join the others that littered the floor around her.

"I don't think I've ever seen someone search so hard for the answer before." Abbot Joseph entered Oya's private study room, holding a tray of refreshments. "Why don't you set aside your search and come have tea with me?"

"I can't," Oya said, her exhaustion echoing in her words. "I don't have time for tea, or sleep, or anything. I have to put the orb back together or everything will be for naught."

Abbot Joseph breathed heavily through his nose and cleared a space for the tray. He watched Oya, already focused on her work once more, and played with the ends of his beard. He walked over to Oya, placing a firm but gentle hand on hers, halting her chaotic scratching. Her head shot up, a retort already building, but stopped short.

"Oya," Abbot Joseph said, his voice low and calm. "You must rest. You won't be able to do anything if you work yourself to death."

Oya opened and closed her mouth several times before lowering her head in defeat. She set aside her sketches and said, "You're right Abbot. Thank you for your invitation."

Abbot Joseph cleared a space next to her and sat down. He poured her a cup of tea first before pouring one for himself. "Help yourself to whatever you like."

Oya didn't mind her tea black, so she left it to cool a bit, opting instead to pick through the samplings on the tray. Meats, cheeses, fruit, breads and cookies, Abbot Joseph filled the tray with just about anything a person could want. She selected a small bunch of green grapes, popping one into her mouth. The grape flesh burst with a satisfying pop, releasing its tart juice.

"Thank you," she said, tossing a few more in before turning to the tea. There was a hint of spice to its aroma, not one she was familiar with. Cautiously, she sipped, finding that she rather enjoyed the flavor.

Abbot Joseph watched her with all the indulgence of a father visiting his daughter after a long stint away. "We must nourish our bodies if we hope to nourish our minds." He picked up a half sketched rune. "What is this?"

Oya made a noise in the back of her throat and reached out for the parchment. "Trying to fill a gap. But it's proving more challenging than I expected." She turned, fishing out a simple notebook from beneath a pile.

"Between Moakwyd and here, I've been able to piece together some workings used to make the relics and the prison orb. But it's not much. All I've figured out is that in order to make the relics and orb, the Ilmarrion had to give up something. One man, the maker of the flute, Song of Heaven, lost his sight. The woman who made the Blood Lamp, her bloodline, died out because no one could have children."

"The world demands balance and sacrifice."

Oya nodded. "Exactly. I understand all that, it's a basic tenet of our magic, but it's the how that eludes me. What runes did they use? What chants? Were there potions or elixirs? Or did they simply force it all into existence?" She sighed, fiddling with the end of a braid.

"I wish Mirra was here. She would see the answer so clearly with that crooked mind of hers."

That earned a chuckle from Abbot Joseph. "I may not have a crooked mind, but I am an outsider. And this is a problem for the entire world, not just the Ilmarrion people. If Mirra and the others fail, we all will suffer for it."

Oya sat back, her face unreadable. Abbot Joseph sat as calm as still water as he waited for Oya to decide. "I don't need to know the specifics exactly," she said after a while, "just enough for me to start. I'm not trying to create something new, like they did. I only want to repair what was broken."

Abbot Joseph sat back, stroking his beard, his eyes staring off into the distance. "Then perhaps you don't need to know how they did it. Like you said, you're only mending what was broken, not bringing something new into the world."

"Yes, but I don't want to accidentally neutralize the orb's effectiveness, or shatter it further because of conflicting magics."

"Who was the Ilmarrion that crafted the orb?"

"High Priestess Thrilla, the last Nexian."

Abbot Joseph's eyes widened for a moment. "And another Nexian has emerged to fight against the Dark One once more." He paused, a thought forming behind his eyes. "I think I know what you need. Come, follow me."

Oya threw her cloak on, ensuring that the deep hood kept her eyes hidden. Abbot Joseph led her to the chamber of Nen, the master of the Binders. "I have a need of you, Brother Nen."

Master Nen, stood, bowing lightly. "I am yours to command. What can I do for you and your friend?"

"In your collection, boast some of the oldest records in existence. Have you come across anything bearing the name Thrilla?"

Master Nen paused, a deep line forming across his brow. "Not that I can remember off the top of my head. Do you know the year or time period?"

"After the forming of the Dead Lands and before the Purge," Oya offered.

Nen's brows shot up. "That's a lot of time. You have nothing that might help narrow the search?"

"Undros was a single city, not a kingdom," Oya said after a moment's thought.

Nen made a face. "That is almost helpful." He made a frustrated noise, and bellowed, "Ka'on!"

A young man of middling years appeared from behind the shelves, as if walking out of shadows. "You're working on the Dead Land scrolls?"

"Yes, Master Nen."

"Take this woman with you. She's looking for something from that era."

Oya acknowledged Master Nen and cast one last glance at the Abbot before trailing Ka'on into the depths of the citadel to safeguard the world's forgotten history.

It was going to be another dreadful night. She'd had many, but the lingering effects of dream weed amplified and highlighted just how shitty her life had become. There was nothing she could do but grit her teeth and try to get some sleep until Em came back from making her semi-false report to Lady Nora. The plan was for her to tell the courtesan that Braelyn had stolen dream weed from the physician and tried to kill herself with it. It was plausible as dream weed, in small doses, was rather harmless and a common tool to put patients under for surgery. Hopefully, it would be enough truth to sate Julian's interest.

The sound of her door opening and closing softly drew her attention away from the growing shadows in her room. Shadows that whispered terrible things as they reached for her with long, bloody claws.

Shuddering, she pulled the blankets closer. "That was fast Em."

"Gotta be more careful than that, princess," Bao said, leaning against the threshold between her common room and bed chambers. "Em's real name is supposed to be a secret."

Heat blossomed across her face and at her core. Pressing her legs tightly against the fire ignited by her drunken memory, Braelyn fought the urge to hide beneath her covers. But royal dignity, for what it was worth, demanded that she face him head on with all the grace she could muster — whilst wearing her nightgown.

"Her fake name is close enough. It could be a nickname."

Bao chuckled, shaking his head. "Rare for others to gain your trust so quickly." He strode into her bedchamber with all the swagger of a man who knows he's desirable. When he sat on a corner of her bed, she pulled her feet in closer.

"I'm sorry." His words were soft, nearly a whisper. His facade crumbled as he hung his head in shame, hands clasped tightly in his lap. "I never meant for any of this to happen to you. I thought...I thought I could keep you safe."

"Nowhere is safe," Braelyn said, frowning. "It wouldn't have mattered if I worked with you or not. I still would have been in trouble. You're probably the only reason I'm still standing right now…so to speak."

Bao laughed softly and pulled out a small, brightly colored box tied with a teal ribbon. "Here, these should help feel better. In my experience, sugar goes a long way to fixing the wrongs of the world. Won't stop the dreams, but it will give your body the strength it needs to recover."

Braelyn accepted the box with a small thanks. The scent of cinnamon and sugar filled her senses the instant she opened the lid. She stared down at the sweet roll, her soul rising toward the light. She set it aside, folding her hands demurely in her lap.

"About the other day. What I asked you to do, I shouldn't have."

Something akin to bitterness flashed across his face, but it was gone too quickly for her to be entirely sure. "No need to explain it, princess. You're a noble and I'm a crime lord, not exactly the best match."

Braelyn sat up straighter, her eyes going wide. His words hurt her far more than they should have. "That's not…what I mean to say…." A heavy sigh. "Bao."

The sound of his name on her lips drew him in like a moth to the flame. The sight of her dressed in nothing more than a thin shift, her hair cascading around her shoulders like rivers of sunlight, nearly did him in. He tried to squash down bits of his dreams where there was nothing between them. No war. No class. Nothing at all.

"Bao, that's not what I meant at all. I don't care where you're from or how you choose to make your way in this world. You're more honest and steadfast than the entire collection of what remains of my parent's court. I should count myself lucky to know you." Her face flushed as she tucked her hair behind an ear.

"It's my behavior that I'm apologizing for. I know I wasn't myself, but that is no excuse for the situation I put you in. And now…" She pressed her lips together to quell their trembling. "And now, everything is at risk. I put the entire operation at risk, all because I thought I was smart enough…again."

She hung her head, hiding her shame and her tears. Strong hands, lined with faint scars, a lifetime of stories etched out on skin, entered her field of vision, gently lifting her chin. Up close, she could see tiny flecks of amber and green she'd never noticed until they were close enough for their breaths to mingle.

"Being smart has nothing to do with it, Braelyn," Bao said, consuming her vision. "And nothing is final until you're dead." His eyes searched hers for a moment longer before he released his grip on her chin and straightened. "But you're right, things have gone south. Perhaps they were always going south and we couldn't see it yet. All we need to do is adjust our strategies and move forward."

"How?"

"Em will fill you in on the finer details later, but the gist of it is that we're leaving. It's too dangerous for us to stay in Verance. If the attempt on you made one thing perfectly clear, it is that there are too many players for me to ensure your safety."

"I will not leave my people in the hands of that creature," Braelyn said with every ounce of anger in her body.

"They're already in his hands, Brae. They were in his hands the moment your parents' blood stained the marble floor. Keeping you here won't make it any easier for them. In fact, it puts them in more danger. He knows that your weakness is your love of your people, your desire to protect them. He'll use that loyalty to hurt your more."

Braelyn scowled, turning her head to stare at the wall. Bao loosened a long, heavy breath, a muscle feathering in his jaw. "Look, you already tried to leave once," he said, switching tactics. "What's the difference now?"

"What's the difference?" Her voice grew cold and sharp. "The difference is that I know the cost of my escape. I wasn't only referring to my parents when I said I've been soaked in the blood of my allies." She cursed the quiver in her voice and the burning in her eyes. She turned her head, clinching both her eyes and lips until she got a rein on her emotions. They sat in tense silence until Bao relented, sliding off her bed.

"And what will he do to you once your brother and Mirra arrive with all the tools needed to lock him away again? How do you think he'll use you to destroy our only chance at winning?"

Braelyn remained silent.

"Just think about it, would you, princess?" Bao walked out of her room as quietly as he entered. Braelyn pulled the box into her lap and took a bite of the sweat roll. Warm buttery crust filled her mouth along with the taste of vanilla, cinnamon, and the bitter tang of regret.

CHAPTER SIXTEEN

Are you certain about the departure time?" Bao's brows knitted together. The sailor in front of him nodded his head vigorously.

"As sure as I know me name, Bossman. Capt'n's got us shoving off night after next right for Zallino. We only got a half a hull, so there's plenty of room for passengers, and the Capt'n appreciate the extra coin." He narrowed his eyes at Bao, cutting glances at his belt.

From his sleeve, Bao pulled out a small pouch and tossed it lightly into the air, with the sound of coins clinking against one another. "Now why should the Captain get a cut of this? You're the one who found me and brokered the deal. Why not say nothing at all and take it all?"

The sailor hesitated, drawing back slightly. "A sailor's only as good as his word. I ain't da kind to turn on them he's sworn to serve."

"I'm not asking you to. I simply wondered why the captain should get a share of your hard work, that's all. I mean, it's one thing to cut him out of the deal when it comes to cargo and goods. But this, this is just a small favor."

Doubt crept into the sailor's face. "You could always take a bit and buy something nice for the captain," Bao said with a shrug, twirling the bag around a finger. "As a way to show your appreciation."

"I guess I could. Might be able to get a better spot on the deck."

"There you go. Now, do we have a deal?"

The sailor frowned once more before spitting into his hand and held it out. Bao flashed a grin and did the same. They shook hands, and the sailor left a little richer than he'd been before. Bao's smile faded as the sailor disappeared into the night. From his pocket, he pulled out a rag and cleaned his hand.

Two days. Not enough time and too long to wait. He still needed to ferret Braelyn and Em out of the castle so no one would question it, at least for a day. Five ships were set for departure within the next couple of days. Bao had brokered passage for himself and the girls on each ship, ensuring that the captains knew nothing. They would question why their fares didn't show, but a lowly sailor who'd gone behind his captain's back for a bit of coin would keep his mouth shut. At least for a time.

He would come back and start gearing up for the war that was brewing on the horizon after he had settled the princess in a safe place. Bao strolled back to the Gilded Lily while casually stuffing his hands in his pockets. Sorro had stayed behind after the engagement celebrations. It felt good to have him back. The old guild was back together, at least as much as they could be.

Bao still believed that part of the reason Sorro left was in part because of Mirra's and Krill's death. At least Mirra had come back from the dead, but Krill. Krill would never again walk these streets, torment the city watch, or laugh and drink with them.

Too caught up in the ghosts of his past, Bao failed to notice the peculiar way some shadows moved, or the soft patter of leather soles against the damp cobblestones. He rounded a corner, stopping short at the large, looming shape in front of him. He shifted back, but was forced to stop again when he heard the sounds of more arriving at his back. The lane was small, made up of the spaces between two rows of semi-dilapidated apartments. The gods themselves could appear and dance naked in the street, and every person would swear to have seen nothing.

Cursing lightly under his breath, he shifted into a wide stance. He kept his body light and loose to give off the impression of good nature, but ready to strike if needed. "Lovely evening we're having, eh lads?"

The men surrounding him said nothing as they continued to encircle him. "Is that the way of it, then? Listen, friends, I'm in no real mood to fight tonight. I got this luscious blonde thing waiting for me at the Lily. She hates it when I drip blood all over her sheets. How about we get around and call it a night?"

The attack from behind came without warning and the only thing that saved Bao was his crooked instincts. Ducking, he spun and drove his fist upwards into the sternum of the closest assailant. He moved again, landing another blow across a jaw before the other attacker fell to the ground.

They converged as one, surrounding Bao. He deflected one blow after another, but time was not on his side. No matter how skilled he was, the numbers were too great, and he couldn't keep fighting forever. And after too many sleepless nights worrying out minute details of half a dozen plans and backups, Bao was nowhere near his prime.

A blow to the ribs knocked the air from his lungs, breaking his defense at last. The goons descended upon Bao like a pack of street dogs, striking without mercy or pause until he collapsed to the ground in a bloody heap. Fighting to maintain consciousness, Bao rolled onto his back, staring up at the night sky. A large, hulking form entered his field of vision, and Bao felt his blood run cold. Bao's world was consumed by the void, and the last thing he witnessed were eyes that seemed to have been plucked from the depths of hell itself.

EM PACED IN THE ANTECHAMBER, CHEWING ON HER thumb. HE missed the rendezvous. Bao never missed the rendezvous, not once. Not even with the city watch hot on his heals. Something must have happened? Did he get caught? Was he betrayed again?

"Em?" Dropping her hand, Em smoothed her hair and dress. For the princess's sake, she'd keep her fears to herself. The dream weed had left her weakened, though her nightmares had ceased.

"Yes, your highness?"

Braelyn's complexion was nearly as white as her bedding. Her hair hung limply around her face and even her eyes seemed to be a shade or two paler than their normal emerald green. "I think I'm up for a bath and a small walk around the gardens."

Em arched a brow. "Bath, yes, walk…I'm not too sure. You have eaten little in the past few days. You've barely been able to hold down simple broths and possets."

"I know, but maybe if I get up and moving, my body will remember that it's supposed to like food."

Em huffed a laugh, earning a shy smile from Braelyn. That smile, that vulnerability, is what undoubtedly finally broke through Mirra's impenetrable wall. It got behind hers, too. She'd do whatever it took to protect that fragile sliver of goodness from the cruelties of the world. "Alright, princess. Let's get you cleaned up and into the fresh air."

It didn't take long for Braelyn to burn through what little strength she had. "Perhaps a walk was ambitious." Her iron grip on Em's arm was the only thing that kept Braelyn upright.

"If you like, we can go to one of the seating areas and I can bring refreshments? Some light tea? Fresh fruit?"

Braelyn flashed a wane smile. "Bring whatever you like, but sitting sounds wonderful right now."

Collapsing into the first available seat, a small mosaic table nestled within the wisteria trellises. Braelyn leaned back and closed her eyes. The heady perfume of the dangling flowers soothed her frayed sense of self as readily as any medicine. She knew she wasn't ready to walk yet. Her legs felt ready to give out on the way to the baths, but she didn't have the luxury to laze about in bed. Especially not after she had time to mull over Bao's words. She couldn't deny the kernels of truth in them. Whether she left or stayed, Julian would use her people to hurt her and to keep her inline. But he would only go so far.

If he had, in fact, poisoned all the nobles who gathered that night, it would have raised enough suspicion that the remaining members of the court would have asked questions. But poisoning a young servant boy, someone only Braelyn would mourn, left them all none the wiser.

She'd been a fool to give in so readily, too wrapped up in her emotions to think clearly, and had been caught in Julian's twisted web. Braelyn groaned softly, leaning back and tilted her head back. Wisteria clusters swayed lightly in the breeze, their pale lavender color catching small patches of sunlight. It was almost peaceful.

From where she sat, no one walking along the main path of the gardens could see her. That also meant that she couldn't see them. She shot up straight when she heard a small group of people approaching her hiding place.

"I'm telling you it's true. My brother has connections in the city watch and they confirmed it." The young male courtier's voice filled with exhilaration.

"I don't know," said another male voice. "How long has the watch been trying to catch him and then suddenly they nab him while he's strolling down the lane?"

The first courtier scoffed. "He wasn't expecting them, Collin. That's the whole point. They finally could make a move without him knowing first."

"I wonder why?"

"Who cares? Now that he's gone, there's going to be a mad scramble for power. For as young as he was, he was more ruthless than any other Bossman and he was smarter than most of them, too."

"It's a shame he lived a life of crime."

The other courtier hummed in agreement. "Do you think we might sneak in and see him? I mean, how often are we going to get the chance to come face to face with the Bossman of the lower streets?"

The courtiers moved beyond Braelyn's range of hearing, unaware of the load they unwittingly dropped. Braelyn clutched her chair with a white knuckled grip. No, this couldn't be true. They had to be mistaken. There's no way Bao would ever get caught, especially by the city watch. He was too smart, too alert for that to happen.

"I made some chamomile tea, and the cook thinks that the cinnamon scones shouldn't upset your stomach too much. What happened?" She set the tray down and crouched in front of Braelyn. "Your highness?"

"They have him," Braelyn said, her voice barely above a whisper. "Julian has Bao."

I TOLD HIM THAT ONE DAY THE FATES WOULD TURN THEIR faces away from him." Sorro scowled from his position along the wall, his arms crossed over his chest.

Tull waved him off. "That's just the nature of the game. Fate's got nothing to do with it. But I'm more worried about why we didn't even hear a whisper. We spend too much coin on the city watch for them to blind side us like this."

"Maybe you've grown too accustomed to being obeyed," Haile commented, picking her nails with a dagger.

Tull glared at her and slapped her boots off the table. He spread out a detailed blueprint of the castle dungeons, both known and secret. "Either way, since they've publicly announced Bao's arrest, I doubt they have in him the catacombs."

"Don't be so sure," Gate said as he leaned against the table, eyeing the blueprint. "They want everyone to know they arrested the Bossman of the Merchant District, but we all know the Viper wants Bao for his connection to the princess. The people don't care what they do to criminals after their arrest."

Tull pressed his lips together. He hated to admit it, but Gate was right, every now and again. He studied the blueprint, his mind already whirling with a dozen distinct possibilities for infiltration and escape. But a tiny sliver of doubt wormed its way through his thoughts. Planning was Bao's thing. He was good at it from the start. Tull was only as good as he was because of the years serving under him. His strength was in solving problems on the fly, right in the thick of when everything went wrong. But he wanted nothing to go wrong. He wanted to get Bao out of the enemy's clutches and to safety.

"Any word from Em?" Sorro asked.

Tull shook his head. "I doubt we'll hear anything from her for another day or so. She's most likely gathering what she can from inside."

Sorro's reply was simple and firm. "Good."

A knock at the door drew everyone's attention. Tull looked at each of the people gathered and they all shrugged. Hands shifted to weapons as Tull opened the door. Two cloaked figures pressed into the room, lowering their hoods as they went.

"God's be damned," breathed Gate at the sight of Braelyn and a priestess from Yulla's temple.

Braelyn pressed forward, blatantly ignoring the hostile air that filled the small room. "This is Sasha. You can trust her."

Haile scoffed. "Beggin' your pardon, princess, I ain't trusting anyone that hasn't earned it."

Braelyn scowled and opened her mouth to argue, but Tull cut her off. "Where's Em?"

"Pretending to be me in the library. Look, I don't have long, but I want to help. I know there's not much I can do, but I know more about the castle than what they ever put to paper."

Gate snorted. Braelyn cut her eyes, and him, turned the blueprint over and motioned for something to write with. "The easiest way to get many people into the castle is through the archive passage. It opens along the base of the cliff, completely hidden from any patrol or estate."

"Are you sure you want to share this?" Braelyn looked up into Tull's face, her jaw set with grim determination.

"Bao has repeatedly stuck his neck out for me. Been there for me. The least I can do is share a few secrets to help him escape." She paused, looking around the room, a furrow between her brows. "Where are the others?"

Sorro made a noise in the back of his throat. "Hiding in their dens until the Sarran is over."

"What's that?"

"It's the five-day period of peace before all hel breaks loose," Gate said. "During the Sarran, no Bossman will make a move for the high seat. It's supposed to be so the uninvolved can clear out before the bloodshed, but it's more commonly used to gather the lads and prepare for war. Unless Bao comes back in the five days, the lower streets with be filled with blood until a new Bossman claims his…"

"Or hers."

Gate rolled his eyes. "Or hers, spot."

Braelyn pursed her lips. "Then that's our timeline."

Sasha stepped forward. "Forgive me, your highness, but I think it would be best if you and your friend fled the city as planned."

"But he was only supposed to help me and then return."

"Not possible anymore," Sorro said. "If the Viper could get to him once without a sign, then he can do it again. No longer will the rest view him as untouchable. They will come at him from all sides," he waved at everyone gathered around the table, "and those loyal to him."

Braelyn fought the urge to squirm under Sorro's dark, penetrating stare. "Either way," she said, bracing against the table, "we need to get him out. I haven't known Bao as long as the rest of you, but I know he will let himself be shattered and die before ever betraying anyone who has placed their trust in him. I can't lose…"

Priestess Sasha placed a gentle hand on the princess's shoulder. "I can pass messages from the castle to you without raising suspicion. If you need to get word to Braelyn, go to the farthest alcove on the western side. There is a loose stone in front of the altar."

Tull nodded. "Find out what you can and leave word in two days."

"I'll do what I can." Braelyn sat back in her carriage and closed her eyes. Everything had gone so wrong so fast. The walls of her gilded cage were slowly closing in around her, crushing the breath from her lungs. She took one long, shaky breath. She couldn't afford to break down now. Not with Bao, depending on her to uphold her end of everything. But the tumultuous sea of emotions deep within her heart beat against the dam of her control. Something needed to give before she burst under the pressure of expectation. Twin streaks ran down her face. An invisible hand clenched around her throat and, for a moment, Braelyn wished she could pass into oblivion.

A LONE FIGURE, CLOTHED IN BLACK, MADE THEIR WAY along the narrow tops of the palace roofs. Their movements were slow and deliberate, moving as fast as they dared. As the figure neared the end of one roof, they picked up the pace, gaining the speed needed to clear the gap to the next. They ran seemingly without fear, leaping into the open air as if they had wings. Tucking their legs close to their chest, their arms trailing behind them. As they fell toward the next rooftop, they spiraled their arms forward, kicking their legs out in front. They landed with a thud, allowing their momentum to carry them forward into a roll. Once, twice, they rolled before coming to their feet once again. The figure trotted further before coming to a stop, their chest heaving with adrenaline and effort.

Braelyn pulled off her head and face coverings, drinking in the cool night air in deep gulps. She tilted her head toward the sky and thanked the gods for letting her stick the landing and for the moonless night. Braelyn wasn't as adept as Em or Sorro, but she couldn't sit idly by any longer. She couldn't be sure what the others were doing in the lower streets, but Em was out gathering up the rumors that ran rampant throughout the castle. Braelyn was supposed to stay in her room. But as the hours progressed painfully slowly, Braelyn gave up on sleep and did something that was equal parts daring and stupid.

Once her breathing returned to normal, Braelyn re-wrapped her head and continued on with her self imposed mission. It would take them longer than two days to find out where Julian kept Bao. He was the master of lies and misdirections and they hadn't the time. The only way they'd be ready to move that quickly was to get it directly from the bastard's mouth. Of course, she would not corner him and ask directly. Even she knew that was bordering on the imbecilic.

Julian and the creature inside him had grown too complacent, too cocky as of late. Perhaps it had come with decades of not getting caught, or because they were nearing the end of their goal. Either way, he failed to notice, or didn't bother hiding, small tells about his routine.

Braelyn smiled beneath her mask. Her mother was right. It truly was beneficial to have friends and connections for all sorts of people. Though she doubted her mother would have approved of the current company, her daughter kept. For the first time since their murder, the memory of her mother drew a ghost of a laugh. Braelyn latched onto that singular granule of fondness and let its warmth fill her like a warm sun on a frozen field in the early days of spring.

The raucous laughter of drunken courtiers drew her back to the task at hand. With one long inhale, Braelyn rushed onward right to the lair of the most dangerous beast on the continent.

The climb up Julian's tower took her longer than she liked. More than once, her grip slipped and the only thing that kept her from falling into the abyss was the small bit of rope tethered by the hook she'd just hammered into the creases between the stones. It had been a long, slow process filled with anxiety so thick that she could have chewed on it like bread.

The watchtower clock chimed three times. Braelyn dared not to hammer in a line so near Julian's window. Instead, she climbed all the way to the top and lowered from the roof's eaves. Swinging out in the open air with nothing more than a bit of rope churned her stomach, but she was done with letting others risk their lives for her. It was time and past for her to return the favor.

"He still refuses to speak?" said a gruff voice she wasn't familiar with.

Julian's cruel laughter sent a shiver down her spine. "It doesn't matter if he speaks or not. All that matters is that he suffers, so she suffers."

The next voice Braelyn heard nearly caused her to lose her grip on the rope. "Um…shouldn't you perhaps be kinder to the woman you've professed to love?"

Lord Kilstan had been her father's most trusted advisor and dearest friend. Until now, she had counted him as a potential ally. So why was he clearly in cahoots with the man responsible for the death of his lifelong friend?"

Julian laughed. "The only reason I'm marrying the princess is because she's more valuable alive than dead. For the moment. The moment she produces my heir and cements my claim to the throne, her usefulness is at an end." He turned a sharp eye to Lord Kilstan. "Does this bother you?"

Braelyn wished she could see Lord Kilstan's face. She hoped he looked guilty, remembering all the times he swept her into his arms as a child. The way she and her brother called him uncle. Every single tear, laughter, and moments of togetherness they'd share. The only bit of satisfaction she received was hearing the way his voice trembled with fear as he answered.

"N-no, my lord. Not in the slightest."

Their conversation shifted onto a dozen other things that had nothing to do with Bao. She tried to file away all the bits of information to pass on, but failed. All she could focus on was the fresh new betrayal and the wicked enjoyment she felt when she marked the weak link in Julian's web of secrets.

Em was absolutely livid. She had been waiting when Braelyn returned scant hours from dawn, and had given her a tongue lashing. The only reason Braelyn wasn't still on the receiving end of a lecture riddled with explicits was the information she learned the night before. Em left to see Tull giving Braelyn explicit instructions to stay put and not involve herself further. But Braelyn was the crowned princess of Undros, heir to the throne and descendent of a long line of royals. She wasn't used to following orders.

The morning dawned with little wind and higher temperatures than normal, driving most of the court out into the gardens. Even with all the windows and doorways open, there wasn't enough breeze to cool inside. At least in the gardens or out in the yards, the rare occasional breeze would kiss their sweat covered brows.

Braelyn chose the thinnest of her dresses in a color that brought out the color in her face, making her appear full of life. Her long hair done up in a simple braid wrapped around her head, secured with a hairpin popular in eastern Zallino, its jeweled flower petals clinking as she walked.

She smiled and inclined her head at courtiers when they bowed, greeting them all with a brightness unseen for sometime. Though several tried to engage her in conversation, Braelyn deftly maneuvered away. She had one target in mind, one person who she wanted to meet. The benign grin on her face took on a slight edge when she finally spied Lord Kilstan walking by himself, locked in deep thought.

"Lord Kilstan," she said brightly, walking faster to reach him.

Lord Kilstan visibly jumped and turned. His guilt was evident briefly before slipping into his mask once more. "Your highness, may I say that you look positively glowing today."

Braelyn waved a hand. "You know flattery will get you nowhere with me, my lord. But I was hoping to get a word with you."

"Of course. What is it you wanted to discuss?"

Braelyn slid her arm into his and gently led him away from the rest of the court. Other than bowing as they passed, no one spared the princess and the former king's advisor a passing glance.

"I fear I must apologize, my lord. I've been so wrapped up in myself that I failed to see how you have been faring these past months. You and my father were as close as brothers. I can't imagine how all of this must be affecting you."

Lord Kilstan paled and swallowed. "It…has been… challenging, your highness."

"Please, call me Braelyn, as you often did before. There's no need for formality between us. After all, we're near family."

Much to her pleasure, Lord Kilstan's distress grew, his face taking on an unhealthy pallor. "Oh forgive me, Uncle. I didn't mean to cause you distress. I simply wanted to reconnect to the closest thing to family I have left. My traitorous brother notwithstanding."

Lord Kilstan's brows shot up. "You honestly believe that your brother could kill your parents for the crown?"

Braelyn made her eyes go wide and tear up, raising a hand to cover her lips. "I was there, my lord. I saw him and will never forget that day as long as I live. If not for Lord Julian, I wouldn't be standing here today."

The confused expression on Lord Kilstan's face told Braelyn everything she needed to know. He knew the truth of it all. Perhaps not Julian's true nature, but he certainly had an active hand in her parent's demise.

"Truth be told, there's something else I much desire to speak to you about." She cast a fervent glance over her shoulder and tugged him into a small gazebo covered in blooming red, white, and pink roses. Not another courtier could be seen or heard, nor was there a wall overhead for a passing guardsman to stroll.

She withdrew her hand from his arm, placing it on Lord Kilstan's chest. His eyes went wide as she pressed him back against the vine covered lattice, pressing her body close to his.

"Braelyn…what are…"

She cut him off by placing her dagger against his throat. She let her mask fall, letting the full force of her rage shine through. "Did you never think I would find out? Did you think your crimes would never come to light?"

"I don't know what you're talking about," he sputtered.

Braelyn scoffed, pressing her dagger harder. "Your lying ends now. You're going to tell me whatever I want to now and then you're going to take this." She backed up enough to pull a vial from her pocket. "Have you ever been to the lower streets in the Merchant District? I'll admit they are rough, not really a hub of polite society, but you can really find just about anything your heart desires. Take this, for example: it's a poison derived from the seeds of apples and peaches. Easy to make, and cheap, but the effects…" She raised her brows and smirked. "Well, let's just say that this concentration is a small mercy. You'll go quickly and painless…for the most part."

Lord Kilstan's face grew whiter than the surrounding roses. He dropped to his knees, headless of her blade, drawing a thin red line against his cheek. "Have mercy, your highness. You don't know how he is. How cruel. How cunning."

Braelyn laughed coldly. "Oh believe me, I do. And still I stand against him as often as I can. There's no hope of saving your pitiful life, but there is for your family."

"My family?"

"Don't you know the punishment for participating in assisting in a regicide?" She leaned in close so that their eyes were level. "I will seize your lands. They will strip your title, marked out of the history books forever. And your family will be led to the gallows right down to the infants, with you being the last so that you can understand what it's like to watch your family die."

A wet spot formed between his legs as Braelyn stood back up like a dark, avenging goddess. "Gods be merciful, I'll do anything, anything you want, just please spare my family. They know nothing of this, I swear on my life."

"Your life has no worth to me."

Lord Kilstan sobbed, dropping to the ground, clutching the hem of her dress. "I know I have no right to ask you to spare my family when I robbed you of yours, but please…for what we once had."

Braelyn wrinkled her nose as if smelling something foul. But the life of someone precious to her hung in the balance. "Fine, but I have two questions for you."

Lord Kilstan whispered a thankful prayer to the gods. "I will answer truthfully."

"Where is the Bossman of the Merchant District being held?"

If her question startled him, he gave no sign. "I have a townhouse in the Divine District. He's being kept in the cellar."

"It's not under your name, is it?"

Lord Kilstan shook his head. "No. I didn't want my wife to find out because…it's where I visit my mistresses. It's registered under the name Carl VonDurist."

Braelyn tossed the vial at him. "I'm going to watch you take that."

He swallowed again, his face blanching again. "What of your second question?"

Her anger fizzled out, leaving Braelyn with nothing but the pain of betrayal. "Why?"

Lord Kilstan blinked several times before he answered. "Your father wanted to change things. Wanted to 'level the playing field' between commoners and nobles. He wanted to build free schools, revitalize the orphanages."

Braelyn stepped back, her arm wrapping around her stomach as if struck. All the times she preached to her father about the inequalities between the classes, he'd dismissed claiming she was too naïve to fully understand. He questioned her to the point of tears about where funding was going to come to not only build the schools, but hire the teachers and support staff. Every time she'd come to him with some kind of social reform, he always seemed to shut her down. And now…now she learned he wasn't trying to dissuade her. He wanted to help her make her visions a reality. And that's what contributed to getting him killed. What turned his friends against him all for the sake of lining their pockets and their continued manipulation of a system that only benefited themselves?

"Braelyn?" Lord Kilstan looked up at her, still holding the vial of poison.

"You look thirsty, Lord Kilstan. Why don't you finish your drink?"

Lord Kilstan cried unabashedly as he unstoppered the vial and tipped the contents down his throat. He cringed against the bitter taste before falling forward, coughing violently clutching his throat. His body began to convulsion as he foamed at the mouth. Braelyn watched with coolheaded detachment until he stopped moving. She walked over and picked up the vial, slipping it into her pocket before resuming her stroll through the gardens.

By nightfall, the entire castle was buzzing with the news of Lord Kilstan's death. A servant had found his body, hoping to take a few moments for themselves before completing their work.

Julian stormed to Braelyn's chambers. His patience with her antics had finally run out. Lord Kilstan's death sent a ripple of unease amongst the nobles, especially those who'd had been with him since he proposed the coup. Kilstan clearly had been poisoned, but they had found nothing with his body. That meant that he hadn't taken his own life in guilt. Someone had moved to take revenge and who knew who'd be next?

Of course, Julian had a pretty good idea who might have been behind Kilstan's death. Just how the princess found out. He couldn't be sure, but if she wanted to play the game of shadows, he'd show her the price needed to win. Guards shattered her door, stepping back to let Julian storm in like death incarnate. "Enough of your games, little girl."

Silence greeted him. The guards pressed in, searching for any sign of the princess or where she'd could have gone. Not finding her in her chambers, the search spread to the rest of the castle. By nightfall, two things were certain. Braelyn most likely handled Lord Kilstan's death, and she had escaped the castle once more.

Julian stood amidst the carnage of Braelyn's chambers, broiling in rage. During the search, the guards had uncovered servants' garments, a dye to change one's eye color, grappling equipment, and a solid black outfit nearly identical to the one he'd given Mirra. He'd underestimated his prey again. Julian roared, blackness erupting from his body in violent waves, turning everything in the room to dust. He'd set the city aflame, hang the bodies of the children, the sick, and the elderly from the walls.

No. A small part of his consciousness pulled back the dark, hungry rage that wanted to be unleashed on the unsuspecting masses. It wouldn't serve their goal to lose control now. Once everything he wanted was his, he'd take his time with the princess. Her screams would be the most delicious meal of his long existence. Of that, he was completely sure.

SHOULDN'T THEY BE BACK BY NOW?" BRAELYN SAID AS SHE paced in Madam Tatinna's parlor.

"Calm yourself," Madam Tatinna said with a sigh. "They've pulled off far more dangerous jobs before."

Braelyn threw herself into a chaise with a long sigh. "I should be with them."

"And then the others would have to split their focus between finishing the job and protecting you. Honestly, Bao said you were intelligent."

Braelyn stuck her tongue out in the most unprincess like fashion, drawing a deep laugh from Madam Tatinna. With the tension finally broken, Braelyn joined in until her sides hurt.

"And here I was thinking you'd be wracked with worry." Tull stood in the doorway, dressed as a member of the city watch. He seemed hale enough, save for the smeared blood on his face and hands.

Braelyn rose to her feet. "He's in the other room," Tull said, pointing his thumb. She rushed past, giving him a small squeeze on the arm in thanks. Tull watched her go with a smirk. "So, do we wanna place bets now?"

She nearly careened into the doctor on his way out in her haste to lay her eyes on Bao. "Excuse me," she said reflectively, but the focus of her attention was on the beaten and battered man on the couch.

"Bao." His name came from her lips like a prayer. He turned his face toward her, giving a weak smile.

"Ya miss me, princess?"

With a great sob, Braelyn threw herself onto the couch, falling onto her knees. She clutched desperately at his ripped and blood-stained clothes, pressing her face against him as she cried. His usual smell of pastries and spices was gone, replaced with unwashed human and blood.

Bao shifted beneath her, gently pulling his clothing free from her iron grip. He made comforting noises as he slowly sat up and pulled her onto the couch next to him. "Hey, now what's all this?" Braelyn shook her head, unable to answer. Bao brushed her hair back from her face and pulled her close. "I'm alright," he said as he rubbed her back. "I'm here because of you and everything's going to be fine. Breath, Brae, breath."

Her breathing slowed, and she loosened her grip on him enough to sit up straight. Her eyes roamed over him, her guilt rising as she cataloged every mark done to him all for knowing her. His skin had taken on an ashen pallor. His lip had been repeatedly torn and one eye was almost entirely swollen shut.

Braelyn bowed her head. "I'm sorry."

"What for? It's not like you gave the order. Stop taking responsibility for what that son of a whore chooses to do."

"But he went after you because of me," she cried.

Bao cursed under his breath and gently lifted her chin with a heavily bandaged hand. "He did it because he takes joy in hurting people and especially in hurting you. He's the only one responsible for the actions he makes. Not me, you, or anyone else. Do you understand?"

Braelyn said nothing, her disbelief clearly written across her face. Bao loosened another heavy sigh, shifted and grimaced. "You shouldn't be sitting up," Braelyn said, moving so she could help him back down. "Are you in pain? Should I fetch the doctor again?"

Bao shook his head. "He's already given what he can. Anymore and I'll be knocked out for days and we need to leave the city as soon as possible."

"You can barely walk, let alone ride a horse."

"I'll make do. Once we reach Xhu'Rozo, I'll be a good little patient and not move until I'm fully healed. Promise." He flashed his trademark smirk as he crossed his heart, though it lacked its usual bluster.

Braelyn gave him a tight-lipped smile before shaking her head. "No, we shouldn't leave the kingdom." She silenced Bao's objection with a hand. "It will take us too long to get back when Mirra and my brother return. Plus, there's no guarantee that Julian won't be able to reach us there. He attacked the Holy Isle. What's another kingdom to him? No, we need to go somewhere he wouldn't dare to tread or be able to reach us if he did."

"And just where is that?"

"Mirra mentioned in a letter that deep in Mystic Woods, there's a ruined Ilmarrion city. Though most of the city is barren, a small number of Ilmarrions, holy people and common alike, live there. They, too, have abilities that can keep whatever that creature inside Julian sends our way. They also might send word to Mirra, letting her know that we're safe. That way, they may move a bit more freely than if we were still under his thumb."

Bao hadn't said a single word while she spoke. She could see him weighing the options. "Do you know where it is, exactly?"

"Not really. Mirra said she reached it fairly quickly after meeting Em. She found a cave and kept walking west until the scouts found them."

"It's not much to go on." His words slurred and his eyes lids fluttered closed.

"I know, but I think it's our best chance." Braelyn smoothed back his hair and moved to stand, but was stopped by Bao, latching onto her wrist, his eyes wide.

"Where are you going?" Braelyn stared down in surprise. Bao's eye were wide and unfocused. The medicine the doctor had given him for the pain and to help him sleep was taking control.

"I'm going to tell the others. You need at least an hour of rest if you even hope to make it out of the city. We can all decide what to do when you wake." She looked about the room, searching for something to cover him with. "I'll get you a change of clothes and a blanket."

Headless of his wounds, Bao lurched to his feet, his eyes fully glazed over. "Don't!" He fell, but Braelyn caught him. She took one look at his panic-stricken face and led him back to the couch. She gently laid him on his side before sliding next to him and wrapped her arms around his waist. Bao wrapped his arms around her, burying his face in her hair.

Tull found them some time later, still entwined together. Bao's hand was tangled in Braelyn's braid. Her face tucked neatly under his chin, with her arms still securely around his waist. He threw the blanket he brought over them, nearly positive that he was going to win the bet.

CHAPTER SEVENTEEN

THERE WASN'T MUCH TO DO ON THE TINY STREET OF Lorithan in the way of entertainment, but the hard faced day workers and mothers with pinched faces made do. Cally Hardwall sat on the pile of bricks that served as her steps, with a washtub between her legs. Her ruddy face was redder with exertion as she scrubbed her husband's heavily mended shirt.

Her neighbor, Widow Molly, spat a thick glob of black spit just shy of Cally's boot. "Dunna know why, ya e'en botha with dat? It gonna get dery da moment he put it on."

Cally sighed, closed her eyes and counted to five, the highest number she knew, before answering. "Long day Widow Molly?"

Widow Molly snorted and lobbed another black spit against the uneven cobblestone. "Ain't dey all?"

Cally made a face, unable to deny the sentiment. A heavy odor of excrement wafted through the narrow street. "Golly, is it time already?"

"Guess so," Widow Molly said, her nose wrinkling against the powerful odor. "Best get da pots, den."

The women disappeared into their homes and retrieved various pots and buckets they used to relieve themselves when they didn't feel like making the three-block trek to the nearest community latrine. By the time they returned to their stoops, the night cart rambled onto their narrow street, with one person at the front and another at the back. Cally emptied her family's refuge as quickly as she could, holding her breath. Widow Molly, however, narrowed her eyes, making her face look even more pinched.

"Kinda early, ain't ya?"

The one in the front shrugged. "If ya say so." He looked around the street for any other people looking to add to the steaming pile of human waste at his back. Seeing none, he bent his knees, picking up the handles of the cart and resumed his unfortunate job. The other, working at the back, inclined his head as they passed. Cally returned the gesture, her eyes going to the strands of golden hair that stuck out from beneath his cap when they caught the small bit of sun that reached them.

It's a shame, Cally thought, returning to her husband's shirt. Such lovely hair would go for a handful of silver, perhaps even a couple of gold, and yet he's pushing my shit away. She shook her head and turned back to the drudgery of her small life.

"I HAVE TO SAY, I'M IMPRESSED, PRINCESS."

Braelyn glared up at Bao from beneath her cap, trying not to vomit in her mouth. Her arms and shoulders ached from pushing the night cart throughout half the lower streets and from shoveling it into a larger wagon.

"Never let it be said that I don't know the effects of an honest day's work."

Bao's laughter turned into a coughing fit. He held a hand up to let her know he was fine. Once his coughing subsided, he turned to the farmer whose cart they were loading, and accepted a small purse. "Thanks Odo. How's that new wife of yours?"

The farmer beamed, easing the hard lines of his face. "She's a doin'. Already got a youngun in her belly. Should be here just before the first harvest."

"Congratulations," Bao said, clapping the farmer on the back.

Odo inclined his head, touching the tip of his cap. "It's da least I can do for ya. After all ya did for me a few years back….well, I wouldn't be here today without it."

Bao waved his hand. "Keep quiet about all this and we're even."

Odo tipped his hat again and shuffled off to talk to the other farmers that gathered to buy loads of waste for their fields. Braelyn returned to shoveling out the muck, swallowing the dozens of questions that bubbled to the surface. Bao took one look at her and chuckled.

"Odo had a poor season a few years back. He'd never had a lot to begin with, but that year wiped him out. He came to me desperate to keep the money lenders from taking the land that had been in his family since his grandfather's grandfather."

Braelyn's brows rose, having some inclination as to the total sum Bao had spent. "And this balances the debt between you?"

"Not quite, but sometimes it's not about recouping all the costs. By helping us, he's placing everything he has on the line.

That kind of daring, of loyalty, is worth far more than a bit of gold or silver."

Braelyn stopped shoveling and stared up at Bao. She'd never met a person so wrapped up in contradictions in her life. He made a living on the suffering of others, but in the same breath doled out more than he'd ever get back. But underneath all his trappings, the masks he put on to play his parts, he was an honest man. A worth knowing, worth standing next to.

Sensing her gaze, he turned, flashing her his signature half grin. "No time to lallygag, my lady. The sooner we finish, the sooner we can be on our way."

Braelyn let loose a curse, earning another laugh from Bao, as she dug back in, a ghost of a smile tugging at her mouth.

THE HOT BATH WAS A GODSEND, EVEN IF SHE HAD TO SIT cross-legged in order to sit in the tub. She welcomed anything that would wash away the stench of the night cart. She lingered until the water cooled, drying with a coarse towel. On one of the two narrow beds sat a set of new clothes. Braelyn picked up the top article of clothing, uncertainty running through her. She didn't care that it wasn't the finest fabrics money could buy or even cut in the latest style. Even when she crept around the castle as a servant girl, she'd been in skirts. Never once in her life had she worn anything that showed her legs. Her mother's words echoed through her head, reminding her that only the lowest of women showed their legs. Even the hint of shape was enough for one to lose all honor.

She snorted. Honor, she'd lost it ages ago. Pressing her lips into a thin line, she dropped the towel and threw on her new underthings. Her hands shook slightly as she slid into the first pair of breeches she'd worn. They were soft, yet durable and wide enough that if she stood with her legs together, no one would know she wasn't in a skirt. She received another pleasant shock with the tunic. Her anxiety reared its head again when she pulled on the tight, long-sleeved undershirt, but the tunic she found lovely. It was fashioned in the style favored in northern Zallino. The color fastened to the side with a simple tie. The sleeves of the tunic stopped at her elbow, allowing for a full range of movement, but her favorite part was the way it split at her hips, long strips of fabric falling in the front and back, stopping just shy of her knees.

Bao, in all his infinite kindness, had found her clothing that she would be comfortable in. A knock at the door drew her attention.

"Yes?"

"It's me," Bao said on the other side.

She unlatched the door, stepping aside to let him in before sliding the bolt in place again. The wooden bolt wouldn't keep agents of Julian out, but it gave her a small sense of security. Bao held two steaming plates of food in one arm and two tankards in the other hand. Braelyn rushed to take one of each before he dropped them.

Bao looked her up and a down. "I knew it would look good on you."

"Thank you for the clothes," she said, suddenly struggling to find the words to express how grateful she was. The roving approval in his gaze ignited heat in her cheeks. She sat on one bed, digging into the food.

"From here on out, we're a newly married couple on the way to my family at their home outside of Konode."

Braelyn coughed on her boiled potatoes. She took a long swig from her tankard, wincing as the bitter beer filled her mouth. Gasping, she opened her mouth to retort, but stopped. Bao stared intently at his own plate, his ears a bright scarlet.

Clearing her throat, she whipped away the wetness around her eyes. "Explains the clothing. I guess I'm a farmer's daughter?"

"Merchant, you're too pretty to be a farmer's daughter. They have earlier signs of wear than most other girls."

She took a fortifying breath. "And just how did we meet?"

"At the markets, of course."

"Did my parents approve?"

A wicked smirk. "Not at all." He lifted his head and met her gaze straight on. She didn't fight the smirk that bloomed on her face.

"Forbidden love then? I wouldn't have pegged you for the romantic sort."

His smirk grew into a grin that promised a litany of wonderfully wicked things. "You don't know all my secrets, princess."

"Husband," she said. "Call me Brea."

An air of mourning hung over Em's farm. Even the chickens were silent, hunkered down in their nests. Braelyn gripped her bag tighter, fighting her growing unease at the surrounding silence.

"Are you sure she's here?"

Bao didn't answer. He scanned the small farm, perhaps searching for secret signals that only he and Em would know. Striding toward the house, his eyes darting quickly up at the smokeless chimney. He didn't bother knocking on the door and entered the dark room. Silence greeted them. After a quick glance at the stairs, he walked to the mantle, running his hand along the bricks. One came free, revealing a small bit of parchment.

"They've gone to be with the rest of Micha's family. She says that whatever we need is ours. Even the land and buildings. She doesn't want to be in the place where he died."

Braelyn's throat burned with unshed tears. She'd felt the same way when Tolin was killed, but unlike Em, she couldn't simply pack up and move. "What are you going to do?"

Bao sighed, rubbing his face, exhaustion written over every inch of his body. "Dunno. Maybe I could retire and live a simple life for once." A bitter chuckle. "As if I ever could."

The sorrow in his words urged Braelyn into movement. She crossed the space between them, wrapping her arms around his waist. She laid her head on his shoulders. Bao took her hands in his, letting go of a long sigh. She was far more comfortable touching him than when they'd first embarked. "You deserve whatever life you desire," she said. "You've given so much and worked so hard for everyone else. Once this is over, go after what you want. What you really want."

Bao gave her hand a squeeze and turned around. "And what if I can't have what I want?"

She felt her own face redden. "You're a smart guy. I'm sure you can figure something out."

Bao laughed through his nose and pulled Braelyn in for one more embrace. "I'll see to the fire if you'll head to the cellar to scrounge up something to eat."

Grateful for the break in tension, Brealyn went outside and turned her face toward the darkening sky. Slowly, she counted to thirty in her mind. For thirty seconds, she opened the floodgates to her emotions and felt it all. Guilt. Worry. Anger. And something far sweeter and far more dangerous than the other three altogether. At the end of her count, Brealyn took a slow breath and slammed down her inner walls once more. Pressure relieved at a more bearable level, she walked around the house to the doors that led to the cellar.

BRAELYN SAT UP IN THE BED WITH THE TASTE OF FEAR IN her mouth. She looked around the darkened room until she remembered where she was. Dropping back with a long breath, she stared up at the ceiling somewhere in the darkness above her and cursed. Another nightmare. At least the details had already vanished like the morning dew. Braelyn tossed and turned for what felt like hours, throwing the blankets back in frustration when sleep would not return.

On silent feet, she padded out into the hallway and stared at the door where Bao slept. From the moment they left Verance until now, they'd shared a bed. Nothing happened, much to her relief and irritation, but she'd grown accustomed to the warmth of his body and the sound of his breathing.

She reached a hand out but stopped just shy of touching the knob. Bao deserved a peaceful night's sleep. It wasn't his fault that her nights were riddled with horrific visages of her failings and the evils of the world left unchecked. Turning away, Braelyn returned to the room and wrapped a woolen blanket around herself. Stepping softly, she crept downstairs, intending to rekindle the fire and spending the rest of the night bathed in its warmth and light.

But it appeared someone else had the same idea. Keeping to the shadows, she stepped down as far as she dared, crouching like a child to peer through the railings. Bao stood before the fire, staring at something that hadn't been there earlier. In the flickering light, she could only make out two vague human shapes and a tall placard between them. Bao had his hands pressed together in prayer, muttering softly. She risked another step. The distinct aroma of incense wafted through the air and the meaning of his actions became clear.

As part of her lessons, Braelyn had learned about the various gods and religious beliefs of the kingdoms around Undros. Throughout most of Zallino, the people prayed to a deity called Onea, The Great All. It was the personification of the will of the universe. But just because you prayed to Onea, didn't mean that what you wanted would come true. If the fates had already determined the outcome, it would happen. The two figures were most likely effigies for his parents. In some regions, the ancestors were worshiped solely or in tandem with other local deities, or Onea, the personification of the universe.

Not wanting to intrude on a private matter, Braelyn slowly eased back up the stairs, but stopped again when she heard Bao speak aloud. It wasn't in the language of her people or the common tongue that helped the various traders communicate with one another, but in his first language. She knew some Zallino, but it was the kind that was spoken amongst the noble families, warlords, and emperors. She couldn't place his dialect, but she could figure out the gist of what was being said alone in the night.

"Honorable Mother and Father. I am sorry for neglecting my duties as your son for these past few weeks. My enemies move faster and with more cunning than a snake. I could barely get out alive. Please let these meager offerings feed your spirits, so you continue to have the strength to appeal to the fates on my behalf. I thank you for all the blessings I have received and I promise to make a more appropriate offering when the world calms again."

"Perhaps I will retire and live the life of a simple farmer here on the same farm where my friend found peace. I know I bring you and the ancestors great shame from this path I must follow. It would be easy if not for her."

It was like a hand wrapped around her throat and squeezed. Swallowing against the tightness, she quickly retreated to the safety of her room and buried her face into the pillow, hoping to muffle her cries.

"Rough night, Brae?"

"A little." She couldn't bring herself to look Bao in the face. Not after what she heard last night. She nearly told him three times to stay behind, but the fear of being alone stole the words from her.

Bao studied her intently, undoubtedly weighing her every movement and facial expressions. Mentally, she clamped down harder on her feelings and slipped into one of her many masks.

"Do you know how long we'll need to go into the woods before we find the city?"

Bao shrugged. "Mirra only said they walked for only a league or so. She mentioned a cave about a day's journey in that we can rest at. She said that we should be able to find the glyphs that will serve as markers."

Apprehension soured her stomach. "I hope they agree to help us."

Bao was not the kind to lay down false hopes. Uncertainty clouded the usual brightness of his face, but he still said, "They will."

Bao felt calmer once they'd reached the safety of the forest. Though he couldn't make out much in the thick vegetation, that also meant that potential threats couldn't see them either. Braelyn walked silently beside him, her eyes firmly on her feet. He frowned. Something happened last night. Something that made her retreat within. He hated it. All his attempts to draw her out had failed, leaving him feeling worse. He was so wrapped up in his thoughts that he failed to notice the bit of unnaturally neat looking roots directly in their path. Braelyn stepped on the first, screaming as the roots wrapped around her calves and hoisted her into the air, like a hunter's trip snare.

"Bao!"

"Brae," he bellowed, reaching for her to only find that he too had roots twining around his legs. The air was knocked from his lungs when the roots pulled his legs out from under him. Blood filled his mouth when he bit his tongue on impact.

Braelyn's frantic cries for him filled the once tranquil forest. He struggled against the roots, to no avail. Reaching for the blades hidden at his wrist, he stabbed the nearest root. He felt the scream in the roots that bound his body. They released their grip long enough for him to scrabble freely.

Braelyn hung upside down next to an ancient-looking birch tree. Her face was pale, despite all the blood that rushed toward her head. She reached out for him, a strange and frantic light in her eye. Bao stumbled for her, reaching out across the distance. Leaving himself wide open for the rock that struck the back of his skull, sending him into darkness with Braelyn's cries echoing in his ears.

Bao crumpled like a rag doll, the bloody stone that struck him falling to the side. Like the day of the garden party, pressure built inside her. Sickening, rolling, burning pressure that threatened to burst her open like an overripe peach if she didn't let go. So that's what she did. Braelyn let go of every steel plated door within herself that kept her true self hidden from a world that would delight in tearing it apart.

It burst from her like a ripple in a pond, wreaking havoc around her. Tree roots shriveled and turned to dust. Lush green leaves turn black as if burnt and fell like black snowfall. The ground became gray and cracked, as all the rich nutrients and moisture evaporated as if they'd never been.

"Stop", cried an unfamiliar voice. A force similar to the one she'd let go, pushed against the destructive wave still rolling out of her.

Braelyn fell to the ground hard as the roots that held her crumbled. Gasping for air and blinking back stars, she crawled to Bao, unaware that she called his name over and over.

Just before her fingers touched a single one of his dark, wavy locks, her world disappeared into nothingness. The last thing she had the sense of mind to recognize was a young man kneeling next to them. His face was unfamiliar, but his eyes…she knew those eyes.

"That's not possible."

"I know what I saw, J'ina. The human woman used Fasht. Go where they tripped the defenses and see for yourself."

"High Priestess, he must be mistaken…right?"

Bao didn't get to hear the high priestess's answer. His consciousness returned with a vengeance, drawing a groan from him before he could stop. The people in the room fell silent. He felt one draw nearer. Not close enough for him to reach, if he had the strength to.

"He appears to still be out," the one he suspected to be, J'ina said.

"Leave us," said a woman whose voice soothed Bao's frayed edges. The other two voiced weak protests but left all the same. The room fell so quiet, so empty that Bao couldn't be sure that the woman hadn't left too. And then she spoke.

"I know you're not asleep, Bao of the Lower Streets, son of Miusa and Johona."

Upon hearing the names of parents, names that only he and one other person knew ended all pretenses. "Who the hel are you?"

The woman was unlike any he'd ever seen before. Her skin bore two distinct colors that did nothing to diminish her regal air or beauty. White locs wrapped in a tall knot on top of her head like a crown, held together by a scrap of scarlet fabric. Her white robes left her arms bare and he could help the way the gem at her throat flickered like blood in glass. Her ice blue gaze offered another shock, especially with the sense of centuries of existence behind them.

A slow smile spread across her face. "I hope you're able to figure out who I am by now."

"High Priestess Usoa," Bao croaked.

The high priestess slightly inclined her head. "Mirra spoke often of you during her brief time here."

The corner of Bao's mouth tugged briefly before he clamped it down. "Where's Braelyn?"

"The princess? She's resting still. I think she might be out for another day or two, depending on how much she channeled."

"What did she channel?"

"The Ilieng."

"But she's human," Bao sputtered. "Only your kind can wield magic."

Usoa shook her head. "There are many kinds of magic in this world. Some that you are quite familiar with and others that remain a mystery — even to me."

"But she's human, mortal," Bao insisted. "Isn't she?"

Usoa smiled faintly and stood back. "Think you're up for a bit of a walk?"

Bao grimaced as he swung his feet onto the floor. But at least he stayed upright. "Lead the way, your holiness."

They walked in silence for a way. Bao couldn't be sure if the high priestess was trying to mess with him by making him break the silence first or if she was simply gathering her thoughts. Perhaps he'd lived amongst the crooked for a tad too long.

Usoa broke the silence first. "When the Dark One first ravaged these lands, my people tried to dispose of him ourselves. He is a creature from another world, brimming with dark and strange magics. High Priestess Thrilla and the heads of the other pillars worked tirelessly to create the relics, the tools to weaken the creature, and the orb, its prison. They gave their lives to create the most powerful magical relics ever created. It was only after they made the relics that we realized we could not use them."

"Why?"

Usoa shrugged. "That has never been clear. Perhaps it was the Ileing's way of maintaining the balance of power in the world. I think that a piece of the creators live within the relics and once they could see the threads of fate, they came to understand that in order to win, we needed to align ourselves with humans. And so the key stones were made and suitable bearers were found."

She led Bao through a half crumbled archway into a sunlit courtyard. Bao blinked against the over brightness of the sun. In the distance, he made out the sounds of clashing staffs and the steady thuds of arrows hitting straw targets. It was then that he noticed signs of fresh scorching on some of the stone pillars.

"Once the wheels of fate resume their turning, nothing can remain still," Usoa said, seeing what drew his attention. "We may not be as strong as we once were, but there is still strength enough to stand against unyielding destruction."

"But will it be enough to finish it?"

Usoa's face remained impassive and unreadable. Without answering his question, they resumed their walk. Bao's face hardened. She didn't know. She wasn't sure that their efforts would be enough to imprison the Dark One again. And why was their only option imprisonment? If the entity squatting inside Lord Julian came into this world, why couldn't they send it back?

"What are keystones and what does any of this have to do with Brae?" Bao asked, tucking his other questions away until he had the time to work them out.

"The keystones open small doorways in humans who can channel the Iliegn. Even today, we're not sure why some humans can channel the Iliegn and others can't. Maybe they have Ilmarrion blood somewhere in the lineage or maybe their will is strong enough to bend the power to their will."

Bao snorted. "The princess has a strong will. The strongest I've ever known. And you think that happened to her?"

High priestess Usoa turned her unnerving gaze on Bao. He shuddered at the weight of ages reflected in their icy sheen. "I know. I felt the ripple of the choosing and the seed's magic flared for the first time in a thousand years."

"But it could be anyone. How do you know it's her?"

Usoa pursed her lips, power rippling around her body like the charge before the lightning. "I mean no disrespect," Bao said quickly, "but there's too wide a margin for error with that line of thinking."

"And you are all knowing," she said with a ghost of a smile. "No need to dig yourself deeper, King of the Crooked. She will want to see you when she wakes." Opening a nondescript door, Usoa ushered Bao into another small room.

He moved for the bed like a moth to the flame, falling to his knees at the sight of the woman sleeping soundly, hale and unharmed. With a knowing smirk, Usao savored the pair once more, recalling a similar moment from her youth, a lifetime ago.

Yes, the fate of the world stood upon the edge of the blade, but she harbored no fear in her heart. A thousand lifetimes she'd lived. She'd seen empires rise and fall, the fall of her people. Usoa also saw the rise of forces long thought lost forever. Surely this meant that the fates would smile on their endeavors. If not, then it was as it always was meant to be, and Usoa stopped fearing death long ago. Stopped longing for it. If her time to rejoin her loved ones in the Nexi was approaching, she'd welcome it like the first rays of sunlight after a long night.

SHE WAS ALIVE. BAO TREMBLED LIKE A HORSE AS HE KNELT beside Braelyn's bed, whispering prayers to every deity and spirit he knew. Raising his head, he studied the lines and curves of her face. The gentle arch of her nose to the tiny lines of laughter and worry at the corners of her eyes. Eyes he so desperately wished would open. A cloud shifted somewhere outside, and the sun poured in through the small window, a broad beam illuminating Braelyn's hair making her look like the goddess of fate.

Bao bowed his head again and accepted the truth he'd fought so hard to ignore. His heart was hers the moment he first laid eyes on her, when she sneaked out of the castle on her own, dressed as a common woman. He took joy from watching the ways her eyes lit up whenever he sneaked up on her. The way her body would relax a little whenever they were together, as if she too, took comfort in being together.

Bitterness filled his heart. But as much as he loved her, they could never be. He was common born and a criminal. His past was too bloody, too dark to ever even dare to dream of a life with someone as kind and courageous as her. He would keep the truth of his heart locked away, if only to spare her the shame of someone like him loving her. Bao knew he couldn't have her, but he could protect her, serve her. Help Braelyn return to the peaceful like she once had. It was the only way he could ever show his love for her.

CHAPTER EIGHTEEN

"I DON'T LIKE THIS," SADRIA SAID FOR THE HUNDREDTH time in as half as many minutes.

Mirra rolled her eyes and sighed, exasperated. "There's no way any horse, no matter how finely bred, can travel through the river lands safely. The only way is by boat, and we don't have the coin to hire one of the larger barges."

Sadria opened her mouth to argue again, but her sister stopped her with a gently placed hand. "Enough sister. It pains me too, but this needed to be done."

Sadria scowled and walked to the stern of the small river boat, staring out at the murky waters. Adria shook her head at her sister's stubbornness. "She has too much stone in her spirit."

"What?" Gaitlan asked, shifting in his seat. He still bore the signs of sickness around his eyes and mouth from his most recent brush with death.

"According to our ariun khün, holy men, Sky Mother and Stone Father create each person using the winds, rains, seed, and stone. But they always use one element a bit more than the others. Because I am gentle and prefer to heal than fight, it is said that I have too much rain. My sister, with her unyielding nature, is too much stone."

Gaitlan looked at her thoughtfully. Adria blushed slightly under his steady gaze. Though what he was doing was considered extremely rude amongst her people, she didn't mind it too much. After all, Gaitlan wasn't a Horse Lord or Stone Clan. He was taniki, a stranger. It wasn't his fault he didn't have any manners.

"And what would you say I am?"

Adria thought for a moment. "I do not know you well enough to guess, but if I must, I would say you have too much wind. You change your mind often, never staying true, until now. At least that's what the lamp showed me," she added quickly when she saw the horrified surprise on his face.

"The 'lamp showed' you?" Mirra joined the pair. "What do you mean by that?"

Adria shrugged. "I can't quite explain it. When I heal someone, I get these…impressions about who they are and their life. I think it might be the lamp's way of letting me see the truth about a person, so I can decide if I still want to give up bits of my life to save them."

Gailtan's look of horror turned awkward. "Thank you."

Adria nodded her head before quickly leaving to join her sister. It had been years since she had to talk so much to someone other than her sister and she suddenly found it exhausting.

Mirra pressed her lips together to restrain her laughter at Gaitlan's distraught expression. "Don't take it personal, princeling. I don't think she's a talker."

He sputtered, crossing his arms defensively. "So how long do you think it will take to find this Shiro?"

Mirra sighed, throwing her head back, the ends of her hair scant inches from the steadily moving waters. Her hand held firm to the copper bead at the end of a small braid, a new and repeated gesture. "I don't know. It took me forever to find him again after we first met, but if I remember correctly, he said that he felt "compelled" to come to my village. Maybe heaven, fate, or whatever drives the flute will compel him to meet us."

"That's it," Gaitlan said through clenched teeth. "We're just going to wander around Zallino and hope that we stumble onto each other?"

"Do you have a better idea?" Mirra snapped. "It's been ten years since I last saw him and the only thing I remember is that he had a long scar on one of his eyes."

Gaitlan snorted, throwing his hands up. "Such an easily recognizable face."

Mirra fought the urge to throw the prince into the river. "What's your idea, oh great and wise prince of nothing?"

Having nothing, Gaitlan frowned, crossing his arms and remained silent. Mirra muttered under her breath and moved to sit on the other side of the riverboat. From the sale of their horses and what gear they couldn't fit into their packs, they purchased passage into the heart of the river lands.

They kept to the major rivers with enough space between its banks that it would take a hundred of their current boat laid out bow to stern to bridge the space. Sometimes they shared river space with large swaths of floating farms, carefully tended by peasants dressed in knee length britches and sleeveless tunics.

The aroma of spicy food scented the air, drawing her attention to the high walled estate on the far right bank. Probably the home of some warlord, nobleman, or merchant, its high stone walls protected the estate from the sometimes sudden rise of the river water because of storms or seasonal changes. The peasants that made their living working in the estates, fishing or tending the floating farms, made do with their homes and villages built on top of long stilts and prayed that they were high enough.

Mirra's stomach rumbled, and she hoped they would reach an inn or tavern soon. She didn't think she could stomach another meal of salted fish and rice. The estate disappeared behind them, keeping the mouth-watering aroma to itself. But as they continued on the river, Mirra noted a rise in other walled estates and stilted houses. The traffic along the river grew, and the banks drew closer until it became a narrow strip just large enough for two boats to pass abreast.

The river didn't widen again until it formed a confluence of three other equally narrow streams. Together they formed a new wide river almost the size of a small lake before splitting off again, creating small islands for small clusters of ash gray stilted homes or walled estates. In the center of the newly conjoined rivers was a large establishment sitting on thick stilts. Half a dozen boats, varying from small round skimmers to travel barges, docked around it. Pale yellow lanterns hung from every place, turning the establishment into a beacon in the growing nightfall.

Mirra nearly sagged with relief when their boat turned gently towards the glowing building. Sadria paid the boatman the rest of their fare the moment they saddled up to a vacant doc. The man took their coin with a bow and headed right up to the upper levels of the establishment.

"What is this place?" Adria asked, taking a red scarf and wrapping it around her head. At her sister's and Mirra's urging, she'd taken to hiding her face whenever they were in crowded areas. Her remaining unseen to Julian and the demon inside him was one of their only advantages.

"Hall of the Silver Crane", Mirra read, earning curious glances from her comrades. "I had an excellent education," she said, shouldering her pack and heading for the first set of stairs she found. The rest fell in line with Adria, sandwiched between Gaitlan and Sadira.

At the first landing, a middle-aged woman wearing a gray wrap overcoat over a darker gray underdress met them. Her hair pulled back into a complex bun with a silver hair stick. Most of her hair was still dark and luminous as freshly made ink, with only the beginnings of silver gray threading through around her temples. She smiled and bowed from behind her podium.

"Welcome travelers. How can we serve you tonight?" Her common was decent with only a few distinctly Zallino sounding vowels.

"Hot meals, baths, and a room for four," Mirra replied. She didn't answer the woman in Zallino. While the rest of the world viewed Zallino as one, collective people, Mirra knew the people didn't. The various regions of the kingdom had long and bloody histories that twisted and tainted allegiances. It made trading difficult, but as long as both parties will set aside differences for a moment, it could be done. Mirra didn't want to welcome any more trouble if she could avoid it.

The woman nodded and called for a young girl that looked so much like Katsumi that Mirra was forced to take a second look. A few patrons looked up as they passed, but pivoted their attention back to their tables. The girl led them up a set of stairs with bamboo railings to the upper floor. It wasn't as noisy there as it was on the ground floor. They walked past room after room of people seated around low tables. Women with pale painted faces and wrap dresses haphazardly tied laughed too brightly as they poured rice wine. They made a game of showing slivers of their skin to the flushed faced men who drank in the sight of a shoulder or the delicate skin of the inner thigh like men dying of thirst.

One woman looked up as they passed and locked eyes with Mirra. For the briefest moment, barely the span of a heartbeat, the woman's mask fell. The light drained from her eyes as she watched Mirra, Sadria, and Adria walk by unfettered with just as much hunger as the men that lusted after her body. Mirra quickly looked away. That could have been her if she hadn't been fast enough, or smart enough, to find a different way to survive.

They went up another set of stairs, and the sound grew dim, almost unnaturally. Tentatively, Mirra stretched out her senses and, sure enough, Ilmarrion magic flowed through the walls. It wasn't much, and the flow had broken in some places. The spell was dying. It made her think of Oya.

She would have known exactly what spell and runes were used to create the barrier against the noise of the lower floors, probably. A ghost of a smile tugged at the corners of her mouth, filling her with an emotion she'd never felt before—longing. She sighed, her hand going for the bead.

"Did your lover give you that?"

Mirra jolted, not hearing Adria's approach. She silently cursed herself for letting her lovesickness get in the way. "Yes."

"Could he not come with you?"

A low laugh. "No, she couldn't. An opportunity rose that only comes once in a lifetime. If she didn't take it then, it would never come again. We both agreed that there was too much at stake for either of us to not take the paths ahead."

Adria's slow blink was the only outward sign that she'd noticed that Mirra spoke of a woman instead of a man. After a long pause, Adria spoke again. "I hope she finds her way back to you, or you to her. To find the other part of your heart is a blessing from the gods. One of the few they gave us."

The tension Mirra didn't know she held eased from her shoulders. "That it is."

"Here is your room," the girl said, stopping shortly. From her pocket she pulled a strange looking key, a long strip of pewter with two prongs of different lengths. "The baths are on the ground floor on the northern side. Only three to a tub." With a bow, she handed the key to Gaitlan and quickly returned to her post, to wait for the next guest.

"Shall we?" Gaitlan said, awkwardly sliding the key into his pocket.

The room was small and sparsely furnished, with only a low table in the center, but it was clean. They walked into the room, dropping their gear near the door. Gaitlan quickly slid the wooden bolt into place and slowly turned to the others.

"Where are we supposed to sleep?" he asked.

Sadria rolled her eyes and pointed to the shelving built into the wall on the other side of the door. Thick, rolled up pallets took up most of the lower shelves with the remaining bearing thin sheets for the warmer months and thick quilted covers for winter.

"All I want is a bath and a hot meal," Adria said, clapping her hands. She dug into her pack for a clean set of clothes, ensuring that the blood lamp was secure in the secret pouch Mirra had Adria make.

Mirra smirked and rummaged through her pack. "Excellent idea. Care to join us, Sadria?"

Sadria shrugged. "As long as he stays and orders the food."

"Why do I have to stay?"

"Three to a bath," Mirra said with a teasing grin, pointing out that they outnumbered him three to one. "And someone needs to order the food and monitor our stuff. I wouldn't trust the locks."

Stunned into silence, Mirra waved to Gaitlan as she followed the sisters out for a nice hot relaxing bath. The sound of the door closing behind them drew Gaitlan from his stunned silence. Gaitlan muttered softly under his breath with little animosity before quickly slipping out to order the most nourishing meal the inn had available.

All three sighed as they submerged their bodies into the faintly perfumed steaming water. Adria slid down as far as she could, keeping her knees close to her chest. Sadria threw her head back, her arms clinging to the outer rim where her muscles and scars sent a silent warning to anyone who'd dare to think them an easy foe. Not that any of the other women gave them as much as a passing glance.

Mirra rolled her neck, working a stiff muscle. A million thoughts tore through her mind like leaves in a storm. She groaned and sunk in further until only her eyes and the top of her head remained above the water.

"Ease your burden?" Adria loosened her death grip on her legs and leaned forward.

Mirra shot up, plastering a simple expression. "Don't bother," Sadria cut in. "That one can lie to the gods."

"That's not nice, sister. We weren't exactly open with her either at first." Adria turned and smiled at Mirra. Mirra thought Adria's smile was like the warm light made by a lone candle in the night. "We are here if you wish to speak." She turned and began talking to her sister in their birth language.

Mirra caught a word here and there, but her mind wasn't on the two sisters. Instead, she was thinking about the last shared bath she had. Moakwyd felt like a thousand years in the past. She tried to pretend that Gaitlan's and Sadria's concerns didn't echo her own. Once more she wondered what force led her to believe that she was in any way of stepping into the role of questing hero. She was a thief trained in the arts of the spy and poisons. She quickly washed before her anxieties and doubt stole what remained of her hunger.

Throwing her clothes on, she muttered something about being tired to the sisters before walking back into the chaos of the ground floor. The crowd was more boisterous than earlier, stirred up by the motley group of musicians standing on a table in the center of the room. Mirra barely noted their appearance and tune as she trudged up the stair. That is until she heard the flute.

All other sounds faded away until only the light, crystal clear notes filled her ears. She couldn't place the tune, but that wasn't what mattered. The more the song filled her consciousness, the more it tugged at her, demanding she turn around and face the will of the gods. With her heart leaping into her throat, Mirra slowly turned around.

The musician playing the flute was a middle-aged Zallino man, his graying hair half pulled back from his weathered face. A long scar ran down the left side of his face, right over his eye. If she hadn't been so enthralled by the song, she would have laughed. They had stumbled upon Shiro, the wielder of Heaven's Song.

OYA JUMPED WHEN THE ACOLYTE SET DOWN A TRAY. "My apologies Master Oya."

"No, it's fine," she said, rubbing her eyes against the burn of exhaustion. "Thank you."

The acolyte bowed and left her in the lone spark of light in the bowels of the archives below the citadel. Three weeks. She'd been lost in the scattered remains of her people's history for three weeks and she was no closer to finding the working to fix the orb. With each passing day, her despair grew until it drove her to forsake the sun and dwell within the realm of darkness.

Dramatic much? Are you sure you're not an actor instead of a priestess? Mirra's presence saddled into the seat next to Oya with that endearingly infuriating smirk on her face. "When the moment calls for it." *Any luck?*

Oya groaned, putting her face into her hands. "No. Not a gods damned thing. Even here, I can only find bits and pieces."

Mirra's visage leaned forward on her elbows, her mischievous eyes scant inches from Oya's. She flicked her tongue out, running along her bottom lip, drawing Oya's gaze. *If there's anyone who can piece together a puzzle, it's you.*

"What?"

The specter of Mirra laughed, leaning forward a bit more. *Yes, taking the bits and putting it together. I think you can manage that.*

A deep crease formed between Oya's dark brows as she pondered Mirra's words. What pieces? What puzzle? She looked at the sea of notes in front of her. Bits of legends only partially translated. Faded symbols whose meaning she'd still couldn't quite figure out, plus everything Usoa told her before she left. Nothing was a clear picture of what she needed to do. It was infuriating. This must have been how Mirra felt before coming to Moakwyd. What she learned, she'd gleaned from half-baked ideas and instinct alone.

Mirra smiled, knowing Oya's line of thought. *That's my girl,* she said before reaching out to gently stroke Oya's face.

Sitting up with a start, Oya pressed her hand to the side of her face, where she felt the fading warmth of Mirra's touch. The light from the lantern had burned down low, nearly extinguished, and the food still sitting on the tray had gone cold. Oya rubbed the sleep from her eyes, wondering when she'd fallen asleep. In the waking world, she looked at the mass of paper, her confidence crumbling once more.

"Still stuck?" Nen casually pushed aside the uneaten food, his nose wrinkling. He picked up a random scrap of paper, turning it this way and that to discern its meaning. "Perhaps this will help."

He handed Oya a scroll of linen. She cleared off a space on the table and together they gently revealed its secrets.

They both cringed slightly when the sound of creaking and crackling filled their ears. They held their breaths until they secured the ends with heavy books and the various empty cups sprinkled around the table. In the fading light of the lantern, Oya peered at the scroll and tears welled in her eyes.

It was a painting, most likely painted sometime during the Nexian Empire. Even though it was centuries old, perhaps even older than Usoa, whose paint looked as vibrant as the day it was painted.

In the center, a woman with long white hair stood, a bright white circle hovering between her hands. "High Priestess Thrilla," Oya breathed, her fingers hovering just above the image.

"The one who made the prison orb?"

Oya nodded. "She gave her life to imprison that demon the first time. As did the others." Her hand drifted over to the images of each master that gave their life to make the relics.

"What about her?" Nen pointed to a dark woman standing in the shadows. Oya leaned over, peering in the fading light.

"I'm not sure. There's only four relics and the orb. I don't know of a sixth thing."

"Aren't the relics forged from the four pillars of affinity?" Oya nodded. "But aren't there actually five?"

For the second time, the thrum of discovery ran through her like an icy river. A question asked for thousands of years slowly rose from the recesses of her mind, and the terrible answer that the painting suggested sent shivers down her spine.

"That's not important right now," she said, leaning back from the painting. "I still don't understand what they did to make the relics. Without that, I can't hope to piece together anything to put the orb back together again."

Nen rubbed his chin. "Would seeing the temple where the relics were originally kept help?"

Oya perked up for the first time. " Absolutely."

The rope ladder swung precariously through the open air. Oya clung to each rung with a white knuckled grip and her eyes shut tight against the vast open air around her.

"The stairs were destroyed ages ago," Nen called out from somewhere below her. "The Abbot is trying to find where the original steps were so we can hopefully excavate them instead of having to carve a new set into the stone."

Oya could only make a noise to let Master Nen know she heard him. A soft chuckle echoed around her. Gritting her teeth, she continued her descent. Reaching the last rung, she clung to the ladder, shaking with equal parts exhalation and apprehension. What if the temple of the relics wasn't what she hoped it to be? She dug enough through ruins to know the bitter pains of disappointment. Swallowing back her fears, Oya stepped off the last rung. The moment her foot touched the mosaic floor, she ceased to exist.

Her body evaporated like the morning dew that clung to the blades of grass in the early hours of dawn. Her mind tumbled about, unable to cling to a single thought, emotion, or fragment of consciousness. If she screamed, she couldn't be sure. She might have cried and sung the songs of her ancestors reserved for only the holiest of occasions.

Millions of images flashed before her. Fragments moving too fast for her to make out. Oya caught glimpses of her time in Moakwyd, her mother's smiling face. She saw old friends and old enemies. She saw things that happened centuries before her birth and centuries after her death. Just when Oya thought she would lose herself to the trappings of eternity, two figures solidified in the chaos dancing around her in a beautifully, horrific dance.

Oya recognized one of them in an instant. Though she was younger than the Mirra she knew, barely out of childhood, there was no mistaking her raven hair, or the hint of mischief tucked into the corners of her mouth. The other was a young Ilmarrion priestess wearing a robe cut in an ancient style. If it wasn't for the paler patches of color standing out against the darkness of her skin like the inner bark of the tree, she wouldn't have known Usoa's face.

The women reached out for Oya, bringing her back into a being of flesh and bone. She sighed as her soul resettled and the chaotic world of time faded away, revealing a dimly lit cavern.

"What the hel was that?" Master Nen's face was pale with a faint sheen that had nothing to do with the climb down.

Oya sat down hard, staring up at the empty pedestal that once held the orb. "I don't know…"

"Perhaps we should head back?"

Oya shook her head. "No, I've read that in the past, we built our temples in places where the pull of the Ileing was strongest. It's likely that they built this temple in such a place."

Master Nen knelt down next to her, placing a hand to her sweat drenched forehead. "Mirra didn't act like this when she found this place."

Oya let out a weak laugh. "Mirra isn't a priestess. She hasn't learned to open herself up to the Ileing. She can barely tap into her full potential." Closing her eyes, Oya settled into a meditative state, humming softly under her breath. Long minutes passed before she felt centered enough to risk exploring the ancient temple once more.

Master Nen sat cross-legged in front of her when she opened her eyes, scribbling into a small leather-bound notebook. He quickly set it aside when he saw she was awake. "Ready to look around?"

Oya nodded and stiffly moved to her feet. She brushed the dust off the back of her tunic and walked over to the mural bearing a necklace she was quite familiar with. The woman in the mural looked down at her with a gentle smile tinged with sadness. As if the woman knew the turmoil rolling through Oya.

"It's a wonder that they're still as bright as they are," Master Nen said, breaking Oya out of her revelry.

Her hand had unconsciously risen, reaching out for the woman. A shudder ran down her spine. Her head throbbed from her initial contact with the power that flowed freely throughout the space. She didn't think she'd be able to come back from a second trip. Bits and pieces still flashed across her inner eye, occasionally tipping her sense of reality.

The pressure in her head grew until her stomach rolled in rebellion. Her vision swam and for the third time, Oya received a shocking revelation. Translucent symbols, runes and sigils shimmered over every inch of the cavern like frost. Oya could recognize a few of the symbols, but most were a mystery to her. One symbol blazed as bright as a star on each of the images of the relics. It consumed her waking vision, searing into her very essence, into the secrets and histories written in her blood.

Oya fell to her knees, touching her forehead to the mosaic floor. Behind her, Master Nen shifted awkwardly behind her, but remained silent. When Oya rose, she felt lighter than she had in days. That symbol was key, the cornerstone from which she could piece together a working that would repair the demon's cage. And then they would send it back to wherever it came from.

THEIR EYES MET, AND THEY BOTH FELT AS THOUGH THEY were suspended in time. Through the smoke from pipes and open fires, they became twin statues, until Mirra shifted forward, drawn by the flute's song. Like the deer that senses a hunter, Shiro bolted, shoving aside the other players without a care. Mirra tore off after him half of a breath later, leaping from table to table. Cries of alarm and outrage range out behind her, along with the sound of breaking dishes.

Shiro barreled down a set of stairs, taking two or three at a time. He reached the next landing at the same time Mirra barreled out the door, right for the railing. She vaulted right over, landing on the next landing with a heavy thud before tearing off after Shiro again.

Patrons of the inn leaped out of their way, shouting curses in their wake. Mirra had a few curses of her own. No matter how hard she ran, or the short cuts she took, Shiro remained a frustrating distance ahead of her.

Mirra cursed and dove into the nearest shadow. For the first time, she was fully conscious of the world between shadows. It was completely void of any sensation. Though she knew she was still running. She felt a tug on her left, pivoted and nosedived into the world of light.

She and Shiro toppled over another railing. Her stomach dropped with the sudden sense of weightlessness. Shiro fought the entire way down, clawing at her iron grip until the dark water below swallowed them whole. The shock was enough to halt Shiro's desperate attempts at freedom. Mirra latched on tighter and rolled.

They fell again, grunting when they met the hardwood flooring of their room. Shiro elbowed her in the sternum, knocking the wind out of her. They broke free, each scrambling back to opposite corners of the room.

"What kind of demon are you?" From behind a curtain of wet hair, Shiro's wide eyes stared back at Mirra.

"I'm no devil," she said with a huff.

"That's still up for debate," Gaitlan said once he recovered from their miraculous arrival.

Mirra rolled her eyes at him before turning her focus back on Shiro. "You may not remember me, but you once gave me some good advice about choosing to live for myself."

The fear receded from Shiro's eyes. He pushed back his long hair, grayer now than when they first met all those years ago. Mirra brushed her hair back from her face before untying the bit of leather she used to cover up the serpent tattoo around her wrist.

Shiro's eyes locked onto the tattoo, a bit of fear resurfacing before the hazy of memory cleared. "You're the little girl that wouldn't stop hunting me."

Mirra flashed him a toothy grin. "All grown up and free."

His eyes narrowed. "How? Julian isn't the sort to let something go."

"He didn't get a say. I have a few more tricks up my sleeve than before." She called up her power, letting it shine through her eyes and tugged the shadows unnaturally closer to them. Shiro flinched away from the shadows and she let them go.

"Look, I don't have a lot of time, so listen closely. Usoa sent me to find you. I'm Ilmarrion too. I know what's been living in Julian and I know how to get rid of it. And that's why I need you."

Shiro blanched. "No."

"You don't have the luxury to say no." Gaitlan crossed his arms. "That thing has killed hundreds, if not thousands, of people. You set it loose on this world, you have an obligation to put it away again."

Shiro shook his head. "There's no way. The orb, its prison, shattered. The spells to make it, or at least mend it, have been lost for thousands of years."

Mirra waved off his objection. "Already got someone working on that."

"You still have to find the other relics and wielder," Shiro said, like a petulant child.

This time it was Gaitlan who flashed a feral smile. "We have most of that under control too." A knock came from the door. His smile took on a harder edge. "Mirra, if you please."

She eyed the prince, his shifting behavior setting off alarm bells in her mind. Not taking her eyes off of Gaitlan, she opened the door and stepped aside. Sadria and Adria slowly entered the room, Sadria quietly moving her sister behind her.

"Who's this?"

"No one," Shiro growled. "You have the wrong person."

"You belong to the Song of Heaven," Adria said firmly, stepping out from behind her sister. "You are bound to it the way I am bound to this." From the pouch at her side, Adria withdrew the Blood Lamp. Shiro's eyes rested on it for a long time. His face went as calm as a lake on a calm day, but that didn't keep Mirra from tasting the rising emotions in the air.

"We only have one more relic and two more wielders to find."

"Just one," Shiro said, his shoulders slumping. "The Phoenix Wing. Your sister is the wielder of the Seed."

"I'm sorry what?"

"Your sister, she bleed on a keystone and became the welder for the Seed. I guess because the others already have...."

Shiro's words were abruptly halted as Gaitlan pushed him into the wall. Gaitlan's face held nothing but murderous intent, his lips pulled back into a snarl. "You leave my sister out of this, you spineless bastard. If you had any honor or balls, you'd have handled this when you first fucked everything up. Instead, you ran away like a god's damned coward, leaving it to us to fix." After his initial shock dissipated, Shiro's expression was nothing more than acceptance.

His head hung low, a strange sight to see on such an older man. Mirra moved to pull the prince off of Shiro before he did something he'd regret when Sadria's snort cut through the tension in the room like a knife. "If you were so worried about your lost honor, you'd perform sekat'su. Instead, here you stand."

"It won't let me," Shiro said, his voice cracking beneath decades of guilt and pain. "I've tried so many times, but this thing, this unholy cursed thing, won't let me!" The last words he shouted, rage replacing emptiness.

"The Song isn't cursed," Adria said, her voice calm and low, the same voice she used whilst healing. "True, it can be a burden to those chosen, even I struggle with my responsibilities. But where you struggle and fight against them, I accept them and the gifts that come along with it."

Shiro sagged against Gaitlan's hold. "I am a slave to its will."

"So, are we all to fate's design?" Adria walked closer, calming, throwing her sister's worried hand off. "No mortal can fight fate, but only you can pull back the veil and see a bit of the dance. You can help shape fate, the small pebble that causes a mighty rockslide. The first drop of rain that ends the long drought. Surrender and be more than what you are."

Tears streamed down Shiro's face as his legs gave out. With a gentle hand, Adria pulled Gaitlan back, letting Shiro fall to the floor. She pulled Gaitlan back several paces before urging him to sit. She knelt beside him, placing her hands in his.

Mirra took a seat next to Shiro. "So…um…how do you know Braelyn is the Seed's wielder?"

"I saw it in a dream," he said.

"A dream?" Gaitlan's rage was barely contained.

"It wasn't a normal one. I know the difference. She's out of the capital and in Moakwyd with Usoa. And a few friends of yours, I think," he said after a pause.

"We can worry about that later," Mirra said, tampering down the rise of questions that threatened to bubble over. "For now, as you can see, we nearly have everything we need to lock that demon up again."

Shiro shook his head. "There's one more thing."

"What now," Gaitlan demanded. "The High Priestess said that we only need to find the relics."

Shiro laughed bitterly. "Even as old as she is, Usoa doesn't know everything."

"What are we missing?", Sadria demanded.

"The binding."

Mirra and Gaitlan shared a worried glance. This was the first either had heard of it. "What is it?"

Shiro looked up at them sharply. "How were you planning on imprisoning the dark one again?"

"I thought we just had to put him in the middle of the relics, charge them up and they'd do their thing," Mirra said, feeling foolish for the first time in a long while. Now that she said it out loud, she'd realized how fool hearted and naïve she sounded.

"Only half right," Shiro said. His words partially soothed her embarrassment. "Before…everything, I was a self proclaimed expert in Mystic mythology. The same for Julian. The real Julian. How else did you think we found the reliquary in the first place?"

A heavy silence fell. "We can worry about that once we find the last wielder and relic," Sadria said, clapping her hands together. "So, old man, are you going to fulfill your obligations or should spill your guts here and now? I'm sure we can find another wielder for the flute."

Shiro blinked up at Sadira. "Has anyone told you that you are unlikable?"

She laughed and smirked. "Since the day I was born, clutching a bit of my mother's womb."

Shaking his head, Shiro sat up straighter, crossing his legs. He held the silver flute in his lap, his fingers sliding along the faint engravings. "Initially, after the accident, I gave the last of the relics to my sister. I couldn't go home, but I wanted her to know that I was sorry. Sorry for bringing shame to our family and for the suffering yet to come. I vowed to never see her again, but fate had other plans. When we crossed paths about eight years ago, she told me that the relic had vanished."

"Was it stolen?"

"I don't think so. The Wing differs from the others. According to mythos, the Wing lives within its wielder from the moment of birth. To only separate upon death. From there, it can either appear in another wielder or present itself as a golden feather."

"Why," Mirra asked. "I never came across anything about the relics. Neither did Oya."

"After his possession, Julian destroyed as much as he could about relics and the demon that lives inside him. Very little remains. But the Wing is closely related to the Song as in it shows you the path you need to take. All you have to do is know where you want to go and the Wing will show you the way. The Song doesn't give you a choice."

"I love a good two-fer," Mirra said, rubbing her hands together. "No time like the present."

"No, there's not," Shiro said. He held the flute, muttering softly under his breath before bringing it to his lips. The tune he played was filled with a sense of searching, yearning. It drudged up feelings of homesickness and longing. When Shiro opened his eyes, they were filled with a soft white light. He played faster and faster, one tune tumbling into another, changing moods as rapidly as the weather in spring.

Mirra felt a familiar tug, the tides of fate, and surrendered to its will. She may not believe in much, but even a godless thief bows in the presence of fate.

CHAPTER NINETEEN

The dead surrounded her. They clawed at her clothing, her hair, starved for the spark of life she carried. It blazed with all the ferocity of a small sun in the middle of her chest. Nothing she did dampened the light. Oya could only flee, tears leaving trails of golden light down her face.

A long clawed hand wrapped around her ankle, causing her to fall face first into the jagged stones. Dry, sandy earth filled her mouth. She rolled onto her back, kicking with the other foot. She screamed, a mixture of survival and revulsion at the sight of the half rotted face, its mouth opened in a silent scream.

Again and again she kicked, gore staining her white robes black. She didn't care that the sharp stones cut her flesh or tore her clothing. All that mattered was escape. She didn't belong here. Nothing belonged here.

A horde of half rotting bodies closed in all around her, biting and clawing, drinking in her life force.

"No! No! No! Get off me! Let me go!" Oya released a great cry and the small sun on her chest blazed to new light. The dead flinched back, shielding their nonexistent eyes while their bloated flesh smoked. Scrambling to her feet, Oya ran.

She ran as fast as her legs could carry her.

She ran until her lungs burned with a wet fire.

She ran until nothing else existed but the sound of her haggard breathing and the pounding of her feet.

In the distance, a lone figure stood alone with a powerful aura of life around him. Weeping with relief, Oya ran for the man, latching onto him like a lifeline. He turned around, a mild look of surprise on his face. Her blood ran cold as she stared into one eye so like her own and the other, darker than the deepest pits of the Danyuwi, the realm of lost souls.

"Now, what do we have here?" Lord Julian asked, an oily smile spreading across his handsome face. The smile stretched to an impossible size with black ooze pouring out from the split skin.

Oya sat up and clamped her mouth shut. Her night shift and sheets were completely soaked through. Her mouth was full of the bitter tang of panic. She looked around her, taking deep breaths. She cataloged the items in the room until her heart ceased trying to burst free. Her calm only lasted one long breath before a fresh wave of horror; he knew who she was, and he was coming.

"Are you sure you can't wait until you return?" Abbot Joseph asked for the tenth time since Oya burst into his private chambers, frantic and demanding a litany of Ilmarrion artifacts.

"No," she said firmly. "Visiting the temple yesterday opened doors I can't even begin to comprehend. The Dark One knows I'm here and possibly why. I cannot wait another moment."

"But you don't have the strength to do this alone."

Oya paused in her work, a frantic hodgepodging of runes to reforge the orb. "That's why I need those artifacts. I can pull threads from the other pillars and use them similarly to the original making."

"And that cost the life of the priestess that made it. I don't think Mirra would want you to throw your life away so carelessly."

Oya closed her eyes, her lips pressing into a thin line. "If it goes well, then I'll be fine."

"And if it doesn't?"

Oya finished the last symbol with a steady stroke. "From the moment I was born, my life was in danger. I could have lost my life to a tribe that thought my eyes and abilities meant I was a demon. I could have died in the City of Water or when I broke my slave collar and fled to Moakwyd. I could have died a hundred times in a hundred different ways. I have lost nearly everything and everyone I hold dear. My people are hunted or are scattered the farthest reaches of the world, ignorant of who they really are."

She folded the parchment and slipped it into her pocket. She slung the satchel that held the fragments of the orb and the artifact Abbot Joseph handed over without a single word of protest over her shoulder. "I am not afraid to die. I will find peace in Sohala and wait for the time when Mirra returns to me."

Abbot Joseph studied her face. "Whatever else you need, simply ask and it shall be yours, Priestess Oya Ironheart of Moakwyd. With your permission, we will record your findings and workings in the annals for those who will come after this."

Straightening her spine, Oya inclined her head. "Thank you."

Abbot Joseph walked with Oya in silence until they reached the forgotten temple. Dawn had yet to fully break, but the dark spaces of sea and sky had already separated. In the gray light, Abbot Joseph took Oya's hands in his and prayed. Though she didn't understand the meaning of his words, she understood their intent. She closed her eyes and offered prayers of her own to the Ileign and to the gods of her childhood.

At the first fisher king's cry, Oya and Abbot Joseph broke apart. "I will be here until the end, whatever it may be."

Oya nodded, her words having run dry. This time, she descended without an ounce of fear. When her foot touched the floor of the temple, she let the power spiral through her, filling her veins with sparkling light; feeling without losing herself to it.

She placed the pieces of the orb in the center of the floor, right where it stood for time beyond memory, until a pair of overly enthusiastic scholars discovered the secret. Next, she laid an artifact onto each corresponding tile on the floor. For Duä, a small Nealtian glass jar holding a thimble full of an oil, the last in existence. Next it was Fasht, with a gold coin inscribed with a rune for growth. In the Su'la spot, she placed another charm meant to protect one's mind from intrusion.

Oya stood before the marking of Haror, her affinity, and cut one of her braids. She gripped it in her hand, her finger rolling the bits of obsidian interwoven between the strands, the fragments of the collar that bound her to the Nealitan queen. It was risky to use something so personal. It would provide a direct line between her and the working. She didn't have to, she still had one more artifact in the bag.

With a long breath, she gently placed her shorn braid down and went back to stand in front of the broken orb. She took one last fortifying breath and then spoke. At first she stumbled over them, but soon the power of the ancient language took over and flowed from her mouth. Her eyes blazed like twin suns, casting stark shadows around the temple space. Lines of power spiraled along her body like shooting stars to pool around her fingers. With glowing fingers she drew one rune after another, layering the working. Something gripped her core with an iron grip and she lost control. Words and runes poured out of her like water. It felt alarmingly similar to when she first stepped foot into the temple. Oya gritted her teeth, clinging to her purpose.

The torrent of magic slowed until she had control again. The once dark cavern shimmered with the light of runes and sigils pulsating to the rhythm of Oya's heart. When she drew a breath, the glow grew brighter. On the exhale, it dimmed. She stayed like this, slowly and deeply breathing, marveling at her connection to the surrounding magic. When the room swayed, she turned her focus onto the broken pieces on the floor. The working was quickly wearing her out and if she didn't hurry, she'd lose it all.

She closed her eyes to avoid blindness as power pooled in her palms, blazing. Pain laced through her, making each word a fight to get out. With the final chant, the runes and sigils that hung in the open air pelted Oya like fallen stars. She didn't hold back her cries of pain. Instead, she used her pain as a focus, a tether to the corporeal world. Her knees gave out first, sending her crashing to the ground. Oya let herself fall, her hands landing in the open spaces between the fragments of the orb.

Arcs like lightning sprang from her and struck the pieces. At first they remained as they were, dull and empty, but as more arcs of energy flowed into them, they changed. The pieces moved, rocking and sliding as if they yearned to be whole. The dark gray transformed into white swirling clouds threaded with golden streams of light.

Oya gathered all the pieces together, tears streaming down her face. As she began the last of the working, she felt a sudden warmth running down the middle of her face. Bright red drops of blood fell onto the fragments, sending the building energy into a frenzy. Hastily wiping away the blood, Oya pressed on, shouting the last of the words as she shoved the pieces together. They fought her like the opposite ends of a magnet until the last vestiges of power flowed from her to the broken orb.

A flash of light, accompanied by a wave of force, sent Oya careening to the opposite wall, knocking the air from her lungs. She slumped to the floor, not knowing if she succeeded or failed. Oya lingered in a world of darkness. Yet, unlike the other world where she finally came face to face with the demon, this world gave her a sense of peace. She floated without a body, simply existing. She breathed in air that wasn't there, expanding lungs she didn't have, and smiled.

A new presence filled her senses, one that was both male and female, and carrying the air of centuries beyond measure. The presence nudged Oya's consciousness downward, and she got the sense that it was sending her back to the realm of the living. She didn't mind. It wasn't her time yet.

Her body was rocking gently, covered with a thick, warm quilt. It took more effort than she'd like to admit opening her eyes. In the semidarkness, she saw the heavy wooden beams and planks. Turning her head, she saw she rested on a small cot in a tiny room. Through the open window, the scent of the sea drifted in. Oya pushed herself into a seated position and, as she did, she spied her satchel tucked in beside her. When she opened the flap, she smiled. Nestled within a swath of fabric sat the Orb of Thrilla as whole as the day it was made.

CHAPTER TWENTY

XHU'ROZO WAS NOT ONLY A BUSTLING PORT, IT WAS ALSO the capital city of Zallino. On the eastern bank, behind high walls, stood the Azule Castle, the home of the Emperor and his court. The compound was nearly large enough to be its own city, with everything it needed from merchants to doctors housed alongside the rest of the court. Mirra briefly wondered how easily she could slip past the imperial guard and refill their dangerously depleted purses. She mulled over the thought for a moment longer, a half-baked plan already crystalizing in her mind.

"Don't even think about it." Gaitlan nudged her shoulder.

"I don't know what you're talking about," she replied, crossing her arms, the plan already gone like ash on the wind.

Gaitlan made a noise like he didn't believe her and re-shouldered his bag. "Shiro's found us a place to stay."

Falling in a half a step behind the prince, Mirra continued her survey of the city. The bustling crowds and merchants shouting their wares in a half a dozen different languages was reminiscent of Undros, but that was where the similarities ended.

Instead of sleek carriages pulled by horses, narrow seats perched precariously on two wheels pulled by lean young men wove easily through the foot traffic. The wealthy wore brightly colored silks or chiffons while the poorer citizens made do with simple cotton dyed with earthy colors. Men and women alike wore their hair long amongst the upper classes, with the only actual difference being the style and types of adornments.

Mirra inhaled deeply, filling her lungs with the scents of lotus, fresh seafood, and spice. Her stomach growled, demanding she fill it with these exotic new flavors. But that would have to wait. Already she felt curious and slightly hostile stares. Not that the citizens of Xhu'Rozo weren't accustomed to seeing foreigners, but she highly doubted they'd ever seen a group like hers. Two Horse Lord women, and two Undrosens with Shiro, who stood out amongst his own people. Mirra couldn't be sure if it was because of the aura of the Song or because he tried, and failed, to make himself small, shame written along every line of his body.

Shiro led them down a set of narrow alleys coming to a small shop with unknown herbs hanging in the window. He led them through without an explanation. Gaitlan slapped his hand over his face the moment the pungent odor of the herbs hit him. Mirra yanked his arm down while Adria and Sadria flashed him a warning glare. Crimson blossoming on his cheeks, Gaitan quietly apologized and schooled his face into polite disinterest.

The wizened man behind the counter either didn't notice or chose not to react, greeting Shiro in his native language. Shiro responded in kind, his hand going up to rub the back of his neck. The man laughed and waved off whatever distress Shiro voiced. The old man's gaze shifted, appraising their group over Shiro's shoulder.

"I don't have much, but you are welcome to hit." The old man's voice was calm and reassuring as he addressed them in thickly accented common.

Adria bowed first. "We are grateful for your hospitality, grandfather. Please let us know in whatever way we can be of use."

The old man's face split into a wide smile. "I like this one, Shiro. A bit too young to be your bride, but I've seen such matches work before."

This time it was Shiro's turn to flush red. "Enough of that Yu Jie. We're only here to rest while we find the Wing."

Yu Jei cackled and hobbled out from around the counter. He poked Shiro with his bamboo cane as he passed. "How many times must I urge you to find humor, boy? Haven't I told you that finding joy in this life is the key to living it well?"

Shiro rolled his eyes. "A million and one times, uncle."

"And still you cannot heed my words." Yu Jei laughed more and motioned for Adria to come closer. "Let's have a look at you, hm?"

Adria stood straighter, lowering her eyes. Yu Jei patted her with his cane. "Eyes up, girl. Those blessed as you are should never lower your eyes to anyone less than yourself." Adria straightened and held her head high with a light smile on her lips. Whatever he saw, Yu Jie approved and grunted before moving onto her sister.

"A fighter here, make no mistake about that." He tapped her arms with his cane. "So like the durian fruit — hard exterior but sweet interior."

Next he turned to Gaitlan. Yu Jie said nothing, but his face conveyed sorrow and pity. Gaitlan swallowed against the sudden tightness in this throat. "I hear it gets easier."

"If at all," Yu Jie said before turning his attention to Mirra.

Surprise and confusion rippled across his face. "Did not think I'd see one of your kind beyond paintings."

"I get that a lot," Mirra said with a smirk. "I'm the stuff of legends."

Yu Jie frowned, his eyes seeing more than the corporeal world around him. "Not quite. The potential is there, as it is for many wrapped up in this ancient dance of preservation and destruction. But as to your role, it has yet to be made clear. There are many hard choices ahead of you, my dear." He took her hands in his and patted the top.

Like Gaitlan, Mirra's throat constricted, tears building like liquid fire. Mirra bowed her head and said in Zallino, "A thousand blessings upon you, grandfather."

Yu Jei smiled sadly, letting her hands go. "Shiro can show you the rooms. I can't leave the shop unattended for long."

Adria perked up. "I know some healing. I can help."

A funny feeling, not quite jealousy, not quite guilt, stirred in Mirra's heart. She knew her fair share about herbs too, though her tutelage came from a darker place. "I'd like to help, if I can?"

Yu Jei regarded her solemnly, but nodded in agreement. A weight she didn't know she carried lifted from her shoulders.

Mirra bowed again and followed the rest of her party up the creaking stairs.

The upper floor comprised a large single room with reed mats on the floor. A partition illustrated with dragons and phoenixes sectioned off the farthest wall. A low table with a metal bowl inlaid in the center sat in the middle of the room with cushions neatly placed around it.

"Yu Jie isn't actually my uncle," Shiro explained. "He found me after…after it happened and helped me to move forward. In all these years of exile, he's the closest thing to family I have."

"You still have your sister," Sadria pointed out.

"Yes, but I can't go near her, not without risking her life and the destruction of all that she holds dear." He shook his head. "No, it's best that I stayed away."

"Perhaps once this is all over, you can return home and explain."

Shiro's face twisted in pain and sadness. "Perhaps."

Shiro dumped his pack along the wall before disappearing behind the partition. When he came out, he held a bundle of clean clothes. He muttered something about going to the bathhouse before disappearing down the stairs. Gaitlan threw his belongings aside and dashed after Shiro, nearly forgetting the change of clothes.

Mirra shouted after him, tossing another bundle. His thudding step echoed down the narrow staircase. "Did I say something wrong?" Adria asked as she worried the edges of her tunic.

"Shame is like a wound that never heals," Mirra said. "It festers and aches until the source is gone. Shiro feels an immense amount of guilt over releasing the Eater into this world again. He was ill-equipped to handle it then, so he ran. He carries all the following years of suffering and bloodshed as if he was the one wielding the blade."

Sadria folded her arms. "He couldn't do anything then because the rest of you weren't born yet. He needed to run so he could be here to help us. It is as the fates have decreed."

Mirra shrugged. "I don't know about fates, but even so, that doesn't erase the emotion."

The room filled with an awkward and somewhat pensive aura. Needing something to do, Adria placed her pack on the wall with the others and set to igniting a small fire in the table hearth. After that she disappeared downstairs, returning shorting with a clay teapot and several cups. She busied herself with making the tea. "We've been traveling hard for some time. We need to take care we don't over-stress our bodies, especially the closer we get to the end."

"Do you know something we don't, sister?"

Adria shrugged. "It's more of a feeling. I feel like the threads of fate are closing in around us, like the wolves when running down their prey."

Mirra chewed over Adria's words. She'd felt something similar but hadn't been able to place it. Her mind's eye drifted across Three Kings Bay, rolling over the green and gentle lands of her home until the visage of Julian, swathed in oily black smoke, consumed her inner eye. Did he feel the same? Could he feel the noose slowly tightening around his neck? Could he sense they were moving fast against him with the only tools able to cause him pain?

"Would you like to go to the bathhouse?" Sadira's question brought Mirra back to herself.

"Sure, it's been a while since I had a good soak."

They found the bathhouse with little trouble. Yu Jei pointed them in the general direction. The bathhouse was easy enough to recognize with women leaving with still damp hair and pink skin. They each paid three coins to the matron on duty and followed an attendant to the bathing areas. First, they were led to the changing rooms where they shed their travel worn clothes for light cotton robes. The dark blue robes would ensure that their modesty remained as they bathed. After they changed their clothes, they were led to an area lined with women sitting on low stools in various stages of undress. The women pulled down sections of their robes and scrubbed their bodies with white cloth thick with soap. When they finished, they ladled lightly steaming water onto their bodies.

"Wash first, then tub," the attendant said in thick common.

They found a bench where they could sit together and began their initial washing. The conversations in the room were light when they first arrived, barely above a whisper, but now they fell silent.

"Is it always like this?" Sadira asked, her body tense and poised for attack.

Mirra shook her head. "I don't think so. Something must have happened, or maybe we're just strange."

They tried to ignore the stares and eventually the conversations resumed. But the underlying tension remained, setting Mirra's teeth on edge.

Once clean, they followed another attendant down a long hallway that opened to an outdoor area. A large, steaming pond surrounded by a tall bamboo fence and dense foliage greeted them. Several women sat either on rocks covered with nothing more than a large towel or lounging against the rocks, peace and relaxation written across their face.

Sadria, Mirra, and Adria looked at each other, shrugged, and discarded their damp blue robes on one of the empty benches before walking into the steaming water as naked as the day they were born.

The water was dark enough that if one politely averted their eyes, they could easily forget that the surrounding others were naked. After finding a small alcove with no other patrons, Mirra and the sisters settled in for a long soak, sighing softly when the heat reached their aching muscles.

Mirra tipped her head back, closing her eyes, and willed the warm water to whisk her away to oblivion. "Initiate Mir?"

Mirra's eyes shot open, seeing the last person she'd ever expected. "Ina?"

Even though Ina wore the local attire with her hair pulled half up into a simple bun, the black blue lines across her face marked her as someone who was "other".

Ina's typically stoic face fell as she ran into the water, headless of her clothing or the shocked stares from the patrons. "You have to help. They took him."

Mirra stood, taking Ina into her arms? "Took who?"

"Kov," Ina sobbed. "The sages took one look at him and stole him away to the Azule Castle."

Mirra opened her mouth to tell Ina that she couldn't help when Sadira silenced her with a hand on Mirra's shoulder. "This is not the place for such conversations." Mirra followed Sadria's pointed gaze and nodded.

They quickly gathered their belongings, hastily changing into their clean clothes. Ina walked out with them, completely ignoring the matron's angry shouts at their back. Back at Yu Jei's, Adria made the tea she set up before they left and they sat around the low table while Ina told them what had transpired.

"The ship we took brought us here after the attack on the Isle," Ina said, her eyes locked onto the dancing flames in the middle of the table. "The court officials questioned each one of us, trying to figure out who would be stupid enough to attack the holy city. A few sages were there too, treating some of our injuries and just examining us as a whole." Her voice became thick with emotion. "I tried, believe me, I tried, to keep Kov with me. But they didn't care. They pulled all the children away from their parents or guardians. I know I'm not the only one who never got them back."

"Dishonorable," Adria said, her hand going to her mouth.

Ina nodded, her eyes turning to stone. "In trying to keep their power, most people lose their honor." She closed her eyes and swallowed. "I need to get Kov out of the Azule Castle and find a safe place for him."

Mirra's blood thrummed at her words. The feeling Adria had just put words to stirred again, coiling around her, tugging Mirra as if to say "yes, you must".

"Why is it so important to free Kov," Mirra said carefully and slowly. The sisters shifted in their seats, picking up on the change in Mirra's tone and posture. Adria's hand went to the small bag where she kept the Blood Lamp.

Ina picked at her thumb. When she looked up, she met Mirra's eyes. "You know why…Ilmarrion. You are not the first of your kind that I've met. I know the stories and I know what Kov…can be to you."

"How?" Sadria asked. "The Phoenix Wing disappeared nearly a decade ago."

"The Wing differs from the others," Ina said. "The other relics always live in the physical world, but the wing…the wing is born with its wielder. Hidden, protected until they die. Then it consumes their body, becoming as real as the others."

"Until another wielder is born."

Ina nodded. "It is like the Song, where it will take you where you need to go, but unlike the Song, the user isn't compelled."

A deep crease formed between Mirra's brows. "How?"

Ina shook her head. "That's all that I know. I only just found out what I told you a month or two before you arrived."

"We're back", Gaitlan called as he and Shiro rounded the corner. He came up short, spying Ina sitting with them. "Pleasure to see you again," he said, his face conveying his confusion.

"I know where the next wielder and relic are," Mirra said. "And you will not like it."

Lord Julian stood in the center of the once dilapidated chamber where he first made the creatures to hunt down Mirra and Gaitlan. He bothered little with it other than to clear out a space for him to work. The death of his agent still left him trembling at times, but now was not the time for weakness. They were getting closer to collecting the weapons made by those infuriating people filled with starlight. They might pull something together to entrap him like before, especially if Mirra led the way.

The demon inside Julian growled. Not a day went by that he didn't curse himself for not pushing her further, for treating her with delicacy whilst trying to unlock her power. Her beautifully dark and angry power, so alike to his own, even with the single speck of light at her center. If she had been the one to free him instead of this useless meat sack, then the world would have already been his. He would finally have the strength to finish what that foolish princess started all those centuries ago and unleash the rest of his brethren upon this succulent world.

At least this time, the fates were on his side. Before, he'd been the one utterly blind to everything, but now he knew what to expect. He knew their limitations and savored the fact that they were working with fragments and whispers. This time, he would come out triumphant. That didn't mean that he would remain idle while they work to imprison him. He still had forces to gather, new worms to make to give his army an edge.

Julian sighed and mindlessly turned the page of an ancient book. Just before his initial imprisonment, he'd had enough foresight to bury it. He stared down at the language no one other than himself could read and pondered in what ways he was going to make the starlight people suffer and to what extent he'd force Mirra to watch. His mouth salivated at the thought of her anguish and horror. Sometimes the anticipation made the meal

that much more enjoyable and this was one meal he looked
forward to savoring down to its last tear stained drop.

CHAPTER TWENTY-ONE

"So that we're all clear, the last relic and wielder are being held captive in the Azule Castle; one of the most secure places in the world. We need to find out where he's being kept, get to him and get out before the imperial guard takes our heads?"

"Sounds about right," Mirra said, leaning back. The twitching of her feet was her only sign of excitement, an old excitement she'd never thought to experience again. "Every place has its weak points, blind spots, and other areas ripe for exploitation. All we need to do is find out what they are."

"Fast," Ina added.

Mirra inclined her head. "Fast."

"So, how are we going to manage that?" Gaitlan's frown only deepened the longer the conversation went on.

Mirra flashed him a smile that promised all sorts of trouble. "I have an idea. Nothing concrete, but it could work after we hash out a couple of things."

"What do you need us to do?" Adria asked.

Mirra paused, sorting her thoughts. "Ina, you said that there are still refugee camps?"

Ina nodded. "It's a standard practice for anyone coming into the city without a seal. Most come by land and are quarantined in the northern portion. I think a few of the camps are still there."

"Go see. Take Sadria with you." Mirra cocked her head, narrowing her eyes as she stared at Gaitlan and Shiro. "Shiro, can you show the prince around the city? Show him things to look out for and map out a couple of escape routes. At least three."

"What about me?" Adria asked.

"I want you to stay here and help Yu Jie. Try to keep yourself as unseen as possible."

"Why?"

"Just in case," Mirra said with a smirk.

Sadria leaned closer to Gaitlan. "Why do I have the feeling that I'm not going to like her plan?"

"You get used to it," Gaitlan said with a long, suffering sigh.

THE WEATHER'S SUDDEN TURN COULDN'T HAVE BEEN better. A gentle rolling storm drove many of the street goers into shops or under the overhangs. With everyone waiting to see when the storm would end, no one noticed Mirra was more interested in the palace gates.

Security wasn't that more strict than the Undrosean castle. Most of the procedures appeared to be similar, but she wasn't willing to bet everything on it.

A group of people dressed in temple garb walked past her, cloistered together under oil-paper umbrellas. One, a young man, noted Mirra standing under the slim awning, with only a shawl wrapped around her head. Mirra ducked her gaze, hiding her one identifying feature, her ice-blue eyes.

He folded his umbrella closed and held it out for her to take. Mirra muttered thanks and took the wet umbrella with both hands. The young man bowed and stepped closer to his companions.

Mirra laughed softly, a corner of her mouth pulling up. Small acts of kindness. She'd received so many little acts that kept her from fully succumbing to the darker parts of herself. She was even more grateful for those acts of kindness now than she had been when she first received them. Mirra held them close to her heart like precious gems.

Brian and her bow. Lady Nora granting her as much freedom as she could. Bao, Em, Tull, Sorro, and Kril. Every second with them, running wild through the lower streets of Undros, was a blessing she didn't deserve.

Oya.

Warmth spread through her limbs, stoking fires she had no way of extinguishing. She felt so light that she wondered if a strong wind would sweep her off her feet and carry her off to a world so unlike anything she'd ever known before. A world that she wanted to protect with every ounce of her abilities.

Thoughts of Julian soured the feelings of serenity that made her want to fly. With him consuming her thoughts, her feet firmly rooted to the wet stones beneath her feet. A curse built on her lips until a small voice in the back of her mind whispered, He's had no one.

Even before he'd been possessed, Julian lived a solitary life. His mother and father died young, having no other children. Neither one of his parents' families had bothered to make an appearance once in his life. It wasn't until he met Shiro that Julian even had a friend. His lonely life undoubtedly made him an easy target for the demon to take root. If he had more support in his life, more people to lean on, to keep him in the light, would things be as bad as they are now?

"Probably," Mirra said aloud. People all over the world suffered and dwelled in darkness. That didn't turn them into monsters. It helped, to be sure. But if you wanted to live in the light bad enough, then even the gods couldn't keep you from it. Pushing useless thoughts aside, Mirra opened the paper umbrella and walked out into the rain.

"Absolutely not!" Sadria banged her fists against the table, causing the dishes to rattle.

"It's the only way." Mirra rubbed her eyes. They'd been at this since everyone returned.

"There's always another way."

"Not always, my sister." Adria's voice rang clear, but she didn't raise her gaze from her bowl of noodles. "And it's not up to you to decide what I will or will not do. I am a grown woman. I've completed my Rites of Khürsen, same as you. I want to do this and you cannot stop me."

The silence after Adria's words was heavy, carrying a sense of finality. Sadria's open mouth expression showed to everyone that her sister had never spoken to her like that before. Mirra took the opening Adria created for her.

"We'll take all the precautions we can," she said, her tone leaving no more room for debate. "Gaitlan will take Adria up the coast to the next town. There, they'll join the rest of the refugees set to arrive in a couple of days." Shiro nodded when she looked at him, confirming the information he gathered. "Ina and I confirmed the sages examine each group. Most likely for illnesses or ill intent. Either way, they're going to "discover" Adria and take her away like they did Kov."

Gaitlan leaned forward. "Are you sure? Maybe taking Kov was a one-time thing? What if they don't sense her ties to the relic or take her? Then what?"

"Fair point," Mirra said. "That's when we fall back on our two strongest tools — my ability to pass through shadow and Shiro."

Shiro shifted on his cushion. "I would rather not, if it can be helped. I can't…always control the effects of the Song. It could end up causing more trouble than actually helping us."

"I understand," Mirra said. "That's why it's our last option. If the first two paths don't work, then we'll have to appeal to fate. It's not like we can leave Kov here. We need him."

"So I get discovered and, hopefully, taken to the Azule Castle," Adria said. "Then what?"

Mirra slid her a scrap of paper with a sigil scrawled on it with a bit of charcoal. "You find a nice dark corner and sketch this symbol on the wall. It will create a link between where you are and its companion mark here."

Sadria looked skeptically at the bit of paper. "You've done this before?"

"Not really," Mirra said with all the confidence she could muster. "If the sages can sense Ilmarrion magic, then I don't want to risk them picking up on me."

"But them picking up on my sister is fine?"

"Calm down, warrior," Yu Jei said, holding up a weathered hand stained with decades of working with herbs. "Sensing a ripple of power from a source they're aware of within their walls is less risky than them sensing it outside. They know of Kov and will know of Adria. They may mark it, but it will be small and fleeting, yes?" Mirra nodded her head. "Then it will not raise any alarm, especially if you move quickly through this bridge."

"You'll need to erase the mark after we go through," Mirra said. "That will sever the connection and lower the risk of anyone getting too curious."

"Sister?" Adria spoke softly as she met her sister's gaze. She would play her role, no matter what Sadria said, but she would feel better about not having a rift between them, should anything go awry.

A muscle worked in Sadria's jaw. "I am with you, as always." Adria smiled at her sister and turned to Mirra, her resolution clearly written on her face.

Mirra clapped her hands together. "It's settled then. Gaitlan and Adria, you leave at first light. Shiro and Sadira, let's see how well you handle city fighting."

"THIS WAY, PLEASE. MEN TO THE LEFT. WOMEN AND children TO the right."

Adria didn't need to fake her apprehension as she followed the other refugee women to the large tent where they would be examined. She knew Gaitlan was somewhere in the surrounding area, but that did nothing to soothe her nerves. All around her was the sound of sniffling and anxious whispers. Those with children or elderly parents clung to each other and wondered if they would ever see their men again. Those alone gravitated towards other single women, taking comfort in solidarity.

"Do not fear," one such woman said when she sat next to Adria. "I heard from my cousin who came a few years ago that we'll only need to stay for a few days. As long as everything is alright, then you'll be with your husband again." She smiled brightly, her moon-shaped face tired, but mostly unmarred by the extreme cruelties of the world. "I'm Lixue. What's your name?"

"Adria."

Lixue cocked her head. "You're from Lorcea, right? The Horse Clans?" Adria nodded. "I'm from the north, near the Gray Seas. Pirates attacked our village. It's gone now, some stayed to rebuild but my family came south to the holy city."

"You said your cousin is already here?"

"Not anymore. She married a merchant sailor and joined him on his ship. I haven't heard from her in a long time. I can only pray to the ancestors that she's happy in the path she's chosen to walk."

Adria said nothing, playing with the edges of her clothing. Lixue's cousin was most likely dead or sold to a brothel. She shook her head. Had she been that naïve before? Or had her recent experiences hardened her and tainted everything with suspicion?

Lixue didn't seem to mind Adria's silence. She chatted lightly with the other unaccompanied women with a light smile on her face. The longer they waited, Adria soon saw the lines of unease along Lixue's body, the tightness around her eyes and mouth when she smiled. Perhaps she wasn't so naïve after all.

Just as the light in the tent faded, a group of imperial officials entered the tent. The women shrank back instinctively, clutching either their loved ones or the person nearest to them. A single man stepped forward. Half his hair had been swept up from his face, save for two long strands that fell before his ears. Though his face appeared kind, there was a shrewdness in his gaze that he couldn't quite hide. He drew his hands from his long sleeves and, with two fingers pointed, made a movement in the air. The lanterns flared to life, chasing away the shadows.

"There now," the official said, "that should make this less frightening for you." the women shrank away further when he took another step into the tent. He either chose not to notice or didn't care. "I am Third Sage Ryuu and I am the one who will assist you during this transition. I know it's disheartening to be separated from your families, but we found this to be the less… challenging way to ensure the health and safety of our great city and its people."

He waved his hand again, stepping back to reveal a line of serving women bearing heavy boxes. The aurora of roasted vegetables and steamed rice filled the tent.

"I know many of you may not have had a decent meal in quite some time. This food is a gift from our holy emperor. We hope you find it nurturing for your spirit and your body." And with that, the line of serving women entered the tent and set the boxes down. They removed the top, revealing a large but simple meal. At first, no one moved toward the food presented. Even Adria didn't want to be the first, but someone had to and her role was to be seen.

Pressing her lips into a thin line, she stepped away from the anonymity and safety of the other women and approached Sage Ryuu and the presented meal. She kept her eyes trained just high enough to not look like she was cowering, but low enough that he couldn't see her eyes and perceive an insult.

Clasping her hands in front of her, she bowed. "I thank the Emperor for this meal." She then accepted a bowl from one of the serving women and allowed them to serve her portion of the food.

She could feel the sage's eyes boring into her back, following her as she returned to her place. Even as the others moved to get their portion, Adria felt his gaze. She didn't lift her head for fear of what dark emotion burned behind his eyes.

Sage Ryuu didn't appear the next day or the one after that. Instead, kindly doctors and court herbalists examined and treated the refugees of any injury or illness. Those women who were about to give birth were the first to be taken away to "provide better care" during their deliveries. Their questions about how their other family members were doing or when they could see them again when unanswered. After day four, Lixue lost her bright smile and spent her time curled up next to a support pole, her face buried in her knees.

Adria tried to keep the mood light, but there was only so much she could do. She was just as much in the dark as they were. Finally, on the fifth day of their quarantine, Sage Ryuu returned to their tent. This time accompanied by what could only be armed guards. The anxiety in the tent spiked dramatically.

Sage Ryuu's smile was nowhere to be seen today. Instead, he looked much like an angry god ready to smite them all with a flick of his wrist. When he saw Adria, he stilled like a cat ready to pounce. He jutted his chin in her direction and two guards stormed into the tent, grabbing her by the arms.

Adria didn't have to fake her panic. "Do not struggle," Sage Ryuu warned her, contempt dripping from his voice. Confusion wracked her brain. What had she done? Did he discover her true intentions? Or perhaps this was all for show, a way to not have too many questions raised by the others? That thought cooled her frantic heart and is what gave her legs the strength to walk out of the tent with her dignity. Behind her, she heard Sage Ryuu addressing the other women.

"There are many who seek to undermine the Emperor and his great works. They sneak in like rats through cracks to sow discourse and mistrust. I implore you to be ever vigilant against those who seek to cause chaos."

He turned and left the women alone, any sense of unity or community burned to ash. Adria let the guards carry her where they willed, their iron grips relaxing when they realized she would not fight them. They led to a small, enclosed rickshaw that looked more like a moving prison, with the iron bars at the windows. They slapped iron shackles around her wrists and shoved her inside. When she righted herself, her hands instinctively going to the Lamp, she received her second shock of the day. An elderly gentleman dressed similarly to Sage Ryuu.

He smiled kindly at her, though not making any effort to help her to her seat. "My apologies for the rough handling," he said. "But we thought it best to keep the reality away from the others."

"What reality?"

The man laughed softly, like a grandfather who knows their grandchild is playing with them. "My dear, let us not waste precious time by denying what you and I both already know. Your body is filled with energy that requires careful cultivation and nourishment to thrive."

Adria shifted. "Instead of worrying about what I have, learn how to better communicate with people who have something you want."

An emotion rippled across the sage's face too fast for Adria to make out. His laughter that bubbled out held no mirth. "You want something from us as well. Why else would a Horse Lord's harlot come crawling to the imperial city?"

Adria clenched her jaw. "To avoid honorless bastards, but I guess they're everywhere."

True ire twisted the sage's face into something dark. The wood around them creaked and groaned. "Careful how you speak to me, woman. I am Yuchi, the First Sage of the imperial court. And it is I that determines whether or not you live as an honored guest, or prisoner."

A shudder ran down Adria's spine. She knew that the man sitting across from her would throw her in the dungeons and let her and her power rot. She prayed that Kov had been smart enough to avoid that fate. She schooled her face into one of fear, a pretty easy feat, and bowed her head. That seemed to appease Sage Yuchi.

"Now then, what is it you can do?"

Adria blinked. "Didn't Sage Ryuu tell you?"

"We can only tell that there's energy present, not how it's directed."

Adria chose her words carefully. "It's not something that I can do many times because it takes a bit of my spirit in exchange."

Sage Yuchi grunted. "No power is created from nothing. To earn you must give."

"Yes, well…I can heal a person of anything, even when they're on the brink of death."

"How?"

"I don't know," Adria lied. "All I know is that I place my hands on them and focus. Sometimes it works and sometimes it doesn't."

"Interesting." Sage Yuchi leaned back, lost in thought. The rest of the ride was quiet. Adria tried to gleam as much information as she could, but the thin bars and privacy screens blocked her view. The only sense she had was smell. But not living in the city meant that the thousand aromas that filtered through meant absolutely nothing to her. With a heavy sigh, she leaned back and wondered if she'd be able to pull it off.

"I DON'T LIKE THIS," SADIRA MUTTERED AS SHE PEERED down AT the wagon, taking her sister further away from her.

"Yes, you've mentioned that…repeatedly," Mirra ground out. "Now shut up and keep up." As lithe as a dancer, Mirra stood and leapt across the open space between two buildings. A heavy thump was the only sign that Sadria followed her.

Mirra missed her old gang, and not for the first time. Bao would have been able to find a half a dozen ways in and out. Em, Kril, Tull, and Sorro would all play their parts without the constant bickering and grumbling. They may not have always believed in the plans, but they believed in Bao. She was never more grateful than now that he had been the one to run their little group. If it had been her, they all might have found their ways to early graves.

They followed the wagon to one of the lesser used gates. Several other court officials walked in and out. "Looks like this is the door officials use instead of going through the main gate."

"Great, now what?" Sadira grumbled.

"We post watches," Mirra said. "Look for patterns. When do the guards change? Are there any officials we can exploit?"

Sadria narrowed her eyes. "That sounds like it will take some time."

Mirra fought the urge to roll her eyes. "Yes, it will. We don't know how long it will take Adria to find Kov, let alone to find the best time to take him. So instead of sitting back at the shop twiddling our thumbs and worrying over "what ifs", we're going to do something constructive and helpful."

Sadria's shoulders crumbled. "I don't mean to be difficult. After our parents died, it was my responsibility to look after her. I was the firstborn. I am the fighter. It's supposed to be me that goes into dangerous places. Not her." Sadria let out a bittersweet laugh. "When we were little, she would always cry when the hunters brought back anything. She would always ask if there was another way to feed ourselves without taking life. She's such a gentle heart."

"I know someone like that too," Mirra said. "Maybe not as gentle as your sister, but caring all the same. At first it was annoying, but then it kinda grew on me, especially after we stopped trying to play parts and simply be ourselves." Mirra fingered the copper bead. "I think that's what you need to do now. Stop trying to fill this role that you've been carrying since you were young. It does nothing but stop you and your sister from growing, becoming who you were."

Sadria stared at Mirra with an expression she couldn't quite read. "You're much wiser than you let on."

Mirra's laughter drew curious stares from below. "Only recently, I assure you. Until a few months ago, I was as pigheaded as you. Now let's head back and set up a watch rotation."

THE ROOM SAGE YUCHI LEFT HER IN WAS THE FINEST room Adria had ever been in. Even with its sparse furnishings. A bed on a low platform was pushed up to one wall. Beneath the hexagonal window stood a small cabinet with a bowl for washing her face and hands. A single person table and chair took the other wall up. They had painted the walls a lovely shade of light blue that helped to make the space feel less small and bright. And the mats beneath her feet were thick and soft.

A soft knock announced a serving girl dressed in a simple spring green robe. She carried a bundle of a similar color in her arms. "Please change into these once you've bathed and report to Fourth Master Herbalist Xe Chan." The serving girl left before Adria could ask her where she was supposed to bathe and where Master Herbalist Xe Chan was.

She started to panic, but then it occurred to Adria that this would provide a good excuse to wander around. She might even run into Kov. Quickly stripping her clothes, Adria slid into the robe. It was cotton but made of the finest quality, nearly as soft as silk. She kept the satchel with the Lamp close to her body beneath the robes. The robes were flowy enough that the slight bulge wasn't too noticeable. Dressed in her new court approved clothes, she slipped through her door and picked a random direction.

Adria tried to walk as if she belonged there, and in some fashion she did. She only received the barest of glances from the people who crossed her path. Most were young men and women dressed as she was. They inclined their heads slightly as they passed, not even registering that she was entirely new.

Coming to a cross section, she paused, uncertainty rising. A peal of laughter came from a bit beyond the gravel path to her left. She followed the sound purely on instinct. The laughter came from a small group of four women, dressed in light pink and peach colored robes, playing a game where they had to hit a small object with a racket.

Adria watched them for a moment before approaching. "Excuse me," she said, bowing. "I am looking for Master Herbalist Xe Chan. Do you know where I could find them?"

The women fell silent, staring at her with unreadable faces. The one in a robe the same shade as the peonies around, then snickered behind her hand. Adria felt the heat rising beneath her collar, but she kept her face as neutral and theirs.

When the silence stretched into an uncomfortable one and it was clear that Adria wasn't leaving without an answer, the woman in the robe that shimmered between pink and pale gold stepped forward.

"You're new, aren't you?"

"Yes, clearly." Adria could be just as rude as they were. The first thing her sister taught her was that in a fight, matching your opponent's initial energy could sometimes prevent it from escalating.

"And clearly you're lacking in manners. Don't you know that when talking to your superiors for the first time, you must give your name first?"

Adria cocked her head. "In what way are you superior to me?"

The girl in pink and gold stalked forward. "I am Lady Hua. I am a lady-in-waiting for the Jade Consort." She sneered at Adria's pale green robe. "You're just an herbalist from the planes." She made an exaggerated sniff. "And you still stink of horseshit."

"Thank you for the introduction, Lady Hua. I am Adria and I'm curious how a fine lady such as yourself could recognize my lineage. Perhaps she has a bit of her own."

Hua's face flushed a horrible shade that clashed with the coloring of her dress once she realized what she'd done and what Adria insinuated. Spinning on her heel, she turned and stormed off. The other three ladies-in-waiting scurried like frightened birds in her wake.

Adria remained where she stood, to calm herself more than anything. A childlike laugh echoed from one bush. "I've never seen her so mad."

A young boy crawled out from beneath the bushes. His robes were a dark blue with a short overcoat rimmed in white. A few strands of hair fell from the tight bun on top of his head. "Don't worry, she's mean to everyone. Come on, I'll take you to Master Herbalist Xe Chan."

The boy, named Lee, chatted the entire way to the Hall of Eternal Summer, where all the herbalists worked. He pointed out the nearly invisible markers that helped mark the routes to various places around the castle grounds. All the information left Adria's head swimming, but Lee assured her she'd find her way in no time.

The Hall of Eternal Summer was decorated much more conservatively than its name suggested. A low wall marked the boundary of the space, but she could see the tops of many trees and hear the low hum of many conversations. Lee left her at the open gate, two tall pillars of green the same shade as her robes. The name placard on top boasted a golden tree inlaid into the wood with a hint of creeping vines.

Adria's mouth ran dry, and she brushed her skirts. With a firm jut of her chin, she walked into the compound with the confidence that would have made her sister proud. Her first impression of the compound was that it was orderly to a fault. Hundreds, if not thousands, of herbs organized into neat little sections. She could only identify about a quarter of the herbs she walked past, and for a moment she forgot the real reason she was there. Tampering down her excitement, she continued up the middle walkway to the largest building she could see.

Incense drifted from somewhere beyond what Adria could see. As she drew closer to the building, her awe grew. Stately but simplistic, tall pillars decorated with flowering vines supported a deep blue tiled roof. Gossamer curtains fluttered in the gentle breeze through the wide openings made by large panels between the pillars that looked like they could swing shut when needed.

Adria took a moment to appreciate a world so different from the one she'd grown up in. She loved her clan and how the sun looked when setting behind the mountains. How the stars seemed so close when she and her sister would ride out on the open plain. Adria even loved the Stone Clan villages, with their simple stone homes with their intricately carved wooden supports. But Zallino, especially the imperial city, had opened her eyes to a wider world. She felt her blood stir, the same blood that drove her ancestors to forever wander the grasslands of Lorcea. She wanted to see more of the world. But in order to do that, she needed to find the boy and seal away the demon with a hunger to consume all life.

She found Master Herbalist Xe Chan seated before a large tapestry illustrating a kindly-looking woman and stern faced man. Between the two of them, a single plant sprouted, illuminated by golden light.

"Wei and Shau. The twin gods of healing and poisons."

"Poisons?" Adria frowned at the Herbalist Xe Chan.

Xe Chan regarded her shrewdly. "The same herbs that heal can also kill. Herbalism is a study that forever balances on the edge of a blade." He stuffed his pipe and lit it with a long bit of wood. He puffed on the pipe twice, releasing a purplish cloud of smoke around his face. "So you've made it. Faster than most. I hope it wasn't by accident."

Adria's frown deepened. "It was a test?"

A fresh cloud of smoke perpetrated Xe Chan's laugh. "You'll soon learn that everything here is a test." He puffed more on his pipe. "Would it surprise you I've already received a complaint about my newest attendant? One that I wasn't even aware of."

"They brought me in today," Adria sputtered. "I knew nothing myself."

She tried to not shift under Herbalist Xe Chan's gaze. It made her feel as if all her protections pulled away. "Plucked from the camps, eh?" Adria nodded. "So they found another one."

"Another what, master?" Adria hoped her excitement didn't show. Herbalist Xe Chan eyed her suspiciously. "I was told that I have energy flowing, but nothing else. I don't know why I'm like this."

Xe Chan sighed. "They never do. The sages think that by keeping those like you in the dark, they can keep some power over you. As to what you are, that remains to be seen. I cannot tell you that. It is something that you must find out for yourself." With a grunt, he stood, tapping his pipe against a brass dish. "Follow me."

Adria scurried to follow, falling into step three paces behind him, as they taught her as a child. He led her to a small room where three other people were processing freshly gathered herbs. At the sight of the Master Herbalist, they stopped their work, turning and bowing, uttering greetings. "Get her settled and show her how we do things. Be sure she understands the rules."

"Yes, Master Herbalist Xe Chan," they said in unison.

Adria felt heat building under her collar when they turned their attention to her. Their eyes were colder and as unreadable as the dark side of the moon. "My name is Adria. It is nice to meet you."

The sun had long set before Adria could return to her little room. She fell into bed, her head swimming with names of new herbs and their usages. Her arms ached from hours spent grinding and mashing herbs against pedestals. Her fingers stung from delicate needle-like hairs and caustic juices. But she was the happiest she'd been in a long while. She almost wished she could stay with the imperial herbalists — almost, but not quite.

Exhaustion pulled her consciousness down, making her limbs take on a weightless quality. I hope I can find the boy soon; she thought as sleep claimed her and carried down its gentle rivers.

By the end of her fifth day, Adria had come no closer to finding Kov. For one, the Master Herbalist kept his people working from sunup to sundown. He had to, if he wanted to tend to the thousands of people that lived within the castle's high walls. This high demand also contributed to her lack of openings to slip out. And by the time she could roam, it took all her strength and willpower to wash and eat before falling into bed — often falling asleep before her head even hit the pillow.

Adria sighed as she poured pale green powder into a dark ambler jar. Picking up a small ink brush, she clumsily scrawled the herb's name and properties onto a slip of paper that she tied around the neck of the jar.

"Missing someone?" asked Kalla, the other herbalist working with her.

Adria shook her head. "Not, really. Just a lot on my mind."

"Don't worry. After a few months, you can take the initial exam and become a full apprentice."

"If you pass." Kalla scowled at Han. Han was older than both of them, with the first threads of silver running through his short cropped hair. Adria swallowed down her initial pity for the man, forever stuck in the preparatory room. The first few times she'd tried to extend a branch of friendship, Han treated her with nothing but derision and disdain. It didn't take her long to ignore the man beyond what she absolutely had to.

Adria ignored her workmates, letting her hands do all the work while her mind tried to puzzle out how she was going to find Kov in a place that housed enough people to be a small city.

"Excuse me, I'm looking for Prepper Adria?" The speaker was a young boy that bore the tale-tale signs of a foreigner. His pale skin lacked the warmth that most Zallino's and Horse Clans had, even at their palest. His eyes were the color of a cloudy sky. Seeing such a child within the Azule Castle was shocking enough, but there was something about the boy that stirred something inside her. The previously hidden part sang as if it had found a missing part of itself; like a lover or long lost family member.

Adria stared at the boy and knew, down to the marrow of her bones, that the boy in front of her was Kov. "I'm Adria."

Kov's eyes went wide, his cheeks turning a rosy pink. "Follow me, please."

Adria stood and followed as if in a dream. She didn't see what path they took or the people they passed. Her world had narrowed to a single point. The boy walking in front of her in dark blue robes.

Eventually, they came to a set of ornate doors, golden and carved with intricate designs. Kov opened the door and led Adria through another set of hallways. Kov stopped in front of a small door, nearly invisible against the gold brocade of the walls. Kov knocked lightly.

"Enter." Adria's spine stiffened. She knew that voice, even though she'd only heard it a few times prior. Sage Yuchi sat behind a desk made of wood so dark it nearly looked black. Twin streams of fragrant smoke snaked and coiled at opposite ends, dissipating into the rafters above. Sage Yuchi didn't look up from his work, his ink brush sliding across the scroll as elegant as any dancer. Satisfied with his work, he set the brush aside and folded his fingers under his chin.

"Ah, yes. My two little headaches. Let us see if we can unravel a bit of your mysteries."

CHAPTER TWENTY-TWO

Three hours later, Adria's back was screaming and in the center of her forehead, a tiny drum beat in rhythm with her pulse. And still, Sage Yuchi continued his interrogation. At first, Adria had feared slipping up, but as the relentless questioning continued, the only thing she'd revealed was that until this moment, she and Kov were complete strangers to one another.

Her heart went out to the boy. His eyes shone with barely contained tears. But there was nothing she could do. If she relented and revealed anything, that would only extend the interrogation. The light within the room had slowly dimmed and she could only hope that with the day coming to a close, Sage Yuchi would give up.

"Now then," Sage Yuchi said, a deep frown on his face. "What can you tell me about a race of people called Ilmarrion?"

Adria had to bite the inside of her cheek to stop from correcting him. She couldn't be sure if he intentionally got the name wrong or if, like in Undros, Mirra people's name had been changed.

"I don't know, Sage Yuchi," Kov answered first, his voice cracking with emotion. "I already answered this question a hundred times."

"I don't know either," Adria said, her exhaustion and irritation making her voice chipped. "Honestly, I have work that I'm supposed to be doing, and he is only a boy. What crimes have we committed to warrant this level of questioning? And what are you even trying to learn?"

Sage Yuchi's eyes flashed with hostility. He was not accustomed to anyone, let alone a foreign woman of no status, speak to him in such a disrespectful way. He pointed the ink brush he'd been using to jot down their answers to his questions at her like a blade. He swelled like a bullfrog, his mouth opening to shout, but was silenced by the Master Herbalist storming into the room.

"So this is where you've been keeping my apprentice."

Sage Yuchi regained his composure and let the ink brush aside. "Your apprentice? Then why doesn't she bear the markings of her rank? All I see is a common laborer."

"The examination is only a formality," Master Herbalist Xe Chan said with a wave of his hand. "I've told you time and time again, you cannot treat my people this way."

"Only the girl is yours, Xe Chan. The boy is part of the scribes, who fall under my care."

Master Herbalist Xe Chan placed himself between Sage Yuchi and Adria and Kov. "That may be, but I am responsible for the health and wellbeing of all within these sacred walls. Do not forget that."

The expression on Sage Yuchi's face could only be described as sour. For a moment, Adria thought he would lash out against the Master Herbalist, but he leaned back in his seat. "Fine, take them. I've finished with them, for now."

Master Herbalist Xe Chan inclined his head just enough to not be insulting. "Enjoy your evening, Sage Yuchi."

Adria and Kov bowed deeply and scrambled to follow their savior. Once they'd reached neutral territory, Master Herbalist Xe Chan spun around and shoved something cold and hard into her hands. "Wear this tomorrow and if anyone gives you grief, come to me."

"Thank you Master Herbalist," Adria said, staring down at the piece of white jade in a thick braid.

"It's the marking of an apprentice herbalist. You clearly have skill healing. The salves and tonics you make are near perfect for someone with no formal training."

"I have training," Adria snapped back before she could stop herself. But instead of being offended, the Master Herbalist apologized.

"I didn't mean to offend. Take the boy and give him something to calm his nerves before getting something to eat. I excuse you both from any evening duties."

He left Adria and Kov alone. Out from beneath the eyes of the masters, Kov's shoulders bowed and the last fragments of his resolve crumbled. He didn't bother to wipe away the tears that streamed down his face. Adria placed a gentle arm around him, pulling him in close.

"You were very brave. Ina would be proud."

Kov pushed away from her, his eyes narrow with suspicion. "How do you know her?"

"Come, let's get you something to eat and a tonic for nerves. Do you know a quiet place we can eat?"

Kov blinked once. "Yes, follow me."

He followed Adria to the now empty room where she worked…used to work. Undoubtedly, her job was about to change. A twinge of guilt ran through her. Master Herbalist Xe Chan had come to her rescue, vouched for her, and given her status within the castle. And she was about to betray all that trust. How could Mirra stand it? She wondered.

"How do you know Inara?" Kov turned, staring Adria down with all the determination a ten-year-old could have.

Adria looked around the open space, unease coiling its way through her. "Are you sure no one will hear us here?"

Kov nodded. "It said we'd be safe…for a while, at least."

"It?"

"The voice in my head. It tells me many things. Like who's lying to me and who I can trust."

Adria cocked her head. "And what does it say about me?"

Kov's eyes unfocused. "You are like me," he said haltingly. "Do you have a voice, too?"

"Not quite," Adria said, her hand going to where she kept the blood lamp hidden beneath her robes. "But like you, it has chosen me to help heal the world. To stop the darkness from spreading and to bring balance back to all nations."

Kov made a face. "I want my family back. Can we make that happen?"

The smallness of his voice tore at Adria's heart. "No. There is no force in this world that can bring someone back from the lands of the dead." Tears welled in Kov's eyes as the last fragment of hope he carried turned to ash. "But you can always make another family. That is what my sister, and I did. We found people we care about and who care about us. We fight and make each other laugh. Doesn't that sound like a family?"

"Yes," Kov answered, his voice thick with sorrow. "But it's not the same."

"Nor is it supposed to be. We will have a dozen different families in our lifetime. Each one is different, but precious."

"Ina reminds me of my mom. She was strong, too. I felt safe with her like I did with my mom."

Adria crossed the space and pulled Kov close. "Then let's get you back to her."

"How?"

"Is there a part of the castle that is dark and where we won't be discovered?" Kov's eyes unfocused again. He tilted his head this way and that as if he was trying to get a better view. After some time, his eyes became clear.

"In three days, it will be the new moon. Most of the palace will be in shadow, especially along the walls. If we go to the southwestern side near the lotus ponds, no one will see us."

"Are you sure?"

"The voice is never wrong," Kov said with conviction. "But sometimes it doesn't tell me everything at once."

"Well then," Adria said, "let's meet by the lotus pond in three days. Will you be able to manage that on your own?"

A small smirk breathed brevity into Kov's face for the first time since she'd met him. "Will you?"

Adria paused, then threw her head back and laughed. Throwing her arm around the young boy, she steered him toward the kitchens, where they begged for a small bowl of rice and smoke fish from the exhausted cooks. Adria then sent Kov on his way, not wanting anyone to see them together longer than necessary lest it get back to Sage Yuchi.

Without the light of the moon, the open areas of the Azule Castle were swallowed by the night. Only the walkways were spared, illuminated in the soft orange glow of paper lanterns. On the walkways, one could imagine themselves on the only sliver of existence in an onyx sea, while those that dared the darkness could watch those who feared the dark unencumbered.

Adria didn't mind the dark. She'd grown up under open skies as her gods demanded. The planes of her people's land were as familiar to her under the blazing sun as it was beneath the silver light of the moon. The Azule Castle was no different. Its wide and sprawling borders were nothing more than a status symbol. Something for the lower masses to stare up in awe and tremble at the thought of betraying their emperor. To the potential invader, it was a labyrinth of hallways and well-manicured lawns. But if you knew what to look for, all you needed to do was follow the signs to find where it was you wanted to go.

It hadn't taken her long to find a decent hiding place. She'd changed back into her original clothing and packed her belongings, leaving the jade piece on her bed. Adria didn't realize how much she wanted the jade piece until she left it behind. Shifting from her seat amongst the branches of a willow tree, she buried her disappointment and focused on keeping an eye out for Kov.

"Are you going to stay up there all night?" Kov's voice called out softly from the darkness, nearly causing her to fall.

"How long have you been here?" Adria said through clenched teeth as she climbed down.

"Not long," Kov said with a shrug. "I asked to get here without being seen and I guess the voice included you, too."

"Do you do that often? Ask the voice for something?"

"Not always. Most of the time it speaks to me without warning, but it always answers when I ask."

"Impressive," Adria said, shouldering her bag. "Well then, shall we?"

She led Kov to the nearest wall, one she'd doubly checked against being spied on. She pulled a charcoal pencil and etched Mirra's symbol onto the wall. She spent her first days memorizing and practicing the symbol until she could replicate it in her sleep.

"What is that?" Kov whispered behind her.

"Our way out. Now back up."

The rune burned darkly, swallowing even the faintest fragments of light. As it gobbled up the light, it grew and transformed, turning into a swirling vortex of pure darkness. Tendrils of cold air spilled out, causing their breath to form tiny clouds in front of their faces. Kov slid next to Adria, hiding partly behind her while clinging to her with all the strength of a terrified child.

The vortex pulsated like the beating of some alien heart, spreading with each pulse until it resembled a doorway. Seconds ticked by like lifetimes and doubt wrapped its icy hand around Adria's heart.

Had something gone wrong? Did she draw the symbol right? What if the others were caught somehow?

Kov's gasp caused Adria to narrow her vision in the center of the gaping void. A slender, pale hand pushed through, followed shortly by an arm, a torso and a leg. Mirra took a deep breath the moment her face broke through the dark, her icy eyes glowing like pale stars.

"Mir?"

"Hello, Kov", she said with a smile. "I brought someone I think you'll be happy to see." She stepped aside, reaching back to pull Ina through the portal.

Kov cried out and threw himself into Ina's arms. "Ina! You came back."

Ina wrapped her arms round the young boy, burying her face, taking in his scents. "I promised, didn't I? I will always find my way back to you, nawelli."

Mirra saddled to Adria. "Please tell your sister that you were treated well here. She promised to cut off my fingers if a 'single hair' on your head was damaged."

Adria softly laughed and shook her head. "I am fine. They treated me well, mostly."

Mirra arched her brow. "Do I need to pay someone a visit?"

"No, no," Adria said quickly, waving her hands. "Nothing like that. It was only a bit of common snobbery." Mirra's eyes bored into hers, as if she was searching for lies under Adria's words. But she had spoken true and, sensing that, Mirra turned to wave them throughout the swirling doorway.

"Let's continue this love fest elsewhere. The door won't last much longer."

Ina loosened her embrace and went to lead Kov through. "Don't worry," she said, "it feels weird, but harmless."

Kov pulled back, shaking his head. His eyes held a faraway glance that Adria recognized in an instant. "We can't leave," he said, his voice echoing slightly. He turned, poised to run, but Mirra got to him first.

"Look, kid, we don't have time for this. Whatever or whoever you got in mind, you're gonna have to make peace leaving."

Adria stepped forward, placing a hand on Mirra's arm and Kov's shoulder. "Peace, Mirra." She eased Kov so that he faced her. "Is it the voice again?" Kov nodded. "Is it important? Do we need this to succeed?" Kov nodded again, his eyes still far away.

"Then take us where the phoenix wants to go," Ina said with a pained expression. "Can you reopen your doorway?"

Mirra shook her head. "Not on the same night. If we don't leave now, we'll have to do it the old-fashioned way. Now, what's this about a voice?"

"Kov is a wielder, like me," Adria explained. "He bears the Wing inside and it…speaks to him. It leads him down the path of least resistance."

"And sometimes it takes him to places or people that we don't know we need yet," Ina said. "But it's never led us astray. At first I thought that coming here was the wrong path, but now…" She glanced between Mirra and Adria. "The threads of fate are tangled around you both. The same for Kov. We needed to come here so you could find us. You need Kov to lead you to the next piece of your journey."

Mirra's showed she wanted to throw the boy over her shoulder and carry him through the quickly evaporating doorway, kicking and screaming if necessary. But her mind, honed by years on the streets and Lord Julian's tutelage, kept her rooted to the spot. The boy's relic worked similarly as Shiro's, but the fundamental difference is that the Wing was more accurate than the Song. The Song could only pull you to the crossroads of your path, the Wing would tell you which one you had to take. She was free to ignore it, of course. But with so much at stake — her friends, the world, her people, Oya — did she dare to risk it?

"Fine," she ground out. "Take me where it wants to go and then let's get the hel out of here."

They made it to the dungeons without so much as seeing another soul. Instead of easing her worry, the relative ease that they made set Mirra's nerves on edge. In her line of work, when things went this smoothly, that usually meant disaster wasn't too far behind.

"Why are we going to the dungeons?" Ina asked as they waited around a darkened corner for a pair of sleepy guards to pass by.

Kov shrugged.

"You don't know," Mirra spat. She grabbed the boy by the collar and spun him around. "Look, kid, I have too much riding on getting you out for you to not know why the relic is leading us to a very convenient place to get caught. Unlike you, I don't relish the idea of sitting in a cell until the end of the world."

"Mirra," Ina and Adria said, their voices echoing with reproach and warning. She paid them no heed, letting Kov feel the entire force of her earnestness.

He swallowed quickly. "Maybe it has something to do with The Old One."

"Who's that?"

Kov peered around the corner and pried Mirra's hands off before stepping out into the hallway again. "I only learned about him a week ago. Sage Yuchi found records of a prisoner that no one seems to remember. He has guards assigned to him and food brought to him, but there's no way he's still alive."

Mirra felt a prickling at the base of her skull. "And why is that?"

"Cause the first records of the prisoner date back all the way to the start of the empire with the very first emperor. Sage Yuchi wanted to see if he still lived, but every person who came in contact with The Old One forgets him as soon as they walk away."

A deep furrow grew between Ina's tattooed brows. "But you remember?"

"Maybe the Wing protected you," Adria said. "Maybe you needed to meet The Old One in order for this path to be open to us."

Mirra had nothing to add, and all conversations fell silent. When they reached the entrance to the dungeons. Mirra had to slide through shadows to incapacitate the guards. She wanted to kill them. That way, they wouldn't have to risk the guards waking and sounding the alarm, but the others were adamant against it. Ina didn't want Kov to be witness to such cruelty and killing people for simply doing their jobs went against Adria's healer's heart. Mirra rolled her eyes but relented, using a set of sleeping darts to ensure that the guards would remain unconscious for at least an hour. Hopefully giving them enough time to find The Old One and get out. Unless the guards were to change in that hour.

Once through the gate, Mirra shrouded her group in semi-darkness. She wasn't about to place all her faith in a little boy, relic wielder or no. But the longer they went, the more it drained her. Her temples throbbed with each step as beads of sweat formed on her brow and neck.

"You'll wear yourself out if you don't let up." Mirra scowled at Adria.

"I'm fine," she snapped.

"You can't do everything on your own." Adria played with the strings of her relic pouch. "Just because you're the first of your kind in a thousand years, doesn't mean you have to carry the weight of this quest alone. Let your friends share the load."

Mirra shook her head. "You can't."

"Why not?"

Mirra remained silent. She didn't have an answer, but something inside kept whispering that success or failure hinged on her. Maybe she was developing a savior's complex?

The walls of the dungeon changed from smooth, carved stone to rough-hewn walls that curved overhead. Mirra hoped human hands and not something else carved them.

"Almost there," Kov said. his voice barely above the whisper.

"Why are there no guards here?" Ina asked.

Kov's answer was simple, if not slightly alarming. "There's no need for them."

They came to the end of the tunnel. Two flickering lanterns framed a set of wooden bars. Mirra spied Ilmarrion runes etched into the glass. The space beyond the lanterns was thrown into shadows with no sign of who or whatever awaited beyond.

While the others hesitated, Kov walked right up to the bars and knelt before bowing his head to the ground. "Greetings Old One."

"It's not time for food, young one," answered a gravelly voice that echoed with the burden of time. "What brings you here?" From the shadows, heavy chains scraped against hard stone. A thin, bald man eased slowly into the light. Deep lines etched his face and hands, unnaturally pale from decades without sunlight. His eyes remained closed, though it hardly mattered. He turned his face to each person gathered in turn. His expression only changed when he turned to Mirra.

"By the stars," he said, sliding all the way to the bars. He opened his eyes, revealing the telltale milky white of blindness. "Tell me, mashta, what clan are you from?"

"Clan?" Mirra looked to Adria, who shrugged as if to say "you'd know better than me".

The Old One's mouth pulled down in a deep frown. He cocked his head side to side and Mirra felt a gentle wave of energy, nearly identical to hers, wash over her. Her own power rose to meet it like a young pup to its elder. Mirra knelt down with her head lowered before she even formed a thought.

"One of the lost ones," the Old One said. "I didn't think your clan survived after it happened. It would have soothed my mother's heart to know that some of the Darkspire clan still walks this earth."

"Darkspire?" Tendrils of excitement and apprehension rolled through Mirra. "Perhaps you can tell me more once we get you out of here, ancient one."

A low chuckle. "I am not leaving, little one."

Surprise ran through the group. "Not leaving?" Mirra slid forward, not trusting that she heard him correctly. "You want to stay imprisoned here…in the dark?"

"My name is Marhoc," the Old One said, settling in his hands folded gently into his lap. "Do not think that because I cannot see that I am blind. Like you, the dark places of this world whisper to me. Through them, I've seen the land change from a vast wilderness to great stone cities and everything in between. This is not a world that I am a part of. And for decades, centuries, I've pleaded with the Ilieng to tell me why it has granted me with long life. And now I know it's because of you."

"Me?" Mirra sat up ramrod straight. Marhoc smiled.

"Yes you. For so long, days beyond measure, I've sat here alone in this tiny world of cold stone. I long stopped caring, stopped caring if I ever left, even when my sight was consumed by the ever pressing darkness. The only thing I had to cling onto was hope. Hope that my family survived in some way…and that I could deliver this to the right person."

From a pocket hidden in his sleeve, Marhoc drew out a small book no larger than the palm of his hand. "My father gave this to me when they left me. He said that I should keep up with my studies while they waited for the demon to be defeated." He thumbed through the pages, his face a mixture of grief and reluctance. Pressing his lips into a thin line, he thrust the booklet between the bars. "This is for you."

Mirra stared at the booklet, her mind and heart warring with each other. If she took what Marhoc offered, she'd finally be able to learn about her heritage, her abilities directly from the source. But…but this was his last link to his family. If she took it, he'd be left with nothing but the ghosts of a time that he walked in the sun.

She shook her head, her throat tight and burning. "I can't take this."

Marhoc's face hardened. "You must. It's your turn to carry our people."

"Mirra," Adria whispered softly at her side. "We were led here. We need this."

Pursing her lips, Mirra reverently took the booklet with two hands. She bowed her head at her elder. "When this is done, I will come back for you."

Marhoc smiled softly. "Take care, young one."

"Mirra. My name is Mirra."

Marhoc inclined his head. "May the Nexi lead you through the dark places in the world safe."

"And may it keep you safe as well, Elder Marhoc," Adria said, bowing her head to the cold stone floor. The other followed suit, murmuring thanks and well wishes for the ancient man before them who sat more regally than any ruler in the world.

As they made the journey back, Kov's gentle sniffling was the only sound they made. No one was happy about leaving the ancient Ilmarrion locked away in his forgotten cell. Mirra pretended that the hot tears streaming down her face resulted from the sharp incline they had to walk up.

"Well now, what do we have here?" Sage Yuchi stood at the entrance to the upper level, a sharp edge to his smile. His eyes narrowed at Adria and Kov. "I knew you were hiding something."

Ina slid Kov behind her with one hand and drew the short sword she'd hidden beneath her robes with the other. "Child stealer", she hissed.

Sage Yuchi laughed bitterly. "How can anyone steal what doesn't belong to another? Anyone with eyes can see that boy isn't yours."

"Family comes in all shapes and colors," Ina spat back. "I am his, and he is mine. And you will not separate us again."

The carefully bemused expression painted on Sage Yuchi's face fell. "Silence woman. Your ilk has no authority here."

Mirra shifted into a fighting stance, daggers in each hand. "Luckily, we don't need your authority. We're leaving with our friends. So you can step aside willingly or we move you."

"Insolent woman," Sage Yuchi spat, pulling his hands free in a swirling motion to free them from his sleeves. He held his hands in front, his first two fingers pointing up. At their tips, a minuscule pearl of white light formed, transforming into a kaleidoscope of rippling light. He moved his hands in a series of motions too precise to be mistaken for anything other than an attack. He flung a grapefruit sized ball of multicolored energy at them.

Mirra shouted and leapt forward, reinforcing her daggers with her magic. The impact of Sage Yuchi's attack thundered through her, pushing her back several inches. Ina surged forward with a shout, her sword poised to remove Sage Yuchi's hands. Sage Yuchi threw her attack back.

"Silly girl, you can't fight Qì with blades." Sage Yuchi laughed. "The boy and the woman will be mine, just like the immortal."

This time it was Mirra's turn to laugh. "You think you have him? The Old One stays because he wants to. He wouldn't even leave with us!"

A strange expression rippled over Sage Yuchi's face. "He spoke to you? I have spent fifteen years trying to draw out a single word from that creature, and he speaks to you?" He cocked his head, eying Mirra in a new light. "What makes you so special?"

Mirra let the shadows swallow her up without a word. She dropped from above Sage Yuchi. He barely conjuring a shield in time. The force of her blow vibrated in her arms. She gritted her teeth and rolled sideways, falling into shadow again to appear where she started.

Sage Yuchi now looked at her in awe. "Yǐng bù. I thought your kind was long gone from this world. That's why it spoke to you. You're one of its people. Perhaps it needs a mate to fully open up. When I finish here, I'll give you to him. I was planning on giving him the boy because he seemed to like him, but this way, I can have a Yǐng bù pup to raise."

Bile rolled in the back of Mirra's throat at Sage Yuchi's wide smile and the slightly deranged gleam in his eye. Marhoc wasn't a person to him. No one was a person to him. That man calmly discussing giving a young boy away as a plaything as one would talk about the weather, or rising prices at the market, and cared for no one but himself. He would gladly watch the world burn just to ease a bit of his boredom.

Deep within her core, Mirra's power rumbled to the surface, filling every spec of her body with dark power. Adria knew something was wrong the moment the shadows just beyond the lanterns began to pulsate and move like wild animals. She pulled Kov in closer and watched Mirra with wide eyes. The woman she'd spent the past month traveling with was gone. In her place stood a primal force poised to shred the world apart for its evils.

"What is this?" Sage Yuchi said, a slight tremor to his voice. "Who are you?"

Mirra stepped forward, her step echoing throughout the Azule Castle. Marhoc wrapped his hands around the bars of his cell and screamed for Mirra to take mercy on the people in the castle.

Mirra ignored Sage Yuchi's question, tampering down on the dark, icy fire that raged through her. She was not that person anymore. Not a beast to lash out against friend and foe. The man standing in front of her wasn't worth the damage her soul would take when she snuffed out his pitiful life. Pouring the last remnants of the dark fire into her daggers, Mirra shifted into a fighting stance, centering herself with three slow, measured breaths before pressing back into the fray.

Sage Yuchi's power was strong, stronger than hers. His spectrum-colored energy dispelled her shadows at every turn, but as their fight continued, one thing became evident; he wasn't a fighter. He might have learned the basics at one point, but Mirra had been fighting for her life since the moment she could stand on her own two feet. And those fights weren't neat and honorable, like in the training ring. Her school of fighting had been brutal, lethal, where one's willingness to play dirty was the only means of survival.

With a firm kick to the side of his knee, she broke his stance, sending Sage Yuchi crashing to the ground. She used their downward momentum to add force to her following strike. He sent a wall of power at her with a thrust of his palm, sending her flying.

She crashed into the opposing wall; the air knocked from her lungs. A roar filled the space as Ina charged forward, dodging the sage's attacks with a graceful ease. He barely scrambled back to his feet before the downward swing of her sword met its target. Instead of his head, Ina caught his long sleeve, her sword slicing cleanly through it.

Sage Yuchi snarled and flung Ina back with another wall of energy. Mirra dropped through the closet shadow, using only as much as she dared. Ina was the only one to see Mirra slide into the darkness like a seal into the water. Ina spat out blood and adjusted her grip on her sword. She breathed deeply, drawing in strength, and charged again. The sage glared at her, raising his hands, shimmering the way the sun danced across the glaciers near her village. She didn't stop when he fired the first bolt at her. His pattern of attack followed a simple repetitive pattern.

Left. Right. Jump. Left again. She learned his steps as quickly as she learned any dance. She'd never had a problem learning new steps. When she was born, the sky spirits shone brighter than before, dancing with delight. Her atta said that was how she could learn dances so quickly, the sky spirits had given her a part of their gift.

Ina hadn't thought about her family in many years. Whenever she had, all she could remember were the sounds of their screams and the smell of smoke and burning hides. The memory of her atta and her wizened face as round as the moon and just as gentle filled her with new resolve. She dodged the sage's next attack, spilling on one foot to bring her sword up and around, poised to remove his hands.

Unnoticed by either, Mirra slowly rose from Sage Yuchi's own shadow. From a pouch at her side, she drew a thin blade, barely longer than her little finger, and stabbed him in the next. The power building at his fingertips flickered and arced like tiny bolts of lightning. A half a breath later, Ina's blade swung down and removed the sage's hands in one fail swoop.

Sage Yuchi screamed, his eyes staring in disbelief at the bloody stumps where his hands used to be. "You hateful whores," he swore as he pressed his bleeding stumps into his chest, staining his white robe red. "I will find you and make you pay for this."

"Then you should know who I am," Ina said, using the piece of the sage's sleeve she'd cut to clean her sword. "I am Ina of the Tsu'loatan, the last surviving member of the Sycukk clan. Come find me on the ice planes if you think you can." She turned to retrieve Kov from Adria, who kept her eye closed in case the Blood Lamp compelled her to heal Sage Yuchi.

Mirra watched them go, kicking the sage in the chest. He cried anew as he fell. Mirra knelt beside him, slicing at his robes until she had several long strands of fabric. "I know you're probably begging for death right now. And if I'd met you when I was younger, I would have given you that reprieve. But I know there's something worse than dying at the hands of your enemy…living with the shame of defeat."

She wrapped a strip of silk around a bleeding stump, cinching it tightly. Sage Yuchi's hiss drew a small smile from her. "I've seen what shame will do to a person, how it eats away until you're nothing more than a shell. I've seen the way it drives you away from the people and places you care about the most, and how it will change you until you are unrecognizable." She continued to tightly wrap the silk strips around the bleeding stumps, slowing the blood flow. "I wouldn't count on using your Qì, was it, anytime soon. I've been very fortunate in my education, unorthodox as it was. That blade coated with a poison concocted by one of my teachers. It blocks the energy flow in the body. Now, as you've learned to work your energy interestingly, it won't kill you like it would a regular person. But I wonder if you'll ever be able to use Qì the same way again."

The whites of Sage Yuchi's eyes grew and his face lost all specs of color to where Mirra felt the need to check the tourniquet around his wrists. "Who are you?"

Mirra stood feeling the last missing piece of herself fall into place. "And by the way, I'll be back for him." She gestured towards Marhoc's cell. "If anything happens to him between now and when I return, I'll make you wish I'd killed you today." She stepped back into shadow, letting it wrap around her like a mother's embrace. Nestled safely in the space between worlds, Mirra loosened a breath, released the last knot that held her back.

THE GUARDS RUSHED INTO THE STUDY AT THE SOUND OF crashing and shattering glass. Lord Julian stood with his hands braced on the desk, his chest heaving.

"My lord?" One guard dared to say, stepping forward.

"Get out, you, idiot!"

The guards quickly returned to their posts outside the study. Julian roared, not caring if it drew the attention of someone outside. Let them come. He'd gladly rip them to shreds, bathing in their blood and fear it that changed what had happened. There was no mistaking it. Mirra and her little band of rebels were gathering the relics, the pieces of his prison. To make matters worse, they were succeeding.

For months on end, he'd felt these fluxes, tiny ripples of Ilmarrion power. And for months he'd thought nothing of it. He'd chalked it up to Mirra trying to learn how to wield her power but, this was much worse.

Oily blackness, like snakes, swarmed up his arms and around his shoulders. Julian closed his eyes and opened up to the energy pathways of the world. A trick he learned while riding in that beautifully, hopefully ignorant princess a millennium ago. Amidst the black planes of his sight, small pinpricks of light blossomed into being. Four were clustered somewhere to the east…Zallino, perhaps. The other two were close, quite close in fact. He turned the full force of his mind onto the two pinpricks of light. Just before he could reach them, a vast wall of ancient power slammed into him, forcing him back into his mortal shell.

Julian snarled and punched the desk, splitting it in two. They had everything they needed to lock him away again. But they weren't together and weren't familiar with the rules and workings of the relics. Of that much, he was certain. An unnaturally wide smile split his face. He would strike them at the knees, for what good was it to have a relic if its wielder was dead?

"Summon the Council of Lords," Julian shouted to the sweating guards outside the door. "Tell them it's time to go to war."

CHAPTER TWENTY-THREE

Oya ran her hand over the crumbling road marker, half hidden by moss. All around her, trees towered over her, leaving the world beneath their branches in semi-darkness. When the wind blew, warm patches of sunlight cause the flowers to erupt in color. She breathed deep, taking in the scents of loam and growing things. It was good to be home. Her hand caressed the bulge in her satchel, and a fierce wave of pride flowed through her. The Orb of Thrilla was remade. Haphazardly, perhaps, but the end results couldn't have been better. Mirra was right. She'd been too focused on recovering what they lost she failed to move forward. She had been the seedling trapped under the ash after a fire until Mirra stirred everything up. Now she was free to grow to new heights, to bear new fruits, and experience a litany of new sensations free from the trappings of the past.

A warm fire ignited in the pit of her stomach, chased by a pang of longing. Who knew when she'd be able to see Mirra again, to brush her raven hair from her face? She missed how easy it was to talk to Mirra when she wasn't being stubborn, or the way her eyes would light up when she was about to do something mischievous. But most of all, Oya missed how easy it was to be around Mirra once they got over their respective issues. Whether they remained lovers or settled for friends, it didn't matter. At least for Oya, it didn't. Mirra was still adept at keeping a wall or two up. But in time, Oya hoped Mirra wouldn't feel the need to keep them up with her.

At long last, she reached the borders of Moakwyd. Longing for home and her own bed, she stepped through the protective barrier. The barrier flowed around her like a warm bath. Minuscule stars danced around her as if the barrier was welcoming her home. Oya held out a hand and filled it with the soft light of dawn. The stars danced and swirled around the tiny sun, whisking it off into the great unknown.

"Welcome back, Oya." Katsumi bowed in greeting, the bell at the end of her long braid jingling. "I've been asked to escort you back to the citadel."

Oya huffed a laugh. "I know where the citadel is. What's going on Kats?"

"Usoa thought it might be better to bring you up to speed before you reach the city proper."

Oya's stomach dropped. "What happened?"

Katsumi waved her hands. "Nothing bad, I swear. It's just… well we have some new visitors." She filled Oya in as they walked and Oya was grateful for Usoa's foresight. It was a lot to take in. First, the princess Braelyn was the wielder of the Seed. Second, she and Bao had stumbled into the city seeking asylum. "I think Bao harbors secret feelings for the princess," Kastumi said, her face alight with a youthful fantasy. "I think she feels the same, but they won't act on it."

"Don't meddle," Oya warned. "Their people do things differently and it's not our place to tell them what to do."

Katsumi pouted. "I wasn't going to do anything. The princess has been spending every waking moment trying to attune to the Seed. Bao just…lurks and watches. He uses one of the practice fields from time to time. But anyone can see he's restless."

Oya made a noncommittal noise. "Well, I surmise events are going to move quickly soon."

Katsumi turned, curiosity written across her face. "Oh, were you successful in your mission?"

Oya smiled and drew the Orb from the satchel. Dark gray clouds swirled inside, docile like calm skies before the storm. Katsumi's eyes went wide. "How…what…is it real?"

Oya laughed. "Yes, it's real. Not new, just mended. But soon Mirra and Gaitlan will find the last of the relics and the wielders and we can finally lock that demon away. Hopefully, for good this time."

"No prison lasts forever," Kastumi said, reaching for the orb. The gray smoke gently swirling cloistered where her fingers hovered. "I'd feel better if we could send it back to wherever it came from. And then seal the door shut."

Oya slipped the orb back into her bag. "One step at a time. First, we need to lock him away and then we'll look into how he came to be in our world. Now that the Holy Isle's citadel is open to us, we might find the answers to all our questions."

"Let's hope we make it that far." Oya glanced at Katsumi. The young acolyte's face had turned sullen, her eyes cast to the ground. Oya pressed her lips together. Because what could she say? It took their ancestors everything they had to originally seal away the Dark One, and still many of them lost their lives. They only had fragments of power and knowledge to achieve the same end. Just how many of them would be left once the dust settled? Her people were already holding onto existence by a thread. Would this be their last stand?

Something uncoiled in her core, rising to the surface the way the sprout unfurls from the seedling. "We will," she said, taking Katsumi's hand into hers. "For thousands of years, the world has tried to stomp out our people, erase us from existence. And yet, here we stand, and here we will always stand. We are born of starlight and were made to stand against the hunger of darkness. Even if we lose here today, there will always be another to take up our mantle, until the end of all things."

Katsumi's eyes widened, tears welling. She bowed low, her hands placed over her heart. For years, Usoa trained Oya to take over as the head of faith, but it wasn't until Katsumi bowed with the reverence typically reserved for the high priestess herself that Oya finally felt secure of her impending role. That didn't mean that she was ready to accept the honorable burden just yet. They still needed to survive the upcoming battle, and it would be a battle.

Oya gently touched the young acolyte's head. Katsumi's moon-shaped face shone with a mixture of awe and reverence. "Take me to Bao, Mirra's friend."

Kastumi's brows furrowed. "Not the princess?"

Oya shook her head. "Leave the wielder for the High Priestess. I think the man that stole away the Dark One's plaything has a unique insight." Oya would see Usoa later, but the tickling in the back of her consciousness warned her that things would move quickly and their defenses were nowhere near ready.

Thump. Thump. Thump.

The hilt of three daggers clustered neatly in the middle of a black circle painted on the chest of a straw dummy. Bao threw without seeing, his mind consumed with a hundred thoughts swirling in his head, each one demanding his full attention. But all he cared about was the ache left behind by the lack of a certain, impossibly amazing, person. Over and over he berated himself for the way his heart demanded that he speak the secret words etched over the very essence of his soul. It didn't help that his traitorous mind replayed every moment shared between them. If he were to be completely honest with himself, Bao would admit that he fell in love with Braelyn from the first moment they met, beneath the branches of the trees. How could he not have, with her inner fire burning brightly despite that bastard's attempts to squash it beneath his heel?

Bao threw another dagger. It joined the others just as neatly. "I can see where Mirra learned her skill with blades."

Startled, Bao turned around to see an Ilmarrion woman he wasn't familiar with. Her clothes were travel worn and salt stained. She wore her dark braids in a messy knot on the top of her head. A hint of a smile tugged at the corners of her full mouth as she waited for Bao's response.

"Some of it," he said, turning around to face the woman. "I take it your trip was successful, Oya?" He gestured to the bulging satchel at her side.

Oya's full smile broke free and he could easily see how she broke through Mirra's walls as if they were nothing. "More or less," she said. "We won't truly know until we draw the demon out like the poison he is."

Bao nodded. "I think the high priestess and the princess are in the citadel."

"I'm actually here for you." Oya pressed her lips to hold back her laughter at Bao's confused expression. "You've done something I don't think anyone's been able to achieve for ages."

Bao chuckled and waved his hand. "Mirra's not that hard to understand. She likes to think she keeps everyone at arm's length, but in all reality, she loves her friends deeply."

Oya laughed, shaking her head, the gems and beads in her hair clacking against each other. "Oh, that I know well enough. I'm talking about deceiving the Dark One. You stole his prey right from under him. Without him knowing."

"I'm not entirely sure about the not knowing bit," Bao said, rubbing the back of his head. "And I'm pretty sure that Mirra did it first."

"Yes she did," Oya said. "But he was so used to getting his way that it never occurred to him that someone could defy him. I guarantee he wasn't about to make the same mistake twice and yet, you not only caused him grief, but stole Braelyn away."

"I almost didn't", he admitted, his words barely above a whisper.

"Thank the gods for small miracles."

Bao snorted. "I don't think Gaitlan or Braelyn would call it 'small'".

"Perhaps not. Either way, I have a need for a man who pulled one over on a demon."

Purpose thrummed through Bao, making his spine straightened. "What need do you have of me, priestess?"

"The tides of fate are rising. Mirra and Gaitlan must have succeeded with their search. I felt the rippling of power on the ship to Undros. I pushed my horse as fast as I could because there's no doubt that he knows too."

She didn't need to elaborate who "he" was. Bao crossed his arms, falling into the role of Bossman. "Again, what do you want with this crooked soul?"

"Like Mirra, you see paths that most do not nor will take. It's that sight that allowed you both to surprise a creature that has lived for eons beyond count."

"We just got lucky," Bao said.

"Then let's hope that you can lend us some of that luck. Because we're going to need it."

SWEAT POURED DOWN BRAELYN'S FLUSHED FACE, MAKING the loose strands of her hair cling to her face. Her eyes were screwed shut and her brow furrowed with concentration. At the edges of her consciousness, she was mildly aware of High Priestess Usoa's soft steps as she walked around the sanctum. Another set of soft steps caught her attention. "Stay focused, your highness," High Priestess Usoa said gently.

Braelyn gritted her teeth and honed in once more on the relic cupped in her hands. The Seed of Life. When High Priestess Usoa first gave her the necklace, Braelyn didn't think it was much. The gem was pretty, a red too dark to be a ruby. Given what happened to the priests and priestess that made the relics, she suspected it may be the blood of the one who created it. Shuddering at the thought, Braelyn pushed all other thoughts away and focused on what she was supposed to be doing — attuning to the Seed.

She still couldn't believe that she was a wielder. Not once in her life had she ever shown any inclination of magic. But apparently, that didn't matter, according to the high priestess. The relics are an entirely different sort of magic than what the Ilmarrions use and any attempts to mix the two were often disastrous.

Braelyn sighed, rubbing a temple. What had started as a pinprick of pain had now blossomed into a full migraine. There was no way she could maintain focus now. Her head pulsed in beat with her heart, sending fresh waves of pain throughout her skull.

"That is enough for today," High Priestess Usoa said. "I suggest you rest, maybe visit Grandmother and we will resume later."

Braelyn mumbled some semblance of a reply and pushed herself to her feet. Her joints screamed in pain as she stood up from the hard stone floor. She slipped the Seed around her neck, tucking under her dress. Not that she thought anyone would try to take it from her, but she didn't like the way the Ilmarrions stared at her. She was used to stares as a princess and as Julian's favorite toy, but there was something about the Ilmarrions that made her feel uneasy. Maybe it had something to do with the same eyes on unfamiliar faces or the weight of power behind the stares. Or perhaps it had nothing to do with the Ilmarrion people, who had been nothing but kind to her, even if they kept their distance. It most likely had to do with the guilt that her ancestors here instrumental in the fall of a once mighty people. All around her she could see what once had been a great city, undoubtedly full of learning and arts.

She briefly wondered how her brother handled this feeling, if he even was of the right mind to perceive it. As she neared the open-air baths, she heard Bao talking with someone. Unbidden, her pace picked up. How many days had it been since they spent any time together? She'd grown accustomed to his presence, to the sound of his voice, his laugh. A soft smile tugged at her mouth as she rounded the corner. But he wasn't alone.

Braelyn's first impression of the woman was that even dressed in worn traveling clothes, she was the most strikingly beautiful woman she's ever seen. She looked like a long forgotten goddess of the night, come down to talk to her chosen mortal. Bao said something, and the woman laughed, throwing her head back. Braelyn's gut twisted. She turned to flee before they spied her.

"Brae," Bao called out. "Come and meet Oya, the woman who tore through Mirra's walls."

The woman, Oya, laughed again, "Not quite. I gave her a bit of grief in the beginning."

Braelyn kept her face neutral as she walked up, still unsure about Oya. "She probably deserved it."

"Only a little," Oya said with a shrug. "But she gives back in turn." The laughter on her face fell. "Have either of you heard from her?"

Bao and Braelyn shook their heads. "I only received the letter she sent from the Holy Isle explaining everything. Since then," Braelyn cut her eyes at Bao, her cheeks warming. "We've been busy."

Oya nodded. "Mirra said you were strong. I'm glad to see that demon didn't break you."

Braelyn ducked her head. "Not completely." Bao shifted beside her. She continued on, unaware of the silent war inside him to maintain the distance between them. "Maybe that's why I can't seem to get this to work for me."

Reaching under her dress, she pulled out the Seed. In the sun's light, the gem came to life, looking more like a drop of blood than a stone. "Maybe the high priestess is wrong and I'm not the wielder."

Oya shook her head. "No, I can feel the connection between you and the Seed. True, it's faint, but it's there."

"But I can't connect to it," Braelyn sighed. "No matter how hard I try, all I get is a headache. I would have better luck trying to walk through walls the way Mirra does."

Much to their surprise, Oya doubled over in laughter. "I'm sorry," she said, wiping her eyes. "You reminded me of Mirra's first attempt to enter The Tower."

Braelyn looked at Bao, who shrugged. "What's The Tower?"

"It's the place where we learn how to master our abilities through the virtues of the pillars of power."

"Oh," Bao said when the silence grew too long. "That makes perfect sense."

Oya smiled and shook her head. "Why don't you join Bao, as he uses his crooked mind to find weak points in our defenses? I fear things will start moving quickly."

Braelyn reached for Bao's sleeve without knowing. "How much longer?"

"I cannot say. All I know is that if I felt the last pieces fall into place, then so did he." Oya pressed her lips into a tight smile. "The end is nearing, one way or another. Until then, all we can do is to prepare and make sure that we savor each moment we have with those who are important to us."

Bao fought the urge to shift under Oya's knowing gaze when she spoke the last words. Was he really that obvious?

"But don't let your thoughts be consumed by fear of what may come. Tonight, there will be a feast. You both should take this time to relax and celebrate."

"Celebrate what?" Braelyn asked.

"Your brother and Mirra were successful in their endeavor. They found the last of the relics and their wielders. The orb of Thrilla is remade and soon the demon squatting inside Lord Julian will be gone from this world and you will get justice for your family and people."

Braelyn clasped the Seed. "As long as I can get this to work."

"You will," Oya said. "Just remember that the Seed is a part of you now. Think of it as an extension of your being, not a tool."

Oya bade them farewell with a curt bow and headed straight for the baths. Braelyn watched after her until Bao spoke, his voice thick with concern. "You alright, princess?"

Braelyn sighed, turning back the way she came. "You don't have to call me that, and no, I'm not." She wrapped her arms around her middle, her shoulders curving inward.

Bao chewed the inside of his cheek. "Come with me." He held his hand out to Braelyn. She took it without question, her despair morphing into light curiosity.

He led her to a tall building near the edge of the city's protective border. It stood taller than any of the other surrounding structures, thick moss nearly covering the entire outer walls. Bao dropped her hand and walked through the door. "Come on, princess, we're not there yet."

Braelyn pouted. "I told you to stop calling me that."

Bao tapped his chin, his face scrunched up with false confusion. "You did? When?"

She opened her mouth, ready to retort, but stopped when Bao laughed. "There she is," he said, leaning against the crumbling door frame. "I was wondering where my Brae had gone."

Warmth blossomed in the middle of her chest at hearing Bao calling her his. She folded her arms over her chest to keep the painfully sweet sensation to herself. "You try having the fate of the world rest on your shoulders."

Something in his gaze darkened. He stepped back out into the sunlight, crossing the distance between them in three long strides. Braelyn held her breath but didn't move. A feeling she couldn't quite place rushed through her. It wasn't fear. Bao was one of the few people she was entirely sure wouldn't hurt her. Bao cocked his head as he stared down at her. She hadn't realized, or had forgotten, how tall he was. If she were to wrap her arms around him, his chin could easily rest on the top of her head.

"I know, Braelyn," he said, his voice low. "I lost my entire world once and nearly lost it again."

Braelyn swallowed. "Again?" She tipped her head up, her mouth slightly parted. The sun had transformed Bao's warm, dark eyes into twin pools of molten amber. Those burning eyes fell to her parted lips, blazing with a hunger that set her flesh aflame. She leaned closer, drawn in by a force that she was tired of fighting.

Lord Tolin was like the first spring sun, gently warming the frozen earth so new life could bloom. Bao burned as well, like the sun in the height of summer, but he was so much more. He was like the quiet nights when the dark held no monsters. He was the stone she clung to amidst a stormy sea, her lifeline, shelter, and so much more.

Her tongue darted across her bottom lip. Bao followed its path. She leaned in closer, their bodies pressing together like the layers of the sweet rolls he loved so much. Bao inhaled sharply, taking a half step back. "Let's go before the sun gets too low."

The sight of Bao's retreating back stung more than she'd like to admit. Scowling, Braelyn followed, wondering what caused him to pull back. He wanted her as much as she wanted him… right?

Bao led them to a set of semi-stable stone stairs. "I've already tested them out. They should hold our weight."

"Should, that's comforting."

Bao snorted and walked up the steps with more confidence than she had. Braelyn watched him walk up the stairs for a bit longer, still not trusting the stone to bear the both of them. When she couldn't wait any longer, she tentatively took the first step. The stone felt sure and steady beneath her foot. Most of her trepidation fell away with each step, but the lack of a railing and knowing that the building had been deteriorating for the better part of a century left her uneasy. Her anxiety skyrocketed when Bao broke the silence again.

"We gotta jump this part. Don't worry. This is the only section that's broken."

"Excuse me," Braelyn said, her knees going weak. Her heart jumped into her throat when Bao lept from where he stood. She didn't breath until he landed on the other side of the wide gap, touching the wall to steady himself. He turned and flashed her a grin that tore at her heart. "Don't worry, I'll catch you."

Braelyn edged as close as she dared to the edge of the gap and looked down. The floor was a terribly long way down. "I don't think I can."

"Don't tell me you've forgotten Sorro's lessons already? You're going to break his heart."

Braelyn blinked once and took a deep breath, breaking up the tightness in her chest. Slowly, she backed down the steps, took one more breath, bouncing lightly on her toes as she shook her arms. With a silent prayer to the gods, she ran. As the toes of her right foot reached the edge of the gap, she pushed, leaping into the open air. For what felt like an eternity, she flew across the gap, her gaze fixated on Bao's outstretched hand. For a heart stopping moment, it felt like she wasn't going to cross the distance, but Bao's powerful hand clasped around her forearm and pulled her across the rest of the way.

Their momentum carried them backwards. She landed on top of Bao with a grunt, breathing heavily until she recognized the intimacy of their position — hands clasped between them, Bao's arm wrapped tightly around her waist, and their legs tangled around each other. Braelyn's heart beat against her chest like a captive bird. She pulled back to see his face, but he held on tighter. "Give me a second."

"Are you hurt?"

"No," he said, "I just need a moment."

Braelyn laid her head down on his chest, listening to the steady but heavy drumming of his heart. All too soon for her liking, he loosened his grip and gently helped Braelyn to her feet first, before getting up. He brushed the dust off the back of his pants, his cheeks and ears a delicate shade of pink "Just a little bit further."

They finished their climb in silence. When they reached the top, there was nothing but the tops of trees and the open sky before them.

"So what did you want to show me?" Braelyn asked, slightly panting.

Bao turned her toward the setting sun and said, "Why don't you see for yourself?"

"My word," Braelyn breathed. Mystic Wood stretched out around them as far as she could see, like an ocean of green. The bits of Moakwyd rose from the emerald sea like spires with the dome of the citadel reflecting the brilliant orange of the sunset.

"I think this was a lookout tower," Bao said, moving to stand beside her. "You can see similar structures, there, there, and there."

Braelyn nodded, seeing the lone stone towers rising partially above the trees. "They might want to put traps there."

"Not a bad idea," Bao said. "Might as well use what's left to our advantage."

Braelyn made a noise of agreement and leaned against the wall of the ancient watchtower. Bao stayed back, burning the memory of her leaning into the last rays of day, her hair blazing like golden threads. Even dressed simply in a plain homespun dress, there was no denying the marks of nobility. She belonged to another world, one where he wasn't welcomed. No matter how they felt. But when she turned, the planes of her face framed by the setting sun, Bao knew that he'd never wanted so desperately than to be by her side for the rest of their lives.

BRAELYN TOOK GREAT PAINS IN HER APPEARANCE. She needed everything to be perfect, if the night was to go how she wanted. After the watchtower, Bao was uncommonly silent, his mind a thousand miles away. She would have thought he was focused on ferreting out weaknesses if not for his expression when she turned around. It was the look of a man prepared to sacrifice his own happiness for the sake of the greater good. She'd seen that look on her father's face a hundred times growing up. It angered her then, and it angered her now.

A knock at the drew drew Braelyn's attention. "Enter."

"How was the rest of your day?" Oya asked, walking through. In her arms, she carried a deep crimson dress. "I thought you might want something special for tonight. Many people are wearing their best clothes."

A broad smile broke across Braelyn's face. "Yes, thank you. And may I say that you look lovely tonight?"

And she did. The white silk dress draped around Oya shone like starlight against the darkness of her skin. Encircled twice around her waist was a wide belt the color of twilight, threaded with gold. She wore her hair half up, twisted into a knot behind her head, secured by a hair piece with spokes like the sun.

Oya bowed. "You're too kind, princess."

"Please call me Braelyn. I feel less like a princess these days."

Oya pressed her lips into a thin line. Braelyn pretended not to notice, running her fingers over the dress. "This is beautiful. And the fabric…I've never touched something so light and soft."

"It was made before the Purging." Sorrow briefly rippled over Oya's expression. "The workings used to make it have protected it against time."

"Are you sure you want me to wear something so precious?"

"This dress was meant to be worn," Oya said. "Before meeting your brother and Mirra, I might feel the way you do. But now, I want to let go of some of the pain of the past. It doesn't serve me or my people." Oya motioned for Braelyn to lift her arms. "You are a wielder of the Seed of Life. And you are a friend of my people. Those two reasons alone are why you should accept this gift."

"Thank you," Braelyn said, tears brimming. Oya motioned for her to lift her arms again. The shift of the dress went on first, smoother than any silk she'd ever worn and as cool as a spring morning. The dress went on next. It was slightly thicker than the shift, but still thin enough that Braelyn didn't think she'd suffer from the sultry summer night.

"Now sit still so I can fix your hair."

Braelyn sat still as commanded, though her hands continued to explore the dress. It was unlike anything she'd ever worn before. The neckline alone would cause a scandal. Wide and swooping, it exposed her shoulders and the tops of her breasts. The sleeves stopped just shy of her elbows before becoming sheer bells that seemed to sparkle whenever she moved.

"There you go," Oya said as she slipped a dark hair stick into Braelyn's hair. "What do you think?"

Braelyn looked into the small mirror and gasped. Most of her hair was pulled back save for two long strands that framed her face with gentle curls. The hair stick held the top part of her hair up while the rest had been lightly braided, secured by a bit of golden thread.

"It's beautiful," she said. "I don't know how to thank you."

As she turned her head in the mirror, marveling at her reflection, a soft knock came at the door. A young apprentice priestess with a long, dark braid with bells at the end entered carrying a small tray of clay jars. "I have some simple cosmetics for you to use, if you like."

"Thank you Katsumi," Oya said, taking the tray and setting it next to Braelyn. "This part I leave to you. See you at the feast."

The pair inclined their heads and swiftly exited the room. "We don't interfere," Katsumi said with a smirk.

"And I'm not," Oya replied. "Even a blind man could see what the princess has planned. I only helped to arm her for battle." Katsumi laughed, threading her arm through Oya's. Tonight was going to be a night to remember for many reasons.

Bao downed the remnants of his drink, unable to remove the image of Braelyn lit by the setting sun out of his mind. If he were a man worthy of standing at her side, he would have dropped to his knees right then and pledged his undying devotion. But he wasn't. He was the son of lowly merchants and a criminal overlord. Instead, he spent the better part of the evening before the feast conversing with Roux, the copper-skinned head of rangers. She immediately commissioned the magical booby-traps and then asked his opinion on locations she'd scouted out for further traps. He had to admit; she was thorough; netted traps, modified hunting snares and pits.

But he feared it wouldn't be enough. The demon using Lord Julian like a puppet still had plenty of tricks up its sleeve. Of that, Bao was certain. He knew you couldn't plan for what you don't know, but the scales weren't exactly tipped in their favor.

"Are the drinks that bad?"

Bao's heart fluttered at the sound of Braelyn's laugh. He turned to answer, and all thoughts vanished like the morning fog when he saw her.

She was a vision, a goddess on earth, dressed in a dark crimson dress with a neckline so low that her shoulders were bare. Fire light danced along her hair, making the brighter strands shine like rivers of stars. Braelyn wore no jewelry, not even the relic, and used only a hint of kohl to line her eyes. Bao could only gape like a fish, frozen before her.

Braelyn pressed her lips together to keep the smirk off her face. She'd have to thank Oya properly once everything was over…and they survived. "Do I look bad?", she said with mock worry.

"No," Bao nearly shouted, reaching for her. His face flushed, and he coughed, composing himself. "No, you look amazing. Breathtaking even." Her smile set him aflame.

"You clean up nicely yourself. Although I already knew that from all the times you snuck into the palace." And she meant every word. The golden yellow color of his undershirt brought out the warmth of his skin. And the muted green overcoat with wide sleeves brought out the flecks of green in his eyes. A braided leather belt over dark, loose trousers and sturdy boots rounded out his outfit for the evening.

Braelyn slid her arm into his and gently steered him away from the crowd. "Come with me. I have something I need to discuss."

Bao allowed himself to be led away, still struggling to form a single coherent thought or word. Braelyn led him inside the citadel to a small alcove just off the main room. She sat down on the granite bench and patted the space beside her.

The collar of Bao's shirt was suddenly too tight. He tugged at it as he sat down. He chided himself mentally. She just doesn't want anyone to hear, he said to himself. No need to get all worked up. "You're not wearing the relic."

Her hand went up, fingers trailing where the necklace usually sat. "I wanted nothing to distract me tonight."

She looked up at him with a look that gave the impression that she wanted to eat him. It made his mouth run dry. "Princess…" he said, barely above a whisper.

"I told you to call me Brea," she reminded him, leaning in closer. "Bao…"

Gods and honorable ancestors, his name on her lips sounded like heaven. It wasn't fair. Jumping to his feet, Bao put some distance between them before he did something he'd regret, no matter how sweet it would be. "I can't…"

"Why?"

Bao struggled to find the words. Braelyn stood and gently turned him to face her. "After Julian murdered my parents, I was afraid to let people in. Even when Tolin," she paused briefly, sorrow flashing across her face, "Even when Tolin and the other lords tried to help me, I kept my distance. Then they died, and I refused to add more blood to my hands."

"You didn't kill them," Bao said.

Braelyn shook her head. "I may as well have. Then you burst into my life, bringing a good deal of chaos in your wake. You brought life back to me in a way I never thought possible. Bao, you're a good man." She cut him off when he tried to argue with her. "The fates left you with very few avenues to take and you made the best of what was available to you. Like Mirra, you're a survivor and should never feel guilty about what you had to do to stay alive. But where others would have taken their hurt and turned it on others, you want to help. You try to take care of everyone, make sure that no one gets to hurt. You want the people close to you to live a life full of happiness. That's why you let Em and Sorro leave."

She reached up and took his face in her hands. "I never wanted a lord or king. I only ever wanted a good man. A man who wouldn't resign me to the role of birthing heirs. One who would listen to me as much as I listened to him. A partner. A friend. And I found all that in you. So don't tell me you're not good enough."

Her gaze burned through him like hot iron. "If you don't feel the same, then I will respect your wishes."

Bao took her hands into his, bringing them down over his heart. "Your brother."

Braelyn snorted. "My brother will respect my wishes or I'll wallop him. And I suspect Mirra would do the same."

"That she would," he chuckled. The voices that screamed he wasn't good enough still echoed in the back of his mind; though much quieter than before. Gently, he reached up, cupping Braelyn's face. She lifted her face like a flower to the sun. "I would like to kiss you."

Braelyn smiled widely. "You'd better."

She tasted as sweet as he'd remembered from that one day. Only this time, he could actually savor it. They deepened their kiss, his hands entangling in her hair and Braelyn bunching his overcoat in her fists.

Braelyn's soul sang, soaring to new heights of joy. She was tired of living in the dark, surrounded by the ghosts of the dead. Her parents wouldn't have wanted that. Tolin wouldn't have either. She opened up to Bao, drinking him in greedily and not giving a single damn about it.

In the dark of Braelyn's room, a tiny pinprick of red light formed in the middle of the Seed of Life. It grew into a steady pulse, similar to the beating of a heart.

CHAPTER TWENTY-FOUR

The Council of Lords conversed amongst one another with tense whispers. Over the course of a week, Lord Julian had trashed the old king's study, nearly beat a maid to death, and they'd seen more executions than all the previous years combined. They knew it had to do with the missing princess. To make matters worse, somehow, word of her disappearance made it to the rest of the city. Commoners, merchants, and other nobles clamored for answers, demanding to see their princess. On top of all that, a new rumor was spreading like wildfire. Some people now speculated that Lord Julian stole the crown from Princess Braelyn, keeping her captive under pain of death. It was quickly becoming too much for the gathered lords, who spent more time with their mistresses and hunting than locked in court intrigues and political climbings. They began to question if they had chosen the wrong side.

The doors to the council room flew open with a loud bang, causing many to jump. Lord Julian stormed into the room as dark and terrible as a storm cloud. Behind him, two new guards followed, sending chills down all who met their dark gazes.

"Be seated," Lord Julian commanded. He took his seat at the head of the table, glowering. "I have news of the princess's whereabouts."

The silence of the chamber erupted into discourse as all the gathered lords clamored for answers. They fell silent when one of Lord Julian's new guards unsheathed his sword. One by one, they fell silent, taking their seats. It was only when the room was calm did the guard put away his blade.

Julian continued, as if the interruption hadn't happened. "My agents have spotted the princess and her captors taking shelter in a ruined city deep within Mystic Woods. They say that it's a small force of antiroyalists, no more than a hundred." He scoffed. "If that. We will march on their base camp in three days. I suggest you hurry to get your affairs in order by then. We will meet at the southern border along the main road."

"Three days? My lands are near Three Kings Bay. It will take me at least twice that time to get there to muster my forces."

Julian turned his focus on the lord who spoke. A faint sheen of sweat broke out across the lord's ruddy face. "Send a bird and make ready or be charged with treason."

A collective uneasy murmur rippled through the lords. To be charged with treason as a noble carried more weight than as a commoner or merchant. If a noble was convicted of treason, everything associated with their house would be burned to the ground. Their entire bloodline would end unless the crown felt merciful to spare the children. Their lands would be salted and their people scattered. It didn't happen often, but when it did, it left a lasting impression.

All other arguments and concerns died away as the men, who once felt so assured of their power, bowed their heads like common servants. Julian opened his mouth and breathed in the delectable flavor of their broken spirits. When he raised his hand, three servers entered, carrying trays with wine and glasses. At Julian's bidding, a glass was set down in front of each lord, then filled with a red wine so dark it was nearly black. "A toast to our future success and to the princess's safe return."

He raised his glass and downed its contents, leaving the others with no other route but to follow suit. Several of the lords cringed at the wine's flavor, something akin to ink and rotting meat. The air in the chamber grew tense, as if the world waited for what was to come next. A startled cry disrupted the tense silence of the chamber as one of the eldest lords doubled over, clutching his stomach.

"You bastard!" shouted a lord, turning to glare at Julian. "You won't get away with this, our people…." The lord's words were swallowed by a strangled cry as he collapsed to the floor.

One by one, the Council of Lords fell to the ground, writhing in agony. Julian watched it all with a delighted expression more appropriate for a play than for the massacre happening in front of him. The room fell silent, save for the ticking clock on the mantel. Julian finished his glass, set it down, and stretched his hand out. The bodies of the lords convulsed, their mouths open in silent screams. Then slowly, as if pulled by marionette strings, they rose to their feet, turned as one and bowed to Julian. When they straightened, Julian looked at his new generals and smiled. It would be different this time. This time he would be victorious and this world would be his and he would feast like he hadn't in a millennium.

If the three hundred soldiers encamped thought anything was amiss with their lord's sudden call to arms, they kept it to themselves, grateful for a moment's rest at last. Anyone would be exhausted with the past three day's mad dash of mustering arms and marching across the kingdom. Now they waited, sharpening their weapons as they waited for their next orders.

The Regent and most of the Council of Lords strode through camp, causing a fury of movement as soldiers scrambled to their feet to bow as they passed. Not a single lord spared a passing glance at the gathered army, even to their own men.

"Bastards," muttered a young archer once the lords were out of hearing. "They haul us away in the middle of the night, without warning, and now ignore us completely."

An older archer with graying hair and a deep scar across his face hit the younger archer on the back of the head. "Hush boy," he scolded. "I heard the princess is in these woods."

"Where d'ya hear that?"

"From some boys that came from the capital," the wizened archer said, gesturing with his thumb. "They said that she's being held captive in some ruins by a bunch of rebels."

A foot soldier snorted as he ran a wet stone along the edge of this battle ax. "If that's what ya want to believe, then you go right ahead."

"What you say?" The older archer's expression darkened. "You callin' me a liar, boy?"

The foot soldier laughed bitterly, setting aside his work. "Not a liar, just gullible. You think the princess was stolen? More like ran away. Wouldn't you if you were held prisoner by the man what killed your kin?"

The young archer chimed in. "That was her brother."

"Lies all of it."

The older archer heaved up the foot soldier by the collar. "I was there. I saw the bodies left by the prince and his followers. Don't tell me it was all lies."

The foot soldier grabbed the archer's arm with one hand and slipped a long dagger free with the other. "Use your brain, ya idjit. If the prince had enough followers to stage a coupe, then why hasn't he attacked again? Why hasn't he reached out to his allies in other kingdoms, twisting everything to his side? He's smart enough to at least do that much."

The tension between the two grew until the younger archer was sure it would come to blows. "It's not up to us to decide what's true or not. We swore an oath to come when called and the call was made. We have to put trust in the lords we swore to."

The sound of the chow bell cut through the tension faster than any words. The two soldiers released their hold on each other, fires still blazing in their faces. But food was food, and they'd had little to eat over the past three days. Still grumbling, they made their way to the three enormous cauldrons near the middle of the camp with three neat lines already formed. The lanterns were lit by the time the trio got their turn, bowls held out for whatever meal had been prepared. But whatever they'd been expecting or hoping for, it definitely wasn't the thick, black gruel the cooks ladled in without a word.

"Gods in hel, what is this slop?"

The cooks said nothing, motioning them to move along with a dripping ladle. Grumbling, they returned to their spot around a small fire, spooning around the suspicious liquid with matching expressions of mistrust and disgust. The old archer caved first with a shrug. He'd eaten worse things whilst in war. He spooned the gruel into his mouth, nearly gagging at the acrid taste that somehow tasted like rotting meat and something else he couldn't place. Since he didn't die with the first bite, the foot soldier and young archer hesitantly spooned it into their own mouths, retching at the flavor.

A hush fell over the camp, not even crickets dared to make their presence known. A single scream of pain and terror cut through the tense quiet, followed quickly by another and another until the entire world seemed to be filled with nothing but the screams of the dying.

In the main tent, Julian looked up from an ancient map, dark eyes gleaming with mirth. "Dinner time." The screams cut off as quickly as they'd risen, the world falling silent once more. "They don't have the forces they once did," Julian said, turning back to the map. "Most of their structures and defenses are gone, pulled back to protect the heart of the city, here."

His face darkened. "They've turned back my previous attempts to break through only because I underestimated them. I won't make the same mistake a third time. Come tomorrow, we will march right to their crumbling city and raise the last of their silly little civilization to the ground. I've grown tired of their meddling nature. Them and their silly little star god." Julian looked at his generals, all silence and still as statues, their black eyes dull.

"Gather your forces, leave all useless human trappings behind. Nothing will slow us down. Nothing will get in our way."

In unison, the lords bowed, leaving Julian alone to glower at the map. He ran a finger from the camp's location to the heart of Mystic Woods, where Moakwyd stood. The paper ripped and curled as if burned in the wake of his finger.

He and the rest of his kind had gone through worlds beyond measure in the quest to state their never ending hunger. Suffering, pain, betrayal, destruction these were as nourishing to him as mother's milk. He'd spent so long enjoying the pile of smoldering ashes in his wake, celebrating wanton destruction with his brethren. But now he was all alone, even now that foolish boy who set him free was nearly gone. Too broken to be any fun, he long stopped screaming over the atrocities done with his body. It was boring.

A slow smile spread across his face. Although, if he were to get his hands on Mirra, then he'd have some fun for the first time in decades. His mouth watered as he imagined the sounds of her screams when he made her kill every single person she loved. Soon. Soon, such delectable pain would be his and he would savor each and every bite.

The sun rose on an eerily quiet camp; fires were left half smoldering. Tents ransacked and goods scattered without care. Horses and dogs pulled against their tethers, desperate for a scrap of food or sip of water and wondering why their masters had abandoned them.

At the edge of the forest, a mass of too still soldiers stood as still as the trees before them. They held their weapons in loose grips, their faces void of any human emotions as they stared ahead with eyes as black as death. At the front of the army stood Lord Julian wreathed in darkness.

He stepped forward and the grass beneath his feet turned yellow, then brown, before breaking into dust in the early morning air. With each step, the wave of decay spread out, an obvious line, all the way to the first of the trees. Julian touched the first of the trees, and just like with the gras, the trees withered and died, crumbling to dust. Grinning widely, Julian pushed onward, cutting a swath of destruction large enough for his army to walk through without hindrance.

With nothing to bar their way, Julian's army reached the first broken watchtower just as the sun passed its zenith. At the sight of the tower, Julian paused, tipping his head back. Though it was faint, he could smell Ilmarrion magic. Perhaps it was a remnant from long ago, or something new. Either way, it didn't appear strong enough to do any real sort of damage. Julian continued on, his army dividing around the tower like the river around an embankment.

There were many benefits to having mindless servants that knew your every will. They couldn't speak, didn't need to eat, and followed orders explicitly. Their only downside was they lacked independent reasoning. One soldier, a wizened archer with a large scar, was jostled by another soldier holding twin battle axes. The old archer fell into the tower, activating the trap with an explosion that sent smoldering chunks of the ancient watchtower raining down on Julian's army.

BRAELYN SAT UP WITH A START WHEN BAO LURCHED FROM her bed. They started sharing the night they finally admitted their feelings for each other. Though they had gone none further than passionately kissing. Bao insisted. Initially, Braelyn wanted to protest, but refrained. He was already pushing beyond what he was comfortable with, just by acknowledging his feelings for her. It didn't truly matter to her in what capacity they were together, just as long as they were.

"Was that thunder?" she asked, rubbing the sleep from her eyes.

Bao slid out of the bed, pulling on the rest of his clothes. "No. Can you use that to see the southern tower?"

All fragments of sleep vanished from her body. Braelyn quickly took the Seed into her hands, opened her mind to see what the flora had to share. She still couldn't believe that she could finally attune to the ancient relic all because she kissed the boy she liked. High Priestess Usoa said it was more likely because Braelyn finally opened herself fully to life, but she liked to think it was the power of true love's kiss.

Chiding herself, she refocused, seeing the world pass through the roots of the noble trees. She nearly dropped the necklace when she came to the place where the southern watchtower and their first boobytrap used to stand. Her skin felt as if on fire because of the burning plant life around the smoking crater. To make matters worse, a terrible taste filled her mouth. Shaking her head and gritting her teeth, Braelyn pushed past the discomforting sensory input, pulling back her mind's eye to get a better picture of what had transpired and what she saw made her stomach recoil more than the foul taste left by the bodies of fallen soldiers.

"He called up the army," Braelyn gasped when she threw her consciousness back into her body. Bao caught her before she could fall.

"Are you sure?" Braelyn nodded, too afraid to speak. "Maybe you can appeal to the lords and get them to switch sides."

"It won't help," Braelyn said, her voice quivering. "He's done something to them. They're gone, filled with whatever's inside him. They won't listen to anyone but Julian."

Bao swore softly, pulling his boots on. "Well, either way, he's come. Let's get you to the citadel."

Panic cut through Braelyn, rooting her where she stood. All she could see was ruin around her with Bao laying dead at her feet, his cooling blood painting her feet red.

"Braelyn!" Bao grasped her by the shoulders, gently shaking her back to reality. He said nothing as he read her face. Her every thought and fear, as clear to him as his very own. Tangling his fingers in her hair, Bao pulled Braelyn close, holding her until the worst of her shaking subsided. "I won't promise that nothing bad will happen. But what I can promise is that I will do everything in my power to get back to you."

"Your brother is on his way. Along with Mirra and the rest of the people, we need to lock this bastard away, for good. But they need us to hold on just a little bit longer. To have faith in them the same way they have faith in us."

Beyond the safety of the walls and Bao's arms, Braelyn heard the city come to life. Those who could fight rushed to their posts while those who couldn't, took shelter within the bowels of the citadel. That's where High Priestess Usoa and Oya were waiting for her. They may not have all the pieces needed to lock away the monster inside Julian, but they were going to be there, waiting for the others. Drawing in a long, shaky breath, Braelyn reluctantly pulled out of Bao's embrace.

She gazed up at him, a thousand things built inside, demanding to be said. In the end, all she could do was bring his face to hers and hope that her kiss would convey all the things words couldn't and that it wouldn't be the last shared between them.

ANOTHER TRAP SENT THE SCATTERED REMNANTS OF Julian's army into the air. He didn't bother to glance behind. He had thousands more to spare. His focus was avoiding the increasingly annoying traps himself. The mortal ones were of no concern to him, but the ones imbued with magic were another matter entirely. He'd taken a risk splitting his essence into so many puppets, but it was one that he deemed necessary. He didn't need warriors with skill, he needed a force large enough to wear down their defenses until nothing was left. That didn't mean with each explosion, pit, or snare, his ire didn't grow.

He felt the barrier before coming onto it. Julian cloaked himself with more power to peer past the physical world. Before him stood a wall and went up several yards before curving like an upside-down bowl. He studied the swirling runes and sigils that made up the barrier, moderately impressed. The last time, it had been nothing for him to shatter the first protective barrier because it was nothing more than a pale replica of older workings that he knew from before. But this barrier was different. There were symbols he'd never seen before, though he could see influences from other cultures woven into the design. A bit of Horse Lords there. There was one that unmistakably came from northern Zallino. He even spied bits of Bardon and Stalmar woven into the designs. Every place where Ilmarrions dwelled or took shelter after the Purging reflected at him in the wall that kept them safe, for now.

Julian raised his hand, a silent command, and his army crashed against the barrier like waves on a rocky shore. Runes and sigils flared with each attack, leaving blackened and splintered flesh in its wake. Julian remained where he stood, his eyes closed, searching. Through each attack, he gained more insight into the barrier's creation.

The first wave fell, a smoldering heap of useless flesh. Julian hissed, clutching his head. No matter how thinly he spread his essence, it still pained him to lose it. But it wouldn't hold him back, not for long. The greenery around Julian blackened and crumbled as he sucked their vitality into himself. Loosening the reins on his power, his dark hunger rippled around him, reaching out to feast on the glorious life forces around him.

Brimming with writhing darkness to the point of his main body being lost from sight, Julian raised his hand toward the sky. More trees, animals, and plants died as their life force collected in the space above Julian's hand. The swirling vortex of energy was at first a resplendent gold, but at its heart, a pearl of darkness bloomed until it took over the golden light. Grunting with effort, Julian heaved the black vortex at the wall.

Bolts of lightning radiated out from where the vortex struck the wall. The vortex didn't fall. It edged in further, causing more bands of lightning that transformed into cracks. Julian stepped forward, pushing the vortex further into the wall. The wall rippled and wavered, the runes and sigils blinking in and out until their light died with one last flare and the barrier disappeared as if it had never been.

I N THE CITADEL'S HEART, H IGH P RIESTESS U SOA STARRED southward. She'd never felt such powerful destruction. It was an affront to everything she stood for, everything she'd fought for. Perhaps this was why the Ilieng hadn't called her home yet. The darkness was ancient, even older than she was. They would need more than rediscovered relics and theoretical understanding to defeat this evil. And time was not on their side.

"Oya, I leave you in charge."

"What?" Unconsciously, Oya clutched the orb of Thrilla closer to her. "Where are you going?"

"Mirra and the others are too far away to be of any help. They need a faster path."

"Then summon…"

Usoa stood to her full height, already loosening the tight grip on her affinity. The grip she maintained for centuries to keep herself hidden from star hunters and to keep her own people from fearing her. "No. This may finally be the end of my journey and I will face it. Help the princess when she arrives, cast the protection circle and make ready."

Usoa walked down the steps of the citadel, the lone beacon of serenity amidst the rising chaos. Those who scurried past her paused in awe at the gold-green light emanating from her proud figure. They spared precious seconds to drop to their knees in reverence. Usoa stopped in front of a large oak tree, the tree at the heart of the city. Pressing her hands against the trunk, she pulled on the thread that she'd hadn't touched since death stole away someone she cared for deeply. And with one last steadying breath, Usoa walked through the great oak, leaving the city for the first time in three hundred years.

Braelyn stood dumbfounded at the top of the stairs. "By the gods," she whispered before hastily making her way inside. Overhead, the once blue sky had turned black, with the tops of the trees turning brown.

"It is time, your highness," Oya said, taking Braelyn gently by the elbow. She steered the princess towards the center of the great room where the last bits of sunlight streamed through the holes in the domed ceiling.

"Did I just see what I thought I did?"

Oya nodded, her expression nearly identical to Braelyn's. "It's not something many can do. It's dangerous and only the most powerful have tried it."

"What did she do?"

"I think she went to get the others," Oya said after some thought. "With demons on our doorstep, we don't have the luxury of waiting for them to arrive."

Braelyn turned, staring at the tree and the growing storm of decay. "Will they get here in time?"

Oya stood beside Braelyn, sliding her hand into the princess's. "I hope so."

"Is there anything we can do?"

Oya gave Braelyn's hand a squeeze. "Pray."

CHAPTER TWENTY-FIVE

THE MOMENT MIRRA'S FOOT TOUCHED UNDROSEAN SOIL, she knew something was wrong. It struck her with the force of a blow to the stomach, almost causing her to lose balance and fall onto Gaitlan.

He caught her, his brow furrowing. "What is it?"

Mirra shook her head. "I don't know."

"Is something wrong?" Sadria asked.

"I'm not sure," Mirra said, sweat breaking out across her brow. "But something feels off, wrong."

Gaitlan's gaze lifted, fixated on a point far beyond the horizon, as if he could see the entirety of the kingdom. Once Mirra's feet stopped threatening to fall out from under her, he went in search of the fastest horses he could find. He was tired of waiting, tired of lying low. He was going to do what he wanted to do the moment his mind was on his own. And he would not stop until Julian's guts stained the ground at his boots, demon possessed or no.

"Come rest here for a moment," Adria said, taking Mirra by the arm. Adria led them to rest under the shade of a lone, tall oak. Ina kept a tight grip on Kov's hand, not that the boy minded. Shiro fiddled with the Song, his face twisted in apprehension.

"It's nearly time," he said. Kov nodded as he clung tighter to Ina. "I can feel the Song's pull to drive us onward."

When the Wing took hold of him, Kov's eyes took on a strange, almost supernatural sheen. "There is only one path ahead. But the end is unclear. We're beyond the sight of fate."

"Great," Sadria mumbled, her hand restlessly going for her weapons. She cut her eyes at her sister. How do you protect someone from fate? It wasn't in her to stand by while her sister's life could be in danger. The wind shifted. Sadria lifted her face to scent the air. It smelled of war, fire, and death. She had a half a mind to throw her sister over her shoulder, toss the gods cursed relic at Mirra and flee back to their homeland.

"Sister?" Sadria sighed and looked down at her sister. Like always, Adria could sense her unease. She also knew, as assuredly as she knew her own name, that Adria wouldn't want to flee. She wants to fight, to do her part. And she was right. This is why the Blood Lamp chose her. Adria was stronger than Sadria in all the ways that mattered most. And it filled Sadria with pride, no matter how it irked her occasionally.

"I'm fine," she said, folding her arms and leaning against the tree. "Just ready to be on the move again."

The half smile that tugged at Adria's mouth showed that she didn't believe her sister's words one bit but would not press further. Everyone could have moments of weakness and doubt.

It was only natural. What mattered was moving on despite your fears and doubt. That was true strength.

Gaitlan returned, his face dark. "I can't find a single damned horse or carriage to take us. Anything large enough is too expensive." He growled, running a hand through his hair. "I have half a mind to tell them who I am and take what we need."

Ina shook her head. "That's not smart. You're wanted for the death of your parents, remember?"

"And you don't need any of that," Usoa said as she walked out of the tree.

Ina shoved Kov behind her at the same time Sadria pulled her sword free. Mirra pushed herself to her feet, trying her best not the gape like the others. Fortunately, no one outside their group seemed to notice the Ilmarrion high priestess's sudden arrival.

"I'm not going to ask," Mirra said before Usoa cut her off.

"There's no time. Julian and his forces are marching on the city. They've already broken through the protective barrier."

"Impossible," Gaitlan said. "It takes months to convince the Council of Lords to muster their armies. Not to mention the time it would take to get there. We weren't gone that long."

"Only if they're still human." Usoa's words hung heavy in the silence that followed. It wasn't like Julian hadn't controlled people before using his dark magic, but to wield control over so many. It was unfathomable.

The high priestess turned to Mirra. "I trust you have everything you need?"

"And a bit more," Mirra said, handing over Marhoc's book. "Can you read this?"

Usoa opened the book, her eyes widening as she flipped through the pages. "Yes, this is high, Marron. The most ancient of our people's language. The last time they used it was during the reign of the Lost Court. I learned it when I was an acolyte in…" She shot her head up. "Where did you find this?"

"Tell you later," Mirra said. "Promise, but do we need this?"

"Only this last page here," Usoa said. "It's a chant used to focus the relic's power on a singular task."

"So we would have failed without this," Gaitlan said, his voice rising.

Usoa shook her head. "Probably not, but it certainly helps. You certainly are full of surprises, Mirra. But the time for such conversations is past." She held out her hands. "Come, join hands and do not let go."

Mirra quickly realized that she preferred traveling through shadows than through whatever this way. Her skin felt raw, as if she were being dragged across splintering wood. It smelled terrible too, though she couldn't quite place what it was. But the worst part was how slow every movement felt. She might as well have been swimming through tree sap for all she knew. To make matters worse, her grip was giving way. And who knew what would happen to her and the others that clung to her just as desperately as she clung to Usoa? When she felt the last of her strength give way, they tumbled into the other side.

Gasping for air, Mirra remained on all fours, willing her stomach to stay where it was. "Please tell me that's not what it's like."

"No," Adria said, placing a warm, gentle hand on the back of Mirra's neck. "Are you alright?"

"It's because of her affinity," Usoa said, her face glistening with sweat. "Our abilities don't mix well. That's why humans have to use the relics. She'll be fine in a moment. Hurry now."

Gaitlan helped Mirra to her feet. "Should I go help with defenses?"

"Don't you want to see your sister?", Usoa said without turning around.

"Braelyn's here?" Gaitlan's touch fell away as he half ran up the stairs of the citadel. All else fell away as he searched for his sister, the one person who kept him going all these long months.

The doors to the citadel were left open with acolytes and fully ordained members rushing in and out. But he saw none of it. His entire world narrowed on the young woman in a simple red dress, her golden hair rippling down her back.

"Braelyn!"

Eyes so similar to his mother's that it tore at his heart, turned to meet his. Silver rimmed the bottom of Braelyn's eyes, her hands rising to cover her mouth. "Gaitlan? Is it really you?"

He held his arms wide and Braelyn ran for them without question. When she crashed into him, Gaitlan felt as if a piece of his heart had finally slipped into place. He swept his sister up in an embrace tight enough that it drew a squeak from Braelyn. When she pushed against him, Gaitlan pulled her in closer. "A little while longer," he pleaded.

"I'm all for that, brother, but I do need to breathe."

Gaitlan reluctantly set his sister down, stepping back far enough to scan for any signs of injury or abuse without fully letting her go. "Did that bastard do anything to you?"

Braelyn's smile faltered, darkness rippling across her face. Gaitlan's hands shook. "Nothing physical," she said finally.

"He relishes the mental anguish more than physical pain," Mirra said as she walked up. "Looking good, princess."

Braelyn pulled herself from her brother's grip. "Thank you," she whispered, pulling Mirra in for a tight embrace. "Thank you for keeping him safe."

Mirra patted Braelyn's back. "I'll charge you later. Is Bao here?" Mirra would have to have been blind to notice the bright pink coloring on Braelyn's face. Mirra silently laughed and swore to find out just what Bao did while she was away.

"He's with Roux, manning the defenses. Probably laying more traps down."

"Good to hear. Did anyone else come with you?"

Braelyn shook her head. "We had to leave in a hurry."

A pointed cough drew Mirra's attention. And there stood Oya, waiting patiently for Mirra, a coy smile on her face. Her feet carried her across the room before she'd realized it. All that mattered was that Oya was there, hale and healthy. When they met each other's embrace, Mirra breathed in Oya's scent of magnolias and the bitter tang of herbs. Oya entangled her fingers into Mirra's hair, pulling back for a kiss.

The others were rooted to their spots, unsure of this unseen side of Mirra. Braelyn was the first to recover, ushering the rest down a hallway to store their belongings and to eat something to eat while everything was calm.

"So, who are the other wielders? I'm Braelyn, wielder of the Seed of Life."

When Mirra and Oya broke apart for air, they were the only two in the vast chamber. Even Usoa found somewhere else to be. "How was your quest?"

"Eventful," Mirra said, weaving her fingers through Oya's. "I met an interesting fellow in a prison under the imperial castle in Zallino."

"You'll have to tell him about him later, after we survive this." The faintest hint of doubt crept into the corners of Oya's face.

"Don't worry, I'll be here. I won't let anything happen to you or the others."

Oya smiled up at Mirra, cupping her face with a free hand. "I know you will."

A crash like thunder shook the ground beneath them, sending bits of plaster raining down. Mirra pulled her lips back into a silent snarl. "I can't wait to see the light fade from that bastard's eyes."

DESTROYING THE BARRIER LEFT HIM NEARLY DEPLETED. Julian stretched out his hand and the soldiers nearest fell to the ground as long black ropes poured from their gaping mouths. The ropes coiled around Julian's arm before sinking beneath the skin. Strength surged through him, his eyes flashing black for a moment before returning to normal. He flexed his hand and breathed deeply until the power settled.

If any of the soldiers at his back had control over their minds, they might have brought up concerns about a lack of response from the Ilmarrions. They continued to march towards the city center without a single sign of a militia or further traps. Not that Julian would have listened. Ever since Mirra broke his brand and disrupted his plans, his normal level headedness had gone out the window. But truth be told, he found it liberating to act in his true nature instead of pretending to be a lowly mortal. His mouth stretched into an unnaturally wide smile. He was having the time of his life.

OYA CALLED BACK TO THE OTHERS THE MOMENT MIRRA fled through the doors. She looked out at the wielders and tried to not let fear creep into her heart. A princess, a healer from the Lorcean plains, middle-aged man with guilt written across every fiber of his being, and a ten-year-old boy. Not exactly what she'd envisioned when thinking about the ones who will lock away the Dark One within his newly reforged prison. But whether they were what she'd wanted or not, they were what the fates had brought to this point.

"This isn't how I wanted us to meet," Oya said, taking command of the room. "But the world doesn't work like that. I wish we had more time to get to know one another and attune to the relics." She gave a quick nod to Braelyn who looked as pale as a sheet.

She pointed toward the open door and the ever darkening sky. "A demon approaches, clothed in the flesh of a mortal. It seeks to destroy everything we love and stand for. I know we come from different places with our own desired outcomes, but there is one thing that holds true for all of us. That creature will not let us live. If we fail today, it will devour our souls and then turn our world to ash."

Oya rubbed her arms against an imagined chill. "I've seen the world it left behind and believe me when I say there's no surviving that level of destruction."

The young boy's guardian slipped her hand around his shoulders. "What do we need to do?"

"We need to summon the demon here, pull him from Lord Julian and then force his essence into the orb," High Priestess Usoa said.

"How are we supposed to do that?" Adria asked.

"There is a chant," Usoa said. "But the rest of you need to leave. I don't care if you join the fight or take shelter with the others below the citadel."

Sadira grabbed onto her sister. "I'm not leaving her defenseless." Her sentiment mirrored by Ina.

"You'll only be in the way," Oya said. "He will use you to weaken our resolve and the odds aren't exactly stacked in our favor to begin with. We're working with only fragments of what it took to initially seal it away."

"Well, that's comforting," Sadria said, tightening her grip on her sister.

"It will be alright, sister." Adria reached up and removed Sadria's hand. "This is what we were born for. If it is my time to join our ancestors in the Fields of Everlife, then I will meet it with my head held high."

Sadria looked as if her entire world had fallen around her, and in some ways, it had. For the longest of time, it had been the two of them, fighting for their place in the world. They'd always fought together, side by side until now. "It's my responsibility to protect you."

"Then keep his forces from interfering."

Sadria stared at her sister, racking her brain for anything she could do to convince her sister to let her stay. After a long pause, Sadria hung her head in defeat before pulling her sister in for a tight embrace, speaking in their mother language.

Ina pressed her lips together and knelt down to face Kov. The fact that he was trying so hard to remain brave despite everything nearly tore her heart out. "I will always find you, remember?" Kov nodded his head. Ina brushed back the hair from his eyes. "Listen to what they tell you to do, but if anything goes wrong, I want you to run. Open yourself completely to that damned thing inside you and let it lead you to safety."

"What about you?"

Ina swallowed against the burning in her throat. "I will be alright," she said. "And I will find you once this is over. I swear it."

Kov buried his face in her chest, no longer caring that tears streamed down his face. Ina murmured gently to him, beseeching the gods and fate to be kind to them today. Ina tore herself from Kov's tight embrace before she stole him away, damning the entire world. She went back the way they came, following the last remaining noncombatants to the shelter. Sadira kissed Adria on the forehead before leaving to join Mirra and the rest of the defending forces.

Braelyn turned to her brother with a forced smile. "No words of comfort for me, brother?"

"No," Gaitlan said. Braelyn tried to keep the hurt from her face, but there was nothing she'd could hide from her brother. He took her hands in his, running a thumb over her knuckles.

"There's so much more that I want to say, things to apologize for."

"You don't need to apologize for anything."

Gaitlan shook his head, keeping his gaze on their hands. "I should have been a better brother, a better prince. I should have…I don't know… done something, anything, to stop that bastard before it got to all this." His head dipped lower, burned with shame. "I've failed you in so many ways, but I have never been so proud of you, little sister. You've sacrificed, survived, and grown stronger than anyone could have imagined."

Braelyn gently pulled her brother in for an embrace. "You haven't failed me. You haven't failed our parents or our country. Julian was never a foe that either of us were equipped to face. You did the best you could with the skills you had. I am proud that you're my brother."

Gaitlan pulled away, shaking. "I've done nothing to make you proud, but I will today." He turned, drawing his sword free, and strode out to settle a debt once and for all. Braelyn watched him go, sending a prayer to Yrd and Yulla to keep her brother safe and let him return to her.

"Let go your fears, your worries, all other thoughts," High Priestess Usoa said, motioning for the wielders to join her. "Let only the thought of sealing this demon away hold true. Let it be the bedrock of your foundation, your guiding light."

Braelyn closed her eyes and breathed deeply. Adria's face seemed paler in the dim light, but she jutted her chin out. Too many emotions rippled across Shiro's face for anyone to make out and poor Kov couldn't stop his shivering.

Usoa hummed a soft tune, swaying gently on her feet. Oya picked up the melody, adding words in a language none of the wielders recognized. As the two women sang, the tightness along their bodies relaxed, their hearts slowed, and they felt more assured of their ability to pull off the binding.

When the song ended, High Priestess Usoa motioned for them to stand around Oya, who held the Orb of Thalla in her hands, its pale, murky clouds rolling lazily inside. "We don't need to have the host in front of us for this to work. If your minds are strong enough, you should be able to pull the demon's essence here. Without a host, he will be weakened, but only for a moment. It is in that moment that you must force him into the orb."

"So, do we think about it hard?" Adria asked.

"Not quite," Usoa said. "I want you all to listen carefully to me and repeat the words exactly as you hear them. Tsua ilnathrin Ileign batha q'yia nor a'na."

Word by word, they slowly repeated the mantra, their accuracy improving with each round. As they chanted, their sense of the outside world faded away and they swayed in time like a dance. The words wrapped around them, pierced their flesh, their souls until they couldn't tell where the words ended and they began.

I should be afraid, but I'm not, Braelyn mused briefly before the words took hold once more.

Light ripple and danced along the relics in a kaleidoscope of colors. The colors wrapped around them like cocoons, before strands of glittering light ran through them, creating a diamond shape. Once the diamond was complete, another strand of glittering light flowed from each relic to the orb. When all the strands touched the orb, it glowed with the same rainbow of light that wrapped around the wielders.

The orb burned hot in Oya's hands, nearly scalding. But she continued chanting. Perhaps there was another person more suited to be the orb's wielder, but there wasn't time to find them. She would have to endure, making sure that the powers of the relics only entered the orb and not her. She didn't think she'd survive the flow of magic, no Ilmarrion could.

CHAPTER TWENTY-SIX

"Bao!" Mirra threw her arms around her friend. "Making yourself at home, I see."

"They practically begged me to take charge," he said with an over dramatic shrug.

"Can you two take nothing seriously?" Roux said with a scowl.

Bao waved her off. "I prefer to spend my last moments in mirth, not malaise."

"If you face it like a warrior, then it won't be your last moments." Bao scowled at Sadria, not sure what to make of the Horse Lord warrior. He raised a brow at Mirra, who gave a look that showed that she trusted Sadria with her life — the highest of praises.

"Then I guess it's a good thing we have you," Bao said with a bow. "We need to set up another barrier right away. Perhaps at the edge of the first houses."

Sadria pushed herself between Bao and Roux. "No, as close to the temple as you can. We need to do everything we can to keep them safe."

"That leaves you nowhere to fall back," Gaitlan interjected.

"Oath breaker," Roux said without her usual malice.

Gaitlan nodded his head in her direction quickly before continuing on. He squatted down, using a dagger to draw a circle in the dirt. "This is the citadel, and here are the training grounds and baths. This is where the living area starts. We should set up another barrier around here," he said, drawing another circle that encompassed about half of what he drew. "If that breaks, it still gives us space to retreat and set up another barrier around the citadel."

"We do not have the people for this."

"Can they set the new barrier, then retreat to the citadel and be ready to throw another up?" This was a side of Gaitlan Mirra had never seen before. The man in front of her was not the same one she'd dragged halfway across the continent, who kissed her, that she fought alongside. This man was the heir to the throne, a king in the making.

"It will take much from them to set up a decent barrier, " Roux said.

"We don't need one as strong as the other," Bao said. "We just need it strong enough to slow them down." He looked at Mirra. "I guess we'll have to get our blades wet."

Mirra palmed a set of daggers. "Just like old times."

Roux remained silent, fixated on the rough sketch in the dirt. The sigh that flowed from her mouth was one of resignation and instilled determination. "The masters should have enough to try again. It may fall the moment the demon's forces strike or it could hold for an hour. The acolytes should set up the one around the citadel. It is their responsibility to protect it. We will leave it to them." She raised a hand and a young Ilmarrion archer appeared. Roux relayed the plans swiftly and then turned back to the others.

"I take it you all intend to fight?"

All four nodded. "Our loved ones are in there", Sadira said. "We will give our very lives if that means they are safe and succeed in their task."

Roux's typically stony expression softened. "Then you'll need weapons that can actually kill those creatures."

Even with all the fighters in Moakwyd armed and ready, a fair number of weapons were still available in the armory. Gaitlan tried to not think too much about the disparity between the Julian's army of possessed and their paltry few fighters. Strapping a low bow to his back, he ran through possible attack points for when the next barrier fell and potential escape routes. He had no intention for his sister to die here today.

"Let me see that first." Startled, Gaitlan handed over the quiver full of arrows to Katsumi. She closed her eyes and focused, brow furrowed. Soft red light shimmered over the quiver briefly before fading away. "Only weapons imbued with Ilmarrion magic can take down the possessed. We started blessing the armories, but very few of us can do it."

"Don't strain yourself," Mirra said. "I can bless blades, too."

Katsumi shook her head. "Only do yours. You need to keep your strength up if you have any hopes of defeating him." The bell at the end of her long braid sounded as she turned to bless

Gaitlan's sword and hunting daggers. "Besides, this is what my affinity used to do. This way, our ancestors can fight with us."

"Tāmen dall'aldilà." Katsumi laughed softly and repeated the phrase Bao uttered. She bowed to Bao as she returned his blessed blades. "Fight well, honorable brother."

He bowed as he accepted them. "Fight well, blessed sister. May the tides of fate be kind to us today."

Mirra added a selection of daggers of all shapes and sizes to the arsenal strapped to her body. She paused with each one, pushing a bit of her shadows into them. The effort left her sweaty, with a mild headache in the middle of her forehead, but she didn't stop. She wanted to take down the creatures with her own powers. She wanted Julian and the demon squatting inside him they didn't break her no matter how hard they tried. She wanted them to feel her strength burn through them as the light drained from their eyes. A small parcel of justice for all those they hurt and manipulated.

THERE WAS SOMETHING IN THE AIR. HE COULD ALMOST taste it, like the dusting of sugar on top of a desert. And he hated it. The blasted fools thought they could keep him out with their fragmented and diminutive magics. He had existed beyond any mortal reckoning, already ancient, when that foolish mortal opened the door. Julian bathed himself in a darkness akin to a sky that never knew the touch of light. The surrounding trees withered and died, crumbling into ash and behind him, more of his army fell and the force inside them returned to him.

Julian smiled, his teeth sharp and mouth too wide for his face. His limbs changed next, the joints cracking and breaking as they twisted into unnatural shapes. His skin splintered and cracked, revealing writing masses of darkness. If they wanted to fight a demon, then he would give them a demon. With a roar that shook the very foundations of the world, he charged, hungering for the taste of flesh, blood, and absolute despair.

His clawed fingers dug into the ground, ripping up dirt and rocks as he ran for the citadel. They would gather their forces there, conserving their resources and protecting the fools who were trying to pull him from his meat suit. He opened his mouth, his black tongue rolling out as he laughed. As if they could. They didn't have the last pieces. Four wielders to five relics, and they didn't know how to activate the relics for their intended purpose. He could almost see it, their rising panic once they realize that it's too late, that they failed and that he would eat their souls along with their flesh. Black ooze dripped from his open maw, sizzling the ground in his wake.

An arrow thudded into the ground, scant inches from the clawed hand. Julian skidded to a halt. He found the archer almost instantaneously. They perched on the roof of a half crumbled house, another arrow notched. The archer let loose, grabbing for the horn around their waist. The arrow struck a soldier at the same time the archer sounded the alarm. Julian's lips pulled back into a toothy laugh until an icy fire blazed through him. Whipping his head around, he saw the soldier falling to the ground, transforming into a bed of flowers.

Magic, Julian snarled. So Mirra passed on what she learned at the Holy Isle? Not that it mattered, the pain he felt was nothing to him. A mild annoyance. They didn't have the firepower to inflict any actual damage to him. He shifted again, settling somewhere between a mix of demon and human.

"That won't help you, little starchild. Your ancestors were ten times as powerful as you, and even they struggled to stop me."

"But they succeeded," the archer shot back, "and so will we, demon."

Julian couldn't help himself and laughed. He loved the strong-willed ones. They were the most fun to break. "Then, by all means, let's see how you hold up." He raised his hand and his army surged forward.

The archer retreated, firing a rapid succession of arrows before turning to run. The soldiers who were struck fell to the ground, becoming a bed of flowers. The flowers quickly wilted and died under the force of Julian's destructive life force, feeding him small bits of suffering. Onward they pursued the Ilmarrion archers until a soldier crashed against an invisible wall, sending waves of gold rippling across its surface.

"Another barrier," Julian sighed. He could already tell that this one wasn't as strong as the first one, most likely thrown up in haste after he shattered the other. His touch sent more ripples of light along the barrier. He could shatter it with half a thought, but what fun would there be in that?

Julian stepped back and watched as a wave of his soldiers crashed into the barrier repeatedly. He pushed the mild stings to the back of his mind, sending a bit more of himself into the attacking soldiers. Eventually they would break through and he doubted that the next barrier, if there was one, wouldn't last against a single touch of his finger. He found it disappointing. He hoped for a better fight than this. Such a let down after they'd given him so much grief. Julian sighed and crossed his arms. Another conflict not worth his time. He was used to it after decades, but it still soured the taste of his imminent victory.

"Don't tell me you're getting bored already. The fun's just started, master." Mirra swaggered to the barrier, a glaive slung across her shoulders, its blade rippling with shadows.

"I was until you arrived, my wayward underling."

Mirra twirled the glaive around, bringing it to rest in front, her grip loose but ready. "I was never your underling. You were nothing more than a long list of people who wanted to use me. And in a little while, you will cease to exist."

Julian's mouth stretched too wide. "Is that so? Well then, let us begin our final dance."

The barrier shattered without him having to touch it. His army of the possessed surged forward. The shadows around the glaive grew, wrapping around her like smoke. A soldier neared her, his sword raised to cleave her in two. Mirra smirked and fell into her own shadow. The soldier fell forward and tumbled. Mirra laughed, walking out from in between two buildings.

"Clever trick," Julian said, "but not enough to stop me."

"Oh, I don't have to stop you", she said, stepping out into the open. "They do." Behind her, Bao, Gaitlan, and Sadria rushed to join her, followed by the rest of the Ilmarrion fighters.

Julian threw his head back and laughed. "I have an army of thousands against what, a few hundred at most."

"It's not always about the size of the army," Gaitlan said as he took up his position next to Mirra. "It's about the ability to use your enemies' weakness against them."

Something tugged at the center of Julian's consciousness, the place where the absolute darkness dwelled. He stumbled forward but remained on his feet. His army stumbled as well, with a few falling and not getting back up. The bits of him used to animate the corpses didn't return to him. He felt it fly toward the citadel, where a pool of power swirled like a whirlpool. A low growl rumbled through his too sharp teeth, his form becoming animalistic and twisted.

Black ooze dripped from his snarling mouth, leaving drops of smoking ichor as he stalked towards the pitiful band of fighters in his way. His back legs bunched, gathering strength, but the tugging resumed. Around him, more of his army fell, the pieces of him flying towards their end.

How, he screamed, how had they gathered everything so quickly? He had his serpents across the continent looking for them. They fell silent after Mirra and the boy entered the Black Marsh. Meer months ago. So how could they have found them all?

Blind to the battle raging around him, Julian turned toward the dome of the citadel, barely visible above the trees. Rage boiled in his gut, sending rivers of molten heat through his body. The time for playing was over. Julian tipped his head back and howled. The army froze, their bodies locked in awkward positions. Mirra and the others struggled to cover their ears without letting go of their weapons. One by one, the soldiers dropped, black bands racing to fill Julian's mouth.

As each tendril returned to its proper place, Julian's monstrous form grew until it was nearly the size of a chart. Black clouds of miasma swirled around on unseen winds, instantly killing anything they touched.

A young Ilmarrion man recovered first, rushing forward. His form rippled and faded, becoming like mist. At first he moved through the miasma with ease, then he stumbled, coughed and fell to his knees. His body solidified only for his flesh to bubble and melt, exposing the tender meat below. He screamed until his throat melted away. He fell to the ground, a horrifying mix of charred bone and cooked flesh.

Gaitlan gritted his teeth and lowered his hands. He felt a sudden rush of warmth pour them as he reached for an arrow from his quiver. His vision darkened as he took aim and let loose, the arrow blazing with light the moment it entered the miasma. His arrow embedded into Julian's shoulder, causing him to roar in pain. The red light of the arrow transformed into flames that raced across Julian's monstrous form.

Julian shook the flames off before they could inflict any substantial damage, but it had stopped him from fully reclaiming the pieces of himself. Nearly half of his army lay dead by his own hands. The other archers scrambled to notch their arrows and let loose. Not willing to feel the flames for a second time, the remaining soldiers threw themselves on top of Julian, shielding him from the arrows. He hissed as the fragments inside the soldiers burned away. A small price to pay. Julian leapt into the air, scattering the corpses of the soldiers like falling leaves. He landed on the edge of the rooftop, his blood thirsty eyes zeroed in on the cracked dome of the citadel. He roared again, his body changing again into nothing more than a mass of acrid smoke, taking off toward the citadel with inhuman speed.

"Mirra, stop him!" Bao shouted, dodging the downward swing of a sword. The remaining army resumed their assault, cutting down the Ilmarrion fighters without mercy. Archers fired one arrow after another, small flames ensuing when they met their targets.

"You won't be able to stop them", Mirra said, ducking and stabbing a soldier in between his ribs right into his heart.

"We don't need to." Sadira's back crushed into Mirra's and the two stood steadfast against four soldiers. "We'll thin them out and retreat to the next position. But you're the only one that can move faster than that demon. Get to the citadel and warn the others. Don't let him stop the ritual."

Sadria spun, pulling Mirra with her, pushing her away from the battle. Before Mirra could recover, another person pulled her away, then another, and another until she was standing at the back of the line, seething. How dare they toss her out like that! She moved to rejoin the fight, but her feet wouldn't obey. They turned and ran for the nearest shadow, sinking into the darkness like water. Mirra was over this hero business. It gave her nothing but headaches.

Mirra reappeared several houses away, bursting into the street. She spied Julian's smoke creature form still rolling over the rooftops, still far ahead. Unlike her, his darkness wasn't limited to areas untouched by the sun's light. But luckily for her, the trees of Moakwyd were tall and wide, providing ample shade for her to travel through. And Julian's own flair for drama had darkened the sky, providing even more avenues for her to traverse.

In and out she moved, taking only a moment or two to regain her breath and lay eyes on the smoke creature rolling over the buildings. Each jump left her head swimming, and she was grateful to have heeded Katsumi's advice. Had she blessed the other's weapons, she might not have had the strength to continue. But she wouldn't for much longer if she couldn't get him on the ground, close enough for her to dig her blades into his back. She got her chance when he finally ran out of buildings and needed to get to the other side.

Pooling energy into the blade of the glaive, Mirra waited until the swirling mass of smoke was in the air, then hurled the glaive like a spear. She knew she struck her target when Julian roared in pain, losing his grip on his smoke form, dropping the street with a heavy thud.

"I'm going to enjoy ripping your throat out," Julian snarled.

"Keep dreaming," Mirra said, running for him, daggers wreathed in shadows already in her hands.

Julian hissed and turned, transforming his hands into long claws. He pulled her glaive from his shoulder and broke the staff, flinging the halves to opposite sides of the street. Mirra shifted into a fighting stance, her legs wide and poised to move in any direction. Without warning, Julian lunged forward faster than Mirra could follow. The demon inside of Julian may have centuries of knowledge and practice to hone its skill, but Mirra had something else. She'd lived the first half of her life acting on pure instinct. Her body knew where to move long before her mind registered that she needed to. And her power rose up independent of her call, always at the right time.

She barely registered the breeze caused by his swing, already twisting her body. One. Two. Her daggers sank into Julian's flesh, black ichor staining her hands. The blood steamed and burned, drawing a hiss from Mirra. Julian roared and swung around. Mirra fell into his shadow, coming out beneath the shade of a tree. She wiped her hands on her clothing to remove the worst of the burning blood. Her hands still stung with a few small blisters.

From down the street, Julian laughed. "What good are weapons if you can't hold them?"

Mirra huffed, half a smirk on her face. "I don't need them." Using two fingers, Mirra drew a rune in the open air. Black streaks, like ink, hovered and took form. Julian ran for her, his claws leaving deep gouges in the cobblestones and hard packed dirt. Shouting the name of the rune, Mirra dove for the bladed half of her broken glaive. The benefit of its reach was gone, but the blade was still imbued with her power. She would need it to keep Julian's claws from ripping her to shreds.

Mirra gritted her teeth and spared a fraction of her consciousness toward the citadel. Come on, she hissed silently, hurry up and drag his sorry ass back to the orb.

THE WIELDERS' EYES WERE OPEN WITHOUT SEEING. THEIR bodies were as still as the stone columns around them. High Priestess Usoa calmly walked around the room, looking for any signs of distress or catastrophic backlash. So far, they were stable. Even Oya had reached a state of mind where she no longer felt the orb glowing in her hands. Usoa felt nothing but pride for her protégé, swearing to take her training to the next levels when they survived this battle; if they survived.

No, like them, I must only picture victory. Anything else would bring defeat. I've survived conflicts much worse than this.

Memories from her childhood rose from the murky depths of her consciousness. The smile of a woman, twisting her locs. The scent of salt air and fresh fish. A grand oak tree, nearly as large as a citadel. Cruel eyes behind gentle smiles. Smoke and destruction. The earth trembling beneath her feet and a white furious rage that threatened to consume her very soul.

Usoa pushed the memories back down into the dark recesses of her mind. This was not the time to dwell on past horrors and mistakes. The sound of shouting rose, and another barrier encircled the courtyard and the citadel. This wasn't good. It was taking them too long to pull it out. They'd been chanting nonstop for sometime now and all they dredged up were a few tendrils that faded away to nothing the moment they passed by the wielders. Sweat poured down the wielders' faces, the color washed out from their face. Even Adria was ashen beneath her golden skin. It may not be a matter of skill or conviction, but of endurance. And Usoa couldn't determine who would outlast the other.

Bright red droplets stained the sand as Mirra coughed. She was running out of stamina, throwing one rune after another. Half the time the shapes were only partially thought through before she flung them at Julian, who had reverted back to his human form. Acrid smoke billowed out from various parts of his body, places where her runes struck true. He wasn't the only one bearing marks of battle. Mirra bore light claw marks across her right arm, left leg, and down her back. The scratch marks burned as if someone poured acid on them, but not enough to incapacitate her.

"Looks like we won't have to worry about locking you away," Mirra taunted, her heart not really in it.

Julian snorted. "You look as if a breeze would knock you over. It's not as easy as you thought, little mage? You may have a tenacity for survival, but to wield magic on this scale takes years, decades to master."

"Then why do you look like shit?"

Murder flashed over Julian's face. His mouth stretched wide and Mirra shifted tiredly back into a fighting stance. Just a little longer. She just needed him occupied for a little longer. Julian took a single step in her direction and fell to the ground, writhing in pain. Even with the distance between them, Mirra could hear his joints popping and cracking, their odd angles causing her stomach to rebel.

When he arched, black coils of night writhed around his body like a swarm of snakes. Slowly and with great pain, they uncoiled, floating toward the citadel. Mirra sank to her knees, nearly weeping with relief. She did it. They did it. The others would draw the demon out and lock it away. Maybe Julian, the real Julian, would die. Maybe he would live and serve as the scapegoat for all the ills the Dark One committed while wearing his skin.

"No", Julian bellowed. "Please."

It was the "please" that made her head shoot up. It sounded nothing like the man she'd known or the monster she fought with. It sounded human. It sounded scared and hurt and ready for release. The demon latched onto one tendril of his soul and pulled it back into himself. He reached out with the other and a fresh wave of black, snake-like tendrils coiled around his arms and body before settling in.

Mirra knew she was in trouble. Until now, she'd been fighting a fraction of the Dark One's might. The last time she saw him like this, the king and queen lay dead at his feet, their blood flowing over the black and white floor.

It took nearly everything she had to get back on her feet. Her broken glaive hung loosely in her hand. She would not make it this time. Her luck had finally run out. She would never get to sail to distant lands. Marhoc would spend another dozen lifetimes trapped in the dark, waiting for her to set him free. Oya. Mirra's throat burned with every bit of regret from a life not lived.

Julian charged at her, eyes alight with an otherworldly glow. She didn't move. She had nothing left, just another pitiful soul who couldn't hack it. Mirra closed her eyes and waited for her death. At least in death she would be free.

Julian roared, and she waited for a blow that never came. When she opened her eyes, Julian was hunched over, a dozen arrows blazing in his back. Behind him stood Bao, Sadria, and Gaitlan, leading the Ilmarrion forces.

"Get up," Bao yelled. "Don't stop. Keep going."

The arrows turned to cinders, and Julian stood tall. "If they want to see me so badly, then who am I to keep them waiting? Thank you for teaching me your little trick. The other one couldn't do it. Maybe you're stronger than she was, even though she was the one to let me in." To everyone's horror, Julian sank into his own shadow.

Mirra moved before her mind could register what happened. The next thing she was aware of was diving headfirst into a darkness that was nothing like her own. This darkness tore at her, lapped at her wounds, pressing around her unlike anything she'd ever felt before. There was no sense of time or space, but she couldn't blindly run through this plane. As much as it sickened her stomach, Mirra took several deep breaths, recentering herself. When she felt steadier than before, she reached out with her senses, searching for the way forward. At first there was nothing but the vast emptiness around her, but then, far in the distance, she felt a pinprick of light. Mirra latched her consciousness on that impossibly small speck of light and will herself forward. She only hoped she'd get there in time.

CHAPTER TWENTY-SEVEN

THE ACOLYTES TOOK TURNS STRENGTHENING THE LAST barrier. Behind them they could feel the ebb and flow of the relics' power as they tried to pull the essence of The Eater to its imprisonment. But ahead of them was an ever-growing sense of destruction and chaos, the likes none of them have seen. Outward they projected calmness and determination, but inside, it took all they had to not flee for shelter.

"It comes to us," someone said.

"May the Ileing guide keep us and guide us," Katsumi said, drawing her long braid over her shoulder. They had barred her from helping with the barrier since she blessed nearly all the weapons used for defense. She could give more, but relented when the elder acolytes gave her a direct order. She puffed out her cheeks and blew, twining her braid around like rope. The bell's disjointed ringing was the perfect reflection of her inner workings.

Something wasn't right. It tugged at her, setting her teeth on edge. There was something about the feeling that made her think it was more than waiting for the Eater's army to reach them.

The ground beneath their feet trembled and rolled. A few acolytes fell to the ground, but most remained standing. Some peered overhead and breathed a sigh of relief when they saw the still intact barrier. That assurance was shattered when the great oak in the courtyard of the citadel burst into a million splinters, forcing the gathered priests and priestesses to take cover.

The bits of smoking wood clung to Julian's shoulders as he strolled through the ruins of the tree. He looked at the cowering acolytes and sneered. "I thought you lot would be a bit more together than the rabble you sent to greet me."

In that second, the world was suspended in anticipation, waiting for what felt like an endless amount of time. Runes of all colors and sizes flew toward Julian. A wall of malicious darkness shot up, absorbing the runes. The wall cracked and splintered, but remained standing. The wall shifted and changed into four large, pitch black serpents. The serpents raised their heads and hissed at the acolytes, stunned into silence below. From their open mouths, blood red droplets fell, burning through anything they touched.

"Protect the wielders!" The war cry went up, urging the priests and priestesses forward, fighting in the best way they knew how. Some attacked with ancient weapons, imbued with the most powerful magic of their age. The splintered bits of the oak tree took new roots, becoming saplings and full-fledged trees in a matter of seconds. The new trees' roots shot up from the ground, dragging the heads of the serpents down so the others could remove them. Elements of water, sunlight and fire lashed out, cutting large sections of the snake's bodies, unfortunately adding more hazardous fluid.

The far right snake lashed out, its jaws latching around the middle of a middle-aged priestess with graying hair. She screamed, stabbing at the snake with a glowing sickle. Her screams became panicked cries as the snake's venom burned through her flesh. Katsumi watched in horror as the cursed black snake opened its mouth further and swallowed the priestess whole.

The serpents snatched more and more priests and priestesses up, their last moments spent fighting in vain. All the while, the demon watched with a bemused face. Immense heat burned in the center of Katsumi's chest. The heat flowed through her until the surrounding air rippled like the sands of the Nealitian desert. She walked down the citadel steps, leaving blackened footprints in her wake. If things continued, there wouldn't be anyone left to keep the ancient ways. Their people would forget who they were and the gifts they were blessed with. They would truly be gone.

"No, don't Katsumi," someone cried.

"It must be done." Flames sparked to life along her skirts, growing and shrinking to the beat of her heart. She didn't go without fear or regret, but neither would help her now. Goodbye mother, father, I will see you again when you leave this world. More flames dance along her now, a trail of smoke billowing behind her like the train of a dress. All four snakes turned their soulless eyes on her. Their bloody maws were open, hungry for more.

"Still hungry? Come have a taste of me." Katsumi raised her hands above her head and let go, fully surrendering the fiery Ileign that coursed through her.

As one, the serpents lunged for Katsumi, pulling back hissing when flames licked their faces. Katsumi was gone. In the very spot where she had been standing, there emerged a towering column of roaring flames. The blaze flickered and danced, taking on a vaguely humanoid form as it consumed the air around it. The heat emanating from the inferno was intense that the remaining priests and priestesses had to shield their eyes and retreat to a safer distance. The flickering, fiery figure extended its ghostly hand and snatched up the writhing serpents, two in each hand. The sizzling sound of the flames intensified as the creature pulled the snakes close. The acrid stench of burnt scales filled the air. The snakes thrashed about to break the fire being's hold, but their venomous fangs had no effect on the fiery figure. Smoldering fire rippled over the serpent's bodies, turning them into ash that broke apart the moment the burning creature released its hold. Ash rained down like flakes of snow, coating the world in blackish gray. With the threat vanquished, the fire being shrunk down until it was nothing more than a wisp of flame before fading away completely, leaving nothing but a half melted bell behind.

"Foolish girl," Julian said, breaking the silence that filled the world after Kastumi's burning form dissipated. "What did that get her? Nothing," Julian said as he lifted his hand and swirled it in the air. A thick cloud of darkness spread across the courtyard. The sound of coughing and gagging filled the air as the remaining priests and priestesses clawed at their burning throats. Julian walked through them, his attention entirely on the open doors at the top of the stairs. They were there. The tugging was incessant, like a persistent child vying for attention. It was long past time to deal with the Ilmarrions once and for all.

From the shadow of a large section of the shattered oak tree, Mirra clawed her way to the surface. She recoiled instantly from the miasma. Cloaking herself with her power, she could withstand the noxious fumes, but not for long. She stared at the destruction around her, trying to piece together what had happened. She didn't want to believe that all the acolytes were dead. Kneeling down, she pressed her fingers into the neck of the closest priest. Though it was faint, there was a heartbeat. She had to believe there was more. Movement drew her eyes to the top of the stairs. Julian strolled up the stairs like a man without a care in the world. And with their last defenses decimated, she only had a matter of seconds before all was lost.

On the ground she quickly sketched the rune they used in Xhu'Rozo adding another, smaller rune at the bottom. She didn't know if it would work or even if she had enough strength to pull it off. But she had to try. Activating the rune, the acolytes vanished into a swirling vortex of shadows. Holding on for as long as she could, Mirra willed the last of the Ilmarrion priests and priestesses to the baths, hoping Grandmother and the other attendants could tend to their injuries enough for them to come back her up.

Gasping for air, Mirra fell to her hands and knees, hissing when her fingers touched the hot metal. Looking up, her blood ran cold. She pried Katsumi's melted bell from the stones, ignoring the pain in her hands. Gently setting the bell on the broken and charred remains of the once great oak, Mirra palmed her daggers and stormed after Julian.

Her rage carried her forward until she was free of the miasma and close enough to hurl a dagger right into the bastard's back. Julian deflected her blade without stopping or turning to look at her. When he reached the top of the stairs, he turned, giving her a short wave before disappearing through the darkened doorway.

Seeing the man responsible for so much of her suffering enter the same space as the one who held her heart broke the last threads of Mirra's reservations. It didn't matter if she burned out her life like a candle burning at both ends as long as Oya remained safe, alive. She had such big plans for her future. If it came down between the two of them, Oya should be the one to live. Mirra could only hope that she'd forgive her.

Severing the threat that kept the power inside from taking over, Mirra became shadow. She didn't need to jump through them. In the time it took her to think of where she wanted to go she was there, solidifying in front of Julian, driving her last dagger into his heart. Right where his heart should be.

Julian looked at her as if she was nothing more than an insect. He swatted her away like one, sending her crashing into one of the stone pillars. All the air left her lungs, stealing away the last vestiges of her strength.

"Look at them," Julian mused. "Trying so hard to only fail. Completely helpless."

Usoa stepped forward, placing herself between Julian and the others, still locked in the ritual. She tried to keep her alarm clamped down. This close to the relics and orb, he should have been drawn out.

"Can't figure it out, can you? You won't have to worry about it for long." A massive black ball of energy careened into Usoa, sending her flying across the chamber. She recovered faster than Mirra, drawing down the vines that grew over the dome. The vines placed her back where she started, then coiled around her arms like whips.

Mirra struggled to get back on her feet. She saw the same wrongness that Usoa did. How was he able to withstand the draw of the relics? Were they missing some crucial piece? Something unknown because it was never written?

Her vision darkened and flickered as she stood on shaking legs. It took everything in her to not succumb to the sweet taste of oblivion. Her vision wavered again, but instead of going black she saw a face. At first it was hard for Mirra to make out who it was, but when the lines of tattoos became clear, she knew. It was the woman who'd been haunting her dreams since she broke free from Julian's hold.

Her stern face and the hard set of her jaw let Mirra know she was not someone to trifle with. She opened her mouth and uttered a single word. Mirra shook her head, not hearing the world. "I don't understand." The woman stepped closer. Mirra shuddered and slipped to her knees. The closer the woman got, the less Mirra could feel. It took her a moment to realize she was dying.

"Not quite, little one," the woman said, in Mirra's voice. "You stand on the edge of life and death. It is the one place where the dead can speak to the living, but we do not have long." She stared at Mirra as if she could burn the meaning of her words into her brain. "The one is stronger than the many."

"Couldn't you tell me plainly?"

The woman's hardened expression cracked, showing a sliver of humor behind the strange tattoos. "You can't learn if the answers are given to you."

Mirra let out a string of curses as the woman faded away. At least she felt better, if only a little. Her dizziness had evaporated. Even the cuts she received from Julian's claws were healed. Mirra flexed her hands, shadows pooling in her palms. "Maybe you're not so bad after all."

The sounds of fighting drew her focus back to the task at hand. *The one is stronger than the many.* Mirra scoffed. She didn't have time to puzzle out the woman's cryptic words, but she couldn't shake them from her mind. *The one. The one. One.*

"I've taken too many hits to the head," Mirra cursed. "Break him apart!"

Mirra wrote a series of runes in the air in rapid succession. With a grunt, she released them. *Julian wasn't the only one who could learn from their enemy.* Smokey snakes slithered through the air. Instead of attaching Julian directly, they flowed through him, taking a bit of his essence with them.

Julian hissed, swiping at Mirra's snakes. They flew just out of reach, right into the center of the diamond. There they let go, and the orb swallowed the black tendrils they stole up. The energy rippling around the relics and the wielders grew brighter, searing Julian's flesh.

Usoa used the vines around her arms, lashing at Julian. With each blow, she tore away a bit of the demon inside. The orb pulled them in as fast as they pulled them out. But there were not bottomless wells of power and the little boost Mirra received while at the border of life and death was gone.

Julian slashed through one of her snakes, summoning the bit back to him. A cruel smile spread across his face as he changed the tendrils' trajectory, sending it right for Kov's unprotected back. Usoa moved, stepping right into its path. It struck her in the middle of her chest. She crumbled, using what was left of her strength to not break the line. Mirra could only watch in horror as black veins spread out from the spot she was struck.

Mirra raced forward screaming, "No!"

Usoa turned, the black lines already streaming up her face. "It's all right. I'm not afraid to die."

Mirra tripped over a bit of broken stone, the taste of blood filling her mouth. She had one chance to save Usoa. The same chance she gave the acolytes. Using her blood, Mirra drew the travel rune and the destination. She slammed her bloody palm down as Julian loomed over Usoa, the sick thrill of killing etched along every line of his body.

A small vortex of swirling night opened beneath Usoa, taking her to safety just as he brought down the killing blow. The stone shattered around his fist and he turned his full ire on Mirra.

"You've disrupted my plans for the last time", he snarled, advancing. Billowing darkness obscured his body from sight, allowing him to move faster than humanly possible. The darkness dissipated when he grabbed Mirra by the throat, slamming her into the ground with enough force that she blacked out for a second or two. Lifting her off her feet, Julian threw her into the pillars again, leaving her frozen as she tried to remember how to breathe. Julian gave her no respite. No sooner than her body slid down the pillar, did he punch her in the face. He broke her nose with a single punch, her hot blood pouring down her face. Again and again Julian slammed her against the pillar, throwing punches to her face and sides.

There was nothing Mirra could do but let him hit her. Let him lose control enough that the orb could finally pull him in. If only they had more time to get a little bit stronger, then maybe it wouldn't have gone sideways so fast. Not wanting the last thing she saw to be Julian's black eyes, Mirra looked over his shoulder to where Oya stood. She looked like a goddess, holding the sun in her hands. Even beaten nearly to death, Oya's beauty drew a smile.

Noticing her smile, Julian turned, his eyes filling with wicked delight. "What good is it to kill someone who's ready to die?" He released his hold around Mirra's throat and turned, walking straight for the other's still locked within the ritual's hold. How much longer would they be able to last before their life forces were burned through?

Julian transformed into a dark, billowing mass, streaking for the unprotected wielders. Mirra cut the tether again, transforming into a living shadow. She crashed into Julian, her darkness battling against his. She'd never felt something so wrong as the Dark One's brand of black. The taste of rotting flesh filled her mouth and clouded her senses.

A part of her mind screamed to let go or she'll die. Mirra tried to push it aside, but her grip slipped when she realized they'd tumbled right into the center of the diamond. Mirra landed hard, instantly scrambling to her feet to put herself between the Dark One and Oya.

Black ropes wrapped around her neck and limbs, pulling her to the floor. Bound and utterly spent, there was nothing she could but watch as Julian lengthened his fingers into claws, heading right for Oya. Wisps of his essence streamed into the orb, but it wasn't enough. They needed more.

Mirra fought against her bonds in vain. The cold hard realization that there was nothing she could do to stop the scene from playing out. Mirra screamed as his claws drew close enough to stroke Oya's braids.

Julian bellowed, arching back. It took Mirra a couple of erratic heart beats to register the golden blazing spear piercing Julian through the back. Julian stumbled back, black blood cascading down his back. Mirra never loved Sadria more than in that moment, illuminated by the light of the relics, her arm still extended. Gaitlan came into view next, already reaching for his sister.

"Stop," Mirra shouted. "We have to finish this."

"How can we," Gaitlan cried. "Look at you. Look at them! They won't last much longer."

Mirra knew it too. Only a blind man would miss the deathly pallor on all their faces. They were already dipping into their life force. Shiro's hair now stark white.

The bonds around her loosened before being drawn into the orb. They needed something stronger than the whips of his power to draw him in, but what could they use? Burning pain spread across her hand. Mirra hissed and lifted her hand from the rapidly spreading blood. Scrambling to her feet, Mirra crossed the space between her and Oya. She wrapped her bloodied hands around the orb. The moment the orb left her grasp, Oya crumbled to the ground like a rag doll. Mirra's spine locked tight, every part of her warring with the innate power of the orb. Please let me do this. You can kill me afterwards. Julian looked up and tried to move, but the golden spear slid deeper, going all the way through his back, its fiery point setting Julian's shirt aflame. His resounding roar, shaking the ancient citadel, sending crumbling bits cascading down on them.

The pain from holding the orb lessened. Giving Mirra the space to breathe. She didn't give herself time to think about what she was attempting to do. Thinking had never been her strong point. She was best when acting on pure instinct, even if she didn't always like the outcome. Kneeling down, Mirra ran her other hand through his blood, clenching her jaw against the searing pain. With both hands covered in his blood, Mirra lifted the orb, using a finger to draw the sigil for the lock. The same sigil that she had to work around at the first door of the tower.

Time itself held its breath as Mirra finished the sigil. "I hope this hurts like hel."

The screams that erupted from Julian's mouth sent rivers of ice down the backs of everyone who heard it. That sound would haunt them for the rest of their days. Slowly at first, broad sheets rose out of Julian's body, spiraling around the orb before being drawn in. The once milky white swirls that lingually rolled within the confines of the sphere were angry storm clouds, trying to break free.

In one last attempt to break free, the Dark One burst from Julian. Outside of Julian's body, the Dark one had no actual form. Though Mirra spied bits of claw and fang through the swirling mass. It screamed without a visible mouth, spreading itself like a ripple in a pond. It pressed against the white lines running from each relic, snarling in pain when he touched.

The pull of the orb continued, slowly drawing in the last of him. Screaming in fury, the Dark One thrashed about, bouncing off the lines. It remolded its body into a thin blade, aimed right at Mirra.

A muscular body crashed into her, knocking Mirra to the floor. Sadria's hand went to her chest, her blood already spilling out from between her fingers. In order to save Mirra, she broke the line. The white lines of energy that connected the relics to each other and to the orb flickered in and out. They were out of time.

The Dark One tried to burrow into Sadria, desperate for a new host to squat in and recover. "No, you don't," Sadira said through clenched teeth. She wrapped her hands around the wiggling thing that penetrated her and pulled. "Hurry."

Mirra scrambled on her hands and knees for Sadria. Using her for support, Mirra clawed her way into a standing position. Slamming the orb down on the scant inches of the Dark One's exposed body. The last fragment of the Dark One disappeared inside the orb, sending a wave of energy cascading through the room. The force of the wave threw Mirra and Sadria back. The last thought through Mirra's mind was to wrap her body around the orb to prevent it from shattering again, undoing everything.

The first sound she heard was crying, and she thought they'd failed after all. Mirra rolled her head toward the sound of the crying but was stopped by a hand that smelled faintly of magnolias.

"Don't move," Oya said, her voice hoarse. "You've got some broken ribs."

"Who's crying?"

Oya made a face Mirra couldn't quite read. Gold light flowed from Oya's hands down Mirra's body. The sharp pains every time she took a breath lessened to a bearable level. "You should be fine to move now, if you take it easy."

Oya slid her hand under Mirra's head and held to ease her into a sitting position. Mirra looked around the room, attempting to make sense of it all. Apparently, sending the acolytes to Grandmother turned out to be a good idea after all. Those in the best condition tended to the rest using herbal remedies, since most of their power used up and spent. She didn't miss the rows of too still bodies lined up neatly to the side furthest from the survivors.

"Where are they?"

"Ina took Kov the moment they opened the doors to the shelter. They're leaving as soon as his strength returns. Braelyn is fine as well. Her brother and Bao are trying to outdo each other." Oya laughed softly, her smile fading as fast as it arrived. "Shiro took the body of Julian the moment he could move. I believe he fears his friend's body will not be treated with respect. He might be right, but for now, everyone is leaving him alone."

"What about the twins?"

Sorrow filled Oya's face as she motioned with her chin. Mirra followed where Oya pointed to. She found the source of the crying. Adria knelt next to her sister's body, wailing. Her hair flowed freely around her face in short, jagged cuts.

Mirra tried to push herself up and nearly fell flat on her face. Oya slid her arms under hers and gently helped her to stand. The walk to the place where Sadria's body laid was longer than any trek Mirra had been forced to do since everything started. Adria didn't look up when Mirra sat on the other side of Sadria's stiff body. Someone had placed a white cloth over the place where the Dark One pierced her.

His last attempt to stay free and his last victim.

Mirra bowed her head and let her tears fall free.

CHAPTER TWENTY-EIGHT

SMOKE BILLOWED THROUGH THE MYSTIC WOODS FOR days now. People from all walks of life eyed the continuous haze with growing apprehension. The only thing they knew was that whatever burned, it wasn't spreading. Of course, it didn't help that the Regent's and Council of Lord's war camp was found ransacked at the edge of the cursed forest. The few brave parties that dared to enter the woods returned empty-handed. They had hastily thrown together a new Council of Lords from the first and second sons of the previous council. Their first act as sitting lords was to lock down Verance. All businesses were to close at sundown, with exceptions for dock workers and doctors. Even the temples canceled their evening masses, each one beseeching their gods for answers. All people were to be inside, with harsh punishments to those caught out after curfew.

The city couldn't stay like this for long. Soon tempers would boil as the tension grew. They needed answers, but more importantly, they needed someone to sit on the throne. But with no remaining members of the previous ruling family, lawyers and court historians tore through thousands of documents to determine their next course of action.

BRAELYN STOOD ALONE, WATCHING THE FUNERAL PYRES burn and smolder. She kept her eyes trained ahead, her arms wrapped tight around her body. She'd only been awake for a day before, the need gripped tight, compelling her to see the burning mounds of the dead. So many lives lost, gone within an instant. They'd won the war, but the cost was high. Hundreds of loyal men, never to return to their homes, their families forever wondering where they went. Nearly half of the remaining Ilmarrion magic users gone, sending their people back generations.

Biting back sobs, she stood and watched. She owed that to them for not being strong enough, for not ending the fight sooner. She would spend the rest of her days making up for the sea of blood at her feet.

"We need to leave," Gaitlan said. His words were gentle, the same tone and cadence he used for when he thought a horse was going to bolt.

"I can't, not yet."

Beside her, Gaitlan sighed. "What else is there for you to do? For us to do? We've paid our respects, but we can't ignore our responsibilities to the rest of our people."

"Our people," Braelyn repeated quietly. She let her brother steer her away from the pyres with a gentle touch at her elbow. The weight of the dead was too much for the living to bear.

A team of horses stood in the middle of the courtyard in front of the citadel. Most of the destruction and carnage had been cleared, though the scorch marks left by Katsumi's sacrifice remained, probably until the end of days.

Adria checked the saddle and bags, her back turned to the siblings. It still shocked Braelyn to see the jagged cuts of her hair, which had undoubtedly been beautiful. Oya approached, holding a jar made of pure silver with delicate swirling designs of water etched across its surface. Adria spied the silver jar and fresh grief washed over her. She took it, clenching it to her chest. Tears streamed down her face and her knees buckled.

Oya moved to catch her, easing Adria down gently. She took the wailing woman into her arms, murmuring quietly. Adria's sobs subsided, and she accepted Oya's help to get back to her feet. "Where will you go?"

Adria placed the jar into her saddlebags with great care. "Back to our tribe. I will spread her ashes on the plains of our people so she may ride again with them in the afterlife."

"And after that?" Adria turned toward Gaitlan, her eyes red rimmed and vacant. "You will always have a place with us."

"Thank you," Adria said, bowing her head. "But I need to find a place where I can entomb the Blood Lamp. I will send word once it is done."

"Take your time," Oya said. "Lay your sister to rest in peace and find it within yourself first." With one last embrace, Oya returned to the citadel where she resumed her work, making more medicine to tend to the remaining injured.

Adria placed her foot into the stirrup, swinging herself into the saddle. "May the next time we meet be under better stars. Gods watch over you."

Braelyn watched the young woman ride away. There had been no time for the two to get to know each other, but she'd traveled with Gaitlan. Fought with him and kept him alive. For that alone, Braelyn would be eternally grateful. Clasping her hands, she offered a prayer of her own. She prayed Adria wouldn't hold on to her grief like Braelyn had and move forward to a new life, even with the gaping hole in her heart.

"I need to leave, too." Bao offered a small half smile to Braelyn when she turned around, her eyes wide. "Gotta make sure the Merchant's District doesn't erupt into flames."

"Back to a life of crime." Braelyn jabbed her brother in the ribs. To say that he wasn't pleased with Braelyn's choice of a lover would be an understatement.

Bao shrugged. "What can I say? I have a very particular skill set."

"One that I would like to use for good instead of personal gain." Bao's gaze narrowed at Gaitlan's words. "First, I have to secure my throne. After that, I will need a new spymaster. Someone who can walk the twisted roads of intrigue while not crossing lines that should never be crossed. But be warned, I won't turn a blind eye like my father."

Gaitlan extended his hand. "The position comes with heaps of headaches, but its fair share of benefits too. Lands and a title for one."

Bao blinked once, cutting his eyes to Braelyn. Try as she might, she couldn't stop the tugging of a smile at the corners of her mouth. Whatever her thoughts, she kept them to herself. This was a decision Bao needed to make for himself. Titled or not, they would be together, regardless of what society said.

"I guess it's a good thing I already have agents lined up," Bao said, taking Gaitlan's offered hand. "Once I make sure the Merchant District is stable, I dig through Julian's tower. You're going to need hard evidence and maybe a couple of witnesses if you hope to keep your head, let alone the throne."

"I look forward to working with you, Lord Bao."

"Same to you, your majesty." Before mounting his horse, Bao pulled Braelyn in for a kiss. Gaitlan groaned, disgusted, and walked away as fast as he could.

"They make a cute couple."

"Could you not, Mirra."

Mirra chuckled. "Awe come on, she's about to come of age next month, ripe for marriage." Gaitlan groaned again, his face turned to the sky. "We did it, princeling."

The shade of guilt Gaitlan carried from the day Mirra pulled him out of a drug induced stupor burned away like fog in the morning sun. A rare, completely inhibited smile filled him with a light that drew so many to him before. Only this time, the light was tempered, no less radiant, but not as wild.

"It's hard to believe that it hasn't even been a year yet."

"It feels like a lifetime ago I had to pretend to be Julian's niece," Mirra said. She hopped up on a toppled pillar, leaning back with her face turned to the sun.

They stood in silence for a time, waving to Bao as he headed back to the capital. "You haven't said if you're coming back with us or not," Gaitlan said, breaking the silence. "I'm sure I could find you a position in the court. I need people I trust at my side."

Mirra paused, carefully choosing her next words. "Thanks, but no thanks." Gaitlan shot her a surprised look. "Don't get me wrong, the offer is tempting, but…" Her gaze slid to the citadel. "There's so much that I want to do. And for the first time in my life, I have the freedom to choose what road I walk down."

"Can't argue with that," Gaitlan said, "but know that the offer stands for as long as you want it to."

Mirra clasped Gaitlan on the shoulder, sliding off the pillar. There was one person she needed to see. Ina and Kov left as soon as the healers said he was strong enough, but Shiro, the ritual, took the most out of him. Usoa speculated it was because he'd had his relic the longest, used it the most. Humans weren't born to use magic. There were bound to be side effects from having the power flowing through for decades.

Shiro's silver hair shone in the sunlight streaming through the window. He sat up in bed, looking better than he had a few days prior. But there was no dyeing the toll the ritual took on him. Deep lines that hadn't been there before seemed to drag his face down, giving him a permeate frown.

"Feeling better today?" Mirra sat at the foot of Shiro's bed.

"In some ways," he said, bone deep exhaustion running through his words. "But the High Priestess says I should be strong enough to return home soon."

That perked Mirra up. "It's about time you went home."

"One has a strong desire to be with family in the end."

The reality of his situation hung heavy in the space between them. "You're dying?"

Shiro nodded. "Fair penance for my sins."

"Stop talking like that," Mirra snipped, rolling her eyes. "Righteous self pity doesn't look good on you. Where's the man

I met by the river calling me a coward for not taking control of my life?"

"He held on longer than he should have, offering his own life for that little savage."

Mirra scrunched her face, embarrassed by the pricking in her throat and the hot tears filling her eyes. "I don't know why I'm crying," she admitted, hastily wiping away the tears.

Shiro took her other hand in his. "It's alright. A lot's happened in the past few months, past days even. Sometimes our bodies need to open up and let it all out."

"Maybe later," said Mirra, getting up. "Take care of yourself and don't die too soon. I want to meet your family."

Shiro said nothing, smiling softly as Mirra closed the door.

The inside of the remedy room was sweltering because of the many pots simmering over open flames. Mirra wove through the crowded room, spying Oya at the grinding table with her back to the room. Mirra slid behind her, wrapping her arms around Oya's waist, resting her head in the crook of her neck.

"I'm awfully sweaty," Oya said, not stopping her work. Back and forth they swayed as Oya worked the grinding wheel.

"I don't mind." She heard Oya's soft laugh in her ear.

"Said all your farewells?"

Mirra hummed yes, turning to place a kiss on Oya's damp neck. "But don't worry, I don't plan on saying goodbye to you for a long, long, long time." Mirra emphasized each long with another kiss.

"Is that so?" Oya said, finally turning around.

Mirra pulled Oya closer, their foreheads pressed together. "Yes," she whispered before capturing Oya's lips in a kiss that melted all else away.

THE CITY HUMMED LIKE A BEEHIVE DESPITE THE RECENT snowfall that made the city look fresh and clean for the time being. But the citizens of Verance wouldn't fully relax until after the crowning. Then everything would be set right and they could get back to living their lives in peace.

Prince Gaitlan's return to the city seven months prior was still a hotly debated topic, with some still believing he killed his parents for greed. But in the days since his return, that number dwindled. There would always be people who saw nothing but the worst of humanity, a reflection of their own hearts rather than truth.

Prince Gaitlan worked tirelessly to placate the people's fears while working hard to rectify the mistakes done in his absence. The princess took over as Regent until the prince's trial, where he was found to be completely innocent. A thorough search of Lord Julian's office revealed countless reports of extortion, poisonings, and murder. Under the promise of immunity, many of Lord Julian's former agents came forward to tell their stories. Lady Nora's revelation caused another scandal. She retreated to her country estate and hadn't been seen since.

But none of that mattered today. Today Prince Gaitlan would be crowned king, and all their trials and tribulations of the past would be laid to rest.

"Make sure you keep your hood up," Mirra reminded Oya for the hundredth time.

Oya waved off Mirra's mothering with a laugh. "I don't think I've ever seen you so nervous. Not even when you faced your trial of Da and nearly drowned."

Crimson painted Mirra's cheeks. "Can you not bring that up again?"

"Who knew that the mighty savior of the world couldn't swim?" Mirra's frown deepened until Oya pressed a kiss on her pouty lips. "And after growing up near the water."

"You go swim in that water and see how fast you catch something." Oya laughed again and Mirra drank it up. She never imagined that she would ever walk the streets of Verance again, free and with someone she cherished more than anything in this world.

"Come on," Mirra said, tugging on Oya's hand. "If we don't hurry, we'll miss the crowning and then Gaitlan will never let us live it down."

They hailed a carriage and rode back to the castle. On the way, Mirra mused over her first arrival in a similar fashion to what felt like a century ago. Back then, she was a shell of a person, changed and forcefully shaped to serve others. Today she was free, an Ilmarrion mage, and living for herself.

Two figures stood in the snow-covered courtyard, waiting for their arrival. "What the hel took you so long?" Bao demanded, his nose and ears bright red.

"You didn't have to wait outside," Mirra laughed.

"That's no way to greet a hero of the realm," Braelyn said, teasing. She opened her arms and gave Oya and Mirra warm embraces. "Come, you must be tired and cold. I have your room prepared. There's still time for a hot bath, should you want it?"

"That sounds wonderful," Oya said, matching Braelyn's steps. She winked over her shoulder as she let the princess lead the way, giving Mirra and Bao time for themselves.

"How's the new job?"

Bao shrugged. "It has its moments. Right now, I'm busy trying to fix everything Julian broke. I have a whole new network to create, spies to train, you know, typical things. What about you?"

"Well, I passed my Düa trial, barely. High Priestess Usoa is working on translating the notebook Marhoc gave me. It's the only way I can learn more about my affinity."

Bao coughed, pulling his coat higher against the biting wind. "Speaking of Marhoc, when are you planning to rescue him?"

Mirra groaned. "Honestly, I do not know. I doubt I'd be able to sneak in again. Sage Yuchi has probably beefed up the defenses by now."

"I might be able to help with that," Bao said, a familiar wicked gleam in his eye. Mirra arched her brow. "You'd be surprised what you can get away with diplomatic immunity."

"Nice to see you haven't lost your twisted mind."

Bao slapped his hand against Mirra's back. "Never, my dearest friend. Never."

The temple of Ydrs looked much as it did on that fateful day. The only actual difference being that Mirra sat in a row near the front. Braelyn had gifted her a dress of dove gray velvet that somehow went perfectly with Oya's dress, the color of the sun reflected on snow.

"All rise for Prince Gaitlan of Undros, prince of the realm!"

The thrum of conversation died, replaced by the sound of hundreds of people moving to their feet. All heads turned, waiting for the prince to walk through the doors to take his rightful place. The gathered nobles and visiting dignitaries bowed and rose like waves at sea when Gaitlan walked past, his long blue robe dragging along behind him.

In the front of the temple, before the altar, stood the High Priest of Yrds and High Priestess of Yulla. Gaitlan knelt before them, the winter sun dancing in his copper hair.

"Do you swear to uphold the laws set for by the gods and by the people?" The High Priest's voice carried through the room, steady and clear.

"I do."

"Do you swear to defend those too weak to defend themselves, no matter their station in life?" The High Priestess's question carried more weight, given everything that had happened in the past year.

Gaitlan's answer came clear and full of conviction. "I do."

Moving together, they picked up the crown from the altar, holding it aloft before placing it on Gaitlan's head. "Then rise," they said in unison. "King Gaitlan and rule well."

Gaitlan turned to face his new subjects. The gathered crowd clapped and cheered, shouting, "Long live the king!" Silence fell across the crowd when Gaitlan raised his hand.

"We have suffered this year, more than any other before and hopefully never again. We must rebuild from the ashes left behind by those that would see us shackled and defeated. We will rise stronger than before. United under a single purpose; prosperity and peace. So I charge all gathered here today, to set aside that which keeps us divided, keeps us tethered in the dark, and walk as one into the light of a new future."

The cheers of the crowd filled the temple, carrying the dreams of a better tomorrow.

THE LAST OF THE REPAIRS TO THE RELIQUARY WERE finally completed. Abbot Joseph led a small procession of Masters to the ancient site, carrying the Orb of Thrilla in a velvet-lined box. They couldn't risk a single crack or the demon that so many died to imprison would be unleashed upon the world again.

Small oil lanterns dotted the room, providing most of the light needed. Once the orb was secure, the Abbot and the Masters would seal away the entrance, leaving the lanterns to burn themselves out.

"It's a shame we have to hide all this again," said Master Nen. "The artwork is stunning."

"Be that as it may, it's best for items as dangerous as this to be kept away from those who'd use for their own means", Abbott Joseph said. They had replaced the pedestal that the orb originally stood on for one with a deep groove cut out the exact size of the orb. Abbott Joseph gently removed the orb and placed it into the groove. Master Nen stepped forward, linking delicate chains of pure iron into four metal rings inlaid into the stone. With the chains, he secured the orb to its new home, handing the key to Abbott Joseph when he was done.

"Let us record what transpired today in preparation of a tomorrow we hope to never see. Then put it from your minds, never speaking of it again." One by one, the masters wore to do as commanded and followed the Abbott out. They laid great stones over the entrance to the reliquary, cutting it off from the light of the known world.

Orange lights danced over ancient mosaic art of a time when a great evil threatened the safety of the world. The mosaics told the story of brave mortals and Ilmarrions who gave everything they had to protect the sanctity of life. It was also in the very room that told the story of their triumph that the evil entity was released, wreaking havoc until another band of heroes sealed it away once more.

As the light of the lanterns shrunk and dimmed, the dark storm clouds swirling within the orb crashed and raged. The sound of fracturing glass coincided with the last flickers of the dying lights.

Acknowledgments

So here we are, at the end of the story, for now. Don't worry my lovelies, there are two more books on the way that will expand on the world and hopefully answer some lingering questions you have about the world and the characters. There will also be a few novellas about some of our favorite characters, because they're stories, while awesome, don't quite fit in with the overall story playing out.

As always, this book would be nothing without the people in my life cheering me on and dragging me up when the impostor syndrome hits. Especially to my every patient husband who honestly I wouldn't be anywhere near where I am without him. For my eternal cheering squad — Aimee, Clare, Jessica, and Christine — thank you for always matching my crazy when I go off on some random detail or plan. A huge thank you to Shelby for helping me polish it all. Your enthusiasm and critical eye were a real life saver.

A special shout out to the amazing designers over on Miblart for not only being able to make this amazing cover, but helped to recreate the originals to match.

A special shout out to Kendal, the best sister in law anyone could ever ask for. You made it very difficult for me to be lazy when it came to marketing. And thanks for pimping me out to every book booth at Comic Con.

And as always a special thank you to everyone who has been with me from the start of this story or who are just now hoping on for the ride. Just knowing that you all are there and that you enjoy reading my little stories means the world to me. I can't thank you enough.

K. N. Timofeev has been a lover of stories for as long as she can remember. Some of her earliest memories involve reading books and making up stories to play with her friends, and sometimes unwilling brother. When not writing, she can usually be found with a book, in her garden or out on the water with her husband (trying desperately to not fall off the paddle board).

You can find more information on her website or on social media. Scan the code below for more.